BIG DEMON ENERGY

Bedeviled AF #1

DEBORAH WILDE

Illustrated Cover by Ben V Funk

Typography by Croco Designs

Issued in print and electronic formats.

ISBN: 978-1-998888-22-1 (paperback)

ISBN: 978-1-988681-71-9 (epub)

Chapter 1

After five months, dozens of sleepless nights, and enough caffeine to fuel a large city, we were so close to capturing our targets, I could almost taste it. The storm clouds had even parted, the full moon beaming its golden light upon my partner and me in encouragement.

That's when a vampire blew in and wrecked our momentum. Unnecessarily gaunt, with nails sharpened to mini spears like some beauty influencer, and black hair lacquered to his skull, all he needed was a drop of blood at the corner of his mouth and he could star in his own B movie. See the Creature of the Night prowl! Scaaarrrrrrry!

"Get thee behind me, asshat!" I splashed through a puddle, waving the irritant away from the entrance to this abandoned laundromat in East Vancouver.

Sachie Saito, my best friend and fellow operative on this investigation, snickered, jumping a piece of loose asphalt in our parking lot mad dash. "Bleh bleh bleh."

Hissing, the vampire cracked his neck and body-checked me. "I'll bleh you first, bitches."

Rude. I regained my footing, ready to take him out, but Sachie was on it.

"Bring it." Sach ripped a thin wooden stake free of its thigh holster and dropped into a fighter's crouch. She looked like a tall warrior pixie with her gamine spiky cut and the stretchy dress she'd worn to the office that morning that matched her fire engine red hair. "Then I'll see how many of your holes I can shove this into in thirty seconds. My current record is seven," she added helpfully.

The vampire furrowed his heavy brow, counting under his breath. He got to three—holes, presumably—then snarled, snatched the stake away, and snapped it with a chilling smile.

We'd had enough bumps in this case without this jerk throwing us off course before we'd reached the finish line. Those two humans we'd been chasing had a slim head start, but every second spent dealing with the bloodsucker added to the odds of them getting away.

I flashed my gold ring identifying me as a Maccabee. "Listen up. A) You have no authority to stop us or demand shit, which the undead landlord of this joint knows, and B—"

Sach grabbed a broken piece of wood back from the vampire and staked him in the heart.

His jaw went slack, his body paralyzed, then he fell apart like puzzle pieces and crumbled to ash.

I wrenched the cracked glass door open from its bloated frame. "B) Never take your eyes off the one with the stake."

"Rookie," Sach spat, barreling inside with a trail of powdery footprints. "We should ask the Spook Squad to find out who his boss is and remind him not to fuck with our portal access."

I shook my head. "It's such a simple concept, yet so hard for some of these vamps to understand."

We raced over dirty cream and mint tiles, sidestepping the broken metal table lying on its side. Fluorescent light fixtures hung down like stalactites between exposed pipes while a lonely washing machine missing its glass was tagged in layers of paint.

Employees of the undead landlords who controlled this three-block radius were already scurrying past the small houses nestled close together and local businesses like the popular taqueria to tattle on the two Maccabee operatives who'd killed a minion and were headed through the rift. Information was power, in the human and supernatural worlds, and the vamps in charge probably had files on us with details down to my shoe size. I filed it under "know thy enemy," but it still freaked me out if I dwelled on it.

My only consolation was that if they knew my biggest secret, the one that could unravel my life, they'd have used it against me by now.

I shielded my eyes with a hand against the harsh glare of sunlight spilling out from the back office. "It's a balmy 'Satan's asshole is steaming' day in the Brink, folks."

"Let's stay safe, partner," Sach said. "And if we can't stay safe, then let's crawl back out before we die. Better benefits for our loved ones."

Closing our eyes so we wouldn't be permanently blinded, we jumped into the rift, a portal to a liminal wasteland called the Brink that served as a barrier between earth and Babel, a vampire-controlled alternate reality.

There were about a dozen or so rifts worldwide; ours had been the last to be discovered about a hundred and fifty years ago, back when Vancouver was a fledgling city. They weren't painful to traverse, more like a tight hug from a clingy relative that you wanted to get away from.

Happily, it only took a couple of seconds to get free of

its embrace. I stepped into the Brink and took a deep breath, the arid atmosphere scorching my lungs, and let my vision adjust.

Heat shimmered off cracked earth which stretched into infinity. Suddenly, bent, wiry husks of trees with needle-sharp ragged bark exploded from the baked dirt, spraying soil and wood chips that almost took out my eyes. In less than two breaths, a dense forest with no protective canopy had been created.

The Brink always kept me on my toes. It presented different challenges each visit, even through the same portal. Last time I'd dealt with snowdrifts. Jury was still out on whether the needle-trees would be better. Both options were such delights.

Sach ran her fingers up the back of her neck, flicking sweat out of her hair. "I feel like I'm being punished for your sins."

"Only six of them," I said mournfully. "Lust hath forsaken me."

"Why dost thou speak old-timey today?"

"I'm a whimsical woman." I pressed the hollow above my left ulna, triggering a steady electric signal paired to my partner's matching implant. It was the best communication solution we'd found since there was no cell reception in the Brink and the chaotic magic reduced walkie-talkies to a staticky nightmare. "Got a signal?"

"Confirmed," she replied. "Happy hunting, Aviva."

"You too."

We split up, Sachie heading left through the tree graveyard while I went right. Unfortunately, there were no footprints to follow or scents of desperation to track.

Coming into the Brink was akin to Theseus entering the Labyrinth—except without any thread to find my way out again. That said, it was a freaking alternate reality, how could I not be enticed? Like the best seductions, it provided a heady emotional cocktail with complex flavors: a shot of disorientation, a generous pinch of anxiety, and a heavy splash of excitement, all shaken and poured into a glass crusted with sweet temptation.

I whipped off my navy suit jacket and draped it over my high, dark brown ponytail, attempting to form a makeshift visor with minimal success. Twenty steps later, my ankle boots and the hem of my slacks were already coated in dust.

I kept catching movement out of the corner of my eye, however, each time I spun to investigate, I came up empty. Just a trick of the light. I hoped. "Heloise, Clément," I called out. "Turn yourselves in. Even if you make it to Babel, it's hardly sanctuary."

Our female suspect was Eishei Kodesh, a human with magic, but her husband had no powers. Not that it mattered; humans didn't survive in the megacity of Babel without iron-clad contracts or protectors. Sometimes not even then.

I tilted my head, straining to hear a reply, but there was nothing save for the low moan of wind. That would have been fine had there actually been any hint of a breeze and not simply an evil, creepy taunt. I pressed forward, determined to find the married couple before anything else did, and wrap up this case.

The Toussaints had been running cons on the art world on three different continents, but my chapter had caught the case because they'd relocated to our city a couple of years back, believing that no one would look for them in Vancouver.

As far as cons went, it was simple: Heloise used her white flame magic to drive up emotions and thus prices on Clément's Z-grade pieces. Not entirely unsurprisingly, what had started as a fraud case had gotten white-hot very quickly, ending in a spree of murders over ownership of a painting that looked like a feral cat vomited chalk on a dirty blackboard.

Sach and I fought to remain the prime investigators. We'd been on this assignment from the start, knew the ins and outs better than anyone, and we'd lived in their heads. This was our chance to prove ourselves on a complex investigation with high stakes, yet we wouldn't have pushed so hard if we'd believed anyone else was more suited to catch the Toussaints.

There'd been a lot of grumbling from more experienced operatives when the director had granted our request—on a probationary basis. Step by step, Sachie and I had built our case and narrowed in on the Toussaints despite every obstacle and red herring they threw our way.

If we lost the fugitives now? I shook my head, refusing to imagine the icy follow-up with our Vancouver chapter head and the massive derailment of our career goals. Failure was not an option.

Not when we'd come this far.

Wiping sweat off my brow, I crept forward, my eyes darting throughout the ghostlike trees, seeking any signs of movement. It would have been great to have water or be wearing cooler clothing, but when Sach and I had arrived at our fugitives' last known location in Vancouver's swanky Shaughnessy neighborhood, we discovered they'd fled to the Brink. There wasn't time to stock up on provisions, let alone change out of our business attire.

Survival would come down to my wits and my blue flame magic.

I pulled my shirt away from my slick skin, sweat rolling between my boobs, and my jacket now a warm, damp weight on my head. Blech. Suddenly, my shoulder blades prickled and my skin was dotted in goose bumps like I'd jumped into a cold swimming pool. My heartbeat sounded like footsteps growing closer, but despite the feeling of being watched and the sense of unease that settled in my gut, no one was there.

No one I could see, at least.

Spinning around for a third time and finding nothing, I touched the brushed gold pillbox ring on my right index finger for confidence. The top of its round compartment featured an embossed flame, the design circled by five tiny gems: one each in red, orange, yellow, white, and blue.

All human Maccabees received their rings upon graduating from Maccababy to level one operative, and we never took them off. The part of our initiation ceremony that meant the most to me was the moment we slid the rings onto our fingers and pledged the Maccabee motto: Tikkun olam. My vow to fix the wrongs in the world.

A large dark shape swooped down with a low, raspy screech, and I ducked, cursing. Supe-vultures were the only creatures native to the Brink. They'd been reported by operatives no matter which rift they came through. However, like everything else in this place, the birds' appearance was random. They might show up seven visits in a row in one location, no matter what the weather or physical environment held, and then not be seen again for the next six months.

Supe-vultures were beady-eyed, sharp of claw, and had feather-free heads—all the better to keep from being matted with blood when they reached inside a carcass. They operated on a cycle of feed, hasten the death of anything that moved too slowly, and feed again. Eerily sentient, they were a by-product of the constant clash in this realm between demon magic and Mother Earth. What a gift.

Three birds circled above, showing their lack of respect with dinosaur-like cries and a strip of white shit that splatted less than two feet away, while the sun beat on me like a crotchety grandma with a wooden spoon greeting her husband, who was late for dinner—again.

Every step was a nightmare of cramping in my leg muscles. I licked salty moisture off my cracked lips, dimly aware that bad as this heat exhaustion was, the next step was full-on heat stroke, then death. Best to live in the moment.

A high, thin cry pierced the air behind me. Pulse spiking, I called out for Sach. When she didn't answer, I tapped my subcutaneous implant, changing it from a single pulse to two rapid pulses followed by a pause. Rinse and repeat.

Three heart-hammering cycles later, the signal returned to its original beat, and I gave a relieved sigh. Sachie was fine. She'd probably desiccated one of the supe-vultures with her orange flame magic.

I glanced up at the birds, tripping over a tree root that hadn't been there ten seconds ago and bashing my shoulder on a listing tree. My jacket tore; my skin didn't. I took the win.

Plus, my pain was rewarded. Sort of.

A badly sunburned Heloise and Clément Toussaint stood defiantly on either side of a doughy vampire, who sheltered them all with a golf umbrella made of some shiny iridescent material. It generated its own breeze and moved incrementally as its users did, so it always provided maximum shade.

The vamp smirked and spun the umbrella, showing off its amazing recalibrating abilities and generally flaunting the incredible technology he'd brought from Babel. Even low-level vamps had access to things humans wouldn't see for ten or more years.

I narrowed my eyes. The vamp's presence complicated things. I couldn't easily slap magic-nulling cuffs on Heloise with him acting as her protector, and I didn't dare pull the small stake from my boot when I'd also have to contend with Heloise's powers.

I surreptitiously tapped my wrist, changing my subcutaneous electric signal to a fast vibration. Code for "Get here now," it lasted about five seconds before reverting to the regular signal, which Sach could follow back to me.

Then I let my magic out to get a better read on the human pair. All Eishei Kodesh were synesthetes. We Blue Flames saw our magic, though neither the synesthetic quality nor the magic itself was visible to anyone else.

My particular talent was illuminating people's weaknesses. Got a scarred liver? A nicotine craving tightening your chest? If I studied a person with my magic sight, their vulnerabilities were illuminated in blue. They weren't all physical, but those were the most basic tells.

Heloise and Clément were awash in blue due to their sunburns. Colored dots rapidly beat at their wrist and throat pulses, and there were navy splotches on the crowns of their heads. Heat stroke, what did I tell you?

A journey that took ten minutes one time in the Brink could take an hour or a day the next. By the looks of the couple, they'd been in here a lot longer than I had before meeting up with the vamp.

Heloise's all-silk ensemble was a ruinous mess of dirt, pit, and crotch stains—ew—while Clément looked like an escapee from an old film noir in his linen suit, complete with cravat and a gold stick pin. Sorry, a villainous escapee. Interesting that for a supposed artist, there were no traces of paint or gesso on his hands, not a single callus, and no sign of skin damage from handling solvents. His nails were buffed to a high sheen, and his skin was pink and plump. Much like the rest of him.

The vamp could have been one blink away from keeling over, but I'd never know. Blue Flames couldn't illuminate the undead.

I crossed my arms. "This is cozy. Did you bring a picnic basket? I enjoy a creamy brie on these outings, but I also prefer it lightly melted, not bubbling liquid, so let's rain check that." I nodded my chin at the vamp. "Hand the humans over and we'll be on our way."

More supe-vultures joined the party with loud, raucous cries.

"Willem is our escort," Clément said in a heavy French accent.

"Like an undead Boy Scout? Cool."

Willem hissed at me, his fangs descending, but even with vamp magic, I could tell he wasn't a skilled fighter like me. We Maccabees worked damn hard to achieve our high level of physical conditioning. I didn't have the muscle mass of some operatives, but my limbs were long and lean, both from training and all the running I did.

I unfurled a cruel smile and beckoned Willem forward. "Want to play?"

Maccabee protocol gave me leave to kill any vamps standing in the way of an investigation—though not at the expense of human casualties. Given that the Toussaints had brought the vampire into this, however, their well-being became a gray area.

Gray areas were such fun.

Willem tensed but didn't move. Yeah, that's what I thought. Only nippers, new vamps, shepherded humans through the Brink, which meant that he didn't have the clout or connections to kill an operative and get away with it. Yet.

Lucky me.

Heloise fanned out her grimy silk blouse, her loose wisps of hair blowing around her face. "Give up, Maccabee."

A sorrow as vast and dark as a sea swept through me. I crashed to my knees, my body hunched over, and wrapped an arm around my middle. She was right. What was the point of continuing? I'd never win. Not the war that mattered most. I was a fool to think otherwise.

"Pauvre chérie," she cooed. "Thinking you stood a chance when you are—what is the word?" She snapped her fingers. "A mosquito playing with lions."

A distant part of my brain insisted that I not let them get away, but who was I to stop them? I knew how the world saw me. Or would if the truth came out. Maybe I was better off lying down to die on the parched, brittle ground?

"Bien." Heloise laughed. "Allons-y." Heloise pivoted, and her heel snapped off. She stumbled, cursing.

A fog lifted off my brain like it had been vacuumed away, my confidence and determination to bring these two to justice flooding back in.

Oh, you cow.

White Flames were all about burning passions; they could amp up an emotion in another or follow their own all-consuming desire. There were a lot of con artists in this group, though it was also where many of the greatest scientists and artists were found.

Heloise, busy slipping her other shoe off and tossing it on the ground with its broken companion, didn't glance up when I pushed to my feet.

"What do you think is going to happen when you get to Babel?" I said.

"Money opens many doors." Clément gave a very Gallic shrug.

Before he finished speaking, I'd lunged for the umbrella.

Willem yanked the titanium handle into his chest, briefly tipping the canopy down and blocking me from his view.

That second was all I needed. I pushed hard on the

canopy, sending Willem and Clément stumbling off-balance, while with my free hand I grabbed the magic-nulling cuffs out of my pocket and slapped them on Heloise.

Too bad that when the umbrella shifted, Willem didn't sizzle like potatoes hitting the deep fryer. Sunlight didn't affect vamps here in the Brink like it did to varying degrees back in the normal plane of existence.

"Whose money would that be?" I said genially. "Heloise's? Vamps aren't as susceptible to cons as humans are, Clément, so what would she need your shitty skills for anymore? You don't even have magic."

"How dare you? We didn't con anyone." Clément blustered like a puffer fish, but my synesthete magic vision revealed his true state: the blue circle over his heart pulsed faster.

A curl of excited energy unfurled inside me.

"My husband is a genius. I would never abandon him," Heloise said loyally, rattling her cuffs like she could shake them off.

The signal between Sach and me grew stronger, indicating my partner was close. I swallowed down my nausea from baking alive out here, conscious of the scavengers circling us like we were the coveted seats in a game of musical chairs.

"You're sticking with Clément through thick and thin?" I stroked my chin, pacing back and forth so I didn't appear too near death. "Then why is Willem standing closer to you than to your husband, his body turned in toward yours? That's not something a stranger does. Got some undead action happening on the side?"

Clément swung his head toward the vampire and his wife, his mouth slackening. Then he narrowed his eyes and clenched his hands into trembling fists.

To be clear, I was incapable of manipulating other

people's emotions or self-perceptions, but feelings were weaknesses, and in certain situations like this one, easy to decipher without my magic.

His wife reached for him, but he turned away.

"I would have gotten away with this if it wasn't for you." Still cuffed, Heloise walloped me with a right cross.

"Fuck!" I staggered back a couple of steps, gingerly probing my eye. *Come on!* The Scooby Gang never suffered bodily harm.

On Heloise's follow-up swing, I grabbed the chain between her cuffs, twisted her wrists over her head, and yanked them down behind her back, though not hard enough to break anything.

She mewled like a kitten.

I pulled harder, practically drinking down the vivid blue rippling off her straining shoulders. "Hit me again and I won't show such restraint. Dislocated shoulders don't only affect the immediate area, you know," I said conversationally. "They can impact muscles, veins, even blood vessels. And if arthritis sets in?" I made a "yikes" face. "Popping and locking aren't just break-dance moves."

A blue splotch flared up over Heloise's heart, accompanied by a silky blue swathe along her side closest to Willem, while Clément's entire body flushed navy. The space between him and the pair lit up in a vivid blue.

Fascinating. Heloise might have held the purse strings, but she was scared to lose Clément and mistrustful of Willem's faithfulness, while her husband was jealous—not only of an alleged affair, but because he saw his human body as inferior to the vampire's dadbod.

"T'es folle," Heloise whimpered.

I forced her arms down behind her back another half inch. "I haven't taken French for a long time," I said, "but I'm pretty sure we're not at the familiar form of address stage. Now, if you'd insulted me with respect, I might have stabilized your pulled shoulder with tape." I patted myself down with one hand. "Except, damn. I didn't bring any."

Heloise was wheezing, her breathing labored like a child who'd run too far. Her torso pulsed with such a vivid blue that it almost hurt to look at; I had her on the ropes.

I pulled her cuffs taut, our skin brushing, and I jumped, zapped by an electric shock of static current. Pure adrenaline coursed through me like wildfire, my dizziness retreated, and my headache dialed down from Riverdance to a soft shuffle.

"As for Willem?" All I had to do was strain Heloise's shoulders one more tiny inch and she'd tip over into a glazed agony. My body tightened in anticipation of that final rush. "He won't stick around, vamps never do. And speaking frankly, this one doesn't look like the sharpest tool in the shed."

Gritting my teeth, I slackened my hold on her chains. No broken shoulders today.

Willem dropped the golf umbrella and sped toward me.

I shoved Heloise away, dropped into a low crouch, and headbutted the vamp in the gut.

Grabby Hands seized my hair in his fist and lifted me off the ground.

I scrabbled on tiptoe, smacking at his hand, and trying to save my poor scalp.

Suddenly, Willem contorted in a series of jolting movements. His skull warped and twisted, his arms shriveled into T-rex-like stumps, and he dropped me.

Ooh, nice. Sachie was using her heat magic to suck the moisture from his body.

Orange Flames radiated heat into or out of things: people, a log, the air, anything really. Sach could force my body heat to radiate out of me to the point of giving me a lethal case of hypothermia. That said, she couldn't freeze a lake. Luckily, few Orange Flames were born with that level of power or had the years of training it would take to unlock widespread popsicle abilities. Which was good, because who wanted some Jack Frost wannabe icing cities?

She twirled a finger, magically pulling heat from the atmosphere to direct it into Willem. Her powers weren't visible, nor did I feel the synesthetic temperature changes that my friend did from her orange flame talents, but the end results were plain to see.

Willem's skin flushed a hot, angry red, and his body curled like bacon sizzling in a pan.

I rubbed my poor, throbbing head. "Cutting it close there, my friend."

"Please. You had a good two or three seconds before your scalp came off." Sachie winked, her cheeks merely flushed pink and not burned thanks to the bubble of cool air she'd magically encased herself with.

"Try anything funny on the way back and you'll get the same treatment." I pointed from the Toussaints to Willem, who was making gurgling noises, bits of blackened flesh dropping off him.

The supe-vultures swooped down to feast.

Heloise vomited.

Jumping out of splatter range, I pulled a stake out of my boots and tossed it to my friend. "Don't say I never gave you anything nice."

"I'm the luckiest girl alive." Sachie grinned, both her cheeks dimpling, then stabbed Willem in the heart, killing him for good.

"Do you plan to behave?" I said to our fugitives.

Clément nodded, his face draining of all color, though Heloise's caterwauling caused my left eye to twitch.

"Good. Mission accomplished," I said, picking up the golf umbrella. I stepped into the welcome coolness of its shadow and gave the handle a dainty twirl. I sighed deeply as the assault of the direct sunlight melted away into nothing. Vampire technology was truly something else.

Sachie wrangled a pair of cuffs onto Clément.

My physical relief was sweetened by the taste of victory.

Two vamps down, two bad guys apprehended, and two well-deserved promotions secured. Once the director congratulated me with the news, I'd treat myself to a great steak, and then, as a level three Maccabee, I'd be placed in charge of a tantalizing new investigation soon enough.

Leader. I breathed in the molten air of the Brink and smiled. It had a nice ring to it.

Chapter 2

Co-leader.

The word rang in my ears, twisting around and around in my brain, failing to fall into anything vaguely resembling me becoming a level three operative. I'd sacrificed any semblance of a personal life, taken on extra training, and pushed myself hard to hit the top rank by the age of thirty. That had been four long months ago.

Today was the day that was supposed to change everything, not make it worse by leaving me a level two, paired up with an as-yet-undisclosed operative who would treat me like a subordinate on whatever case the director had in mind for us.

Numb, I followed Chapter Director Michael Fleischer into the spacious lobby of the Vancouver Maccabee headquarters. Our five-story building occupied an entire city block on the border with Burnaby. Below the surface, it even boasted a secret basement and subbasements.

The place had begun life as a garment factory in the late 1800s, but when that business went belly-up in the Great Depression, the local Maccabees took it over. Thankfully, the previous techno-futuristic interior design popular with dot-com start-ups in the '90s had finally been renovated to give us a comfortable working environment. Gone were the modular plastic furniture not designed for human asses and all the stark white that conveyed the vague impression a Clockwork Orange–style reprogramming was imminent.

I'd timed my arrival at HQ today to Michael's, and admittedly, straight up pestered her for her decision, despite her telling me it could wait until we'd gotten to her office.

"Stop gogging. It's unseemly." Michael wore her customary outfit of a severely tailored pantsuit, today's number softened with an emerald blouse that matched her green eyes. Her silver hair was pulled back into a chignon and hammered gold earrings shaped like leaves dangled from her lobes. Yes, she was stylish, but the long pins securing her hair were lethal projectiles, and the points of her earrings could slice zip ties—or flesh.

I rubbed a faint scar at the base of my thumb. "'Gogging' isn't a word," I said dully.

"It's not?" She paused midway through the lobby to pull out her phone and look it up.

I scrubbed a hand through my wavy hair, then did my breathing exercises—counting to twenty, inhaling through my nose, then exhaling hard through my mouth.

It didn't help.

I glanced around in hopes of finding something to calm me down enough to continue this conversation in a professional manner, because if I let my emotions get the best of me, it was game over.

My pickings were slim. The reception area looked more like it belonged to a corporation than a magic police branch. Large abstract bronze sculptures flanked the glass doors to the part of the building accessible to the general public. It handled all concerns from processing Eishei

Kodesh criminals to magic community members paying parking tickets.

Everything from the walls to the marble reception desk to the concrete floor and bolted-down plastic chairs in the waiting area was cream.

The only blaze of color was the enormous mural dominating one wall depicting five flames: red, orange, yellow, white, and blue with the words "Tikkun olam" across the top.

The Hebrew phrase and Maccabee motto was originally a mystical approach to all mitzvot, or good deeds. Broadly, it referred to the responsibility of Jews, now extended to all operatives, to fix the wrongs in the world, while the flames represented the magic of the Eishei Kodesh, or, translated from the Hebrew, the Holy Fire People.

Humans hadn't always had inherent magic abilities, though thousands of years ago Jews had played around with spells and power words to very limited success. Much more notable was when innate fire-based magic came into being around 150 BCE. There was only one type at first, and it didn't have a color classification.

The magic spread over the centuries through other races and religions, and, like many a trait, changed and evolved. Maccabees catalogued the new powers using a system of colors seen from largest to smallest in a flame: red (the original power), orange, yellow, white, and blue. They coincided with the order of the most common power to the rarest, and from the least skill involved in using an ability to the most.

Jump forward to the 1700s, after the Salem witch trials.

Magic had become prevalent enough, and witch hunting was out of control. The Maccabees, who'd taken their name from the heroes of the Hanukkah miracle—

honoring them and their flame that formed the basis of our magic—stepped out of the shadows as a formal global organization to police humans with abilities.

There were days I'd dreaded coming through the doors, others I'd sailed in all smiles, but not once in the seven years since I'd passed the test to become a Maccabee had I regretted my decision. Not even today, though if Michael figured this was a done deal, she was badly mistaken.

"Oh, 'gogging' is a word all right." Michael tapped her screen with a slight shudder, continuing toward our receptionist, Vera, with a smile and a wave. "I suggest you never search it."

I followed her, gripping my employee lanyard hard enough for the edge of the plastic laminate to dig into my palm.

Vera, a perky young woman with blond hair and cornflower blue eyes, nodded at us, busy filling out a courier slip while on the phone. She wasn't only our receptionist, but a very capable Red Flame. That magic devoured matter and burned things away. Instant incineration—provided users could touch their target.

It was very useful for destroying shedim (or, as most civilians called them, demons), the creatures who wanted to devour humans and the reason magic was first introduced into the world by a group of Jews, since humans had no way of fighting shedim without it.

Every Maccabee HQ, and most pro-magic corporations, placed Red Flames in lobbies as the first line of defense, because even ones who could barely set a piece of paper ablaze could cause a lot of damage. A couple memorable office rampages had proven that. That's why they were the most highly trained in terms of control. They remained the majority of the magic community to this day and had the only powers visible to the naked eye.

Sadly, it had become depressingly common to also see Red Flames safeguarding medical clinics with any focus on reproductive health.

I stalked behind Michael, my hands half curled into claws. "Getting back to this co-leader status?"

The director pressed her thumb against the scanner on the wall behind Vera's desk with a short, sharp gesture, and the door to the employee-only area buzzed open. "I'm not sure what there is to discuss." She strode into the corridor, not bothering to check if I'd followed.

The door clipped me on the shoulder, making me wince, but I hurried over to the elevator and jabbed the call button six times, imagining it was Michael's head. "Any other level two who'd shown the same commitment to their job as I have and had the same excellent record of case closures, especially after this last investigation, would have been promoted immediately."

Michael preceded me into the car. "Not an operative with the number of complaints against them that you have. Mrs. Toussaint ended up with a hairline fracture in her shoulder."

"After she gave me a black eye." I pushed the button for the fifth floor. "Would you like the receipt for the extra-strength concealer I had to purchase until a healer could slot me in for an appointment?" *Cry me a river.* "No suspect likes being brought in. Every single one of us ends up with a charge of excessive force at some point."

"It's not just one though, is it?" She didn't even spare me a perfunctory glance, her attention on the riveting sight of the doors closing. "We all deal with aggression; I'll allow you that much. But it goes further than that with you."

Ladies and gentlemen, my mother. Never one to pull punches.

My stomach twisted with the knowledge of why I'd

never be promoted—danced around and alluded to by Michael—but never spoken out loud. No, the reason was best kept hidden, like a snake coiled in the shadows. My jaw clenched so tightly that the muscles twitched beneath my skin.

My mother was a Yellow Flame, their talents predicated upon the cleansing properties of flames. Specifically, they cleansed complicated ideas and systems, anything ranging from the body or brain to an alloy, a building, or water. Unsurprisingly, a lot of them became healers or went into research on viruses and pathogens.

Unlike me, they couldn't see weakness or illness; their synesthesia was scent based. Kind of like dogs who could sniff out cancer, though they despised the comparison. Software development and engineering were also big draws for that crowd.

Michael had used her purifying magic to root out a decades-long systemic corruption here in Vancouver, becoming a director with the reputation of being a bastion of righteousness, fighting the good fight on every front.

Well, every front except one: I remained her greatest failure.

The thing about Yellow Flames? Any impurity they couldn't cleanse, they became masters at hiding. Perfectionism at its finest.

I stepped in front of her, my light brown eyes clashing with her green ones. If I sought any sign of myself in her more patrician features, it was only for a second. Other than our full lips and thick wavy hair, there was no obvious resemblance. I was broader through the shoulders with a heart-shaped face, she had narrow hips and sharper cheekbones. My entire life I'd been subjected to an endless loop of people's surprise that we were related, but unlike when I was younger, I no longer bothered to insist that yes, she was my mom.

"Come on, Michael," I prompted snarkily. "You can get more specific than that. Why is it more than aggression with me?"

The elevator stopped on the third floor, and a young female operative came in. She gave a nervous head bob to the director, then kept her gaze fixed on the doors until we reached the fourth floor, and she hurried out.

I rolled my eyes. That level one would get less anxious around Michael. Eventually.

As the doors closed, leaving us alone once more, Michael gave an impatient sigh. "The charges themselves are dismissible, but more than one complainant has reported on your willingness, no, your eagerness to push things further than necessary."

"Say it." My voice was tight.

"I'm not unaware of your leadership potential," she said in the oh-so-rational tone of voice she'd used on me when I was a kid that still made my shoulders tense up and my teeth grind together. "But if you want to lead," she continued, "you've got to sort out this tendency to inflame people."

"Targets, not teammates." I clenched my fists. "I have *never* used my magic to read a partner's weaknesses unless they were injured so badly that they couldn't speak, and I had to know how to help them." It was a hard and fast rule that I'd never broken, and Michael damn well knew it. "Say it," I growled. "For once in your life, be honest about what's going on. You owe it to me."

The elevator slowed to a stop on five and the doors opened.

"I owe you?" Michael said in a mild voice that sent warning bells screaming in my head. She motioned for me to move aside.

I smacked the button to close the doors again. I'd already jumped off the metaphoric cliff. Might as well fully say my piece before I smashed into the ground. "You can't stand to admit it, can you? You had a wild night with some dude, then he skipped town, and you were pregnant."

It was almost impossible (and gross) to imagine my mother having a crazy sex-fueled hookup, but shedim excelled at encouraging people's animal desires to win out. Vamps, despite their strength and brutality, had a reputation for being refined and elegant, where demons were unhinged abominations who coerced people into behaviors that they never would ordinarily engage in.

What a bunch of bullshit. Shedim weren't unearthing any desire that a person didn't have inside them to begin with. For some these urges were already close to the surface, and for others, they were deeply buried within their subconscious, but they didn't spring out of nowhere.

Generally, if you knew where to look, these desires weren't even that hard to spot, so a demon would have no trouble tapping into them. Take my mother, for example. I didn't develop my love of those 1970s punk goddesses like Blondie and Joan Jett because I was on some retro musical kick.

My mother wore out the grooves playing her favorite songs like "Bad Reputation" and "One Way or Another" on repeat and teaching me the lyrics to the adrenaline fueled, female driven, transgressive anthems.

I often wondered if shedim chose their victims because they sensed which people would be most receptive to their particular persuasion. After all, the demon who'd trysted with Mom hadn't incited her to violence or into conning other people, and I doubted one could. He'd simply coaxed her bad girl side out for the first and only time in her life.

I wasn't defending shedim. They toyed with people for their own sick amusement, and never left them better than they found them. They also had the power to work their evil mojo on a large scale and were behind some of the worst atrocities in human history. I just didn't believe their targets were free of those impulses to begin with.

"The extra-special surprise that your baby daddy was a shedim didn't get revealed until later," I said.

"That's because most infernals don't survive past the first trimester," Michael lobbed back. "Who could have known that you'd be the rare exception?"

My mouth fell open. The fact that most half demon, half human fetuses didn't make it to birth wasn't news to me, but she'd never voiced it, and certainly not with a dryness that made my pulse speed up and my hands get clammy.

"Would I be standing here now if you'd known what he was? What *I* was? After the first trimester, that is."

Michael shook her head, an annoyed expression on her face. "Don't talk nonsense."

Was it though? She hadn't referred to my half-demon side at all since I was a teen.

My mother had raised me with a tough-love curriculum, training me to keep my shedim nature hidden while constantly pressing home the danger should I be found out. When I turned fifteen, however, she announced she trusted me to keep it under wraps on my own.

Or she simply wished to ignore the entire business by that point.

She'd taught me well; I'd give her that.

I was a master at hiding the fact that I was a half shedim. No one suspected that my "tendency" to occasionally go too far was due to anything other than my ability to illuminate weakness combined with Blue Flames' reputed lack of control. And according to some people who weren't fans of mine, a reckless personality.

Michael reached past me to hit the open-door button,

then walked briskly onto the executive floor in a tease of citrus and vanilla that my brain would forever associate with the smell of power. It complemented the tasteful art and furniture upholstered in muted colors.

I stomped behind her, waiting for some surge of perverse satisfaction that I'd gotten her to broach the topic. All I felt was a dull, hollow ache.

We passed a couple of hush pods—soundproofed glass modules with two cushioned benches and a table. One was empty, but in the other, our HR manager was explaining something to a slightly bewildered young man gripping a coffee mug like a lifeline.

Too bad my mother wasn't amenable to a good bribe. I'd have brought her a London Fog to start her day. To be fair, she was generally open to a well-thought-out appeal, but if you failed, you'd be speared with the Look. The one that sent tough-as-nails level three operatives and vampires scurrying to do Michael's bidding.

The Look expressed a bone-deep disappointment that even if you saved the world seven times over, Michael would still think less of you. The last time I'd received it was six years ago when I'd asked for her to intervene with a particularly harsh trainer who was helping me focus my blue flame magic.

Blue Flames were the illuminators of the magic community. Essentially, we shone light on that which was hidden, applying our powers to everything from mineral veins deep underground to flaws in existing physical structures or technology. Some even illuminated esoteric concepts like personal boundaries. (Popular with Blue Flames working in mental health.)

As Eishei Kodesh, we had only one area of expertise each however, and mine was people. I illuminated their weaknesses, anything out of the ordinary whether physiological or mental.

The limited shedim powers I had were totally separate.

I wouldn't ordinarily have asked Michael to intercede on my behalf—I'd signed on for the training after all—but I was in a very raw place at the time, and the pace and depth of the training was more than I could handle considering getting dressed was a major accomplishment. I'd merely wanted to let up on the full-tilt pace a bit, and I'd thought… I'd hoped…

I shrugged. It didn't matter. The request was refused, and I never asked again.

However, I wasn't asking for a handout or a favor now. I'd earned this promotion.

Michael warmly greeted her executive assistant, Louis, making a joke about the stack of files and phone message slips in his arms. Louis was my mother's guard dog and he bristled whenever anyone he perceived as a threat got close to her. Including me. We gave each other cool chin nods in acknowledgment.

Michael asked me to give her five minutes, disappearing into her office with him. How did she expect me to wait when everything I'd worked my butt off for hung in the balance?

Co-leader. No power, no respect. Not good enough. Michael was throwing me scraps, and I wasn't going to take them.

I snapped a thread off the hem of my skirt. Anger wasn't uncommon when it came to our relationship, but this was ridiculous. If she was placing her Starbucks order while I simmered out here, I would lose my shit.

"Psst. Aviva." Sachie beckoned at me dramatically from around the corner, a shock of fire engine red hair falling into her face.

Despite my roiling emotions, I smiled at the memory of my best friend's one and only theatrical experience.

Sach had imbued her role of zucchini in our grade three play to Shakespearean heights. A framed photo of a swooning fuzzy vegetable with chubby cheeks hung in her parents' hallway, next to the one of Sachie in a kimono when her family went back to Japan for her coming-of-age ceremony.

Michael's door remained shut, so I headed over to my friend, who was with another level two, Gemma Huang.

My bestie leaned in, her voice lowered. "Can you find out more about the new guy from Michael?"

Operatives were a gossipy bunch—it was a miracle that anything was kept secret.

"Get us the first intel on the fresh meat," Gemma said, doing squats while in a skirt and heels. I'd never seen her simply stand like normal people did.

Sachie wrinkled her brow. "Do vamps count as fresh?"

"Depends if anyone has broken him in yet," the other operative said.

"This isn't about sex." Sach planted her hands on her hips.

Gemma shrugged and stretched out her hip flexor. "It would be better if it was. I'll never understand why you want to be transferred to the Spook Squad."

There were far fewer vamp Maccabees across the globe than human operatives, and they weren't designated levels. All undead operatives went into a general pool at their chapter called a Spook Squad. These squads were given cases to investigate, same as any operative, but they focused on rogue vamps and shedim activity, not policing Eishei Kodesh.

Unlike the rest of us, Spook Squad operatives got to combine all the fun challenges of solving crimes with more fighting and stabbing. Plus, there weren't the same strict protocols around arrests since their targets weren't human. All of that appealed to my bloodthirsty bestie, who'd been working on a transfer to Vancouver's Spook Squad for some time now.

"Why willingly expose yourself to shedim?" Gemma gave an exaggerated shudder.

"To keep the world safe by tracking them down and killing them," Sachie said. "It's not like I'm licking lepers."

I'd been around anti-shedim sentiment my entire life; I even shared it. But it never got easier hearing it from my best friend. I wanted to scream that not everything shedim-adjacent was bad, but since I couldn't go there, I went for the argument I could make.

"You're such a hypocrite," I said to Gemma. "Hot for vampires and death to shedim. Some vamps, hell, some humans are as evil as demons. But the wicked among the living and the undead get fetishized, while demons remain despised."

"Because they're pure evil." Gemma switched her stretch to her other leg. "We don't get a lot of absolutes in life. This is a real easy one. All demons are bad. They're nasty freaks. In the streets, not in the sheets like vamps." She fanned herself.

"Way to miss the point," I snapped.

Sachie stared at me, her brow furrowed at my tone.

I shook my head. "No one evil should be admired. Not demons, vamps, *or* humans, but there's a double standard. That's all I'm saying."

"Whatever," Gemma said, throwing me a dirty look. "Check if he's hot. Us hypocrites want to know."

"We hypocrites," I said sweetly.

"Don't be a bitch, Fleischer," she retorted, finishing her stretch. She smoothed down her skirt. "I know the genes are against you, but do try."

If only she knew what genes I had to fight against in that moment. They sure as hell weren't Michael's.

Sach made a scoffing noise. "I don't care if this new operative is the world's biggest schlub—"

I pressed my hands against my heart. "Look at you dropping Yiddish words. I'm all verklempt."

"If you would all give me two seconds to speak," Sach said, crossing her arms. "The rumor is he's been given carte blanche." She pressed her hands to her cheek with a dreamy two-dimple smile. "Will you find out for me? I want to join whatever case brought him to town."

"A vamp with carte blanche." Gemma snickered. "Michael is going to love that."

"Love what?" Michael had snuck up on us, an amused sparkle in her intelligent gaze.

Thanks, Gemma. You spoke her name and she was summoned. Like a demon. Sadly, saying Michael's name three times à la Beetlejuice didn't send her away. I'd tried.

Not that I wanted her sent away. Necessarily. It was just that she'd dropped the co-leader bombshell on me, then made me wait, and now she'd startled me. I had to get back into the zone.

"Can we get on with our meeting now?" I said.

"I'm all yours."

And that was the problem. Of all the DNA donors I could have gotten in this life, I'd ended up with one who'd pulled a runner and the other who was, well, Michael.

I guess this was why they said to never work with family.

Chapter 3

Michael sat across the wide expanse of desk from me. "Despite the childish fantasies you've woven starring me as the villain, Avi, I'm not."

My mother hadn't used my nickname in… I furrowed my brows. It was long before I'd joined the Maccabees, before my wayward teen years even, back when she was still my protector and the mom who'd fight the world to keep it from hurting me. That version of her seemed like a distant memory now. It felt like forever ago that she'd switched sides, trying instead to keep me from hurting the world.

"I'm not the villain either," I said, as collected as I could make myself. "You saw how hard I worked on that case. Sachie and I handled an escape attempt that even level threes would have found challenging. You know how much time and effort I put into closing it, and you know I deserve better than being named co-leader with whoever you plan to pair me up with."

Michael tapped her silver pen against the desk in a rapid staccato. She was generally unflappable, so this was the equivalent of her running around in circles like a chicken with its head cut off. "Gossip certainly made the rounds quickly about the new vampire. What did Sachie and Gemma say?"

Why was she avoiding the subject of my co-leadership? Oh fuck, she wasn't planning to stick me with Jesse, that humorless black void, was she?

I leaned back in my chair and crossed my ankles, trying to find a semblance of calm. I was a genius at compartmentalizing my identity, but my emotions, not so much.

Everything in this office was designed with serenity in mind, but nothing was helping. The row of living green bamboo reeds against the left wall? Nope. The plush light gray throw rug that my heels sank into? Nope. The framed parchment on the exposed brick wall certifying Michael Hannah Fleischer's appointment as director? Definitely not.

"All Sach knows is that some vamp is here on a big case and he has carte blanche." I left out that Sachie saw this as her opportunity to work with him. Michael was aware of my friend's ambitions.

"Have you ever heard of that happening before?" My mother stopped tapping the pen and started clicking it. "I mean, with anyone, much less a vampire?"

I swallowed a groan. Barely. Did she really think now was the time to indulge in her love of questions and teachable moments? Though it was more insulting if this was a stalling tactic to calm me down, like my perfectly reasonable frustration was an off-the-charts demonic response.

However, once my mother had settled on a plan of action, she was nothing if not committed, so I sighed and went along for the ride until I could get a concrete answer about who I was being partnered with.

"No," I said. "Maccabees love their structure and rules."

Carte blanche was unheard of. For anyone, but especially vamp operatives.

"Exactly." Her clicking grew faster and more annoying.

"Michael," I said, frustrated, and nodded at the pen.

She looked down at her hand like she'd forgotten she was holding the writing implement, then tossed it on the desk. "Anyone working out of a chapter office, even visiting operatives, answers to the director."

Okay, enough was enough.

"No disrespect," I said, "but I neither give a damn about this vampire nor need you to explain how your job works. I'm aware. Right now, I deserve more of an explanation for you kiboshing my promotion than you've given."

Her office phone buzzed.

I gripped the armrests.

Michael held up one hand while she picked up the receiver, listened for a moment, then said to alert her the moment he arrived. When she hung up, she closed her eyes, strain etched on her face.

One day I'd separate out our relationship as director and operative from mother and child as effectively as she did, but today was not that day. "Mom," I said softly.

She opened her eyes.

"What's got you so worried about this vampire? This is clearly not normal. Is he related to someone on the Authority?"

Authority Council members, or in common vernacular for the executive body, the Authority, were elected to their positions. The buck stopped with them. I expected my mother to become one sooner rather than later.

"There have been some murders. One of the victims was Aleksander Pederson." Michael scrubbed a hand over her face, her Maccabee ring glinting in the light. "He was only thirteen, a cousin to the Authority secretary. He was killed a couple of weeks ago."

"That's horrible, but what's the connection? Was he killed here?"

"No, in Copenhagen, but his death was...unusual. The investigator believes it was related to two similar ones that occurred six weeks apart as well as one that occurred in Vancouver two days ago."

There hadn't been even a whisper about a strange death here in town. Not on the news and not through the grapevine. "You hushed it up?"

"I was ordered to until the investigator arrived." Michael's lips compressed into a thin line. "I don't like having a free agent in my territory."

The penny dropped. Like from the top of the Empire State Building, slamming into my skull, dropped. "You're sending me in to play spy?" I looked up at the ceiling and gave a bitter laugh. "Well, I've got to hand it to you. I didn't think I could feel worse about this situation but look at that. Thanks, Michael. That's outstanding. Even me being a crappy co-leader is bogus."

"No, it isn't."

"Really? Because if he's backed by a Council member, he holds the cards, not you. He doesn't need to accept me on any basis, much less as co-leader. He'll know I'm a plant."

"Let him." Michael silenced a notification that beeped. "I'll give him carte blanche as ordered, but what a shame that our coroner is backed up and budgets are already allocated for all resources for the remainder of the year."

"How Machiavellian," I said with grudging admiration. "Front-of-the-line access and funds in exchange for your mole being on the team. What's in it for me?"

"You get to prove your leadership abilities. Keep me in

the loop, make sure this investigation plays by the rules, and I give you my word that once it's wrapped up, or the vampire leaves, you get your promotion. Level three, no strings attached."

It was the best deal I was going to get, but how could I trust that she wouldn't keep pulling her promises, like Lucy pulling the football from Charlie Brown?

"You wouldn't give me the promotion I deserve because I'm inflammatory," I said, "but you're willing to partner me up with a vampire to solve multiple murders that I'm guessing involve either other vamps or shedim?"

"We're not sure who or what they involve."

I didn't have Spidey senses, but I could tell when people were being cagey. I pushed my curiosity about the case aside. "Michael, why do you want your half-demon child on this?"

"Because you're the only one I trust." She met my gaze calmly with no hint of tension or anything to suggest that was a lie. "Are you in or out? I'd like to have your agreement before I call him in and present him with the fine print."

I believed her on that front, yet I was missing something vital. "Who's the operative?"

She reached for her silver pen again, thought better of it, then said the name in a resigned sigh. "Ezra Cardoso."

My body went cold. The world lurched nauseatingly, the ground under my feet turning to quicksand.

Cherry Bomb, the Brimstone Baroness, perked her head up from the dark pool deep inside me where she lived. Maybe it was weird naming my shedim side and referring to her in the third person, but guys did the same with their penises, and unlike most of them, I wasn't deluded about Cherry's prowess.

Through training, strength of will, and feeding her urges so she didn't become too ravenous to control, I kept

Cherry in line, but at the sound of Ezra's name, every carefully crafted mental binding snapped, and my entire body throbbed like a starving prisoner whose cell had just opened.

"He's not an operative. He's a—" Party boy? Mafia heir? Scourge who should be ruthlessly eradicated?

"He is and has been for the past four years." She held up her hand at my outraged gasp. "I only learned about it. He started gathering intel for us a couple years after the two of you..." She cleared her throat. "His involvement was on a need-to-know basis."

When we met, Ezra had spent his life keeping a low profile. He claimed that when anyone learned he was one of the only born vampires, a Prime, the attention made him feel like a tiger on display at the zoo.

The parade of gorgeous women; the skiing runs in Gstaad; the free climbing in Utah—all of that had been Ezra's cover story as an operative? When rumors surfaced about a year after our breakup that he was the enforcer for his dad's Mafia I'd figured it was a work hard/play hard kind of deal. That since his hits took him around the globe, he blew off steam wherever he found himself.

That version of Ezra hadn't gelled with my experiences, but it certainly made it easier to cast him as my evil ex. Not that I cared if he was offing other asshole vamps.

But how did him being a Mafia assassin work if he was an operative? Was he a double agent?

Was he already an assassin when we were together and never told me? My head pounded.

Maybe whoever he'd been when we were together was the lie, maybe the person he was now was the facade.

I no longer cared.

"Aviva." Michael rapped on her desk, watching me expectantly.

I closed my gaping mouth. Wait. She couldn't honestly

expect me to go through with this. "Are you insane?" I stood up, gripping the back of the chair for balance. Cherry lingered at the edges of my consciousness like a predator at the edge of a jungle. Judging. Waiting. "Or just cruel?"

"I meant what I said about you being the only one I can trust."

"You were there. You saw how badly he hurt me. I know you're ambitious. You always have been, but surely there are limits to that. Surely you wouldn't make me do this, knowing what happened?"

Michael stretched her hand out to me. "Please sit down." When I didn't answer or comply, she dropped her hand. "You know him better than others."

I snorted. "I really don't."

"Then let me put it this way. Everyone else is too blinded by his reputation."

"Which one? The Prime Playboy or the Crimson Prince?"

"Either?" My mother gave me a wry smile. "You don't want him or fear him."

"True, I'm more likely to stake him and be done with it." A dark surge of glee snaked through me; I shoved it down with my metaphoric fingernails.

Michael pressed her lips together then fussed with her monitor. Neither of which was the rebuttal I expected.

"Holy shit!" I tightened my hold on the chair enough to turn my fingers white. "You're hoping for that?"

"Don't be ridiculous. I did have to factor it in as one of many possible outcomes, given your history—"

"I'm out of here." I strode for the door.

"But I dismissed it. You want this shot, Operative Fleischer. Work with Cardoso or make him leave. I don't care. Just get him out of my territory."

My hand on the doorknob, I glanced back, my eyebrows raised.

"Not in a shop vac." She took off her earrings and rubbed the lobes. "I may be the only person who trusts him less than you do."

No, that would be Sachie. My hand tightened on the knob. Oh fuck. What did this mean for her plans?

Damn you, Michael. I wanted this opportunity, conditions and all, but at the expense of my heart bleeding out on the floor again?

The Brimstone Baroness clapped her claws together, and my eyes tingled faintly. Not enough to signal that they'd changed to their demonic color, but rather Cherry testing my control in the wake of this first Ezra-sized detonation.

I dug the nails of my free hand into my palm, wanting the clarity the sting could bring, but the Baroness had always relished those blurred lines between pleasure and pain, and she lapped the sharp bite up. I rested my head against the door. How could I face my ex without thoroughly unleashing Cherry Bomb?

Would that be so bad?

Down, girl, I snarled.

"I haven't forgotten what he did to you." The anger in my mother's voice startled me enough to turn and face her. "Nor will I ever forgive him for it. You haven't been the same since."

"Gee, thanks. I'm also proud of how I've pieced my life back together."

"This is your chance to heal." She stood up, her chair creaking, and approached me. "You're stronger than you think."

"I have no doubts about that." I had questions about what I might aspire to magic-wise if I didn't have to constantly keep Cherry Bomb in check, but my beliefs in my strength—and my control—were rock solid.

In my head, Cherry flipped on her belly like a cat stretching in the warmth of the sun. I might fight with the Baroness, but I didn't hate her. Not anymore. I'd accepted her presence.

Too bad my mother hadn't. Forget me anthropomorphizing Cherry and interacting with her, Michael didn't accept my demon side at all. And no one else could know about her.

My mother reached out to touch me, but I put my hands up and she stepped away, leaving an oddly cold gap. "I appreciate that you're in an impossible position. Your Eishei Kodesh magic illuminates weakness in others, then your shedim genetics feeds off that, demanding you push it to an extreme."

True, but that symbiosis worked in my favor. Growing up, I'd seen Trad doctors (self-labeled Traditionals or people without magic) rather than healers in case my demon magic was detected, but when I'd become a Maccabee—against Michael's wishes—that wasn't an option. Yet not once had anyone spotted that I was an infernal.

"Despite that constant struggle," Michael continued, "I don't see a trail of bodies in your wake. Perhaps I haven't expressed my pride in your control before, but I'm doing so now."

"What a timely compliment." I pressed my palms against the cool wood behind my back. "My entire life I've suffocated under the weight of this secret, not even telling my best friends. Now you're willing to risk that part of me getting the upper hand because it works in your favor?"

"It doesn't work in my favor." She shook her head. "Your career will be destroyed if anyone finds out. I'd hate to lose a good operative."

Same as if I was any Maccabee and not her only child. I bit the inside of my cheek. "As will yours."

Michael nodded in acknowledgment. "Since most infernals don't make it to term, few have ever been found. Or outed." She licked her lips nervously, an uncharacteristic gesture. "The world isn't kind to them or those who sheltered them, but I don't think your secret is in any danger of being exposed." The intercom buzzed again, and she strode back to her desk. "In or out, Aviva?"

Vamps hadn't been accepted without a lot of fear and bloodshed, and that was with the best of them stepping out of the shadows in the 1960s. Some were good, others weren't, but mostly they were universally embraced.

The world feared and despised shedim. As they should. There was no such thing as a good demon. The shitty thing was that people believed that the pure evil inherited from a shedim overrode any possible humanity in an infernal. It was statistically impossible that I was the only one of my kind out there, however, I could hardly seek others out, given the torture and scientific experiments that other infernals had suffered.

But I was so sick and tired of hiding.

Some Maccabees chose to remain level two operatives forever, not wanting the responsibility that came with being level three, which had nothing to do with magic ability, by the way. But for me, that status was a crucial milestone.

In becoming the youngest operative ever to make it to level three, I could start to prove myself as one of the great Maccabees, both in regularly solving hard-hitting cases and mentoring those under me to help them achieve their own greatness to keep humanity safe.

I'd be such a force for good that when the day arrived that I came clean about my shedim side to other Maccabees, I'd have a better outcome than villagers coming after me with torches and pitchforks. Even people like Gemma would be forced to see the good in me.

Sadly, I couldn't appeal to Michael with my reasons for this promotion because she was the one who'd drummed it into my head that I had to keep my secret at all costs. She'd strip me of my level two rank and bounce me back to Maccababy should she learn I planned to eventually go public.

However, with Maccabees on board and supporting me, I could change the rest of the world's antipathy toward us. People would have to finally admit that infernals—I chafed at the name—couldn't be painted with a single brush.

No half shedim would ever suffer the same shame and fear I had, because I'd make a mark as indelible as the stars in the sky. Tikkun olam. Fix the wrongs in the world.

I squeezed my gold ring, my talisman on my path to acceptance. Could I stay detached and play the long game while working with my ex?

Eezzzzrrrraaaaa, Cherry hissed. A veritable catalogue of wooden stakes flashed through my mind. *Look at the glossy sharp toys. So pretty…*

I shook off those images. I was good at keeping secrets, but could I keep one of demonic proportions from being exposed if I was constantly around my ex?

Gathering all my reserves, I mentally re-bound Cherry, driving her further and further into the inky depths, but it was tougher than usual to make her retreat. I sighed. I'd have to let her out later.

"Aviva," Michael said sharply, the receiver against her chest.

I smoothed a hand over my hair, cataloguing how I looked: shirt that made my rack look great, good hair day, tasteful makeup.

This reunion wouldn't be the stuff of my fantasies.

That involved Ezra lying on the ground bleeding out. He'd look up to see me backlit like an angel, but I'd step over his dying body (wearing fabulous heels) while holding the hand of my hot lover. Ezra would then expire of severe dumper's regret. And possibly blood loss, though I hoped that came second.

Then again, this also wasn't my nightmare where I ran into him wearing trackpants and a sweatshirt that was only slightly less flattering than a straitjacket either.

I worried my bottom lip between my teeth. Ezra had annihilated me, but I'd scraped up the shards of my old self and hardened them into forged steel. I didn't break when hard things hit me anymore.

I wouldn't break now either. I could do this.

I sat back down and pasted on a calm expression. "You have a deal."

Michael smiled and spoke into the phone. "Let Mr. Cardoso in."

Chapter 4

Sources speculated that the reason Ezra Cardoso was ridiculously photogenic was because he was a Prime. He never exhibited a wonky eye, an unfortunate double chin, or a flat out "burn it" picture like the rest of us mere mortals. Even so, photos failed to capture how the mere quirk of his lips could express ten thousand words of amusement or how when he leaned in, totally intent on whatever you were saying, he made you feel seen in a way no one else ever had.

I braced myself for the force of him live, but the person who strode through the door was so unlike my first love that it was almost like seeing a stranger.

Any softness in Ezra's face was gone, replaced by a ruggedness in his straight nose, full lips, and well-defined jawline that better fit the image of a man raised to be heir to a vampire Mafia.

He'd bulked up, his formerly lean frame now a V shape. The jacket of his blue three-piece suit hugged his ripped biceps and broad shoulders like he was a modern-day conqueror and this was his bespoke armor.

The Ezra I'd known wouldn't have been caught dead in this outfit.

Or undead.

Michael smiled. "Do come in."

I frowned at the way he studied her like a lion determining a threat or prey, every inch the Crimson Prince, then realized it was Ezra's silvery-blue eyes under his thick arched eyebrows that made it both easier and a million times harder to look at him. Where once they'd caught the light, rippling and ever changing, they were now hard crystals promising knifelike edges, despite the easy grin he bestowed on my mother.

"Director," he said.

One word in that smooth, low baritone and my heart exploded against my ribs so hard I was positive it drowned out all other sound in the room.

His gaze lasered on to me and he went stock-still, his eyes never leaving mine.

A shiver ran down my spine. I crossed one leg over the other, blessing the fates for having worn the wine-colored pencil skirt (that I'd bought as an early celebration gift) with my sheer black hose, and high heels with a bright pop of scarlet on the soles. My tailored white shirt with three-quarter sleeves and a teasing hint of cleavage completed the look.

Something flickered in the depths of his gaze, but it was gone in an instant. "Aviva," he said in a bland voice.

I waited for some awkward follow up small talk but got nothing. It was as if he couldn't be bothered to find out how I'd been.

All right. Two could play that game.

"Cardoso," I replied coolly.

I'd have relished his tight expression, but I was busy telling myself his brush-off didn't matter. It was the first exposure and would be the worst. Now, like a virus, I'd been infected and could build my immunity.

He transferred the gift bag he held to his other hand. "Am I interrupting something?"

"Not at all." Michael motioned to a seat.

Ezra took the chair next to mine with no hesitation. My presence didn't disturb him a whit.

I'd have brushed him off just as easily, but I caught a whiff of his cologne with its notes of cardamom, cloves, and bergamot, a spicy orange smell. It was mixed with the fresh, cool scent of a windswept summer breeze that was all him, and I was hurled back to all the times he'd teased me for pressing my nose to his T-shirts to sniff him.

I dug in my skirt pocket for a package of mints, practically huffing the candies before popping one in my mouth.

He raked a wayward lock off his forehead. His black curls had grown out since we were together, now slightly untamed. (Primes could grow their hair, all other vamps were stuck with the length they had at death.) This longer style lent him a rakish air, yet there was a maturity to him that he wore well. Combined with his close-cropped black beard and mustache, he resembled a pirate. Or the physical representation of sin.

Big deal. It had been six years. He changed; I'd changed.

I crunched my mint into dust.

Ezra set his gift bag, with the neck of a wax-sealed wine bottle protruding, on Michael's desk. "I was in the caves of Saint-Marcel for a wine tasting and this one reminded me of you."

"Do tell," she said drolly.

My ex got an impish expression on his face that I recognized from the many "What? Me do something naughty?" pics that kept popping up on my social media feeds despite my best efforts to block them. "Layered and intense."

Michael chuckled.

Ezra didn't wear a tie, that apparently was still a step too far even for him, and the first couple buttons of his crisp white shirt were undone, exposing a triangle of brown skin.

Vamps kept the same skin color they'd had when alive. They looked totally normal in photos, but if you were in the same room and noticed they weren't breathing, or you felt their gaze on your back, your flight response was pinged.

Not that running was a smart idea. Too many of them took it as an invitation.

"It's a token of my gratitude for accommodating my requests at such short notice," Ezra said.

I squelched the memory of running through my apartment, laughing, while he play-hunted me, and shifted in my seat to shake off my squirminess. He'd certainly pinged me in ways that my operative training hadn't prepared me for.

I wasn't the only one. Whether yachting in Saint-Tropez, diving the Great Barrier Reef, or getting together with celeb pals for a charity hockey game, where Ezra Cardoso went, the paparazzi followed. His antics were the definition of clickbait, and his groupies (Ezracurriculars) were rabid, fanning themselves over each scandalous venture.

Michael pulled the bottle out of the gift bag and gave an impressed nod. "Thank you. I'll enjoy a glass tonight. Now, we have much to discuss."

"I can't imagine what's left to work out," Ezra said. "The terms of my assignment here are fairly straightforward."

"Actually," I piped up, meeting his gaze levelly, "it's not

so much a discussion as a directive." I tapped my finger against my chin. "You're familiar with those." I paused. Smiled. "From all your work as a Maccabee, of course. I just learned we were fellow operatives, but what exciting assignments you must have had."

"And you, the picture of a legacy princess."

My smile hardened. How dare he throw that at me when I'd shared my fears of never amounting to more than Michael's daughter in this organization, instead of a damn good operative earning my reputation via intelligence and hard work?

"Though I will say." He casually crossed one leg over the other. "A directive saves the trouble of time-wasting repetition when the outcome is a predetermined conclusion."

Sadly, since he was a vamp, I couldn't read him for weakness, and Michael would bitch if I jammed a pen through his throat and messed up her fancy Eames chairs. Not that I would, consummate professional that I was.

"Predetermined conclusions. Right." I picked up her silver pen and danced it over my knuckles. "In that case, it's polite to give the other party a well-reasoned explanation and some processing time." I clicked the pen. "A little tip I've picked up as a clear communicator."

One side of Ezra's mouth quirked up. "You definitely keep talking until your point is conceded. Sometimes, however, people refuse to accept reality, in which case, it's best for one party to lay down the law and move on."

Perhaps my next click of the pen was a bit violent because Michael raised a hand. "Speaking of how it has to be." She shot me a warning look. "You're in my home now, Mr. Cardoso, and regardless of what anyone has led you to believe, you will answer to me."

"I wouldn't have assumed anything else," he said smoothly.

"Good." My mother gave a Cheshire Cat smile. "I'm pleased to put all our chapter resources at your disposal and approve your off-site office rental. In return, you'll work with a team of my choosing."

The vampire draped an arm over the back of the chair. "I'd hate to pull your people away for this. I know how stretched local branches are. I've brought my own man."

I eagerly swung my head back to my mother.

"He's most welcome here," she said, "but the other members are nonnegotiable."

Ezra slid his gaze to me, almost like he was making sure I wouldn't bite before replying. "Having Aviva working for me might distract from the investigation at hand. I'm sure you want to have it resolved as quickly as possible and get me out of your hair."

Michael didn't even blink at his smug look. She nodded at me.

I got to deliver the news? I almost jumped up and punched the air, instead, I tsked Ezra. "You misunderstand. I'm not a team member." I gave him one exquisite moment of relief before driving the knife in. "I'm your co-leader."

He opened his mouth. Closed it. Blinked.

"That was a directive, but I can repeat it if it helps," I said sweetly.

"Sticking me with someone who'll report back to you doesn't surprise me," Ezra said, "but using your own daughter? This misguided motherly payback has no place on a mission."

The director's expression turned to granite, but I calmly set the pen on the desk, chin up and posture immaculate.

"Contrary to your insulting insinuation that I'm a

pawn being moved around by her mommy, I chose this assignment."

Ezra Cardoso, my first love and ex-boyfriend, wasn't a virus. Building immunity to him wouldn't save me. I'd been prepared to play nice, but he'd escalated this to a cage match, the two of us locked in combat for the duration of this investigation. Ooh. Maybe I could give him a catchy supervillain/personal nemesis nickname like they had in wrestling.

Piledriver Cardoso. *Ezra, fucking me into the mattress, his eyes wild, one hand pinning my hip down and—* Definitely not that moniker.

"Meanwhile," I said, moving on with steely resolve, "while you apparently have quite the familiarity with murder—"

"You only have murderous impulses?" He tugged nonchalantly on one of his cuffs to straighten it.

I paled, my eyes shooting to Michael, who was thankfully responding to a text she'd received and hadn't paid attention to his allusion to Cherry Bomb.

"That was low, even for a playboy-hitman vampire, or whatever other extracurricular activities you've got going on," I hissed.

"After all these years, I think we're both mature enough to admit that you probably have a voodoo doll in my likeness," he said smoothly.

A knot unwound in my chest. I'd have been grateful, but it was his fault it had cropped up in the first place. "My understanding is that *investigating* murders is not your area of expertise. That would be…"

His eyes flashed in warning at my pause.

"Using your socialite cover to gather intel on rich and powerful shitheads," I said with an innocent expression. "Therefore, you're not more experienced than me, and I have the contacts in Vancouver to be effective. You and I share the same goal of solving this as quickly as possible, so accept the directive and play nice, Cardoso, because this is happening."

Ezra studied me like he was trying to solve an equation that didn't add up. He walked over to the window and leaned against the sill. "Why?"

"Why what?"

"Would you want to partner up with me?"

"You're a stepping stone to something better," I said. His flinch was almost imperceptible, but I caught it. I scratched my forearm, the skin on my body oppressively tight.

"As for my 'misguided motherly payback,'" Michael said, setting her phone down, "you're as wrong as you are condescending. I made this decision as director, accounting for a number of elements."

Ezra smiled thinly. "Including my father."

"As I said." She spread her hands wide. "I assessed many things, including your exceptional work with this organization, which is why I've only imposed a single condition on you."

I watched with mad respect. Say what I might about her, the woman was damn good. Well, when it came to other people.

"Much like a sniper using only a single bullet," Ezra said.

"Or one perfectly sharpened wooden stake," I said with a saccharine smile.

Ezra pushed aside the partially open blind. His hands hadn't changed. I suppressed a shiver at the unwanted memory of him tracing endearments over my skin, his butterfly touch turning deliciously forceful afterward.

The night we'd met, I'd been at a local bar with a bunch of operatives, including Sachie, all of us celebrating our newly minted rise from Maccababy to level one operative, when Ezra approached me and asked to buy me a drink. He was only supposed to be in Vancouver for one night before leaving on a two-week kayaking trip in the wilderness. We stayed up all night talking and walking around the city, and the next morning, he ditched his trip.

Days turned into weeks. Ezra spent the rest of that summer while I was at work enjoying his downtime. He explored the city and rock climbed the Chief, a massive cliff face in Squamish, about an hour north of Vancouver. When September rolled around, he deferred the MBA program he hadn't wished to attend in the first place, taking classes in anything and everything that interested him, from mechanics to cooking.

There was some kind of strain between him and his dad. I'd overheard one tense fight about Ezra coming home, but he'd assured me all was well.

What can I say? I was twenty-four, in love, and thought we'd last forever.

Our whirlwind romance lasted six months, and for a parting gift, he burned my world to ashes.

Was Ezra also remembering our past? Was that why he gazed out the window like the downtown skyline was the most interesting sight in the world?

For some reason, being born with fire magic in one form or another tempered the effects of sunlight once a person was turned. There was a strong correlation between the strength of their powers when human and their ability to survive sunshine.

Trad vamps couldn't go out during daylight hours at all. They fell asleep at dawn and woke at dusk.

As a born vamp of two Eishei Kodesh parents, Ezra could move freely in sunlight except when it was noon on a summer's day. Then he'd crisp up nicely.

It was 10AM on a cloudy October morning. More's the pity.

He pushed off the windowsill. "Who else is on the team?"

"Sachie Saito and a vampire operative called Darsh," Michael said.

I turned my strangled laugh into a cough.

Michael opened her desk drawer and put her fancy pen away. "I trust that won't be a problem?"

Not if I didn't have to tell Sachie that her desire to work with the new guy came with a huge asterisk. She'd been there through the post-breakup apocalypse and I wouldn't have survived without her, but it left her rather biased against Ezra. Kind of how Walder Frey was biased against Robb Stark in *Game of Thrones*.

I shook my head. "No problem at all."

Ezra, who'd met my best friend many times back then, looked faintly ill. "I don't remember meeting Darsh," he said.

I smirked. Darsh's default mode with new people was "cat toys with mouse."

"Oh, you didn't," I said cheerfully. "We only got to know him a couple of years ago when Sach befriended the Spook Squad. She intends to work with them eventually." I stood up. "Come on, co-leader, let's gather the team."

"Let's," he said in a carefully neutral voice, but it was no coincidence that we reached the door at the same time. He was already jockeying for power, trying to take the lead. I made it out into the hallway first with a vicious thrill. Game on.

Chapter 5

The temperature of the average iceberg was several degrees warmer than our vibe during the elevator ride to the basement.

"Prime Playboy, Crimson Prince, Maccabee operative." I ticked the list off on my fingers. "So many sides to you, how do you ever keep them straight?"

Ezra kept his eyes on the numbers crawling past. "Are you going to plague me with sarcasm the entire time we work together or just while we're enclosed in this metal box?"

"It's hardly plaguing. I'm determining how I'm supposed to trust you if I can't be sure that some other secret identity won't spring free and put me and the team in danger."

He gave a quarter turn, enough for me to see the disdain etched into his features. "First of all, I've not kept anything secret other than my undercover operative work, which was not mine to share."

"Bullshit," I said. "You never told me about being your dad's enforcer when we were together."

"Because I wasn't."

"Really?" I widened my eyes. "The night we met, you were supposed to be going kayaking for a couple weeks, but suddenly you stayed. For six months." And I was stupid enough to believe it was all for me. "Did you have a target you were hunting? Was I your cover story?"

"Trust me, if I'd needed a cover story, I could do better than shacking up with some girl. And you've got a lot of nerve bringing up trust."

"Excuse me?"

"Have you trusted any of your close friends or operative partners with what you are? Does Sachie even know?"

A muscle ticked in my jaw. "That's different."

"Of course," he mocked.

"Hey." I grabbed his arm to make him look at me directly. "My secret is for *my* protection."

"Ah yes. The old 'the world isn't kind to infernals' lament. You have no idea how easy you have it."

"Awww, which part of your life is hardest for you, sugar? Being a Prime and an assassin so no one dares mess with you? Jet-setting around the world, going to fabulous parties, and meeting celebs as part of your cover?" I mimed playing the world's smallest violin. "And fuck you for implying I'm on some pity trip. I stated an objective truth about my reality. It *is* different. You don't get to invalidate that."

"Here's another truth. You live in a constant state of controlling Cherry. Are you willing to gamble that you'll never slip up?" he said. "Not even when you get tired or so emotionally invested in a case that you can't banish the images from your head?"

"I never have before, so yeah. I'm confident I'll be okay."

"Heading an investigation hits you differently from working it, especially when it involves serial killings. Should you mess up, your teammates' lives are on the line." He leaned back against the railing and spread his arms wide. "Whereas I've never made a secret of what I am personally. *Who* I am."

"Wish I had that luxury," I shot back.

"Regardless," he steamrolled on, "anyone I work with is confident that I don't take unnecessary risks nor am I rash or impulsive."

Ezra's words punched into me like heavyweight champion blows in the final round. I'd never given him reason to doubt that I was a good person, so his belief that I was reckless or uncaring or plain stupid stemmed from one thing and one thing only.

And so, we came full circle.

"I'm not Cherry's mindless puppet. Is that what you really think?"

"Of course not." Oh good. Not a puppet, just an abomination.

I crossed my arms. "Like you, I've been thoroughly trained to assess risk and calculate for the optimum outcome with the least harm. I've certainly never acted rashly or impulsively."

"Bullshit," he parroted back.

"Name once."

He met my gaze. "Los Angeles."

I caught my hand before I rubbed my heart. *You bastard.* Flying to the States to confront him a few months after he dumped me remained my biggest regret and deepest shame. Only Sach knew I'd done it.

"That wasn't work," I said tightly.

"It was for me." His gaze was a cold slap.

I fiddled with my Maccabee ring. "I didn't know."

"I told you to go home."

"I deserved a proper explanation."

He cocked his head. "We all deserve things we don't get, princess, but you didn't want to listen, and you put other people in danger. Fundamentally, I don't care if your behavior is because of Cherry or that's how you are. Either way, you shouldn't be on this case."

How dare he throw my lowest moment—one of his making—back in my face and act like it was relevant to my exemplary career as an operative? "I've earned this and I'm not going anywhere."

He jabbed a finger at me. "Trusting you with this investigation and a team is impossible so long as you keep lying to everyone. Tell Michael you're stepping down."

"You mean the same director who knows the truth about me and still assigned me because she doesn't trust *you*? Let's see. That makes two of us in the 'distrust Ezra' column and only one on the 'distrust Aviva' side."

"Only because you're not giving anyone else the choice to make up their own minds."

I didn't take my decision to keep Cherry hidden lightly. I'd spent hours obsessing over whether I was doing the right thing, but every time I convinced myself that I should fess up to my nearest and dearest, there was a random comment or throwaway slight against shedim that was so damning, it reinforced my belief that the world wasn't ready to change its mind on infernals. Just like there had been today.

Still, the bitter hurt that washed over me at Ezra's words was like an ocean. It had monsters with sharp teeth swimming in its depths, underwater volcanos full of fire, and riptides that could drown a person in seconds.

I steeled myself—for the rest of this conversation. For working with someone who had once been my haven but was now a barbed wire fence. "Is that a threat that you'll out me?"

The past six years I'd lived with the constant fear that Ezra would use Cherry against me. It was almost a relief to have it out in the open.

"Don't compromise my case and we won't have to find out."

My laugh had a bladed edge. "If my shedim nature was a danger to anyone, you wouldn't exist anymore."

"Like you could take me."

"I'd dare you to find out, but you're of more use to me undead than dead."

The elevator doors opened. Ezra stepped past me into the open area where the Spook Squad worked out of and took a deep breath. Since he didn't require oxygen, acting like he needed some fresh, non-Aviva air was a mega diss. I'd remember it.

I looked up at the ceiling, taking a moment to wrap myself in calm feelings.

All of the perforated factory tiles, which had been brown with age, were gone, the ceiling now a smooth white plaster from which hung multicolored silk lanterns hand painted in delicate flowers, throwing bright pools of light.

Ezra took in the space with a single assessing glance. "Colorful."

It was. Delightfully so. For years, the basement had been a furniture graveyard, spanning pieces from wobbly threadbare Art Deco chairs to bloated 1980s mahogany executive desks. They'd been cleared out and replaced with oversize couches and chairs in sumptuous bright fabrics that were sturdy enough to bear the brunt of two vamps in full brawl.

However, I couldn't tell if he was being snarky. I shoved the last threads of my anger aside, opting for a more jocular tone to reset our dynamic. "It beats other Spook Squads' design aesthetics."

"Not into red velvet bordello?"

"I mean, once you've seen one. And motorcycle club toxic masculinity gets redundant, am I right?"

Hearing voices coming from the kitchen at the back, I headed that way, patting the large unicorn stuffie riding a stumpy palm tree planted in a pot covered in mosaic tiles from Italy. "Looking good, Bentley."

We passed streamlined adjustable computer stands, a couple with open laptops, and a reinforced iron door leading to the single holding cell, which nulled vamp magic. Most got staked before they got anywhere near the cell. Shedim ended up in jail even more rarely.

Our chapter basement didn't have windows, courtesy of the original garment factory. The vamp operatives would have been fine with them because they were all former Eishei Kodesh, but no one wanted any Trad vamp suspect to be fried mid-interrogation.

Ezra glanced at the row of offices on the left, each with ergonomic chairs and modular workspaces, his stride loose and relaxed like meeting a group who'd only know him as a thrill-seeking social media darling, and therefore be hostile to learning he had unheard-of carte blanche, was a regular occurrence.

Sachie's laugh floated out from the kitchen. It was not the sound of someone who knew she'd been transferred to a team with her best friend's personal holocaust.

But just in case she was keeping up appearances… I glanced at Ezra. Even a six-foot shark in a designer suit could be injured, and I couldn't have my first act as co-leader be sweeping up my counterpart's remains.

The paperwork would be hell.

I sprinted past a confused Ezra to pat my bestie down for weapons.

She was with two of the three undead operatives in Vancouver's Spook Squad, all of them arranged in a semi-circle around a new vamp. Well, I think it was a vamp. I saw only his toned ass in tight denim sticking out from under the kitchen sink and his ridiculously large hard thighs. If the rest of him was appropriately proportioned, how did he fit in the cupboard under the sink?

Or in those jeans? I glanced at his motorcycle boots. Size thirteen? Fourteen? Big feet, big—

Cherry Bomb sat up.

The stranger made hmming noises and reached backward for a wrench in the toolbox. Big hands too.

"Hey," I said, keeping my distance in the doorway.

Sachie brandished a wickedly sharp cleaver in my direction, nary a dimple in sight. "I heard the news."

Oh yay. Michael worked fast.

I checked over my shoulder, but Ezra hadn't arrived yet. I dropped my voice to a whisper, hoping he wouldn't hear. "Maybe lower the—" I gestured at the blade.

"Knives aren't for vampires. They're for people who willingly throw themselves back into self-destruction." She smiled wider. "Know anyone like that?"

Our friend Darsh lounged on the counter like a slinky lemur, all long limbs and big brownish-gold eyes ringed in dark liner, a crackling energy radiating off his porcelain skin. He was the palest being I'd ever met, a result of vanity, not vampirism. With his shoulder-length tumble of silky brown hair, fuzzy cropped sweater, and cargo pants with an embarrassment of buckles, it would be easy to underestimate him. Or at the very least, be flustered by him.

Darsh generally counted on both being true.

His overall air of mystery helped with that. He'd shared with Sachie and me that he was Roma and he spoke Romani, a language descended from Sanskrit—also the origin of his name—but not much more. Many Roma kept their ethnicity secret because those people were highly discriminated against and persecuted even today, but Darsh wore it like a badge of pride. Why shouldn't he? He was top of the food chain, and people who disrespected his community found out how much lower they were.

"Apparently, I've been transferred too?" Darsh spun the beads woven into his black leather wrist cuff. "Huzzah."

I grimaced. The last time he'd uttered that word in that dangerous purr, a shedim had ended up begging for death.

"Michael is full of surprises," Ezra said from behind me.

Sachie readjusted her grip on the cleaver.

Darsh slitted his lashes. "Careful, darling. You don't want to antagonize the Crimson Prince."

"I'm not here to hurt anyone," Ezra said mildly.

Sachie quickly flicked her gaze at me, then away. "No?"

I massaged my temples. *So it begins.* Okay, she wouldn't stab Ezra with the knife. It was too big to be effective and he'd get it away from her. Besides, she was an Orange Flame. She could turn him to vamp jerky and really make him suffer.

Shit. She wasn't kidding that the knife was for me.

"For the tenth time," Cécile Tremblay said, tightening her blond ponytail. "Requisition a plumber." The whip thin Québécoise vampire and most senior operative of the Spook Squad pressed her lips together in a line as sharp as the creases on her khaki pants.

"A plumber would take a week to show up," Sach said.

"It's no problem at all, ma'am," the voice attached to the butt said in a Southern drawl that was slow and thick like molasses. "I'm happy to help."

"Non. This is most unorthodox." Cécile crossed her arms, turning to face Ezra and me. "As is losing Darsh to this investigation. I couldn't believe it when Michael told me last night that Ezra Cardoso was one of ours."

"Imagine my joy at learning it five minutes ago," Darsh said.

"Indescribable joy," Sach chimed in.

Ignoring my friends, I clasped my hands behind my back so I didn't rub them together in glee. Cécile had been a human operative who was turned when she was attacked off-duty. She'd chosen to remain with the organization, though she no longer wore her ring. Vamp powers made the magic in the ring unpredictable, so undead Maccabees were released from that part of their oath.

Cécile was also a stickler for rules and regulations. Ezra was about to get a strip torn off him.

Ezra placed a hand to his heart and said something to her in French.

My mouth fell open at the words in his low, husky voice falling from his lips like honey. He spoke French?

Sach twisted the cleaver to catch the light, momentarily blinding me.

I blinked. Right. Yes. The important fact was that his BS charm act on this no-nonsense woman was going to fail so hard.

Cécile blushed. "We're Maccabees. We serve the good of humanity together."

Say what?!

"That we do," Ezra said somberly, but the second Cécile turned back to the sink, he smirked at my scowl.

Something clanked from inside the cupboard, and the enormous man uttered a soft "dang it."

"Tabernac." Cécile shook her head, already halfway to the door. "I'm finding Michael."

And then there were four.

"Almost done," Sink Vamp said. "I look forward to meeting y'all properly when I've got this drain unclogged."

Right, five.

"What a Boy Scout," Darsh murmured.

"No rush, Silas," Ezra said. He smiled at Sachie. "Good to see you again."

"Delighted you think so," she said, stroking a finger over the needle-sharp knife blade.

As her best friend, this pleased me to no end. However, as her direct superior, it was a tad problematic.

I clapped my hands together. "Darsh, allow me to properly introduce Ezra Cardoso."

"The Mafia heir turned knight in shining armor. It's so surprising it is almost unbelievable." Darsh shrugged. "But far be it from me to judge." He threw Ezra a brilliant smile and held out his hand in the manner of a pope expecting his ring to be kissed. Well, a pope who reigned in dark purple nail polish. "Enchanté."

Ezra shook his hand without hesitation. "I read up on you."

Darsh broke the grip. "A fan. How sweet." His demure tone was at odds with the steely glint in his eyes.

As co-leader, I should shut this down. Darsh was almost six feet of cobra about to strike, and I'd normally give him the easy odds, but Ezra hadn't known they'd be teamed up.

During our time together, Cardoso—I really needed a supervillain name—had actively sussed out exits and potential dangers like most vamps, but he'd shown up today already informed about Darsh? That was forethought threat determination.

I frowned. Had Ezra read up on all of our Spook Squad, guessing that Michael would assign one of those vamps to work with him? Or was learning about Darsh merely some extension of Ezra researching me?

What exactly might he have read about me? Or had he not bothered?

"I was more curious than a fan," Ezra said. "You're

the only vampire to ever strike a deal with the Maccabees to become an operative and escape punishment."

Sachie's knife clattered to the ground, and I sucked in a breath. We were Darsh's best friends and this was news to us. Surely you'd tell your besties if you'd committed a heinous enough crime to get the Maccabees called on you? Yes, he kept mum about other personal details—even his age was a giant question mark—but he trusted us. He'd been a Maccabee for decades, posted all around the world, and no one had ever said that his being on our side was involuntary or part of a deal.

What else was he hiding from us if Ezra was right?

"That's old news," Darsh said flippantly. His blasé attitude sounded a bit too tight to ring true.

"Yes, seeing as it happened seventy years ago in a city lost to an earthquake." Ezra threw him a bland smile. "With all the specifics conveniently long gone."

"It doesn't matter," Sach said immediately.

Did it? Had the lazy Sunday mornings where Sach and I sprawled on Darsh's sofa watching *The Great British Bake Off* while he fed us mimosas been a lie? What about when he dressed us up and gave us crazy glitter-filled makeovers for our nights out together dancing? Or those rare moments when his natural sparkle vanished, leaving an inexplicable sadness weighing down his shoulders that he didn't hide from us?

"No," I said firmly. "It doesn't." Darsh was allowed his secrets, and I wasn't going to judge him on anything other than his actions during our friendship. It didn't matter how or why he'd gotten here; he was a valuable operative and a good friend. People could hold secrets and still be trusted by the ones closest to them.

But how had Ezra unearthed this? Was it a testament to his intel gathering, his Mafia connections, or did he have access to Maccabee information that not even my mother did?

Unease snaked through me.

Ezra had partied with the rich and famous for the past four years, collecting intelligence on powerful people who kept their skeletons in tightly locked closets. Yet somehow, he'd maintained his cover while being dogged by paparazzi, and while his reputation as the Crimson Prince followed him everywhere? Not to mention, he'd never been charged with any crime, much less arrested.

Had being raised by a Mafia don father taught him how to spot a mask? I hadn't known anything about that part of his life when we'd been together. He'd fooled everyone—including me. Was murder investigator his latest disguise?

My fate was tied to this case. If this was some con Ezra was running, he'd rue the day he showed up here.

Darsh hopped off the counter to retrieve the cleaver that Sach had dropped. "I'm a mystery wrapped in a pretty package."

I grabbed it before he could, earning an amused snort.

"You're right." Ezra shrugged. "It's ancient history. Far be it from me to judge."

If Darsh was a cobra, Ezra had proven himself a mongoose, striking his blow with ninja stealth.

I unclenched my jaw. Michael had uncharitably taken the *vacuuming Ezra's remains up with a shop vac* option off the table, so now I'd have to keep him safe from *two* individuals who wished him dead if I was to earn my level three status.

I could make him disappear, Cherry crooned in my head. I'd have hushed her, but a good operative had to keep an open mind. We'd call that plan B.

Chapter 6

The new vamp, Silas, finally scooted out from under the sink, rubbing a smudge of oil off his hand with a rag. "Should be good to go. It was just a trap issue."

I did not expect the cropped dark red hair and smattering of freckles across his broken nose paired with the brightest hazel eyes I'd ever seen. Whatever vamp age he was, he'd been turned in his mid-twenties and never lost his boyish good looks.

Silas stood up to test the faucet, and I swear his shadow blotted out half the room. He probably bench-pressed oxen. The guy was so jacked that Ezra looked a bit scrawny next to him and Darsh looked like a hunger strike victim.

Not that I'd ever say that out loud.

"Hi." I held out my hand. "I'm Aviva Fleischer. Your new co-leader." The "co" part stuck in my throat. What can I say? I was an only child; I was never good at sharing.

Silas stuffed the rag in his back pocket and shook, his hand swallowing mine. Contrary to popular belief, not all vamps were cold to the touch. That only happened when they were hungry. "Silas," he said affably, his skin thankfully warm. "Nice to meet you, ma'am."

Ezra laughed at my horrified expression. The corners of his eyes crinkled, and his white teeth flashed like a beacon of joy against his brown skin. His unfettered merriment drew me like a moth to a flame, and I took a step back to keep from getting zapped. "Silas has never shaken off his old-fashioned upbringing," he said.

"Call me Aviva," I said kindly.

"Sorry, ma—I mean, Aviva," Silas said, his cheeks flushing faintly pink.

This wasn't my first rodeo with a vamp. My expression had nothing to do with his manners, but the sum total of his reaction to me. Ezra had brought Silas along as his team member. He was someone my ex trusted to have his back; they would have swapped personal stories yet Silas hadn't shown any reaction to meeting me.

Did Ezra shed personal entanglements as easily as each of the skins he wore? Or had he never felt anything for me at all?

Sachie pried the knife from my white-knuckled grip and set it on the counter.

Ezra clapped Silas on the shoulder. "This guy has been with me through thick and thin these past few years. You couldn't ask for a better operative."

"It doesn't get better than Sachie and Darsh," I retorted.

"Now that we're one big happy family," Darsh said, crossing his arms, "what's the deal? Sach and I were only told we were working on a top-secret case."

Ezra and Silas exchanged somber looks.

"Multiple murders." Ezra looked around. "In the interests of privacy, I've rented us a workspace elsewhere." He rattled off an address. "Let's reconvene at midnight, and I'll walk you through the details. Wear boots and warm clothes."

Ooh. A nighttime adventure. This was going to fuck with my sleep schedule, but I was always up for a good nap. "We'll be there."

"Where should I put this?" Silas picked up the toolbox.

"Leave it," Darsh said. "I'll put it away."

"No," Silas said. "My mother raised me to clean up after myself."

Darsh opened his mouth, but Sach pushed past him, stepping on his foot as she did so.

"I'll show you," she said.

"Thank you, Miz Sachie."

She blushed. "Right. Well. This way."

Silas nodded at Darsh and me. "Nice meeting you. I'll see y'all later. Ez, I'll wait by the main entrance." He followed Sachie out.

"Oh, I've got to see this," Darsh muttered and headed off after them.

I watched them leave. It was late morning, which meant Silas had been Eishei Kodesh in life since he was awake. I wouldn't be sure how comfortable he was outside until I saw how he moved about there, but I suspected he'd been fairly powerful before he was turned. Not that he'd still have his flame magic.

Once an Eishei Kodesh was turned, that magic was supplanted by their vamp abilities of enhanced hearing, smell, speed, and strength, plus compulsion abilities that deepened with age. A vampire of twenty years could compel a small bird or rodent, but not affect a human until they had a couple hundred years under their belts. Regardless, all changed vamps, whether Trad or Eishei Kodesh, possessed the same abilities, with the exception of their sun tolerance.

That was another reason that people had a much harder time reconciling the existence of demons. Shedim magic took many forms, all geared toward amping aggression and sowing chaos.

"Will you and Sachie be all right working so late tonight?" Ezra smothered a yawn. "We normally won't have to meet at night, but I'm jet-lagged and my internal clock is messed up." He headed back through the now-empty main room.

"Don't worry about us, just make sure you're in peak form. Co-leader," I added pointedly.

"Look, Avi, I—"

"Aviva," I corrected. I'd been Avi to him through our entire relationship. Well, almost all of it. If he sought to disarm me by falling back into a personal connection, my nemesis (Crusher Cardoso? Nah, that sounded like a monster truck) was in for a grave disappointment. "Let's keep this professional," I said coolly.

"Does Cherry Bomb agree with that?" he said.

Inside my head, the Baroness hissed.

I ground my teeth together, taking off a layer of enamel, but I'd concealed my flinch. I'd never had a choice about my mother knowing my secret, but there was one person I'd *chosen* to trust with it.

It was so ingrained in me to keep the word "infernal" quiet that it took me three tries to say it aloud that night, but Ezra had been sweet and solicitous, concerned only about the strain of hiding that part of myself from the world. Not once during that talk had he expressed scorn or derision.

As one of the only Primes in existence, someone who'd been born a vampire rather than turned into one, he was a curiosity within the vamp community, and a freak in his own way. He'd understood.

I'd fallen asleep in a state of bliss, certain in my heart

of hearts that I'd done the right thing. I'd even decided that Michael was wrong, or at least overly paranoid, and I resolved to bring Sachie into the circle of trust. A weight had lifted off me, my outlook on life blooming into a glorious Technicolor, like Dorothy landing in Oz.

The next morning, Ezra dumped me with no real explanation. That was the first time he used my full name. Our breakup was as brutal as Buffy finally sleeping with Angel only to wake up to Angelus. Except there was no curse on Ezra's soul to blame or explain it away.

I'd finally shown my true self, and I'd been cast off like garbage. It had taken me a long time to recover from that and even longer to fully believe in myself, *all* of myself, again.

The lesson had been hammered home, and no one, not even my mother, knew that I had learned it.

"Your threat when we were in the elevator to expose Cherry was received loud and clear." I veered around a club chair. "I'd appreciate you not bringing it up on a regular basis."

Ezra scrubbed his fingers through his hair, which annoyingly only made it look more windswept and sexy instead of like he'd stuck his finger in a socket. Ooh. Maybe I could drive him to electrocution and be done with him once and for all. "What I said before… I was tired and it slipped out," he said. "I promised I'd never say anything, and I meant it."

"Ah, but that was then," I said nonchalantly, following close on his heels. "I wouldn't dare presume your character now. Don't speak ill of the dead, etc."

He stopped so suddenly at the elevator that I bashed my nose on his spine.

Rubbing it, I stepped back, suppressing a chuckle. Ezra haaaated being called dead.

"This investigation isn't a joke," he snapped and hit

the call button. "Four people have been brutally murdered, and I expect more will follow."

Excellent reasons to treat this case with the utmost gravitas, but honed instinct from years of experience and training told me there was more to this. He'd avoided Vancouver for six years. Now, he'd taken a break from being a spy with a playboy lifestyle to come solve a murder case? Had he been coerced? Or was he made an offer that meant as much to him as attaining level three did to me?

Time would tell.

"I'll say this once, so listen carefully," I said. "I'm an exceptional Maccabee, and I take my job and my responsibility to keep people safe more seriously than you can imagine. As far as I'm concerned, when I step through our office door at midnight you will simply be a new colleague working an important case with me. I'll pull my weight and have your back. Any history we have?" I snapped my fingers. "Forgotten."

The elevator doors opened, and Ezra stepped inside. "Same for me."

No, I'm pretty sure you forgot it the moment you walked away six years ago. I matched Ezra's cool gaze. Good thing I was such an expert liar. My heart gave a single twitch, but I'd long ago reinforced that precious organ, and she held firm until the doors closed.

I exhaled slowly.

"The man has exceptional taste in suits," Darsh said, pushing out of the stairwell door. "But the rest of him is rubbish."

I jumped with a shriek. "I thought you left."

"Now I'm back."

Sachie followed him. "Apparently, I failed to adequately entertain Darsh." She tagged me on the shoulder. "Your turn."

Our friend threw himself onto a purple velvet sofa.

"Yes, do better than Miz Sachie and Cowpoke." He mimicked Silas's accent.

Sach whipped a cushion at him. "What did you expect me to do to Silas? Dry hump his leg? Climb him like a monkey?"

Thrilled as I was that we weren't going to get into the weeds of me working with Ezra, this was not my desired team bonding. "All right, you two."

"Either would have been preferable to that dull conversation you had." Darsh tucked the cushion behind his back.

"We were discussing free soloing." Sachie dropped into a chair and crossed her legs, swinging one Doc Marten-clad foot. "What part of rock climbing without any ropes is dull?"

"On another note—" I began.

"Nothing if you're talking about overhangs or fingertip grip things," Darsh said. "He went on about chalk. For five minutes straight."

I put two fingers in my mouth and let out an ear-piercing whistle. "Are you done?"

"Apparently." Darsh sniffed.

"I love the two of you beyond anything—"

"Oh boy," Sachie muttered.

"That's a 'but' sentence if I ever heard one," Darsh said.

"Did either of you hear the part where I was made co-leader on this assignment?"

"Between my horror of working alongside Fuckboy and Cowpoke?" Darsh scratched his nose. "Vaguely?"

"Is that going to be weird? Me being your boss?"

"Aw, it's cute you think we'll treat you that way," Sachie said.

I stuck my tongue out at her.

"Well, I feel very secure following someone with those

leadership skills," she said. "Kidding aside, I'm thrilled for you, if confused about what the unholy hell Michael was thinking."

"Inside voice," Darsh murmured.

"No. There is no inside voice." She stabbed a finger at me. "I saw how you looked at him when he spoke French. You are not going down that road again. Walk away from this. For the sake of my sanity. I beg you."

"I'm not a masochist, and I'm not going to fall for him again. But if I walk away, then he's dictating my life as much as when I couldn't get out of bed for weeks."

Darsh flashed me a heart sign, and I smiled. He'd heard the details of the crash and burn.

Sach picked a piece of lint off her dress. "Avi—"

"No."

"But it doesn't mean—" She held up a hand to cut off my further protests. "You don't need to be the youngest level three."

"This isn't about ego."

She frowned. "Then what is it about? What happens when you hit this goal? What becomes the next thing you live for?"

I sat down and steepled my fingers in contemplation. "World domination."

"Uzai!" She stomped her foot.

I wagged a finger at her. "I'm not annoying. And perhaps the woman intent on a far more dangerous career path than me should not judge."

Her open desire to work with the Spook Squad had lost her friends among the human operatives, though she claimed not to care. What would this cost her? I tamped down my worry. If this was her dream, I'd have her back, same as always.

Sach made a snarky face. "Don't judge. Exercise regularly. Eat breakfast. You're always putting conditions on our friendship." When that got a laugh out of me, her expression softened. "I'm simply saying there's more to life than work."

I spread my hands wide. "If life would care to show me otherwise, it knows where to find me. Until that happens, I'd like the fruits of my hard labor now, please. Okay?"

Besides, she was wrong about why I was so determined to move up.

"Okay. Dumbass." She shook her head, but I got a fond smile—one showing both her cheek dimples—so all was well. "It probably won't matter anyway," she added. "I give you five days before you stake Count von Cardoso."

I perked up. Now there was a strong contender for a supervillain name.

"I get the Count Dracula reference," I said, "but what's up with the 'von'?"

Sach grinned. "It makes him sound eviler."

"Yeah," I said musingly. "That's it. Count von Cardoso, suuuupeeeervillain." I said it the way a wrestling announcer would, liking the sound of it.

Sach slapped her hand on an oversize ottoman. "Pretend that's a twenty. Five days till he goes down."

"Bet making is so dull in this electronic age," Darsh said. "Oh, for the days when you could toss the keys to the castle down on the felt and then look into the haunted eyes of your opponent as you swept your winnings from the table."

"Do we need to revisit whatever landed you in our organization?" I winked at him.

"And here I was about to demonstrate my faith in you and give you a full week until you cracked." Darsh snapped his fingers at me. "Lend me twenty, AF."

I slapped my hand on the ottoman. "I'll take your

insulting bets and kick butt. If I resolve this case successfully, then I have level three in the bag. Obviously, I'm going to outlast him."

I didn't mention that driving Ezra out of town was also an acceptable outcome for Michael. I had to work the case and find the killer, not manage my friends' schemes to rid us of Ezra's presence.

For all their snark, Sachie and Darsh were committed investigators, but their protective instincts might derail their honorable intentions.

"Now, will you both please behave for my sake?" I pressed my hands together in a pleading formation. "Sach, no staking Ezra. Darsh, no needling anyone. Metaphorically or literally."

"And you won't call him Count von Cardoso," Sachie said.

"To his face," I conceded.

"Fair."

"I, for one, shall be on my best behavior." Darsh crossed his heart, rattling the black beads woven into his leather wrist cuff.

Sachie stood up and stretched. "I guess drinks night is out, but Michael released me from paperwork duty." She punched the air in triumph. "I'm going to go home and sleep. Avi, you coming?"

I hadn't driven this morning because my car was in the shop. Given Sach and I were roommates, I might as well hitch a ride.

"Yeah." I had to lead my first team meeting as co-leader this evening and contend with my ex. On top of that, I had to stay alert in case my best friend started wielding pointy things. It was going to be a long night.

Chapter 7

A nap wasn't the only thing on my agenda.

I'd been up for a while, trying and failing to read a book until it grew late enough for my purposes. Finally, at 9PM, I layered up with a white reflective jacket over my T-shirt and compression tights, slipped on my runner's headlamp, and laced up my current favorite sneakers. I filled up my hydration pack with a sports drink—electrolytes were essential—strapped it around my bicep and headed into the living room. "Going out for a run."

Sachie paused the K-drama on her laptop, put her burrito on the plate, and raked an assessing glance over me. She hated that I ran at night, but she'd conceded the losing battle years ago. So long as I was lit to her standards, she was appeased enough that she'd come identify my body in case of a mishap.

"Wait." She swung her long legs off the textured sectional sofa and pressed the invisible latch on our reclaimed oak coffee table, releasing the drawer. Taking another bite of her burrito, my multitasking friend found and tossed me a thin yet lethally sharp wooden stake. Sach described her training to get onto the Spook Squad as committed. I'd add enthusiastic to that. Regardless, we had stakes, bear spray, and good old brass knuckles stashed all over.

My friend refused to only rely on magic because if she got hurt or tired, she'd be too drained to finish off an opponent. She included her ring in that policy—in case its magic ran out at a critical juncture. Instead, she practiced religiously with weapons and made me do it too.

They didn't go with her condo's expansive view of Sunset Beach or the cool artisanal furniture, but defense over design. Besides, what her parents couldn't see when they came for dinner wouldn't result in another lecture about the dangers of her career plans and my friend's eye twitch kicking in for the next day or so.

Ben and Reina called this place the "failed bribe." When Sachie graduated university with a degree in criminal studies, they offered to give her the down payment for a condo if she didn't become an operative. She took them up on it, though she made it clear that she was still going to become a Maccabee. However, if they didn't want her living in some shithole on a Maccababy's wages (Vancouver was ridiculously expensive), she'd like the down payment as well, please and thank you.

She didn't tell any of us back then that joining the Spook Squad was part of her plan.

More than once over the years, I wondered if Sach suspected what I was and that arming me wasn't merely to keep me safe but to help me blow off steam. I didn't ask and she didn't tell.

"Be back by eleven if you plan on showering before work," she said.

"No, I'd like to show up for my first meeting as a hot stinky mess. Really nail my unprofessionalism with the added bonus of looking like shit in front of my ex."

She took a bite of her burrito, grimaced, and then

used her magic to pull warmth from the air and reheat it since she was too lazy to walk to the microwave. I'd seen her do this countless times before. Satisfied with her next bite, she restarted the show.

If Cherry hadn't been pulsing against my tender insides, abrasive like a scouring pad, I'd have stuck around to watch. Oh well, I'd get a recap later.

After locking up, I headed past the other five doors to the elevator. It was always quiet here on the ninth floor. Not that our neighbors rocked noise control, just that the place had stellar soundproofing. It was one of the main reasons that Sachie had opted for this condo over the others they'd checked out.

I waved at a couple of strata members chatting by the mailboxes in the marble lobby and pushed outside, looking up at the stars before stretching.

It was a gorgeous night. The weather had been clear and dry for the past few days, but there was that bite in the air made for wearing skirts and boots, and all the trees in the city had exploded in a brilliance of color.

Once I was sufficiently warmed up, I broke into a slow jog until I hit my stride.

I dropped some of my internal safeguards, and the Brimstone Baroness bounded to the forefront of my consciousness like a dog who'd been cooped up too long. She directed the leash, but I held the other end. Cherry hummed, her excitement soothing the rawness of her earlier mood.

Cherry steered me to our favorite route along the seawall to English Bay and into the darkness of Stanley Park. A beloved staple of our city, it was about a fifth larger than Central Park, housing an aquarium, an outdoor theater, rose gardens, and acres and acres of forest with trails. Since it was an urban retreat and home to many animals deserving a natural light cycle, the park itself was poorly lit.

It was perfect on every level.

I jogged past the outdoor pool at Second Beach. My demon genetics didn't spare me from the aches and pains of running, but in talking to other athletes, I'd gathered that my high came on faster and deeper. Like I could jog a few blocks and hit a marathoner's level of euphoria, making any workout feel more fulfilling.

The waves lapped gently against the side of the seawall, keeping us company until we reached the stone stairs at Third Beach, which led to the rest of the park. I headed up, jumping the stairs two at a time, and quickly crossed the empty parking lot. The only sound that existed was my breathing and the rhythm of my long, even strides, each footfall a percussive vibration keeping time with my heartbeat.

Once in the forest on spongier ground, I adjusted my speed to one appropriate for a woman cognizant of jogging alone at night while paying attention to tree roots or rocks that could trip me up on the dirt trail.

An owl hooted, its gold eyes gleaming curiously at me from a ruffle of white feathers, and I hooted back. People assumed that nighttime meant shadows, but from all my time spent outdoors in the dark I'd learned to see the amazing color palette laid out before me: silvery ferns, stands of dark green cathedral-like Douglas firs, and the reddish peeling bark of a split-trunk arbutus, all bathed in the yellow-orange glow of moonlight.

My runner's watch beeped to warn me to head home, but first, I lifted my arm and drank deeply from the hydration pack strapped to it.

Cherry sulked for the first part of our return journey since she hadn't fed yet—i.e. gotten her energy rush out of me beating the shit out of something supernatural—but she perked up with each new rustle, each new possibility that a monster had come calling.

Being a half shedim didn't come with enhanced senses like vamps had, but Cherry recognized when full demons were present. However, I only got that ability when I let her take the lead, experiencing it as a huge spike in her excitement.

I'd made it out of the forest and onto the sidewalk that ran along the road above the seawall when a surge of adrenaline speared through me so hard that I stumbled, my pulse going haywire. Sadly, it wasn't like Cherry pinpointed shedim. It was more, "Aha! There be danger in the general vicinity. Have at it."

I slowed to a walk, doing some shoulder stretches and scanning the darkness around me. A twig snapped off to my left, and I pivoted sharply, reaching for the wooden stake concealed against the small of my back, but it was only a raccoon chasing a mouse across the street.

I dropped my hand.

Footsteps pounded steadily behind me.

"Hello?" I called out tremulously, glancing over my shoulder.

"Hi." A man in a orange nylon jacket with the logo of a local aid organization splashed across the front waved at me. His leashed Doberman trotted beside him.

Hello, puppy, the Baroness hummed.

Damn it, Cherry. The major downside of her Spidey senses was that an animal she decided would be fun to tangle with caused the same spike. Or a human with a gun. Shedim, bear, same same to the Baroness. As the one with higher cognitive function, I chose other options. I wasn't about to wrestle a grizzly or stare into the death end of a 9mm Glock to feed her cravings for violence and chaos. The disadvantages of that talent outweighed the benefits, which is why it was trotted out only under specific conditions.

Nor would I harm a dog.

The man reached into his pocket.

I crossed into the middle of the street, keeping up the charade of being a regular woman avoiding a man in a deserted location.

He pulled out a set of keys and dangled them. "Didn't mean to scare you. Just heading home." He pointed at a panel van parked up ahead bearing the same bright logo. I was familiar with this nonprofit group. They worked with Vancouver's homeless population, many of whom lived here in the park, distributing food, medicine, and even blankets and coats if needed.

"Drive safely." I mentally ordered Cherry to stand down, bringing her to heel like any good dog owner.

"I will. Thanks."

I made it another half dozen steps forward, then stopped, something nagging at me.

The aid worker was unlocking the van's door, his pet sitting patiently at his side.

Animals reacted differently to vampires or full demons depending on where they fell on the food chain: deer fled, bears attacked. No surprise that cats either ignored them or curled up on Satan's lap if it suited them.

Dogs generally went apeshit at the major supernatural beings but they barked and growled at infernals. It was a background noise to my life.

There was only one reason why this one hadn't.

In my head, Cherry cackled.

I snuck up to the rear of the vehicle, checking to see that the man wasn't about to drive off. He was busy removing his jacket and tossing it on the passenger seat, so I eased the doors open and gasped.

The inside of the van looked like it had been finger-painted in blood and shit. It smelled that way too and unless the lone calf and foot tossed on the dirty floor was some new high protein meal being tested out, this monster had gotten close to his prey under the guise of helping people, only to kill and eat them.

I grabbed a rock, leapt around the side of the van and launched the projectile, nailing the man between the shoulders and knocking him down.

He sprawled on the sidewalk, curled into a ball and covering his head with his arms. "Please don't hurt me," he cried piteously.

I didn't have time to worry if I'd badly misjudged the situation and hurt an innocent human because his Doberman lunged for me.

I let Cherry fully rise—though still leashed—to the surface, an inhuman growl tearing from my throat.

The dog yelped, its paws skidding on the concrete as it tried to stop. Its nose bashed my hip.

"Down!" I rumbled, pointing at the grass.

The dog dropped to its belly on the ordained spot.

Sighing, the aid worker pushed to his feet, his glamour dissipating to reveal a misshapen creature about five feet high, with four arms, and skin the color and texture of clotted cream. I'd never seen or heard of this type of shedim before; there were too many to be familiar with them all. One day, I'd add all my first-hand knowledge to the Maccabee databases, but for now, with no other information at hand, I was stuck winging it.

"You know how hard it was to train that dumb mutt to shut his yap around me?" The demon had the dulcet tones of a seagull who'd swallowed sandpaper.

"I hope he bit you in the balls." I whipped out the wooden stake and slammed it into the shedim's shoulder. It splintered and broke off with no damage to the demon.

"I'm not a vampire," he snarled. "Amateur."

Not really. I'd learned an important detail. I'd have to conserve my energy accordingly because he wasn't going down with a single blow.

The shedim gripped my torso with three hands, using his fourth to painfully grab my chin and yank my head up. "You're either brave or stupid."

I gagged. His breath was a mix of rotting flesh and sweaty feet. The odds it killed me before any physical assault were high.

Shedim couldn't detect half demons, which worked in my favor. Who wanted a constant target on their back like that? However, if he kept squeezing, my jaw would break.

I relaxed my brutal grip on Cherry, giving her a modicum of control over my body. Her presence inside me became as palpable as a black storm cloud, so heavy and powerful that my bones shivered from its weight. The sensation covered me like a blanket, bringing with it an odd sense of pleasure that I normally wouldn't let myself indulge in.

My eyes got a tingly pins and needles sensation that made my nose twitch.

The shedim blinked at my suddenly glowing acid-green irises that were the color of poison. "You're an infernal? Yum. A delicacy."

I slammed my forehead against his nose, but he knocked me sideways before I connected, so I grabbed his wrist and snapped it, the appendage dangling at a grotesque angle. Admittedly, that left him with three more, but it also allowed me to break free.

The shedim smiled cruelly, exposing a row of crooked jagged teeth against gums blackened with decay, and kicked me in the kidneys.

The air was knocked from my lungs, startling me into relinquishing more control to Cherry. A faint scent of brine shimmered off our skin. We flexed our puny human fingers, admiring the sharp claws on our left hand.

Tasting violence on our tongue like the sweetest honey, we flared our nostrils, threw our head to the sky, and howled, the muscles in our neck corded. A dreamy smile bloomed on our face.

The shedim's twelve eyes narrowed.

We were Neo in *The Matrix*, the world slowing down around us. We barely felt the skin on our knuckles split when we punched him in the gut, or our flesh bruise under his blows.

Full demons didn't like physical combat. They preferred to let their magic do the heavy lifting, but this shedim hadn't been able to sink his insidious powers into us. He was out of practice from hunting a weaker, marginalized population that didn't require much exertion on his part to victimize.

With each blow we landed, his clotted cream skin texture grew more and more curdled. He gnashed his teeth and roared.

Cherry and I snickered. If we were Neo, our opponent was King of the Wild Things. We chucked the demon under his wobbly chin.

He clamped on to us with three hands and swung us into the road.

We bounced on our ass like a rubber ball, rolled over, hit the curb, and fell still. Our hydration pack armband flew into the darkness, and one of our runners lay in the middle of the asphalt. Every part of us throbbed, but we were in it to win it.

His shadow fell over us before we could push to our knees. The demon pressed a foot onto our chest, and white-hot pain shot through our body. The magic he sunk into us cranked our need for violence to the fury of a rioting crowd.

Blood seeped from our nostrils and tear ducts, smearing our vision into an angry red blur. Our heartbeat pounded through us like a war drum.

Our attacker hovered above us, sensing our battle lust and smiling. "You know what they say about too much of a good thing."

It's perfect, Cherry thought.

A low hum, like a million thrumming locusts, coursed through our veins. Every part of us felt plucked and drawn out, like we'd been laid out on a rack.

The shedim jerked his hands away. He glared at the crimson gashes that slit his palms. "Unnatural spawn. You should have been drowned at birth."

Fear slammed into me like a wrecking ball.

Sharp-edged scales frosted in the same toxic green as my eyes now striped my skin. My green eyes and the claws on my left hand were my usual changes. I'd only lost control enough to hit this next stage of my demon side once before: on my bedroom floor after Ezra had gone scorched earth on me.

I fought Cherry, clawing my way back to become fully human, but she and I teetered on a seesaw.

One blow from my multi-handed physical opponent would send me crashing to the ground, my humanity splintered and the Brimstone Baroness ruling in its stead.

In my head I was screaming, but I couldn't work my throat. I could barely move my limbs. Half-blind, I threw my attacker off, and stood up in jerky movements, battling my foe's dark magic coursing inside me that was a siren's song to Cherry.

There was no point begging her to dial down her own cravings and give me a fighting chance. She didn't care that her total satiation meant my destruction. She was the drunk girl at the bar with too-bright eyes and a too-wide smile, too far gone to realize that one more sip was going to make the good times end hard and fast.

I had seconds to turn this around, but if I'd misjudged the extent of the shedim's injuries and not tenderized him enough when I activated my ring, its magic would release uselessly into the air.

That would suck for so many reasons.

I couldn't allow a shedim to brag about nailing an infernal. Sure, I'd be dead, but it would make life difficult not only for my mother, but for anyone who was close to me. It wouldn't be any better if I lived and he got away either, because my life would no longer be my own. Best case scenario, the Maccabees locked me up and experimented on me for the rest of my life.

I shakily dodged an elbow strike, but the demon caught me in a wrestling hold. I grappled with him, trying to get free and deploy my ring, but darkness pressed in on me. I couldn't draw a breath, and I still couldn't see fuck all.

Digging into the last of my energy reserves, I grabbed one of his four arms and bit down hard. Warm coppery liquid filled my mouth. Demon blood was gross, and some types were toxic, but either I hadn't encountered those shedim or I was immune.

Disgusted, I pushed him away and spat out his blood, but I was free. Quickly wiping my eyes, I swiped a finger clockwise over the five tiny gemstones embedded in the ring, activating it, flipped into my synesthete vision, and sighed in relief.

A tapestry of blue polka dots lit up his body along with a single white circle that flared hotter and brighter than the others.

His critical weak spot.

Bullseye. Giving silent thanks to the Blue Flame whose

magic was helping to save my life, I slammed the front of the ring against the white dot.

A thin stream of fire blazed into it; the red gemstone had kicked in. Even though it only lasted a few seconds, that was long enough.

The demon let out a howled curse and grabbed me. Too bad he now had all the strength of a wet paper towel.

I easily stepped out of reach and braced my hands on my thighs, panting and watching the magic process unfold with vicious glee.

It was the orange stone's turn. Now glowing, it drew all the heat out of the shedim. His body twisted, curling like a piece of paper that had been set aflame, his skin the texture of old leather.

The white gem on my ring kicked in, amplifying his emotions, and further weakening him. The demon's cry was the agony of a mother losing a child, the fear of a young soldier sent into enemy gunfire, the hate of a prisoner for their sadistic jailer.

A sated Cherry sang along.

Finally, the yellow gem shone like the sun, its cleansing magic extinguishing the shedim's powers.

The feeling of extreme violence that he'd injected me with loosened its grip. My legs buckled, and I crashed to my knees, my tears washing away the blood in my eyes. With the demon's powers obliterated, the magic vise around my ribs also disappeared, and I sucked down a huge breath of cool air.

Then came the grand finale: the shedim shriveled up in a blur, until the only thing left of him was a paper-thin whorl of skin the size of my forearm.

All five gems on my ring went dark.

The Doberman meekly approached and nosed at my sleeve. Once I'd ensured my skin was back to normal, my claws were gone, and I wouldn't hurt the dog, I scratched the top of its ears with a trembling hand. "I'll get you somewhere safe, buddy."

Back when Maccabees first created Eishei Kodesh magic, when everyone was a Red Flame, they'd expected to incinerate both vamps and shedim with their powers. Later, once Eishei Kodesh had evolved other types of magic, they tested those out too.

I retrieved my sneaker and put it on, the dog sticking close.

The Maccabees quickly realized that none of the new powers killed vamps. Blue Flames couldn't even illuminate their weak spots, which made sense. Why evolve a function that wasn't necessary? Maccabees already knew that vampires had to either be staked through the heart with wood, have their heads cut off, or be incinerated. We already had their weak spots.

So Red Flames used their magic, and everyone else used stakes or blades.

Unfortunately, demons didn't respond to fire magic as nicely as the undead. It took a long time for Red Flames to kill shedim, and some of those fiends had the audacity to enjoy being torched like it was a deluxe spa treatment. Since those operatives had to remain in physical contact with the demons to use their powers, this was a costly lesson to learn.

Maccabees continued to hunt shedim, but positive outcomes were spotty. Until they created the magic cocktail stored in our rings.

I fumbled in my hoodie pocket for a travel-sized package of wipes.

As a half shedim, I'd wondered if I could kill a full demon without the help of my ring, but I'd never tried. Honestly, I wasn't sure I wanted to know the answer, because if I used the ring, I was the same as any other human operative.

That wasn't my main concern tonight, however. I'd been afforded a terrifying glimpse of one potential future. When a shedim considered me an abomination, was there anything I could do to gain approval from my fellow Maccabees, much less the rest of the world?

Would that choice even be mine or would I reveal my demon side publicly out of hurt or fear and damn myself?

No. Fucking Ezra. I'd let him get under my skin and plant doubts in my mind about my well-thought-out survival strategy.

I tore a handful of damp cloths from the plastic container and scrubbed at the blood clotting my nostrils until I was satisfied my face was clean. My eyes had instantly lost their pins and needles sensation when the shedim died, which meant my irises had returned to their regular light brown color. I ran a finger over my arm, seeking reassurance that I had smooth skin and not sharp scales. I did it twice more before my brain was convinced.

My human body wasn't a glamour; it was my natural state. However, the more I let Cherry take control in the short-term, the more I developed certain physical demonic attributes.

I checked the time. I'd have to take an extremely fast shower to make the midnight meeting, but first I called Maccabee HQ to report a suspicious van I'd seen on my run. Leaving out all mention of the shedim, I explained the back door had been open, described the grisly remains inside, and gave them a landmark to find the van, since the park was enormous. I ended the conversation by saying that I'd lock up and hide the keys in the wheel well.

Once that was done, I reversed my hoodie to hide the blood and gore, fixed my ponytail, and picked up the leash. "Wanna run?"

The dog wagged its tail.

I did a quick search for the closest no-kill animal shelter, then the Doberman and I raced each other.

Cherry was silent. After these escapades she went into digestion mode, much like an anaconda who'd swallowed a jaguar. My whole body was sore, but if the fight kept her powered down for a few weeks, the injuries were worth it.

I took the seawall most of the way, since there were no streetlights and I'd encounter few people. Still, I was relieved when I dropped the Doberman off and none of the employees recoiled at the sight of me.

Thanks to the second wind from Cherry's feeding session, I sprinted home.

Eishei Kodesh's magic was a fire-based system. The same flame that burned for eight days and nights in the Hanukkah miracle was used in a ritual now lost in the fog of time to create inherent magic ability.

However, fire was vitally important in Judaism in many other ways. We had Moses and the burning bush, we lit candles every Friday at sunset to usher in our Sabbath, there was an everlasting fire burning on the altar in the Temple of Jerusalem back in ancient times, and we believed in the perpetual flame within the heart of every Jew, which had to be constantly stirred and kept alive.

After a lot of demon-killing failures, some wise Maccabees went back to the idea of fire, hypothesizing that if Jews had to stoke their internal fire, conversely, we had to snuff out the fire within shedim.

But practically speaking, what did that mean? Was there a literal physical source of the demon's fire, their life force? The closest we'd come was their kill spot, but the first problem was that Blue Flames who could illuminate weakness in a demon were rare. Like "in every generation a Slayer is born" rare.

I was not one of them. My Eishei Kodesh magic only worked on people.

When that type of Blue Flame was found, however, the Maccabees basically drove a money truck (or money horse and cart) up to them, milking them like a dairy cow for the rest of their life, their magic distributed in our rings.

A couple of blocks from the condo tower, I slowed to a walk. I was confident that breaking out my demon sensing abilities on the job would result in a pay bump, but I kept my mouth shut because that talent didn't stem from being a Blue Flame.

Somewhere in the 1600s, the Maccabees nailed the demon-killing formula, placing a magic cocktail in the compartments of our rings. The jewelry had been part of the organization from the beginning, but until that point, they only had the embossed flame on the top of the pillbox.

I flicked my finger against the ring. Weirdly, the magic inside was sloshy, allowing an operative to tell when the stash needed to be reupped—after about four uses. I was down to one.

It took only a minuscule drop of each of the five magic types to kill a demon, but due to the rarity of Blue Flames with the right properties, the stash wasn't infinite.

Lots of Maccabees went their entire lives without using the magic contained in their ring, while others had to top it up more frequently. Not every city with a Maccabee chapter had vamps working there, so it was left to the humans to handle rogue vamps and shedim. Although we had a Spook Squad in Vancouver, even a human operative might run into demons in the course of a job. We were allowed to refill as needed, but it was also tracked.

I relied on the override access codes, which weren't logged, and which Michael had "conveniently" left out for me to see years ago to get into the secured room with the dispenser.

Since vampire operatives couldn't wear the rings, it was fortunate that their enhanced strength and senses made them highly capable demon killers.

I got home to find Sach unloading the dishwasher and already dressed for work. "Your hoodie's inside out. Was it that good a run?"

I examined a tear on my sleeve. "Except the part where I ran into some guy and his dog." I shook my head. "Doberman." Technically, I wasn't lying. I just wasn't being clear.

"I'm glad it wasn't worse. Leaving in twenty, okay?"

I nodded. One day, I'd get through a post-run interaction without my gut cramping up. Or better yet, create a world where I didn't have to dance around the truth in the first place. I hoped. Well, for tonight, I had a happy demon inside me. I took the win and headed for a hot shower.

Chapter 8

Any expectation that my new professional digs would match—if not exceed—the comfort and style of Maccabee HQ were dashed when Sachie drove up to the run-down two-story building in South Vancouver located across from not one, but two gas stations.

Maccabee chapters were found across the globe, in medium-to-large cities where the majority of Eishei Kodesh lived. We also maintained a minor presence anywhere a Brink was located.

No one could say for certain when the Brink had first sprung up, but it had taken a long time to identify all dozen or so rifts. Some were in cities, others in the middle of nowhere, and Maccabees constantly monitored for new ones.

I double-checked the address that Ezra had given me. "We're in the right place."

We exited the car, and Sach eyed the cannabis store that occupied the ground floor—one of many in Vancouver. "Well, if we feel the need to get stoned?" She waved a hand at the gas stations. "There's no shortage of chips."

"Good attitude." I hit the buzzer next to the dented metal door.

There was a rush of static and something that might have been Ezra's voice.

"It's us," I said.

The door unlocked with a buzz and a click, and we headed up the narrow stairwell. It smelled like an old person's home that had been closed up for too long, and the nicked walls were painted an unfortunate pea green.

Sach hit the tiny landing at the top and entered first.

I hesitated before following, doing a quick once-over. I'd used topical yellow flame ointment to rid myself of the worst of the bruising. The midnight blue long-sleeved turtleneck concealed any bruises that hadn't totally faded, plus I'd worn my dark, wavy hair down as extra cover. The bleeding from my nose and tear ducts had stopped more than an hour ago, and I'd taken a hot shower, but vamps could sniff out the tiniest trace of blood, and there were three of them beyond that door.

My fingers twitched but I didn't have a stake. That would have been rude, and besides, I wasn't worried. Darsh could have killed me many times over had he been so inclined, Ezra wasn't coming for me under these circumstances, and I doubted that any vamp who called me ma'am posed a threat from the faintest whiff of blood.

I'd trained and worked with vamps for ages, and conversely, our undead operatives had practiced controlling their bloodlust. This would be fine, but if it went sideways, at least I wouldn't be outed, since Cherry Bomb, currently in the equivalent of a food coma, would be of no use.

I opened the door.

The space was larger than I expected, though mostly bare of furniture. A whiteboard dominated one wall next to a scratched-up conference table with six serviceable chairs, but there was an unplugged coffee maker in the galley kitchen next to an old fridge, so at least we were equipped with the basics.

Three sets of vampire eyes shot in my direction, and while I automatically assessed them, it was all rather matter-of-fact. *Grizzly-sized vamp in red plaid shirt at three o'clock, sleek panther at eleven o'clock, King of the Jungle at four thirty.*

Ezra's icy expression was an all-too-familiar—and potent—reminder that there were far worse injuries than physical ones.

A bead of sweat rolled down the back of my neck. "Quit eyeing me like bloodhounds," I said evenly. "I went for a run and had a mishap with a dog."

Darsh, sitting on the windowsill, flapped a hand at me. "You missed a spot, babe. Want me to lick it clean?"

"Big talker," I said, grinning. Our friendship was completely platonic with a lot of teasing, but Darsh was very touchy-feely and dropped endearments with lots of people.

Ezra frowned. He'd changed from a suit to a fitted green Henley with the sleeves rolled up and dark jeans that hugged his thighs like an environmental protester chained to a tree. "If you're done with the chitchat," he said, "perhaps we could get to the reason we're all here."

Sure thing, Count von Cardoso. I smothered a snicker.

"It's five minutes to midnight," I said, "so while I appreciate the urgency of this case, let's start as we mean to continue, with respectful adult communication instead of snark."

"Much appreciated guidelines," Silas said and shot Darsh a pointed look from the corner where he lifted a large monitor next to its twin like it was a tissue box. He placed it on the folding table he was using for a desk. Cables snaked down over to the computer tower on the floor next to discarded boxes and Styrofoam packaging.

Wondering how much trouble my friend had stirred up before we'd arrived, I narrowed my eyes at him, receiving a cherubic smile as he grabbed a chair at the end of the conference table.

Ezra didn't bother to reply to my comment. He moved to the short filing cabinet under the whiteboard and fished out a package of dry-erase markers.

Sachie was jiggling each of the green vinyl chairs in turn around the conference table. She selected one and carefully sat down. She'd broken a shitty chair in high school by sitting on it and now was a fiend for stability. Ironically, only in furniture though. She slapped a notepad and pen on the table. "Ready."

I crossed the room, dropped my puffy coat on a chair across from Sach, and set my laptop bag down.

Car brakes screeched loudly outside followed by several horns honking.

"Interesting digs," Darsh said.

Silas blushed, crouching down by his makeshift desk to tidy up the packaging. "That's my fault. I'd never been to Vancouver before, so I asked someone familiar with the city to help secure a space." He stuffed Styrofoam into one of the monitor boxes. "Apparently, he's still holding a grudge and, uh, we got stuck with this place."

Sachie and Darsh perked up at that tidbit like sharks scenting blood.

"It's better than if we were in a tower downtown," Ezra said. "No surveillance cameras, not a lot of places to hide and watch our comings and goings. We can spruce it up if need be."

We wouldn't be here long enough to require that. I opened my laptop, offering to take written notes.

A picture of each victim in happier times was affixed

to the whiteboard, above each of the four neat columns delineated by red marker. From the open leather briefcase bulging with papers on one of the chairs, Ezra planned to set the rest of the murder board up while he talked us through the crimes.

Sachie flipped open her notebook and clicked her pen, the picture of a bright-eyed, bushy-tailed pupil.

Ezra uncapped a red marker. "Silas knows all this since I brought him on right after I started, but I'm going to run you through it the same way I did with him. I'll introduce the victims before getting into the details of their murders. Throw out any character assessments you have. We're casting a wide net of observations."

"The murders hadn't even been linked until we came on board, a week after Aleksander's death," Silas said. "We only had third-party reports to go on until now."

Ezra wrote "Alison Hamlin" under the picture on the left of a white woman.

Sach bent her head over her notebook. It looked like she was taking notes, but I knew better. She was drawing. It was hard for her to sit still when absorbing information. Our high school teachers got mad at her doodling and failure to pay attention until she trotted out her perfect recall of everything they'd said. They left her alone after that.

"Alison was forty-two." Ezra wrote the facts down in bullet points on the board. "Australian. Atheist. She was an environmental scientist who lived in Sydney, and our first victim, killed back in July."

"She's athletic," Darsh said. "Look at the panoramic vista in the background. That photo was taken on top of a mountain."

"Her tan is from a love of the outdoors, not fake-and-bake sessions," Sachie said, briefly glancing up. "That hat of hers is a Tilley, classic gear for outdoor adventurers."

"She was a happy person," I said. "She enjoyed her work and enjoyed life. That's not just a smile for the camera, those laugh lines crinkle up the corners of her eyes. Did she have a romantic partner?"

"No," Silas said. "Lots of friends, no romantic entanglements."

Ezra added all that to the board, while I entered them into my notes.

"Anything else?" When we shook our heads, he moved to the next photo depicting a Brown man in a salwar kameez leaning on a cane who was posed more formally in front of a lake in an arid valley. "Zayn Mirwani. A seventy-two-year-old Sunni Muslim who lived in—"

"Balochistan. Probably Quetta," Darsh said.

"Y-yes." Ezra blinked at his paper, then at Darsh. "How did you know?"

"His Pakistani surname denotes him as Brahui and most live in Balochistan. Quetta is the largest city in the region so it's a reasonable assumption."

Silas joined us at the conference table. "Why do you know that?"

Darsh shrugged. "Spent some time there."

Neither Sachie nor I were surprised by the breadth of Darsh's knowledge anymore. I peered across the table. She'd completed the outline of a dragon. One of its talons skewed too large for the rest of it, but otherwise, a solid likeness.

"What did Mr. Mirwani do?" she said.

Ezra must have remembered her need to occupy herself while consuming details from when he'd first met her, because he didn't comment on her drawing during this meeting.

"He was the retired founder of an NGO dedicated to securing educational opportunities for rural communities."

Ezra wrote "educational NGO" on the board under the other details.

"I'm guessing he's widowed," I said. "That's a vacation photo. If a wife had taken it, she would have told him to smile, or more likely, been in the photo with him and asked someone else to take the picture."

Some mothers took their little kids to museums or swimming lessons. Michael had done all that with me, but every outing was overlaid with lessons in how to read people for the tiniest sign that they'd uncovered my Cherry bombshell.

Mama Yoda in a power suit and pearl earrings.

If I hadn't become an operative, I'd have made a killing on the professional poker circuit.

Huh. Mom might have preferred that.

"Zayn was a widower," Ezra confirmed—somewhat begrudgingly, in my opinion.

"His posture denotes a dignified man," Darsh said. "He wasn't proud out of arrogance."

Sachie studied the photo for a moment, clicking her pen. "He's stately, like a figure from a bygone era. He didn't go on that trip by himself or with a tour group either. A son or daughter took that picture." She shaded in the scales on the dragon.

"They dragged him on vacation," Darsh said.

"I agree." My fingers flew over the keys. "Nobody works in NGOs to get rich. He probably was a workaholic, married first and foremost to his cause, and now that he's retired, he doesn't relax easily. I bet he still did some consulting to have a hand in the game."

"I'm not sure about the consulting," Ezra said, writing down what we'd said, "but it's possible, and he does have a daughter. Zayn was murdered six weeks after Alison."

When no one had anything else to add, Ezra pointed

at the photo of the boy, the third of our four victims. "Aleksander Pederson."

He was a slender blond boy with glasses and a serious expression.

I sprayed some cleaner on a microfiber cloth from my laptop bag and wiped off my screen. "Michael told me he was only thirteen."

"Barely worth noticing," Darsh said. "I mean, considering the accomplishments of the other two. What's the appeal to the murderer?" He tapped his finger against his lip, his expression thoughtful.

"It's awful when a child is killed," Silas said. "For any reason."

"Some might say you're just a child," Darsh replied.

Silas laughed. "I'm one hundred and seventy-two."

"Barely worth noticing," Darsh said. "Hypothetically, were one murdering vampires based on accrued accomplishments."

"Really?" Silas nodded at Ezra. "Well, he's only thirty-two."

"That hardly matters," Ezra said. "To quote Mark Twain, 'It's not the size of the dog in the fight, it's the size of the fight in the dog.'" He winked.

Sach chuckled.

So coy, Cardoso. I leveled a flat stare at my computer screen instead of his head.

"Would you say Ezra's barely worth noticing as well?" Silas asked Darsh. "From this hypothetical murderer's perspective, that is?"

"He's not worth noticing at all." Darsh smiled, removing precisely zero percent of the sting from his words.

"Hypothetically," I said, trying to turn the smirk that had burst free into a glare at Darsh. "From the murderer's perspective."

Ezra had followed the discussion without comment, but his gaze snagged on mine. "Respectful adult communication, hmm?"

I inclined my head. *Touché.* "Targeting people based on their accomplishments is a stretch for this case though, isn't it?" I folded the microfiber cloth. "Had these murders happened in close proximity, then yes. To someone with a far-right agenda, targeting a scientist working on climate change and a BIPOC man providing educational opportunities to marginalized communities has merit as a motive. But these murders occurred on different continents. Let's not get tied into a specific reason yet."

"Plus, Aleksander had barely hit puberty," Sachie said, coloring in the dragon's wings. "At his age, my biggest achievements were my Girl Scout badges." She pointed at Darsh. "Make a crack and die."

He pressed a hand to his heart. "I'm all about respectful adult communication."

"I completely agree about not limiting our thinking on this case," Ezra said, "but Aleksander wasn't your regular teenager. He competed in young inventor tournaments and had patented nanotechnology to retrain a patient's brain to develop new pathways for people dealing with obsessive compulsive disorder."

"That would have been covered in the media," Sachie said. "How high profile were the others?"

"Search their names," Ezra said, "and you get hits. Not tons, but it's a way to find them."

"It's inefficient." Silas shook his head. "It's not like anyone plugging 'good people' into a browser gets these three as their top results. We already ran that line of inquiry."

I sat up straighter. I'd found my first thread to pull on and a livewire hum coursed through me. "Funding. Scientific research, an NGO, even those inventor competitions.

They all rely on some form of external funding, like grants, either government or foundation based. Can we hunt that down and see if there's a common source?"

"On it," Silas said.

Darsh quirked an eyebrow. "An accomplished hacker, are you?"

To the other vamp's credit, he didn't blush or look away. He met Darsh's gaze straight on. "Yes."

I opened my mouth to stop any snarky retort, but my friend surprised me.

"Good for you," he said seriously. "I'm useless at that sort of thing."

Sachie and I exchanged pleased—and relieved—looks.

"That brings us to our latest vic," Ezra said. "Kyle Epstein. He was killed Monday night." He wrote the name under the photo. The man's face was heavily lined, his wiry brown hair was tangled, and his bushy beard was unkempt.

"A Jewish Kyle?" I wrinkled my nose. "That's different."

"I, for one, commend him for the Charles Manson vibe he's rocking," Darsh said. "Homeless?" he asked in a more somber tone.

"Close. He lived in one of those single room occupancy hotels," Ezra replied.

"We found it hard to guess his age by simply looking at him," Silas said. "He looks fifty, but being one step away from living on the streets puts the mileage on pretty darn quickly." There was a thread of darkness underlying the sorrow in his voice. "He's only thirty-three."

Sachie whistled. "Only three years older than Avi and me. What happened to him?"

"The paper mill he worked in up north closed down about four years ago due to a fire and never reopened," Ezra said.

"Was it the main source of employment for his town?" I said. Off Ezra's nod, I continued. "It made sense for him to move to the Lower Mainland to find work."

"It's common for people in those situations to end up relying on day labor jobs or short stints in construction," Sachie said.

"I have autopsy reports for the first three victims," Ezra said, "but I asked the coroner to hold off on Kyle until we walk the crime scene. I'll visit the body in the morgue afterward, then authorize the report."

"Mill worker doesn't fit the good deed profile of the others," Darsh said.

"He saved two co-workers from the fire," Ezra said. "Almost lost his own life doing so."

"Were all our murder victims Eishei Kodesh?" I said.

"Yes," he replied. "They were all White Flames, except Kyle, who was Orange." He reached into his leather briefcase, his mouth pressed into a grim line. "These are the photos of the victims. Again, I'd like your observations. Whatever comes to mind." He spread the pictures out on the table, and the rest of us got up to better examine them.

"I haven't seen the ones of Mr. Epstein yet," Silas said, peering over Sachie's shoulder.

I picked up Alison's photo and winced. "Fuck."

The woman's eyes had been removed, their sockets like a bottomless well into her soul. I almost couldn't look directly into them, just like I'd never look straight into the sun, because it was painful and dangerous. But I forced myself to bear witness to this atrocity.

Her corpse was the calm color of natural candle wax, but her chest had been cut open with surgical precision where the heart was located. Rather, where the heart *had* been located. It, too, was gone.

"Are they collecting trophies?" Darsh asked.

"These are ritual killings, but we have no leads on why the heart and eyes were taken," Ezra said, a growl threading through his words.

"The victims were also drained of blood," Silas said, "but there's no vamp bite."

"A strong Yellow Flame could remove any trace of that," I said. "Look at the color of the skin. No lines, no wrinkles, no birthmarks. This body was purified with yellow flame magic. Not an ointment, but an actual Yellow Flame cleansing the body after the victim was cut open."

"Since they were cleansed," Darsh said, "there's no way to tell what actually killed them."

"That's one of our big problems," Ezra said.

I studied the other photos. "Do we throw a demon on the suspect list? Forcing an Eishei Kodesh to do their bidding?"

Sachie scratched her neck with the top of her pen. "Shedim like games, but, Ezra, you said they were ritual killings. That means the murders were staged in some way." She shook her head. "In my experience, demons aren't interested in showy gestures like that."

Silas frowned. "Agreed, but what did they need chains for?"

"There aren't any chains in these photos," Ezra said. "Or markings of such."

"Yeah, there are." Silas pushed a photo of Kyle closer to his friend. "Look at the side of his foot. That's a faint imprint of a chain link. This could be an important break."

I couldn't see anything, and from Sachie's shrug, she didn't either.

Ezra's face was scrunched up. "You sure?"

Silas clapped him on the shoulder. "Told you before, you need glasses."

Darsh plucked the photo out of Ezra's hand, angling it to the light. "I don't see it."

"Guess it's left to those of us barely worth noticing to do the actual noticing," Silas said in an "aw shucks" voice.

Yup, this respectful adult communication was going swimmingly.

Chapter 9

Rather than show us photos of the first three crime scenes, it was boots on the ground to the site of Kyle's murder, which neither Ezra nor Silas had seen yet.

Ezra had rented a luxury SUV for us to all pile into. It fit seven, and although there were only five of us, Silas counted as one of Sach and me combined. He took the front passenger seat, while Ezra drove since he was the second largest and he was familiar enough with Vancouver to navigate.

Sachie and I took the middle row while Darsh settled himself elegantly in the back seat. The drive was mostly silent. I stared out the window, wondering what awaited us.

Ezra drove across the Second Narrows Bridge to North Vancouver, eventually arriving at North Shore River Park. This was a high-traffic area during the day, popular with hikers for the gorgeous forest trails, and kayakers and fishermen enjoying the Capilano River.

We walked single file along the wide concrete path winding through this part of the park, with Ezra in front and Silas bringing up the rear. It hadn't been raining, but the night air was damp in the temperate rainforest, and the tree trunks seemed to stretch up for miles. The roar of the river nearby was a wash of white noise, punctuated by the rustle of leaves.

Ezra checked his phone, then veered off the path into the woods. Moonlight filtered through the canopy, and massive fallen logs played host to fragile shoots and carpet-like patches of moss. The forest was steeped in a reverence that I longed to bathe in.

Less than two minutes later, however, he stopped.

Crowded between the trees was a white forensics tent measuring about twenty feet by ten. Tall enough for even Silas to stand up and not brush the peaked top, it preserved the crime scene and shielded bodies from gawkers. Two young men guarded the tent, bundled up in heavy coats against the chill. I recognized one. Poor level one. I so did not miss these grunt assignments.

I identified myself. "Who found the body?"

"A couple of hikers," the unfamiliar operative replied. "Trads."

Michael had been ordered to keep this murder under wraps, which meant that even though magic itself was known to all, in this specific case, some Yellow Flame operative had "cleansed" the Trads' memories of the findings. To be fair, the director would have ordered the same thing had an Eishei Kodesh found Kyle.

Memory wiping wasn't one of Michael's talents. Trust me, I'd have forced her to use it on me six years ago. I glanced at Ezra. "Shall we go in?"

The guards distributed shoe coverings and latex gloves to us, then unzipped the tent and stepped aside.

Ezra pulled a powerful flashlight out of his pocket and flicked it on. He'd given me one back at the SUV, so I powered it up.

We all hurriedly entered, shivering at the freezer-like temperature, then Ezra closed the tent up behind us.

Sach gasped, one latex-gloved hand flying to her mouth and nose. "*Kimoi.*"

I gagged.

Kyle's body had been removed to the morgue at Maccabee HQ, so there was no corpse. That wasn't what unnerved me.

The air was saturated with evil as palpable as a cat rubbing its fur against my bare skin. The smell was thick enough to chew, a combination of blood and salt that blended with the natural botanicals. Everything about the aroma was wrong, like puzzle pieces shoved together without a care that the edges had been mashed up and bent to make them fit into a single picture.

"What in holy heck is that smell?" Silas said, his voice muffled by the sleeve of his jacket.

"I vote for Hell's asshole," Darsh said, carefully picking his way around the edge of the tent. "Trads have it easy."

The forensic tents used by Trads didn't magically seal in all particulates like ours did, which was achieved via cutting-edge tech, orange flame magic that did something with the temperature to preserve the air and any organic material, and blue flame magic whose continued illumination of the scent preserved it. That's why this crime scene still smelled fresh after almost three days. Much to the dismay of my poor olfactory system.

Darsh reached up, snagged a handful of leaves from a cedar tree, and stuffed some of the feathery fronds up his nose. "Yes, it looks ridiculous," he said at our expressions, "but it'll block out the Eau de Death."

He held the rest of the handful out. All of us except Ezra helped ourselves to his stash. Foliage apparently wasn't the correct accessory for cashmere trench coats.

The pungent cedar tickled my nostrils, but it was also a one thousand percent improvement.

"This looks exactly like the photos of the other crime scenes," Silas said. "They're consistent if nothing else."

Sach stomped on the ground a couple times. "It's not muddy, but it is damp and there aren't any footprints." She jostled my arm to train the light on the ground. "Look at the faint lines. They raked over the dirt to cover their tracks."

The tent had been custom fit around several trees, including a spruce that had a symbol carved into its bark.

I walked over and traced the symbol. "This looks like a Hebrew letter. Can anyone identify it?"

Ezra's face drained of all color, and a muscle ticked in his jaw. "It's 'he.'" He used the Hebrew pronunciation "hey," his voice tight. "¡Carajo!"

I forgot that he'd grown up speaking Spanish with his Venezuelan father and tended to swear in that language instead of English, but it wasn't his foreign language usage, or even the fact that he'd had the same realization that I had—we'd missed a murder—that made me step back until I hit the tent canvas.

Ezra's affable charm had been ripped away with a savage swiftness leaving a barely leashed violence carved into his tight shoulders. His silvery-blue eyes hardened into glaciers, and his mouth compressed into a thin slash. Ezra's fury was a whip that lashed against my skin.

If my magic illuminated vampire weakness, he'd be a solid dark blue pulsating dot. I tasted his rage at the back of my throat.

It even woke Cherry Bomb, who, quite frankly, should have been sleeping like a baby after that shedim battle. My demon side sprang to the forefront of my consciousness and wrestled one of the reins of my self-discipline away before I had time to process it.

Cherry urged me to push Ezra further, to unleash the rage and self-loathing obviously bubbling under his skin and turn it back on him.

Turn it on the others.

On me.

Cherry didn't care so long as I broke his control. She pushed at me harder.

I dropped my gaze to the dirt, half closing my lids a split second ahead of the tingly pins and needles sensation. My heart rate spiked. I swear my glowing acid-green gaze was illuminating the space like a lighthouse.

I plastered myself to the tent's fabric, my body shaking, fighting to put Cherry back in her place. For thirty years, my Brimstone Baroness and I had engaged in a dance where letting her lead occasionally was less important than staying on the dance floor itself, because the pretty patterned tiles kept us moving to a melody of compassion, remorse, and humanity.

Should that music stop, and our steps take us past my hard-won boundaries, our dance would turn from a waltz to a mosh pit where cruelty was pleasure, power was joy, and all of it cost me my soul.

"Avi." Sachie was speaking to me, but she didn't take her eyes off Ezra. She crept one hand to the small of her back where she kept a thin stake. "What's going on?"

Careful to keep my face averted, I held up a hand, asking her to give me a minute, my vision unfocused, and my chest tight.

No one had commented on my eyes. Someone would have had they been noticeable. My heart rate calmed down enough for me to wrest back enough control and make my demonic eyes return to their usual light brown.

"Are you having a panic attack?" Silas inquired solicitously. Great, three vampires who were aware of my sped-up heartbeat.

"Well, duh. She's breathing in murder particles, Captain Sensitive." Darsh snapped off a twig and tucked it into his hair like it was a flower, but my friend's ridiculousness ratcheted down my nerves a couple of levels.

Sach studied Ezra for a long moment before dropping her hand away from her concealed weapon.

Ezra tugged on the cuffs of his coat, his posture stiff. "I apologize if my outburst scared—"

"Don't be ridiculous." Did I sound too loud? Too fake? I couldn't tell. "I didn't go through a childhood of Jewish summer camp without remembering that 'he' is the fifth letter of the Hebrew alphabet. We only have four victims though."

"We missed one?" Sachie's eyes widened. "Which?"

"The fourth," Ezra said. "Alef, bet, gimel. But no dalet." He'd torn a thick strip of bark off a tree and was decimating it in one fist to dust.

I sucked up all my anger and shame at my internal reaction to Ezra's outburst and used it like a battering ram to shove Cherry back into her deep, dark pool. I resolutely ignored the hurt she emanated that I wasn't letting my beautiful non-human side be free—yet again. In my head, I whispered to her that one day I'd bring her into the light, but she had to trust me. Let me do my job.

My shedim self finally complied, but not before she gave a last pinched ache.

"Hebrew letters are common to all the crimes so far," Silas said.

"Israelis most often use the same roman numerals as in the English language," Ezra said, "but sometimes this other system of using letters to number things is preferred." He snapped a photo of the carving with his phone. "Each body was positioned under a spruce with a letter carved into the trunk. Different varieties, but all spruce, nonetheless.

"Why spruce?" Darsh counted off footsteps from the base of the tree to the chalk outline of where Kyle's body had lain. "Four feet. Is that consistent?"

"Only roughly." Ezra paced like a caged tiger. "Ancient Greeks called spruces the tree of life and associated them with renewal, resurgence, and resilience. What it means in this context is anybody's guess."

Silas crouched down by the chalk outline and touched a finger to the soil before sniffing it. "Metal. Told you."

Darsh squatted down beside the other vamp and ran a finger through the dirt. "He's right. The smell permeates all the soil within this outline."

Silas dusted off his jeans and paced slowly across the enclosed space, sniffing deeply. "Here." He stopped suddenly and pointed at a spot by a different tree. "They dumped the chain at some point."

Ezra joined him, the two quietly discussing possibilities.

Sach borrowed the flashlight from me to investigate the tent on the other side of the spruce. "Uh, guys?" she said a moment later. "You need to see this."

We hurried over and pulled up short.

Sach crouched under a sturdy maple branch next to salt crystals scattered over the dirt.

"Why wasn't this documented in the three other murders?" Ezra looked like his head was about to explode.

"The killer might have cleaned it up the other times," Silas offered. "Or it was overlooked."

"Yellow flame magic and salt," I said. "That's speaks to purification. But why the chain?" I shone the flashlight on a maple branch above me and frowned, going on tiptoe to brush a gloved finger against the splintered bark. "Something was screwed in here."

Ezra nudged me aside, shining his light up. He was tall

enough that his face was only a couple of inches from the branch. "A hook."

I shouldn't have been able to smell anything other than the cedar stuffed up my nostrils, but his woodsy cologne had saturated the air. It hadn't even been this bad enclosed in the car with him.

"A hook and salt?" Silas rubbed his chin. "Were they curing the bodies?"

I marched back to the cedar tree and reupped my nose blockers. "Oh, fuck me. The Hebrew letters. Were they making the bodies kosher?"

"Don't they have to slaughter would-be kosher meat in one clean swipe?" Darsh said, trailing a finger across his pale throat. "A laceration like that would be too much for most Yellow Flames, even powerful ones, to heal with no trace of the wound."

Silas squatted down. "Train the light here, please." When Ezra obliged, he rubbed some crumbly dirt between his fingers. "There's a fair bit of blood in the soil but not enough to account for a human body's worth. They collected most of it in something."

Ezra clenched his hand holding the phone so hard that he cracked the screen. "Pendejos."

"It takes a long time to exsanguinate a person," Darsh said, "but given the stench of blood here, they risked doing it at the murder site."

"The killer didn't kill with a single knife cut, so they don't care about actual kosher procedures," Sachie said. "This was a ritual purification. They killed their victim, removed the blood, heart, and eyes, then purified and laid the victim under the spruce within a single ceremony. They believed this was necessary, otherwise, the risk of discovery makes no sense."

"That speaks to a higher purpose," Ezra said in a clipped voice.

"Remember, this is drawing on a specifically Jewish process with Hebrew letters at the crime scene," I said. "Is the killer Jewish? Because Kyle Epstein is the only Jewish victim. It's one more question for the list." I walked the crime scene from the outline of the body back to the salt crystals. "These people weren't murdered by slitting their throats, and if their skulls had been bashed in, again, that's not something that could be cleansed away."

"They weren't shot either," Silas said. "My vote is poison or maybe choking them. If the killer was acting alone, they had to be strong."

Ezra took a long, deep breath. "Let's break this down." His anger lingered in the snipped edges of his words. "The victims are killed in a forest and their blood is collected in something. Their eyes and hearts are cut out." He made notes on his cracked phone. "A purification ritual using aspects of the kosher process like hanging and salting the body is performed, but some of the blood is spilled on the ground. Probably on purpose. An offering of some sort."

"With the transformation complete, the victims are laid by a spruce symbolizing birth or renewal," Darsh said. "Renewal or birth of who?"

Ezra's shoulders slumped. His jaw was tight, and he clenched and unclenched his free hand, but his eyes looked tired and sad.

I'd seen that look in the mirror before Sach and I had found the clue in the Toussaint investigation that we'd required to break it open. Yeah, well, when you dealt with horrific crimes, tired and sad were job expectations. Ezra was a Maccabee; he didn't need a hug.

"Blood, eyes, and heart." I shone the light over the salt crystals like they were tea leaves I could divine answers from. "In fringe circles that'd be considered quite the mystical cocktail. Human body parts have been used in other crackpot potions like for immortality or strength enhancement, but not with any results."

"There are those who continue to believe in them," Silas said. "For the purposes of these murders, it doesn't matter if this potion works, only what our killers think they're using it for. Which is what?"

"That's the problem," Darsh said. "They might believe it will restore hair loss."

Sach furrowed her brows. "The organs were removed by someone with surgical training, and the incisions in the photos were clean cuts. I doubt it's as superficial as hair loss."

"Which loops us back to a higher purpose," I said. "Something big."

Darsh took off his latex gloves and rolled them into a ball. "Well," he said brightly, "I've seen enough."

"Me too," Sach said.

A moment later the zipper was opened. They didn't bother closing it behind them when they left the tent since we'd walked the entire crime scene and gotten all we needed.

Silas took Ezra's phone and waved it at him. "What did I tell you back in Singapore about this case getting to you? We're entering sock season. I can feel it."

Ezra threw Silas a grin with a shadow of its usual charm. "You never know. Might be sweater season."

Huh? I swung my light back to Silas, hoping for clarification, but his warm amber eyes had frozen to a hard resin.

He tossed his friend the phone back. "It's the reason for the season that I'm most concerned about, Ez. Don't brush this off."

"I'm just tired, chamo," Ezra said with a ragged sigh.

Silas didn't reply, so I took that as the end of their conversation.

"Could you give us a minute, please, Silas?" Tempting as it was to tell my co-leader that he had to keep his rage in check during this investigation so I didn't go shedim screwy, I'd rather gnaw off my arm than hand Ezra any ammunition. Especially this soon in our working relationship.

However, his earlier outburst and Silas's comment raised questions about my co-leader's stability. Being haunted by an investigation and driven to solve it was one thing, but if Ezra was going to lose his shit and compromise this case—and my chances of becoming a level three operative—then I had the right to know.

Silas opened his mouth, clearly to refuse, but I fixed him with the Look. It involved a delicate balance of an encouraging smile with enough coolness to showcase my disbelief that you could handle such a task, topped off with both eyebrows raised and my head tilted. I crossed my arms too. Do the Look wrong and I looked like I'd been goosed, but I'd practiced that puppy until it was second nature.

"Su-sure," Silas said. He backed up, stumbled over a tangled ball of roots poking up from the ground, then bolted so fast that I swear I saw cartoon puffs of dirt blaze behind him.

I pulled the cedar leaves out from my nostrils and threw them down. Better to suffer the Ghost of Cologne Past and the Eau de Death than have this talk with tree bits dripping out my nose like snot. I strode to the tent exit, making sure that everyone else was out of vamp hearing range. "Do I have to worry about you being emotionally compromised?"

"Get real," Ezra replied.

"Then what's the actual reason you're investigating this? Why did Secretary Pederson ask you out of everyone to take this case? And skip the hurt posturing.

Five ritual killings? That's way outside your wheelhouse."

"It was three at the time."

I waited patiently, the Look firmly in place.

"That doesn't work on me," he said.

"Why? Because I'm not intimidating?"

"No. Because I've seen you naked, laughing so hard that you snorted water out your nose," he said calmly. "It dilutes the menace factor."

We'd been holed up in my bedroom, roasting because the AC was on the fritz and Vancouver was having a heat wave. Ezra ran a piece of ice from his water glass down my sweaty back, I'd shrieked about the cold, and the ice fight was on, the two of us chasing each other around the room, until we fell onto the bed, still laughing. He'd leaned in to kiss me and—

In my head, an audience "oooohed." *Ladies and gentlemen, Count von Cardoso has slammed Queen AF against the cage and she's down!*

"You swore to forget our history," I hissed.

"I lied." A sly expression slid across his face. "I suspect the same is true of you."

When replaying our best moments had sent me down a spiral of masochism and martinis, I'd proceeded to Marie Kondo those non-joy-bringing fuckers. His presence now was what was bringing them back, not any wistful thinking on my part.

I tapped my foot against the floor. "Answer my question."

Ezra stared at the dirt for a moment. "You know why the Maccabees approached me?"

"Slow week and desperation?"

He locked eyes with me. "Because I was a hitman."

"No shit, Crimson Prince. So's Darsh. So is everyone

who works on a Spook Squad. Sach and I have killed vamps before, too, you know."

He speared me with a mixture of contempt and pity. What was I missing?

Ezra's dad, Natán Cardoso was a former Maccabee and a former good friend of my mom's. After being turned, he swiftly and ruthlessly rose to become one of the top Mafioso in Babel.

I hadn't really considered what being raised as heir to his father's empire entailed because by the time I discovered that fact, Ezra was my ex. I'd blithely dismissed him executing undead criminals, but perhaps killing fellow vampires had damaged Ezra?

The thing is, it wasn't like working for the Maccabees, even in an intel gathering position got him away from that. Necessarily.

"Were you ordered to go after innocent vampires?" I said. "Individuals Natán dictated he wanted gone for whatever reason?

"I killed humans," Ezra said flatly, with an expression so blank it seemed like dissociation.

A couple years after our break-up, I binged a ton of Mafia movies and all of *The Sopranos*. Dons didn't care if their hits included the family members of their enemies or if anyone in the general community was caught in the crossfire. Hell, even their own people were expendable in their quest to gain and hold power.

What atrocities had Natán forced Ezra to do? Did Ezra live with a stain on his soul, born of killing innocent humans? His broken phone screen tonight was a testament to his protective streak regarding people. Had Natán not seen his only child clearly enough to grasp how brutal this would be on his son's psyche? Or had he twisted a perceived weakness into a fucked up tough love program?

Too bad Natán and Mom were no longer friends by

that point. They could have swapped notes. Okay, not fair. Mom didn't make me kill people. Just myself, little by little.

"Hang on." I did a double take. "The Maccabees asked you to assassinate humans? Who?"

"Coño, not fellow operatives." Ezra raised his hands to calm me.

"That hadn't even occurred to me, but thanks for planting that image."

"Don't worry, Aviva," he said darkly, "if I ever come for you, you'll know it."

"I have no doubt."

This was surprising, but not? Did Maccabees have to follow the same laws and justice system as Trad cops where humans were involved? Yes. Did I believe that governments had black ops targeting shitty powerful people and that the Maccabees probably did too? Also, yes. I'd never heard of such a thing in our organization, but I hadn't known about Ezra being a Maccabee either.

"You've been playing spy and executioner?" I scrambled to remember a time and place that I could put Ezra at which coincided with the death of a public figure but couldn't. "For both the Maccabees and your father?"

"Natán has other people to gather dirt."

This felt like a test of my reaction, but it also felt true. Okay, so why was I scrambling to catch up, like I remained one step behind in this conversation?

"You solve this case, catch the perps, and the Maccabees help you get free of that life?" That had to be it, right? Yes, Ezra had destroyed me when he dumped me, but I'd still been breathing.

Maybe that wasn't the best example.

His laughter was edged in ice. "No, Aviva. I solve this case, catch the perps, make sure that no word of it leaks out and panics the general public worldwide, and I get to *keep* killing people."

"You're lying."

"Believe what you will. However, Secretary Pederson didn't ask me to come on board this case. I offered because they wanted to retire me, and I have other plans. Don't ascribe any nobility to me," he said harshly and walked out.

I was so shocked that I stood there dumbly for a moment. Even Cherry didn't make any comment from the peanut gallery. So, Ezra Cardoso was the Eager Executioner? Maybe, but my gut said otherwise. There was more than one mystery going on here. Only one of them led me closer to my personal goals, but damned if I wasn't going to solve both.

I'd always been an overachiever.

Chapter 10

We broke into different investigation teams back at the new office. Silas finished setting up his computers to dig into any common funding sources between the four known victims, since even the food banks or social services that Kyle used relied heavily on external financing. Our internet hadn't been set up yet, so he was working off the data on his phone.

Since Sachie's and Darsh's laptops were at HQ where they could get online, they offered to go back and comb through all the databases, like legal directories, police records, and global newspaper files that Maccabees had access to, for any murders bearing similar hallmarks to the other four.

It was about 5AM on Thursday morning, but chapters ran 24-7, so that wasn't an issue.

Ezra and I headed to Vancouver's Downtown Eastside to interview workers at the single room occupancy hotel where Kyle had lived. They were Vancouver's version of skid row housing.

The historic heart of our city was traditionally a community of low-income families with many resources geared to their well-being. There were still vibrant pockets but sadly, the most disenfranchised who'd called the Downtown Eastside home were being packed into smaller and smaller areas. SROs now butted up against million-dollar condos with a barrage of security.

I was truly grateful for Sach's West End apartment and being able to share her mortgage payments, otherwise, I'd be paying a fortune for a tiny place that wasn't half as nice. Our city was squeezing out the middle class, while those with addiction or untreated mental health challenges often ended up on the streets.

The neighborhood was quiet, though there were still a few people sitting on curbs openly shooting heroin, and trash from the unofficial flea markets littered a few blocks along Hastings Street. These markets sprung up daily and sold everything from stolen goods to clothing and even CDs and VHS tapes.

I took it all in from my privileged position in a luxury car with heated seats and was nauseous. Being in constant survival mode meant these people were easy prey, not only for vamps or demons, but other humans. I'd regularly patrolled down here when I was a level one and the stories that I heard from the community would stay with me forever.

Cherry and I would sometimes come down here on our nighttime feeding runs to find non-human prey lurking in the area and give them a taste of their own medicine.

Once we rolled up to the SRO, we agreed that Ezra would stay outside so he didn't frighten the workers or residents, given his hulking presence. (My words, not his.) The harried employee at the front desk hadn't seen Kyle in the past couple weeks. She checked with a resident who confirmed it.

"Disappointing but not a dead end," I said when I

reported back to my frowning co-leader. "This is where my contacts come in handy."

I led him to a grungy all-night diner, slowing down to peer through the glass. Although I didn't see any familiar faces, I pulled the door open. Happily, the inside smelled much better than it looked, redolent with cinnamon and bacon.

"How do you feel about chop shops?" I said.

Ezra looked down at his cashmere trench coat. "Overdressed?"

I ordered a dozen assorted doughnuts to go from the sleepy woman behind the counter who packed them with zero panache in a brown paper bag. "Is there really the perfect outfit for visiting illegal automotive establishments?"

Purchase in hand, we were again on our way.

"Leather. And a bike." Ezra slowed his pace along the sidewalk to match mine.

"You mean like fingerless gloves and a cute ten-speed with a bell?" I smirked. "I don't think that would cut it."

"Speaking from personal experience, are you?"

"Don't forget the glittery basket and ribbons on the handlebars. I was the envy of Jamieson Elementary's grade two girls." Two blocks over, I turned into an alley, striding halfway down to bang on a corrugated loading bay door. "Let me do the talking."

When the door didn't open, I put both fingers in my mouth and whistled loud enough to bounce the sound along the alley walls.

"Nice trick," Ezra said.

"One of many."

The door rose up with a mechanical hum, ZZ Top blasting out from somewhere in the garage's depths. Behind it were cars and motorcycles in various stages of dissection.

Jordy Green, a burly man in his late twenties with an impressive beard, strode to the entrance. He wore a stained Rolling Stones T-shirt and gripped a wrench in his hand. "No."

I shook the bag of doughnuts. "Come on. I'm her favorite person."

"She gets *ideas* whenever you're here," he growled.

"Yeah, like she's too good for you. I've got her eighty-five percent of the way there, but I'm hoping to go the distance tonight."

With a roar, Jordy rushed me.

Ezra blurred in front of Jordy before the man could touch me and lifted him by the scruff of his neck like he was a puppy. "Manners."

Jordy flailed in his hold. "What the hell, Avi?"

Hearing my nickname, Ezra dropped his captive, and turned to me accusingly. "Avi?"

"Did I or did I not say to let me do the talking?" I handed the other man the doughnuts. "Sorry, Jord."

He checked inside the bag. "No worries, but only because you remembered the cinnamon sugar ones." He bit into the flavor in question, calling out through a mouthful, "Rukhsana! You've got company." Munching contentedly, he headed back to the bike he'd been dismantling.

Ezra crossed his arms. "Maybe if you'd filled your partner in that—"

I cut him off with a sharp head shake. "Maybe if you'd trusted that I could take care of myself since I'd obviously been here before. Would you do that to Silas?"

"If I sensed a threat? You bet."

"Yeah, I was in real dire straits." I waved a hand at Jordy. He'd already finished the first doughnut, his beard and shirtfront dusted in cinnamon sugar. Chocolate smeared his upper lip from his next treat. "No offense."

He shrugged good-naturedly. "I did have a wrench, but I can see how our schtick might be misconstrued by outsiders."

"I'm not an outsider, am I, Avi?" Ezra purred dangerously, showing a hint of fang.

Queen AF has Count von Cardoso in a chokehold, ladies and gentlemen.

The click of heels interrupted my happy musings.

"Quelle surprise. Someone brought me a much more interesting gift than doughnuts," a woman drawled in French-accented English.

Damn.

Rukhsana Gill had multiple piercings, a brown bald head tattooed with a coiled snake, and eyes that had seen far too much for her twenty-six years. Her voice was honey-rich and all five feet of her was lush curves.

"Now you've done it," I hissed at Ezra. "Whatever you think you're seeing, Rukhsana? It's not interesting at all. In fact, it's boring to the point of comatose."

"Then you lead a much more exciting life than I gave you credit for. Introduce me to Ezra Cardoso."

I groaned. It hadn't occurred to me that she'd recognize him. More fool me.

"Enchanté." Ezra bowed low over her hand and kissed it.

I mimed shooting myself in the head.

Rukhsana slitted her eyes, a Cheshire Cat grin with fuck-me red lipstick spreading across her face. "You're even more delectable in person. Stay awhile." She was already divesting Ezra of his trench coat, her hands lingering on his biceps and pecs.

His surprise at being manhandled was amusing; the way he turned in her arms, giving her a long look at his tight ass, less so.

"This isn't a social call," I said.

She tossed me Ezra's coat and looped her arm through his, leading him off to the narrow staircase along the side wall. "Don't be rude, chère. There's always time for pleasantries."

I gaped at her. This from the woman who had literally set a timer on my past visits. I stomped after them, eyeing a sledgehammer leaning against an SUV before heading up the stairs into her leopard-print lair.

The guys in the chop shop answered to her. She played boss, mom, and matchmaker in equal amounts to her boys. My sum knowledge of her past was that she'd immigrated from Lyon in her teens, had never met a car she couldn't hotwire, and was a social butterfly who was plugged into circles at every level in our city.

She wasn't personally acquainted with Kyle Epstein, but she made a few calls, then poured us each a tumbler of whiskey while we waited for answers. I didn't like that kind of alcohol, but she and Ezra went off on a tangent discussing distilling methods and complexity of flavor.

He drank whiskey and enjoyed it enough to have developed opinions on it? Since when? The Ezra I'd known had once stumbled through a liquor store with me, both of us tipsy. We'd boggled over names and varieties of that alcohol, laughing ourselves silly by exaggeratedly pronouncing and mispronouncing them to each other. Now he was saying "blended bourbon" as if that had never been an inside joke.

Rukhsana, unaware of this internal war I was dealing with, draped her legs over the arm of her wingback chair, charming gossip out of Ezra about his famous pals, both human and vampire. He indulged her with a litany of secret scandals that I listened to with a bored expression but planned on sharing with Sach later.

Entranced, Rukhsana trailed a finger along her décolletage, insisting on a more personal story. Ezra indulged her with a tale about one night in Glasgow and a dare involving some supermodel and a cloak.

He sat close by her, all the better for her to keep touching him, while he sipped on a blood chaser. When we first got together, it was weird to enjoy a coffee while he had a cup of blood, but I'd gotten used to it. Most operatives did, and those that didn't kept their distance from the Spook Squad.

Eating and drinking were hotly contested subjects in the vamp world. Only blood sustained vampires so anything else was purely for taste or because they missed that habit. There were purists who had killed over their fervent belief in an all-blood diet. I hadn't seen Ezra eat when we'd been together, but he'd enjoyed a good drink.

Apparently, that wasn't all he enjoyed.

Touchy-feely was Rukhsana's default mode. She behaved that way with all men, women, and nonbinary individuals who she was friends with, unless they were obviously uncomfortable with the physical contact.

She and I weren't friends, which was fine; our relationship was business oriented and transactional, but by extension, so was Ezra's. He hadn't behaved this way with any of our team, and if this was the new normal he'd developed since we'd last been in contact, I was going to have to start taking anti-nausea medication.

Cherry opened her eyes, watching Rukhsana to determine her threat level—as a competitor, not an enemy.

I loosened my grip on my tumbler to set it on a coaster and cleared my throat. "We don't have all night, so if you could follow up about Kyle now?"

Ezra sighed heavily. "Fleischer's right. We should get back to work."

Poor Prime Playboy. I so loathed cutting into your socializing.

I gouged my fingernails into the armrest, but did not

say a word, since we'd agreed we didn't have any past history, and I, at least, was not one to break my word.

Rukhsana swung her feet to the floor and pulled a face. "Mom's cranky."

I did not snap that I was hardly a mother figure given I was intimately acquainted with the feeling of Ezra pushing inside me, filling me up. How he'd flex his fingers against the curve of my hips like he was checking that this was real, that *we* were real, gazing upon me in reverence with eyes as hot and bright as supernovas.

Rukhsana made one more call, which yielded a much-needed break. Apparently, Kyle had befriended some guy who'd offered him a couple months' work doing repairs at Arbutus Campground now that the high season was over.

I pulled out my wallet to pay her for the information like I always did, but she waved it away.

"This one's on the house." She trailed a finger down Ezra's arm. "Provided you promise to come back and finish our conversation."

I did more gaping. Gogging even, to quote Michael. I was repurposing the word for these multiple fish impressions I was doing, but seriously? Cash was a perfectly adequate payment system that did not leave me with a bad taste in my mouth.

"I'd be delighted." Ezra and Rukhsana hugged like one of them was moving to Mars.

Jordy saw us out. I got a high-five goodbye and Ezra got a bare minimum chin nod. That was nice.

I hustled it back to the car, silently damning Ezra's easy strides that didn't allow me to shake him.

"I should introduce Rukhsana to some of those Silicon Valley bros," he said. "Let her whip them into shape." He chuckled.

"You certainly enjoyed her company."

"I recognized a valuable ally and cultivated that relationship," he said mildly. "It's what I do."

It's what I do, I mimicked in my head. I took a deep breath. "You're right. I apologize."

I swear Cherry gave a disgusted huff, but I ignored her. I couldn't demonstrate my leadership abilities if I was incapable of admitting when I was wrong. In my opinion, the best leaders operated from a point of respect, not belittlement or bullying.

"No need," he said.

No shit.

Arbutus Campground was a forty-minute drive away, not far from the site of Kyle's murder.

Ezra put on *Greatest Hits* by The Doors. His mom, Eva, had been obsessed with their music when she was a teen growing up in Tel Aviv. During our relationship, he'd confided that other than the black hair and darker Middle Eastern complexion he'd inherited from his Mizrahi Jewish mother, the only other thing he had left of Eva after her death was their shared love of classic rock. Ezra's few memories of her were of her dancing with him to The Doors.

Between the smoothness of the ride and Morrison's velvet voice, I was lulled to sleep in minutes. Well, I rested with my eyes closed until we'd parked, and Ezra left the car. I let him, curious if he really intended to go off without me, but when I opened my eyes, barely thirty seconds later, it became clear that he did. I flipped him off, out of view of the windows.

The early morning sky had transformed from a murky smoke gray to a brighter but no less gray color, and misty raindrops rolled down the window. Ugh. Mist was the worst. Too fine for an umbrella but still wet.

Our SUV was parked along the side of a road leading to the campground's entrance, which was blocked off by a yellow metal safety gate.

Getting out of the vehicle, I scanned the surrounding woods for any sign of Ezra, but with his speed and stealth, he could be five miles away or hiding in front of me and I'd never know. I inhaled deeply and filled my lungs with the scent of pine, letting any residual irritation at him wash away.

I hopped the gate and started up the packed dirt road leading to the modular trailer that served as the check-in building. My breath came out in white puffs, and I tucked my cold fingers into my pockets, but there was something precious and wonderful about being out here in nature without any city noises. Under different circumstances, I would have picked a trail and run through the trees, crunching over the frosty grass, but instead, I silently made a circuit of the grounds, sticking to the shadows when possible.

Arbutus Campgrounds wasn't in bad shape: some branches had blown down and damaged the small gazebo next to the playground, one of the bathrooms was missing a gutter, and a couple of the half dozen or so cabins for rent needed their roofs replaced. Whoever had approached Kyle with the job offer hadn't lied about the necessary repairs, but why go into the Downtown Eastside to find a laborer? North Vancouver was a much closer town where men could be hired. Was it because the population in the Downtown Eastside was more transient and more vulnerable?

Or was Kyle chosen for another reason?

Ezra still hadn't shown himself, but a light was on in the reception cabin, so I walked up the wide plank stairs, not bothering to be stealthy, and rapped on the locked door.

A grizzled man in a green army jacket and a camouflage-patterned toque, which he'd pulled down low over his brow, answered the door. "Yeah?" He sucked on a cigarette, held with nicotine-stained fingers.

"Aviva Fleischer." I showed him my Maccabee ring.

He blew out the smoke. "Yeah?"

Stellar conversationalist. I fanned the second-hand cancer away.

"I'm looking for Kyle Epstein. He missed calling his mom on their weekly chat and she's asked us to track him down." I shrugged. "Moms, right?"

"Can't help you."

I deployed my magic vision. The blue circle over the man's heart was doing a fast marimba, and his back was a series of blue dots, streaking down like rain on a windshield. Increased beats per minute and sweating.

I stuck my boot in the door, blocking him from closing it. "I'm sure it's nothing, but I heard he'd taken a job here and I was hoping you could put me in touch with him?" I shivered. "Perhaps we could discuss this inside? It's cold out here."

Magic blue swirls zinged around the man's brain.

Something was clearly bothering him about me. But what?

He narrowed his eyes and took another drag, coming to some conclusion. "Kyle," he said in disgust. He threw down his cigarette butt and ground it into the porch boards. "Come on in."

"Much appreciate it," I said, the door thwapping shut behind me.

The ancient brown ceiling fan fit right in with the lumpy floral couch under the window, the calendar of a scantily clad woman hawking car parts, and a linoleum floor whose color I could only describe as somewhere between beige and not beige. This was likely from the years of cigarette smoke baked into every inch of the place, which gave the room a delicate ashtray ambiance.

The man held up an electric kettle. He had quite the tight grip on it because his fingers pulsed blue. "Tea?"

"No, thank you, Mr....?"

"Call me Roy." He plugged it in. "Have some. It'll warm you up."

I blew on my hands and wriggled my toes to get the circulation going. It was cold in here too, and sometimes it was good to accept gifts from people in order to build rapport. "Tea would be great."

"Need a cup." He disappeared through a doorway with a brown beaded curtain and a small plaque saying "Office" nailed above the frame.

I glanced at the side table on my way to the counter. The sun-bleached women's magazine on top of the stack proclaimed "shoulder pads and perms the power look of the decade."

Roy returned minus his cigarette, holding a Styrofoam cup that had the tea bag string trailing out of it. The blue dot over his heart was still hammering. "I gave you sugar. Got no milk."

"That's fine, thanks. So, Kyle?"

"He stayed for about ten days, then took off during his coffee break." Roy ranted for a full minute about young people's lack of a work ethic nowadays.

"What day was this?" I said.

Roy scratched his nose, his face screwed up in thought. "The generator was low on diesel, and I had to go to one of them big-box stores instead of Phil's because he opens his place later. Takes the wife for chemo those mornings, you know."

"So, which day?"

"Monday." The same day that Kyle was killed.

"Did you report his absence?"

Roy stared at me like he didn't understand the question.

The kettle clicked off, and he poured boiling water into the cup. He stirred it with a plastic spoon, then set it down in front of me with the tea bag still steeping.

"Do you usually hire people from the Downtown Eastside?" I said.

"My regular guy moved to Ontario with the wife." Roy's heart rate slowed to normal and he wasn't sweating anymore. This was a familiar topic for him. A truthful answer.

I couldn't detect lies (or rather illuminate truth), since that was a different and extremely rare specialization. A seasoned liar could tell me up was down, have me believe it, and not demonstrate any weakness through my magic vision while doing so.

Roy's behavior, on the other hand, didn't really require magic to decipher. He'd been nervous about my appearance, now he wasn't.

I waited for him to answer my previous question about his hiring practices.

He didn't.

"Why did you hire Kyle?" I said. "Specifically?"

Roy shrugged. "Winter's coming on. People down there ain't got it easy." He sounded like this was first-hand experience, not an observation. "Figured someone might like a place to stay and a regular paycheck. Saw Kyle first. He said yes." How many years had Roy been extending his gruff kindness to others? Maybe paying forward the helping hand that someone else had once given him?

Roy nodded at the cup. "Drink up."

I took a sip and gagged. "Sweet," I coughed.

He nodded and pulled another cigarette out from behind one ear. "Kyle seemed reliable. Guess you can never tell."

"Did you get a chance to talk to him much?" The tea

was strong, but it was also hot and I was warming up. I drank some more.

"Sure, plenty of times packing up the—the tools and such." What was up with that slip? "How's the tea?"

I drank a bit more. "Good, thanks."

Roy nodded, smiling. "Some people swear by coffee," he said, "but make tea right and it'll put hair on your chest."

The runner-up slogan of the British East India Company.

I blotted my forehead with the back of my hand. "Do you have Kyle's phone number?"

"He ain't answering."

No, he wasn't. And how much did Roy have to do with that? "I'd still appreciate it."

He sighed like I'd asked him to empty the ocean with a teaspoon and headed for the back office. "Let me find it."

"Thank you." Did I have cotton in my mouth? Was this what it was like to speak around fangs? I laughed, but that made the room swim around me, so I made my way to the sofa and collapsed heavily onto it. Hopefully Roy would forgive my less-than-professional behavior but better I was on the couch than on the ground. I unzipped my coat and fanned out my turtleneck, sweat running down the back of my neck. "Roy? You got that number?"

"One minute," he called out.

I ran my tongue around the inside of my dry mouth. My blue flame synesthete vision was blurring, and when I glanced down at my body, blue streaks ran through my rubbery limbs.

"How you doing?" Roy peered down at me.

I opened my mouth. That felt funny so I did it a few more times.

"That's what I thought," he said.

Then everything went black.

Chapter 11

I opened my eyes, shivering in the dark, despite still wearing my heavy coat, and searched my pockets. Roy had taken the mini stun gun and the flashlight but left my phone. Ipso facto, there was no cell service here.

After checking and confirming I was right, I turned on the light on my phone. Look at that. I was in a windowless cellar. Metal shelving units contained boxes of canning jars next to canned fruit with labels written in spidery handwriting. Sausages dried in a string along the ceiling, and a metal barrel in a corner with a dark splotch of concrete under the spigot emitted the stench of wine.

I gingerly moved my limbs. My body felt heavy, but I wasn't bound in any way.

Always use cuffs, man. I smiled thinly. *Roy, you amateur.*

Cherry Bomb was also awake. Even though I always felt the changes in her awareness, I'd spent ages as a kid using my synesthete vision to find physical proof of her existence. My reasoning was that I was a Blue Flame Eishei Kodesh, whose particular talents illuminated weakness in humans and being a half shedim was the ultimate deficiency.

That's what I surmised, anyway, based on people's perceptions of infernals.

To be clear, I didn't view Cherry as a weakness, but it wasn't like I could argue that point with my Blue Flame magic.

Of course, it was all just conjecture until one day in my teens, when, armed with two mirrors and my synesthete vision, I saw shifting blue shadows in my hindbrain, and freaked out in the best possible way.

How did I know that this magic mark denoted Cherry's existence and wasn't a tumor or something? Well, the section at the back of my head where I found the shadows was called the primal brain. It was responsible for survival, drive, and instinct. When a person operated from a loss of rationality, overpowered by strong emotions, they were living in their primal brain.

Combine all that with the fact that those shifting shadows didn't exist anywhere else on my person and I had no symptoms of any disease, and this was as conclusive as it got. It wasn't like I had anyone to ask—even Michael couldn't tell me much, and she'd combed the infuriatingly sparse Maccabee documentation on the subject perhaps more times than I had. The lack of information all came back to there being so few of us—the thorny "most infernals don't survive past the first trimester" issue.

I rubbed the back of my skull, seeking reassurance that all was well with the Baroness after the sedatives Roy fed us. Without the mirrors, I couldn't see the shifting shadows to make a determination that they'd regained their normal speed, but hopefully they'd recovered from any sluggish drift back to their usual swift slide.

I got drunk about as easily as any other social drinker my size and weight, but thanks to my demon genetics, if I consciously willed it, I could sober up at the drop of a hat. Best hangover cure ever: never get one in the first place.

What this meant was that I had a similar ability to flush sedatives out of my system. I had no idea what type of shedim my deadbeat demon daddy was. The physical traits he'd passed down and that came out when I let Cherry take control were common to more than one type of demon. Other than those, all I'd gotten from him was my propensity for violence, which was level one evil shit, my demon-sensing radar, and this weird metabolizing, which didn't work on food.

A five-day all-cookie diet when I was a kid had proven that. Michael didn't even let me run off the four pounds I'd gained, since I enjoyed running. No, she sent me to some nightmare bootcamp for kids for a week. It was never about body shaming me, but hammering in that I couldn't afford to lose control on any front. That those abilities were never a perk.

Either way, it sucked.

Given Roy's rapid heartbeat and sweating, his pre-added sugar—excellent for masking any trace of bitterness from a crushed-up sleeping pill—and that odd slip of the tongue, it was a no brainer to accept the drink and let Roy think he'd hoodwinked me.

My phone battery was almost dead, so I had to use it judiciously. I quickly yet thoroughly scoured every inch of the floor and walls for a crack or broken seam, but the cellar was solidly built, and the metal door was locked from the outside.

I didn't waste my energy yelling. There weren't any campers, Roy wasn't going to free me, and these walls were too thick for even Ezra to hear me.

Unfortunately, vampires didn't have the subcutaneous transmitter that human operatives used in the Brink, because their magic shorted out the implant. So, I couldn't send Ezra a signal and have him find me now. Well, I didn't seem to be in immediate danger. I'd stay calm and break down the situation until I had a way to free myself.

Whatever Roy was paranoid about me finding, it wasn't here. Nor was the cellar intended to double as a prison. My guess was that he panicked when a Maccabee showed up, drugged me, and stuffed me in here without much of a plan.

That didn't make him any less dangerous, but I doubted he was involved in Kyle's murder. Admittedly, the fact that Roy had something to drug me with close to hand *and* that it was his first instinct didn't look good for his innocence. However, I was still alive, and maybe Kyle hadn't come back to work because the real killers had taken him.

Hmm. A sedative slipped into a drink was an easy way to help a "drunk or sick friend" without arousing suspicion. Too much and our victim would OD in a bloodless death. The nonviolence of it lined up with the ritual killings, but those required forethought. If Roy was our guy, he wouldn't have thrown me in a cellar. Or rather, there would be signs that Kyle had been here as well.

First things first. I had to get out of here.

I visualized the reception trailer. It sat on blocks atop a concrete pad to support its weight. No cellar there. However, I doubted Roy had taken me far, especially since Ezra would have shut that right down. Losing me on day one was not worth Michael pulling his investigation privileges. Which raised the question of where he was.

I set aside my worry that something bad had happened to Ezra until there was proof of that and eyed the metal door. Cherry couldn't break it down. I touched my ring and sighed. The Maccabees weren't aware of how often I reupped, but Michael was. This charade of mine to get captured and then use the magic in my ring to free myself was not going to go over well.

Screw it. Better to ask for forgiveness than permission.

I ran my finger clockwise over the gems, and the blue stone began its glowing pulsation. It didn't illuminate shit since there was no demon present, but I appreciated its sacrifice and gave it a smart salute.

Next, I placed the ring against the lock. The brief stream of red flame fire was hot enough to partially melt it, the orange flame magic further twisting the metal.

The white and yellow flame magic also went to waste, but that couldn't be helped.

I bashed the glowing lock free, using my sleeve to keep from blistering my skin. It fell outside with a dull thud, and I pushed the door open into a tunnel, about fifty feet long, that sloped upward. Its walls were made of packed dirt, and the entire structure was braced with wooden beams. The flat light of an overcast day streamed in from the far end.

"Fleischer!" Ezra's silhouette filled the mouth of the tunnel and he strode toward me, his coat flapping around his legs like a superhero cape. That was the second time tonight he'd used my last name. Was this passive-aggressive payback for Jordy using my nickname when I'd forbidden Ezra from doing the same? My left eye twitched, and I wanted to kick in him the groin.

"Where have you been?" he said.

"I signed up for a vacation package, but there's no Wi-Fi or room service. Zero out of ten, don't recommend." I waved my hand at the cellar, and he peered inside.

He leaned his forearm against the wall, smirking down at me. "Got caught, did you?"

I backed up. "I deliberately allowed myself to be imprisoned after scanning Roy, the man who hired Kyle. He had something to hide."

"Solid C+ for effort." Ezra scratched his bearded jaw. "But I beat you to the punch. The man has a greenhouse full of strange plants about a kilometer from here in the forest at the edge of his property and quite the chemistry setup inside. Lots of hidden cameras in the woods too. Did such a good job that I almost didn't see them."

"Ooh, a drug lab? Roy, you Heisenberg wannabe. Did you question him?"

"There was no one to question."

"Did a runner, did he?" Luckily, there was a cell signal in the tunnel, so I phoned Michael and told her to liaise with the Trad cops to track down Roy Reynolds, the name on the labels of his magazines. I informed her of the drug lab and how he might be dangerous, so to approach with caution.

Ezra waited patiently until I completed the call. "Why do you believe Reynolds is Trad?"

"An Eishei Kodesh would rely on their magic. Roy drugged me with a sedative."

"He what?" Ezra snarled.

"Did you think he put me in the cellar through a feat of physical strength? No chance. He's a wiry old dude." I rolled my eyes. "It wasn't like I didn't know he was drugging me."

"And you let him?" His fangs had descended.

"Save your breath. I burned it out of my system before I became completely unconscious and played possum to see if this was part of a pre-established plan for dealing with unwanted visitors." I set off along the tunnel, explaining my theory about sedative use to abduct and kill the victims. "Roy's not involved in Kyle's murder though."

"Why not?" Ezra had put away his fangs like a civilized vamp. His hands were slung in his coat pockets, his strides were loose, yet there was purpose and intent propelling each step forward, which was different to his easygoing vibe of six years ago.

"His rant on the evils of slackers was genuine, plus if he imprisoned me in this cellar, it's where he would have put Kyle. There was no sign of that. Roy simply panicked because he assumed I was onto the drugs and improvised. Oh, and I confirmed that Kyle was taken the same day he was murdered."

"No possibility of a missing persons report being filed," Ezra said before I could.

It had always been that way with us. One would say something and the other would run with it. We'd traded quips and argued opinions at lightning speed; I'd forgotten that.

"The killer stalked their victims beforehand. Became familiar with their patterns." There was a bounce in Ezra's step, and his eyes warmed in excitement to that almost eerily glowing blue that I'd fallen dreamily into during our endless conversations on everything from magic to music. "But did they clock the hidden cameras?"

I'd never been in sync with anyone like I had with him. Not even Sachie.

I toyed with my Maccabee ring while Ezra made a follow-up call to Michael requesting tech people come to the campground and secure all footage before the Trad cops arrived. He'd swing by in a bit and go through it.

My ex remained the sexiest man I'd ever seen, but I could resist physical urges. It was these other connections that were messing with me.

I grew more and more waspish about it, but since I couldn't voice what was really bugging me, about two-thirds of the way through the tunnel, I snapped at Ezra to slow down. It's not like I needed him going first to protect me.

No, you only need protection from yourself, Cherry whispered.

Nonsense.

Is it? You pride yourself on your control, but you talk to yourself like there's another personality in you. Some would call that madness. Cherry's voice became Michael's.

"But there is. There's Cherry," I heard my ten-year-old self say. What was happening? I ran my hand along the dirt wall, anchoring myself.

"Your shedim half isn't a kitten, Aviva." Michael turned from the stove, spatula in hand. The kitchen was filled with the scent of garlicky meatballs searing in the pan. "She's not a pet to name."

I looked up from my math workbook, my stomach hurting like it always did when Mom had that prickly worried voice. "You named me. Why can't I name Cherry?"

"It's not the same thing," my mother said tightly. She flipped over the meatballs before speaking again. "If you love her, she'll weaken you. That's what demons do." She took a long sip from her wineglass. "You must stay strong. Stay *human*. Do you understand?"

I shrank back against the scary gleam in her eyes, but I nodded.

Her expression softened. "I want to keep you safe. If you don't control that side, your shedim genetics will constantly drive you to do dangerous and foolhardy things to sate its needs. Someone will find out and..." She shook her head sharply. "Promise me you'll stop thinking of her like a friend and see this part of you for what it really is."

I erased the seven I'd written on my subtraction problem and changed it to a six. "I promise." *I promise not to hurt you, Cherry.*

Cherry didn't make me weak. She made me strong. Mom didn't get it. I liked hamburgers and humans killed cows for that meat. I'm sure the cows wished they were alive, eating grass and pooping in meadows. But unlike some people, Cherry had never killed anyone. I made sure of that. Yes, she was me, but I had to feed that part of myself differently if I wanted to survive. Mom didn't get it.

Cherry and I were a team. Not quite human, not quite demon.

A hand came down on my shoulder and I started, the apple blossom wallpaper in the kitchen crumbling into dirt.

"Move it, slowpoke," Ezra said.

I'd exited the tunnel into a wooded area that I presumed was still on the campground property. However, I stood there, stuck in the edges of that memory involving my mother, its wisps clinging to me like spiderweb strands. Shaking them off, I resumed my trek, but I stumbled over an uneven patch of ground. My hand slapped against a bramble of blackberry bushes, the meaty part of my palm slicing across a thorn.

I hissed, the pain blazing a path through my brain that was like a clean streak being rubbed into a dirty mirror. Roy had drugged me. I thought I'd gotten it out of my system, but he must have mixed a sedative with a hallucinogen or something that dredged up long-forgotten memories. When I metabolized the drug, I only blew away the sedative part.

My mind was very clear now.

"Take me with you to the morgue." I hurried to match Ezra's strides, wet overgrown blades of grass clinging to the hem of my trousers. "These victims being killed all over the globe with no discerning pattern is unusual." Just like my and Cherry's co-existence. "Since Kyle's body has been preserved, perhaps there's something that the photos missed that I can pick up on with my magic. Something that can narrow down this hypothesized higher purpose."

Ezra loomed over me. "Why did you confront Roy alone?"

I elbowed past him and kept walking. "Did you hear anything I said?"

"Yes. Kyle's body was cleansed. We all agreed on that point."

"So? It's still worth me having a look."

"You have experience using your magic post-mortem?" Ezra said.

"No." Not once in my training or studies had anything suggested that my particular Eishei Kodesh talents would work in that situation. Then again, I'd developed my skill set faster and was more precise than others with the equivalent ability because I'd trained my butt off to achieve that expertise. Why not test it now?

A bat flew out of a tree, winging its way up into the clouds.

"Considering our slim leads," I said, "it's worth a shot. Also, I didn't exactly see a note telling me where you'd gone when I woke up in the car."

"You were faking it."

"Get that a lot, do you?" I said dryly.

"You had a phone. I had a phone. I'd have returned immediately." Our history said otherwise, but my bland expression didn't waver. "You should have told me where you were going," he added.

I spread my hands wide. "You had a phone. I had a phone."

"You have a history of not playing well with partners."

"Sachie would disagree." I jammed my hands into my coat pockets to warm them up. "Did you read any unbiased reports about me or just cherry-pick the ones to cement your preconceived notions?"

"I read lots of things," he said.

"How literate of you." I slow clapped him. "A couple

of my male partners didn't like that I was smarter and got results faster. I certainly never stabbed them in the back."

We left the wooded area for a clearing filled with overgrown grass. Unfortunately, I didn't know where the car was, so I had to let Ezra lead.

"Admit it." I sought somewhere to look that wasn't his piercing silver blue eyes or full lips. His nose. There. It was perfectly adequate and uninspiring. Except it led back to his eyes and mouth. "You don't give a shit about me asking questions without you. You want me off this case."

"Don't flatter yourself," he said. "I want Sachie and Darsh off it just as much."

We crested a small rise, and the luxury SUV came into view.

"Right." I stepped over a trail of slug slime. "Everyone who's part of the Vancouver branch who doesn't possess any abject loyalty to you. That's not suspicious or anything."

"Look, you have good instincts," he said. "But how much energy are you spending keeping part of yourself hidden? Energy that might slow down your reflexes in a crucial moment or impair your judgment?"

Did he think I didn't continually wonder that? I was doing my best to fit into the world so that one day I could open it up for people like me.

"I've spent my life training and keeping my shedim side in check. I've kept it secret, while you've been celebrated for being a Prime, a playboy, and a Mafia enforcer."

Ezra beeped the fob at the car. "That's reductionist. I'm celebrated for much more than that."

I hurried around to the passenger side, biting the inside of my cheek to keep my smile from getting loose. My brain had obviously glitched because there was no way I was amused. "People know you're a powerful supernatural being, and instead of being afraid, your Ezracurriculars get all hot and bothered hoping they can make baby vamps with you."

The second I blurted it out, I winced. That was a tactical mistake.

Ezra smirked, one arm braced on the top of his open car door. "Read my fan forums, do you?"

"Only when I want to bore myself into sleeping. How can I be sure that if you get super stressed or upset that you'll still be able to control yourself? I can't. I'm not recusing myself from this case. I've demonstrated a quick grasp of the facts and brought up some good conclusions and strong avenues to investigate."

"You also got kidnapped—"

"Presented with a unique undercover opportunity." I got in the car and fastened my seat belt while Ezra started the engine. "You have no latitude to harass me when your outburst back at the crime scene caused Sachie to second guess whether you were fit to lead. Tell me you didn't notice it."

"I'd have disarmed her before she ever pulled a weapon on me."

Incredible. "Whether or not that's true—"

He snorted.

"Sach is highly trained and very comfortable working with vampires. Michael wouldn't have assigned her to our team otherwise. The same goes for Darsh controlling any extreme behavior he might fall prey to. You and Silas are the unknown elements here."

"Says the infernal."

"You can drone on about my shortcomings all you want. Yes, I'm part demon but I'm also half-human and my humanity will always prevail. Too bad you can't say the same."

Ezra's composure shattered for a blink around his

edges: a sharp slump of his shoulders swiftly remedied, a flash of pain clouding his eyes before they resumed their cool disinterest, a sucked-in gasp he didn't fully swallow.

A stark, pained silence fell around us as if the entire universe had paused to mark my arrow hitting its target. The moment lasted a long time—as did my uneasy mixture of victory and guilt.

He pulled a sharp U-turn that had me clutch the "oh shit" handle, and we bounced over a pothole, sending a light spray of mud onto the trees at the side of the road. "You're still choosing to hide Cherry."

"It's not by choice," I said, smacking my thigh in frustration.

"Everything is a choice."

I stared out the window, my jaw tight. "What do you want from me?"

Ezra clicked on his turning signal and merged onto the paved road leading back to the highway. "I don't know," he said quietly.

My heart thudded hollowly against my chest. "Are we going directly to the morgue?"

"No. If you're going to try and illuminate Kyle's corpse, then get some sleep, eat something, and do it when you're fresh and fully powered."

I unzipped my coat partway. "I wasn't using 'we' in the royal sense. Are you going without me?"

"No. I'll let you suss things out first but check in and give me your findings right after. Meantime, I'll go through the footage from the campground after I take you home."

I nodded and gave him my address, but he cut me off.

"I remember where you live. Unless you moved?"

"Why would I?" I said defiantly.

"I don't know," he said tiredly. "You and Sachie have

been living together a long time. Perhaps you wanted your own place?"

"I'm happy where I am."

The resulting silence was awkward in the way that a dog licking its balls was: looking away wasn't enough to escape the cringey reality. I put on a talk radio program about pesticides, listening to it during the drive back like I was cramming for a test on endocrine system disruption in wildlife.

Ezra pulled up to the curb in front of my condo building, set the emergency brake, and turned off the engine. "Here we are." He yawned.

I quickly unfastened my seat belt. "I'll hop out. No point in you parking."

I'd rather endure a colonoscopy with a ghost pepper solution than invite him upstairs for a coffee, which he tended to drink boiling hot and black because the weirdo loved the bitter taste. Not that I had the picky bastard's favorite Sumatran dark roast on hand.

Anymore. And I certainly didn't keep synthetic blood in my fridge.

So no, despite the blurry glaze in his eyes, his short beard looking a bit unkempt, and him rubbing some knot in his neck, I had nothing to perk him up before sending him on his way.

That didn't make me a bad partner. Quite the opposite, I was a good partner, upholding a boundary that allowed me to function around him and bring my all to this investigation.

I'd had to replace all my bedroom furniture and undergo months of therapy to erase his presence from my home. Had I lived with anyone other than Sachie, I'd have moved, but our place had always been filled with laughter and friends. It was my happy place, and I refused to give that up. If it changed for a while, well, I'd claw my way back to it again.

Plus, I'd recently bought my first set of fancy bedding. Not that he'd ever be in my bedroom again, but his near proximity could contaminate the plush linens, and I wasn't made of money. Replacing them was not an option.

"Until later," I said, inclining my head like a stately ruler. Inwardly, I groaned.

"Until then," he agreed, bowing his upper body low and pretending to roll an invisible hat off his head with an outlandish gesture like the most obsequious of courtiers.

I turned away before he saw me grin.

Chapter 12

I returned to Maccabee HQ that afternoon needing a caffeine fix, so I headed for the third floor before hitting the morgue. I stepped off the elevator, passing a man with a mop of brown hair and fat white headphones who was hunched over his laptop.

Ryan's terrible posture and predilection for decorative beard ornaments during the holidays aside, this lanky Trad was the whip-smart head of IT. He'd claimed the coveted cushy wingback chair by the wall of live greenery instead of holing up in his department at the back of the floor, but that wouldn't last long. The second he got called away for assistance, others would jostle for possession of the seat.

You'd think Michael would arrange for more quality seating, but I suspected the constant vigilance required to keep tabs on the chair amused her.

Not all support staff who worked for the Maccabees were Eishei Kodesh, but all the human operatives were. Anything regarding Trad law and order was handled by regular police while magic law and justice was dealt with by the Maccabees. If I had a complaint about a Trad person, I'd go to the police, not the Maccabees, since the suspect didn't have magic.

We didn't have the same rank system as Trad police officers. After novices graduated from training school to operative, we had three levels we progressed through before becoming upper management, with the chapter director being the top boss at a local level.

Level ones dealt with the public the most. They patrolled, investigated assaults, traffic accidents, home invasions, and assisted higher-level operatives. It was street-level work where we cut our chops.

All lower-level jobs for human operatives were assigned by level threes, the top operative rank. They kept the juicy stuff like murder or gang crimes for themselves. Some recruited specific level twos to work with them on a more permanent basis, others chose to partner up with fellow level threes on a case or solve it on their own. They worked up on the fifth floor.

Once we reached level two operative, which was where the bulk of us were, we got to take on more interesting cases, like the Toussaints' fraud spree. Marilyn, my superior, who'd assigned Sachie and me that assignment, had not been pleased once it became a homicide investigation, and Michael granted us dispensation for the two of us to remain the leads.

I shouldered through a frosted glass door into what had previously been a huge cubicle farm. The enormous space had been opened and flooded with natural light, its accent wall painted a tranquil light green. It boasted a kitchen, throw rugs, bookcases with all manner of titles, and a mix of workstations and living room furniture to make us feel more at home.

Regardless of level, everyone ended up at the kitchen on third because it had a coffee bar and baked goods delivered fresh each day. Good snacks were imperative to Maccabee happiness.

I hit the button on the high-end automatic espresso machine, listening impatiently to the clanking and grinding sounds while I waited for my mid-afternoon fix.

The machine buzzed, releasing an aromatic double shot into my glass mug. With every last drop expelled, I slid the mug under the milk-frothing arm and watched the foamy liquid blend in a swirl with the dark roasted caffeine. Get in my belly.

A plate with a coveted apple fritter appeared on the counter by my elbow. Operatives claimed these buttery flakey tart crescents like moms snagging the hottest toy for Christmas. Bruising was not uncommon.

"I saved one for you in case you were coming in." Gemma leaned back against the kitchen island, doing biceps curls. Her blue wrap dress clung to her curves like fancy wrapping paper on an expensive gift.

"You either intend to poison me with absolutely no subtlety, or you want something. Either way, not interested." I pushed the plate away.

"Hear me out." She shot me a fetching smile. Damn she had great skin.

The zit at my hairline pulsed. Screw you, adult acne. I took a sip of my latte, savoring the notes of caramel, and motioned for her to speak.

"Introduce me to Ezra Cardoso."

I cough-choked, every atom in my body flaring in a giant "Hell, no" and Cherry whispering suggestions for where we could shove that fritter. I opted not to take her up on them—yet. A good leader did not allow personal prejudice or snap judgments to cloud their actions, and this might be a purely professional request. I cleared my throat. "Why do you wish to speak to him?"

A wicked grin lit up Gemma's face, though she kept on with her arm regime. "I want to ride him like a mechanical bull. I mean, have you read what they say about his—"

"He's a fellow operative," I gasped. All I needed was a set of pearls to clutch—when had I become such a prude? I didn't mind friendly banter, but wasn't this too much? Weren't we entitled to a little more respect from each other than discussing bedroom details? I mean, I knew Ezra's bedroom details and Gemma didn't, and yet, I was respecting her by not smirking or shoving the fritter up her—

"Why do you think I'm asking? I'll never have the chance to get this close to him again." She frowned. "I've never believed that you pulled the nepotism card with Michael before, but I don't understand why you were assigned to co-lead with him otherwise."

Gemma knew nothing of my past with Ezra, so she wasn't saying this out of concern for my well-being, and I'd hit my limit of being polite with this woman. She'd subjected me to years of subtle and not-so-subtle jabs, and yes, at times, I gave as good as I got with her, but this diss had not only crossed the line, it had rubbed it out and kicked dirt over it.

I smiled thinly, running a finger around the rim of my mug. "Are you insulting my ability as an operative? I take my reputation very seriously, so I would think twice about what you say next." I fired the words into her like darts.

Her shoulders twitched. Heh.

"No," she said petulantly. "It's just… Oh, forget it."

"Already forgotten." I stared her down until she left.

She'd killed any desire for my latte, so I dumped it down the sink and placed the glass in the dishwasher. The Maccabees had been an Ezra-free refuge and now he'd ruined it. He didn't even have to be present for me to be forced to deal with the emotional fallout of him working here, and I hated it. I was mad. At him, at Gemma, at Michael for putting me in this situation. There was plenty of blame to go around.

Sachie wasn't anywhere on this floor, so I grabbed the fritter and headed to the basement. As I suspected, she was hanging out down in the Spook Squad's digs.

Darsh was taping a large handwritten sign to the wall that read, "Ask us about Ezra at your own risk." Under the words was a bloody lip print. With fang.

"Ooh." I clapped my hands together. "Could I get that on a T-shirt?"

While my friends hadn't slept yet, they had showered and both changed into one of the many spare outfits they kept at HQ. Sach's hair was pinned off her face with glittery barrettes, and she'd paired her Docs with denim cargo pants and an electric blue knit sweater.

Darsh, as was his wont, was brilliantly attired, decked out in leather pants and a skintight top covered in blue sequins. The ridges of his absurdly cut ab muscles peeked out in the gap between his pants and his shirt, his brown hair was tucked in a messy bun on his head, and a winged eyeliner application that I envied made his brownish-gold eyes pop.

Darsh called himself and Sach the butterflies to my designer caterpillar. I'd foregone a skirt for a pale pink pantsuit and matching heels, with a double-breasted vest that was cut demurely enough to be worn without a shirt.

Sachie absently munched around the edges of a dry cheese sandwich, her bleary eyes glued to her laptop screen, and three oversize mugs of half-drained mocha lattes sat on her desk like sentries.

I handed her the apple fritter. "Here."

Even with my nap, hot shower, and a homecooked nutritious meal, my eyes were gritty, and my body felt sluggish, so it was a wonder my bestie was still awake at all.

"You're a goddess," Sachie said, practically inhaling the pastry. She listed closer to the screen, all twisted and hunched over.

"Keep sitting that way and the left side of your neck will collapse into your shoulder," I said.

Darsh wrinkled his nose. "She'll have to wear large bows around her throat to distract people."

Sach shot us both the finger without looking up—or sitting up.

I gently grasped her elbow and pulled her to her feet. "Take a break and come with me to the morgue."

"Because who isn't refreshed by formaldehyde and lifeless meatsacks?" Sach said.

I raised an eyebrow. "Meatsacks? You are spending too much time with vamps."

"No such thing, darling." Darsh cracked his lower back before sitting down at his computer.

"Agree to disagree," I said and tugged Sach into the elevator.

"So." My friend side-eyed me. "How was working with the ex? Do I need to bust out the Disney villains karaoke playlist when we get home?"

"God, no. If I never duet 'Gaston' again, I'll die happy."

"Get over yourself. You made me do the heavy lifting on that one."

I nudged her with my hip. "I made you do *all* the heavy lifting during that darkest timeline. I'd have wasted away to a sad, shriveled lump under my covers without you, lost in a fog of despair."

"A *dirty*, sad, shriveled—"

"Yup. Got it."

"I burned that flannel robe of yours, you know."

"You told me you drove it into the country to live with a nice family."

We both cracked smiles, but Sach turned it into a frown and jutted up her chin. "Yeah, well, if you choose to wreck your life, I will not put your Humpty Dumpty ass together again. And forget about me keeping you company at kickboxing lessons. You can go all by yourself and have to partner up with some rando who smells like garlic."

I swallowed through a tight throat and nodded.

The elevator doors opened and Sachie caught my hand. "Don't fall for him again. Please. It killed me to see you like that."

I nodded, my eyes damp, and squeezed her in a one-armed hug.

"Now, let's go see meatsacks," she said cheerily and breezed out.

The morgue at Maccabee HQ was located one floor up from the Spook Squad's basement digs. Despite the fresh coat of white paint on the walls and the gleaming stainless-steel tables and sinks, it was the little things that pulled focus: the orange biohazard buckets under the tables, the tang of formaldehyde, and the whir of the exhaust fan on full.

Oh, and the wall of sealed cooler drawers housing the decedents.

Sach and I put on surgical caps and latex gloves, waiting for the coroner to come back.

I tucked an errant strand back under my cap, idly scanning the plastic signs with body part names on them, which hung alongside a chalkboard positioned next to a scale. Under my breath I hummed "The Ballad of Sweeney Todd."

Sach snickered.

Vancouver didn't have a lot of homicides, hell, last year's murder count in our entire province barely cracked 120 for Trads and Eishei Kodesh combined. Our morgue served the magic community, but as importantly, it was where slain operatives ended up before burial.

I traced a finger over one of the latched refrigeration drawers, the metal handle cool even through the gloves I wore. Goose bumps dotted my skin, and not from the lowered temperature that kept smells from stagnating.

Would I end up here one day, an empty shell in a cold metal box? Sure, I'd be dead so who cared if I was in there or laid out on a bed of roses, but what would happen to a Maccabee who turned out to be a half shedim? Would they even get the dignity of a burial or would they be dumped in an unmarked grave as a warning or a dirty secret?

"Hello, ladies."

I jumped at Dr. Malika Ayad's singsong greeting.

"Worried about ghosts? I'll protect you," she teased. The Maccabee coroner pulled on a fresh pair of latex gloves. She wore her customary scrubs and hijab.

"Is that offer good in the event of a zombie apocalypse?" I joked.

"No. Then it's on Sachie to save us both."

Sach rested her elbow on my shoulder. Five-foot-eight to my five-five, she used me as an elbow holder on a regular basis. "Just because I enjoy a good vamp tussle now and then doesn't mean I'm into grabby brain guzzlers. You're on your own."

I shrugged her off. "Could we please see Kyle Epstein? I'd like to check him out with my blue flame vision."

"Of course." Malika walked over to the wall of drawers and unlatched the one next to me. "Decomposition has been negligible. This is almost exactly the state he was brought in." She pulled back the sheet.

Sach and I leaned in.

If you ignored Kyle Epstein's empty eye sockets and heart cavity, the man looked rather peaceful. His skin was a creamy alabaster from the magic cleansing, with no sign of any laceration.

Fully aware that this was a long shot, I slid into my synesthete vision. Huh. Kyle actually had a blue mark, but it wasn't a dot. It was a fat double knot occupying much of his upper chest. I closed one eye then the other, wondering if it was some post-mortem weirdness conflicting with my power, but the knot remained steady.

"Hey." Sachie nudged me. "What are you seeing?"

"Kyle has this double knot in his chest. I've never seen or heard of anything like it, but I'll check the archives. It might be indicative of a blood or heart disorder?" I shook my head. "It's really odd."

"Tell me what you find," Malika said, sliding the body back into the cubby and latching the door. "I should have you view all the bodies. Might make my job easier."

I shuddered. "I'll pass, thanks."

"Can't blame a woman for trying. Now, since you've seen the victim, Mr. Cardoso has requested I start the autopsy." She raised an eyebrow. "Is he as handsome in person as he is charming on the phone?"

There was a big difference between Gemma wanting an introduction to Ezra and Malika asking about him. Namely that Gemma never normally asked my opinion or requested help with anything, while Malika and I respected each other's professional abilities and had a good rapport. This was simple curiosity, not Malika using me for anything. Also, she was happily married to her high school sweetheart.

I shrugged. "He thinks he is."

"Well, no other vamp has ever sent me a gift basket full of my favorite teas to thank me in advance for my assistance," Malika said.

"What a prince." Sach managed to say it without a trace of sarcasm. *Of Darkness*, she mouthed at me.

I tamped down a smirk.

"We won't keep you any longer," I said. "Thanks for letting me see the vic."

"Anytime," Malika said.

I trailed Sachie into the elevator and she hit the button for the basement.

"What's with the frown?" she said.

"Is this knot a result of the Yellow Flame's magic? Is it relevant to this murder case at all? It's not like I can check the other vics and see if they have that mark."

Alison had been cremated, and I wasn't about to dig up Mr. Mirwani or Aleksander. Besides, they'd be decomposing already, whereas Kyle was newly dead and preserved in a sealed drawer. The chances of seeing anything on those other corpses were negligible.

"You'll figure it out."

I smiled. "Thanks for the vote of confidence. And for being the ultimate best friend in the world."

She patted my shoulder. "I'm a gift."

Chapter 13

There was nothing in the Maccabee library about a fat double knot seen via blue flame vision, not even anecdotally. I also searched out diseases or abnormalities that Yellow Flames were unable to cleanse to explain it, perhaps some scars or tumors. There were a few that left a magic mark post-mortem, including a couple types of cancer and certain rib segmentations, but Ezra and Silas had seen the post-mortems for the other victims. If they were ill or injured before being abducted, Ezra would have informed us.

One way or another, I had to determine what this meant.

I was stretching out my stiff lower back and pondering how to find answers when Ezra sent a text to the team to meet at the new office in an hour.

Sach and I grabbed an early dinner at a fast-food drive-thru on the way.

We were in my old hatchback, which I'd picked up from the garage with a minor heart attack at the cost of the repairs. While I drove, my friend told me about the latest woman that her mom, Reina, wanted to set her up with. When Sach had come out as bisexual in university, Reina had taken this to mean she had twice as many opportunities to get Sachie settled with someone who'd talk her daughter out of her dangerous Maccabee lifestyle.

Sach permitted it, because some of the people her mom thrust at her were hot, and she'd had some memorable hookups. I mean, her dad, Ben, was a stone-cold fox; Reina had good taste.

"All I'm saying…" Sach stuffed a handful of fries in her mouth, speaking with bulging cheeks. "I asked how tall this woman is." She sighed. "She's unnecessarily short."

I tossed the crust and soggy lettuce remnant of my cheeseburger onto the wrapper sitting on the dashboard and flicked on my turn signal. "Is there ever a necessary shortness?"

She considered that while she finished her chicken strips. "How about when you have to limbo under a death laser that's mere feet off the ground?"

"That's a situation you foresee coming up often in a relationship, do you?" I said, checking the side mirror for oncoming cyclists before turning.

"I mean, I'm not going to rule it out." She popped the button on her cargo jeans with a groan. "I'm not sure what's worse, my unrealistic expectation that I could metabolize that combo meal without busting out of my pants like I swallowed a horse, or the fact that I still ate every last morsel."

"Hard to say." I was buzzing on grease, fatty protein, and enough aspartame to run a marathon. Both a gross and delightful sensation. "Are you going to meet the unnecessarily short woman or not?"

"I considered it until she proposed the waffle restaurant on Lougheed."

I grimaced. "The one where hope goes to die? Hard pass."

"Maybe it was an ironic suggestion?"

I slowed to a stop at the yellow light. "Ah. So, she's bangable hot and you're trying to justify her questionable taste."

"They have real maple syrup there," Sach said weakly.

"This is Canada. That's not a unique selling point."

She grabbed the crumpled-up take-out bag. "I'm finishing the rest of your fries," she muttered.

"Oooh, hate-eat them, baby." I waggled my tongue, making my friend laugh and show both her dimples.

Other than internet access secure enough to connect to all the databases at Maccabee HQ, the office hadn't been outfitted with anything new. Conference table it was.

Ezra stocked the fridge with individual servings of blood, mostly synthetic but with a couple bright packages of animal blood. "I'm waiting for a text regarding some of the footage we obtained from the campground," he said. He'd trimmed and groomed his beard back to Hollywood pirate perfection, and his silvery-blue eyes were bright and clear, versus my bleary red ones. "We'll start the meeting once I have that update."

Tattooed script on his left biceps peeked out of his soft green T-shirt. It was difficult, albeit possible for vamps to get inked, and not have their healing magic automatically wipe away the tattoo as the artist created it. There were powerful Yellow Flames who specialized in that.

The words were too obscured by the fabric to read them, and he hadn't had any ink six years ago, claiming that between being one of the only Primes in existence, and a Sephardic Jew (tattooing was forbidden in our religion), he had no interest in doing anything that might bring more attention to himself.

Oh, how times had changed.

I glanced away, refusing to speculate if he had others and where they might be. Also, what a load of crap given how he'd embraced his public persona readily enough. Even once it came out that Ezra was a Mafia enforcer, he hadn't hidden. Almost the opposite, in fact. It was like he doubled down on his refusal to hide, because there was a tidal wave of photos in the aftermath. I couldn't escape images of him attending the Grammys with rockstar pals or alone at a vamp café reading a book.

Vampire cafés were nothing like maid cafés in Tokyo because no one was in costume. In fact, showing up to one of these places dressed like a wannabe Count Dracula was a bad idea. Though you might provide that special ingredient in an award-winning concoction at a blood barista competition.

Anyway, that photo of Ezra, his head bowed over some novel with a curl escaping out of his black knit cap and into his eyes, almost broke the internet.

I tore the tape off a box of weapons that we'd brought over from HQ. Sach helped me unpack them into a cupboard that we commandeered.

Darsh poked his index finger with a stiletto blade. "Ouch." He pouted and sucked on the bead of blood.

Sach smacked him across the top of the head. "How many times do I have to tell you not to touch things that can kill you?"

Darsh blinked at her innocently. "But I so love the thrill."

Silas, casually dressed in a fitted sweater and dark jeans, tested an oak stake. By tested, I mean he flexed it like it was a bendy toy to right before its breaking point, then nodded in approval. "That'll do." He sauntered over to the fridge, grabbed a synthetic drink, removed the straw, and neatly popped it into the package before taking a sip.

Darsh snickered.

"What?" Silas said.

"You look like a child sucking on a juice box." My friend grimaced. "With synthetic blood to complete the toddler look."

Sach put away a Taser, rolling her eyes.

With the weapons stored, I plugged my laptop in. I'd given my speech about respectful adult communication, and I didn't see my co-leader feeling the need to parent out all the group dynamics, so I was hardly going to step in and play Mom. Darsh behaved this way with everyone, and it was on Silas to shut him down.

Silas waved at the fridge. "You want animal blood, be my guest. There's a few of those in there."

A wasp flew into the room through a partially open window.

I fanned away the stinging beast. Bees were cute. Wasps were evil.

"You might like rustling heifer blood," Darsh said, "but I prefer to drink it the way the devil intended. Cardoso's reasons for drinking the fake crap are obvious, given Jewish prohibitions on consuming blood, but what's your excuse, Cowpoke?"

"It's inhuman and an abuse of power. And don't speak to me like I'm an idiot."

Given that Southern accent, those boyish looks and freckles, and his enormous size, it would be easy to dismiss Silas's intelligence. He'd probably been battling that in life and undeath. I'd seen otherwise, and Ezra wouldn't have anyone watching his back who wasn't incredibly smart.

"*We're* inhuman," Darsh countered. "You can drink all the fake plasma you want, but don't delude yourself on that score."

"Mierda," Ezra muttered. He flattened the cardboard box that the blood had come in, using it to wave away the wasp. "Is there a point to this besides insulting my friend?"

"I'm not insulting him." Darsh dragged a finger over

the side table set out with snacks. No ketchup chips though, which Sach would be rectifying. "I'm getting a measure of the man."

"You want me to admit I'm inhuman because I drink blood at all?" Silas crossed his arms, each of his biceps popping to approximately the size of Australia. His half-finished drink dangled from one hand. "I can't help what I am or what I do to survive."

"Amen," I muttered.

Ezra crossed over to the conference table, the wasp buzzing around his head. He did this weird little hop dance, swatting at the insect with more force than necessary.

Darsh stopped in front of Silas. "I want you to understand why it's *important* to drink human blood."

"Whatever, man." Silas turned away.

Darsh grabbed his arm. "When I feel a person's rapid pulse vibrating through my fangs?" Darsh swiped his tongue over his teeth. "When I see the excitement and fear in a person's gaze as they dance with death?" He tilted his head up since Silas had a good four or five inches on him. "The thump of their heart under my palm?" He placed his hand on Silas's chest.

Silas stared him down, poker-faced.

"It's only when we're faced with the reminders of what we've lost in this long immortal life of ours, when we hold a person's fragile existence in the palm of our hand..." Darsh curled his fingers inward, all of us tracking the movement. "And choose to preserve their life by keeping ourselves in check and letting them walk away? That's how we prevent ourselves from falling over the edge into monstrosity. So yes, Silas. I drink from humans." Darsh swiped the half-finished blood package away. "That said, this is inherently preferable to animal blood." He took a sip. "Mmm, spicy." He licked his lips, shoved the drink back at Silas, and sauntered over to the conference table.

Darsh had an interesting point. He, too, was doing what he had to, both to survive and to keep from descending into madness during his immortal existence. It would be so easy for him to snuff out human life, yet he chose to continually remind himself of its value and affirm that while he wasn't human, he wasn't a monster either.

Silas stared at the container like it was a hand grenade with the pin pulled, while Ezra said something in Spanish that I'm certain was an insult, along with Michael's name.

Count von Cardoso's smack talk game is strong.

Ezra's phone sounded with the text he'd been waiting for, so smirking at the announcer's voice in my head, I started the meeting.

Once we'd all taken our seats, Ezra opened his leather messenger bag, but what he pulled out was not a laptop.

It was a ball of purple fuzzy yarn attached to a partially knitted project cast in a triangle onto three small green metal needles with double-pointed ends.

Ezra settled back in his chair, pulled a fourth empty needle out of the ball and, needles clicking, began casting and purling or whatever the hell he was doing. He worked fast by human standards, creating perfectly even stitches, though for a vamp it was a relaxing pace.

I gaped at him.

I wasn't the only one. Sach wore an expression like she'd swallowed the wasp currently buzzing angrily around the ceiling light.

Darsh narrowed his eyes. "How cocky for a vamp to pick up a hobby with tools that could kill him."

"Takes one to know one," Sachie chirped.

"They're metal, not wood," Ezra said.

I was more mystified about why he was sharing this pastime with us. Did he view himself as top dog of the group and not care about any teasing? Was this a gesture of trust, opening himself up, or was it another mask? Which Ezra was the real one?

Had I fallen in love with and had my heart broken by an illusion?

I got a bottle of water from the fridge and pressed the cool plastic to my forehead before I drank deeply.

Ezra moved the needle that had been filling up with stitches to the right of the three in use and tapped his thumb against its tip. "It would take more than these to take me out."

"Ooh, I love dares." Darsh batted his lashes.

"They look sharp enough," Sachie said. "Leave them on a chair and it's an emergency room trip waiting to happen."

"And the start of a new urban legend," Darsh said.

Silas didn't look surprised. Not at my friends' reactions or Ezra's hobby.

I shook my head sharply. "Is this stress knitting or something you do regularly?"

"Hard to separate them," Silas said wryly. "Ask me how many pairs of woolen socks I own for a vampire based in Charleston?"

Ezra frowned at him and Silas chuckled. My ex thrust the tip of the empty needle into a loop and commenced a new row. "Knitting has a fascinating history. Men used to knit socks for themselves in the army, women added coded messages in their knitting during times of war, and surgeons use it to keep their fingers nimble and improve their hand-eye coordination."

"Methinks the vamp doth protest too much," Sachie said.

"Old-timey. Nice." I flashed her a thumbs-up.

"It started as a joke," Silas said. "Then Ez discovered it was great for being underestimated." He clucked his tongue. "It's amazing how many people have outdated ideas of masculinity."

Darsh swatted the wasp away. "Don't look at me. I bloomed into a post-masculine state ages ago."

Ezra had already finished his row and moved on without even looking at what he was doing. "Being underestimated can be fun."

"Right," Silas said. "Women falling in a puddle at your feet when they see you is simply a side benefit." He laughed. "Not Orly though. She threatened to jam a needle up your ass if you gift her with any more creations."

Creations, plural. Orly must be very close to Ezra. I twisted my fingers in my lap.

"What can I say?" Ezra shrugged and grinned, but his eyes slid sideways to me, the corners crinkling a tiny bit, almost like he was in pain.

"We've gotten off track," I said curtly.

"Well, we've got good news," Sachie said. "I think we found the fourth murder!" She held up her hand and Darsh high-fived her.

"Holy shit!" I grabbed a dry-erase marker off the pile on the table and moved over to the whiteboard to add in these new details.

Ezra nodded. "Excellent work."

Their break had occurred due to a combination of luck, smarts, and a lot of patience. After hours of combing various databases for any similarities to the other murders, Sach and Darsh tried a different tack and plotted out the known murder locations. The killer had been moving north and west from the first death in Sydney to the second in Quetta. The direction remained consistent to Copenhagen, though the distance shortened.

However, somewhere between the third and fifth murders, the killer ended up due west in Vancouver. There were no reports from the east coast of Canada that were a possible match, so Sach and Darsh speculated on where the NW trajectory had changed. When they took the shortened distances between the first three locations into account and stuck with a NW movement, it put the site of the next murder in Greenland.

Contrary to popular belief, there are cities there, but a ritual murder in a place that sparsely inhabited would have made international news.

Nothing showed in any news files, but guess what Greenland did have? Spruce trees.

My friends turned to missing persons reports during the time frame between Aleksander's and Kyle's murders and found something odd. A female coma patient, Lynd Rasmussen, had been stolen from a hospital in Nuuk, Greenland, and never found. That was strange enough, but there was also a fire in that same time frame in a tiny corner of the Qinngua Valley that destroyed a swath of trees including some spruce.

"The fire in Greenland wasn't deliberately set," Sachie was saying. "It was due to a rare lightning strike, but if it happened after the murder, that would have erased any trace of the body."

"Did Lynd fit the humanitarian profile?" I said.

"She was a high school teacher. Depending on what you think of teenagers, then yes. Apparently, she wasn't a bad person, but we didn't find any notable philanthropy either. Maybe she was a nice neighbor. I don't know, but she's the most likely victim."

"Yellow Flames can't wake coma patients." Silas scratched his chin. "Our suspect must have taken Miz Rasmussen out of the hospital while she was still unconscious. No one noticed?"

"Apparently not," Sach said.

Ezra placed his knitting on the table, the empty

needle once more secured in the ball of yarn. "My gut says you're right about her being the fourth victim. Was there hospital footage of the kidnapping?"

"No," Darsh replied. "Though a hospital ties into our working theory that this Yellow Flame has surgical training. Who better to sneak a patient out than someone familiar with that environment?"

Ezra rested his chin on his folded hands. "A trip to Greenland is in order."

"Are you going to be coy about that text about the security footage," Sachie said, "or fill us in already?"

"I wish I could say that we caught someone's full face on at least one camera," Ezra said, "but all that we have is a blurred figure."

A chill ran down my spine, and I stopped writing. My mind raced with questions at this implication, most notably, how badly would this complicate the investigation, and how much danger would it put us in? "A vamp is one of our killers?"

"Yeah," he said. "I think—"

"Someone believes the old legend that you can cure vampirism with the blood of the righteous," I finished. My unease was reflected in the grim silence of my team members.

Ezra, who was directly in my line of sight, stared into the middle distance, his gaze unfocused as if he was struggling to absorb the weight of this troubling news.

Silas gave a heavy sigh, and Darsh looked positively murderous.

Sach whistled softly. "Hello, higher purpose."

The wasp buzzed by my ear, and I yelped, swatting it away vigorously. It flew off, only to circle back. I ducked, waving my hands around.

Something suddenly whipped over me so close to the

top of my head that it ruffled my hair when it whistled past.

The buzzing fell silent. One of Ezra's knitting needles quivered from where he'd sunk it halfway into the wall—and skewered the wasp in the process.

"I don't like them either," he said mildly.

Silas tore his eyes away from the dead insect. "We better hope there's some other reason for these murders," he said somberly, "because if the Eishei Kodesh is using a potion made from good people to rid the world of vampires, regardless of whether or not it actually does anything, you know what will happen."

Darsh nodded. "War."

Chapter 14

What would war mean? Where would our vamps' loyalties lie? With the Maccabees or their own kind?

If pressed, I couldn't take up arms against a friend, undead or not.

Sach gnawed on her lip, looking vaguely ill.

One of the things that Maccabees had managed to put into law in most countries was the mandatory registration of any vamp on earth. Some, like Darsh, were vehemently against being put on registries like sex offenders, regardless of whether they'd actually broken any law. Other vampires didn't mind.

Humans were all for it, however, because it allowed Maccabees to determine whether vamps were keeping to blood laws and more or less keep track of them, given they couldn't monitor comings and goings to Babel.

I appreciated both sides, but this was the first time I'd been in a room where vamps outnumbered the humans, and it hit me differently. This Yellow Flame we sought wasn't monitored, their every move scrutinized, and they were a serial killer. Why should these operatives be subjected to that, just for being undead?

"It's an urban legend," Sachie said. "There is no cure for vampirism."

"That we know of." Ezra walked over to the wall and yanked his needle out. "But what if the Eishei Kodesh has truly found a way? They'd have to administer this potion to every vamp."

"Forcibly administer," Silas said darkly.

Ezra nodded and flicked the wasp corpse into the trash. "Their mixture would have to behave like a virus and spread through the global vampire community, nullifying the magic that lets us turn humans."

"You better watch your back if that happens," Darsh said. "A Prime is the only vampire who can have biological vampire babies. You'll be a target." He made a face. "Might not be your back you'd need to watch though."

"Thank you for elaborating," Ezra said dryly. He washed off his needle at the kitchen sink and dried it on his jeans.

"It doesn't matter how it could work," Sachie said, "since it won't. The chances that the killers have managed to succeed where countless others have failed are infinitesimal. It's the *belief* that a working cure exists that's the danger."

We could put all the laws in place establishing consent for feeding on or changing a person, including a notarization that the changee was a willing participant, but there would always be rogue vamps who did as they pleased with humans.

Some newly undead didn't handle the change well and offed themselves. Fire was a popular though painful choice for Trads. Former Eishei Kodesh who wanted off this plane of existence had it easy: they simply walked into the bright light of day.

Just because someone wholeheartedly embraced the idea of immortality didn't mean they were prepared for what they were getting into. Not really. We'd all heard the stories of old undead criminals who had accumulated immense wealth, experienced every pleasure, but no longer felt anything. Many went mad.

While stopping vampirism from happening in the first place was different from killing the undead, it still left me uneasy. I had no doubt that if there was a way to stop half shedim from being born, those procedures would be hardened into law.

"The killers are on a quest for their own holy grail." Silas tipped his chair forward and back down again. "It doesn't matter whether they actually can or can't pull this off. Fanatics can twist themselves into knots and still insist it's a straight line."

I nodded. "All it takes is enough vamps or humans hearing about it and believing it's happening and war will break out."

How much did the truth matter versus personal belief? Were our thoughts our reality? Was that why Ezra hadn't told me about his Mafia family back then? He'd been fleeing one reality and trying to create another? I shook my head. No, because he'd become an enforcer after our time together.

What was the truth versus Ezra's own beliefs now, and where did being on this murder investigation play into them?

"Humans won't condone killing other humans," Sach said. "Not even to cure vampirism."

"Your innocence is adorable," Darsh said.

"Kyle Epstein was abducted during the day," Silas said, "so it wasn't a Trad vamp who did it. Is this vampire running the show, or is the Yellow Flame an equal partner?"

Ezra sat back down, dancing the small knitting needle

over his knuckles. "Does one way make it better or worse?"

Silas scrubbed a hand through his hair. "I'm just looking for angles."

Ezra sighed. "I know, chamo."

"Either way, the vamp is there willingly." I drummed a dry-erase marker on the table. "Hard to force a vampire to do anything they don't want to."

I honestly hadn't meant anything except in a general sense that humans, even ones with magic, couldn't strong-arm vamps, but Ezra tensed.

He immediately shook it off and carried on smoothly. "Get the person with super speed to abduct the victims and evade detection."

"The vamp killed them." Darsh uncapped a dry-erase marker that had rolled across the table, sniffed it, and made a face. "The Yellow Flame wiped away the bite mark."

"I'm hoping to find out which vamp," Ezra said. "That's what the text was about. We pulled a close-up of the vamp's hand when he broke one of the cameras."

"In the most likely place that Kyle was kidnapped?" I said.

Ezra pointed a needle at me. "Yes. The vamp definitely is male, and his sleeve had fallen back revealing part of a stylized tattoo. The Maccabee techs identified it. So handy of British football teams to place their names on their logos. Our suspect supports Manchester."

"Could you see if the hand had any white hair or age spots on it?" Silas said. "What about loose skin or brittle nails?"

"Have a fetish, do you?" Darsh said.

"They're ways of narrowing down the age range," Silas said. "And if you have nothing meaningful to contribute, then hush up."

Darsh shivered. "Ooh, I've been told off now."

"Naw, sweetheart," Silas drawled. "If that had happened, you wouldn't still be standing."

Darsh blinked, and I smothered a laugh. Good for Silas.

"I'd guess he's not above his forties," Ezra said, attempting to get us back on topic.

"Okay," Silas said. "I'll run the age range, get a suspect pool of registered vamps from London HQ, and then contact tattoo artists in Manchester to see if anyone recognizes the artwork. There can't be many who are capable of inking vampires."

"It could easily be an unregistered vampire." Sachie looked up from her drawing. "Get me a photo of the tattoo and let me visit them. Establish rapport." Sachie's name meant "happiness" or "good luck" in Japanese, but another meaning was "branch," and she had a magnificent tree inked on her back. "Unless you have any tattoos of your own to bond with them over?"

Silas shook his head. "Happy to hand this over."

"Did you get anywhere tracking the funding?" I asked. "Any possible connection to this hospital?"

Long story short, the funding was a bust. There were no similarities between any organizations that the victims had worked for, or, in Kyle's case, had used personally.

Darsh leaned back in his chair and swung his pointy black leather shoes onto the table. "I had a thought."

"Lucky us," Silas said. He retrieved a bunch of loose power cords and connector cables from his makeshift desk.

Darsh's lips quirked.

Ezra steepled his hands under his chin. "What's on your mind?"

"What if the ritual killings are a smokescreen?" Darsh said.

Sach, once more drawing, yawned. "Sorry."

Darsh gave an exaggerated pained sigh but continued. "I'm not sure about eyes, but blood and healthy hearts have value on the black market, and vamps have organ trafficking cornered."

"You want to go to Babel and check it out?" Silas said dubiously, wrapping each cord into its own neat pile.

"Yes!" At my overly enthusiastic pronouncement, everyone stared at me. "I'll go with him."

It was a good idea, but that's not why I was so excited. I'd never had the opportunity to go to the Crypt, the black market in Babel, since I'd never had an undead escort into the vamp megacity before. The Crypt was shrouded in mystery and rumors, and I was dying to find out if any of them were true. Okay, not literally, universe. That wasn't a challenge.

Most importantly though, Maccabee archives hadn't turned up anything about that blue double knot in Kyle's chest, but a black market was the perfect place to find someone with knowledge of odd magical marks—and crackpot potions.

I was about to explain that to everyone when Ezra crossed his arms over his puffed-up chest. "Over my dead body," he said.

I raised my eyebrows.

"You know what I mean," he grumbled.

"Let me accompany Darsh," Sachie said, adding a mushroom to the alien landscape she was sketching. "I'm trained to fight vamps, and I've wanted to go to Babel forever. I can hop over to the North Yorkshire Moors portal from Manchester."

"No." Ezra stood up, all the better to loom over us. "No humans and that's final."

"Why don't we discuss—" Silas said.

I stood up. Ezra could loom, I'd bristle. "Says the man who doesn't outrank me."

Ezra pointed at the door. "How about says the man who could physically twist the handle so you can't leave?"

"Try it and I'll shove a stake up your ass."

"Discuss it like civilized people." Silas sighed and picked up another cable.

Darsh thudded his feet back on the ground. "Oh no, let's keep going like this."

"I want to ask around about that mark," I said to Sachie. "You focus on the tattoo shops."

"What mark?" Silas said.

"Don't you trust me to keep Avi safe?" Darsh said.

Ezra stiffened at my friend's use of my nickname. I doubt anyone else noticed, but I was woefully attuned to the most minuscule of his gestures. "Don't start with me," he growled.

"I *am* going to focus on the tattoo shops." Sachie shaded the mushroom in with angry strokes. "Then I can go to the Crypt and ask around on your behalf."

"You pulled an all-nighter, so you're not going anywhere until you've gotten some rest," I said. "Lack of sleep is a liability."

"I'll sleep on the plane," she countered. "Before I go to Babel."

"What mark?" Silas repeated.

"You saw a mark?" Ezra said.

"Yes, you were too busy being a jackass to hear me. Sach, you can't check if anyone else has it." While I didn't want to pull rank… "I'm going and that's final."

Sachie put down her pen and saluted me. "Aye, aye, captain."

It was always better when Sachie yelled. This tightly controlled tone of voice meant she was deeply and seriously angry. Well, so was I. "You're being unreasonable. Think of what's best for the investigation."

"My experience being around more vamps," she said.

I waved a hand around the table, where I was currently sitting with three of them. "You were saying?"

"Apparently I was saying nothing since you've already decided."

Jesus. I rolled my eyes.

Ezra jabbed a finger at Darsh. "Should any of the Kosher Nostra find her—"

"Your father's goons won't know we're there," Darsh said.

"Right." Ezra laughed harshly. "Natán didn't get to his exalted position without an exceptional network of informants."

Darsh shrugged. "Then call your dad and tell him to back off."

"He doesn't control all the vampires in the black market, much less all of Babel, so what about the rest of them?" Ezra gathered up the dry-erase markers. "Babel is dangerous enough for humans without taking them to the Crypt. That place is the opposite of neutral ground. This is a pointless risk, Aviva. Darsh doesn't need you there. He can ask about the mark."

I clenched my fists. "It's not pointless."

Ezra capped one marker so hard that the plastic shattered.

"I've never been to the Crypt," Silas said. "Nor would I want to go. Whatever's there won't be pretty. You ready to handle any trauma from that?"

That gave me pause, but I nodded.

"Do you admit it *is* a risk for you to go there?" Silas said.

"Yes," I conceded.

"Then explain why you have to go, beyond being the one who can see this thing. You could describe it and Darsh could look into it." Silas stacked the wound cables in a pile. "You're my team leader, Aviva. I have a right to know that you've thought the risks through and aren't a thrill seeker who might endanger her operatives."

Ezra looked mollified—somewhat. Sachie gave me a defiant glare, waiting for me to answer, and Darsh blinked like a cat mildly interested in the antics of its lowly person.

"There was a fat double knot in Kyle's upper chest, which I saw with my blue synesthete magic. I couldn't identify it, which bothered me. My search in the library at HQ didn't find any matches for it, but then Darsh mentioned the Crypt and I saw a way to determine if it was significant. Any vamp dealing in human organs will have clients making some of these potions, and perhaps the knot is relevant to another type of so-called cure or enhancer? This weakness is either a disease that remained in the body post-mortem or something the Yellow Flame did during the purification ritual. If I can narrow it down to one of those things, perhaps we avoid war when this gets out."

Ezra shook his head. "That's more of what you already said."

I crossed my arms so I didn't grab one of his knitting needles and test how much damage metal could do to the undead. "The fact that I'm the only one who can see the knot should be the end of this discussion. However, if you require more reasons, how about this? If someone asks follow-up questions like how it compares to other blue dots, who here can answer them? Me. What if a vamp says that they've heard the double knot appears in hearts or livers or is indicative of a genetic marker? Who here has the training to extrapolate any further information we need? We're racing the clock against another murder, and I'm the best person for the job."

"That's fair," Silas said.

"Nothing about this is fair," I said waspishly. "I'd already explained about the double knot and that I was the only one who could see it. I shouldn't have to justify myself further. Ezra, if you'd announced that you were going with Darsh, no one would have questioned you."

Ezra blinked at me. "That's a good idea."

"Think again," Darsh said. "I'm not going to the Crypt with you. I don't need a babysitter or a partner."

"You're right." Ezra crossed his arms. "I'll go on my own."

"Absolutely not," Silas said. A vein throbbed in his forehead. "No one should go there alone. Not even you."

"Look, while we want to find a different motive for these murders, we also want to do it with the least possible collateral damage," Ezra said. "I'm the only one guaranteed to walk away unharmed. Darsh, you'll go to Greenland."

"Thanks so much, Aviva," my friend sniped.

"Sorry. That wasn't my intent." I jutted up my chin. "Regardless, I'm still going. *Co-leader.*"

"You and I have very different capabilities," Ezra said, not unkindly. "I'm sorry if that's not fair, but it's true. Everyone in Babel will detect your heartbeat. The second you step into that city you're marked as prey, and it's a million times more dangerous inside the Crypt. Especially if you're looking for answers to unusual questions."

"I'm sure vamps have human clients with stranger requests," I snapped. "You and I may have different capabilities, but your father runs one of the main vampire Mafias in Babel, and you're going in on Maccabee business. How does that make it safer for you?"

"They only know I'm an enforcer. No one will risk my death down there." He sat down with a smug look like this was all settled, gathered up his knitting, and tucked it into his messenger bag.

"Avi's right," Sachie said. My best friend shook her head at the grateful look I gave her. "I'm still mad at you because there was no need to be an asshole." She threw her pen, striking me in the chest. "And don't apologize yet. I get to stay mad until I say otherwise."

"Well, so do I." I fired the pen back at her. And missed. "I'll draw on every bit of my training and experience to keep myself safe," I said. "It's a risk, yes, but I honestly believe it is one worth taking. Let's vote. All in favor of me going with Ezra?" I raised my hand.

"What happens if Ezra is given a direct order to hurt you?" Darsh said. "Who do you think he'll choose?" He flinched like he'd been kicked under the table and glared at Sachie. "It's a fair question."

"My father wouldn't move against Michael's daughter," Ezra said.

"But if he did?" I said in a cold voice. I was so tense that my muscles had knotted and cramped, and my veins burned like they were filled with acid.

"If you're so worried about it," Ezra tossed out, "don't come."

"Nah, I doubt you'd kill me," I said. "It would mean paperwork in triplicate."

"There are worse things than death," Ezra said darkly.

I met his eyes. "Yes, you're excellent at inflicting them. But I don't break easily."

Water carved out canyons and carbon was pressurized into diamonds all while Ezra remained silent. The others looked back and forth between Count von Cardoso and Queen AF.

Ezra pinched the bridge of his nose. "Fine."

"Thanks for your blessing, O Beneficent One," I said snarkily. I shoved my laptop in my bag so hard that I broke one of the metal clips for the leather strap. "Fucking great."

Ezra gruffly ordered Silas to get some sleep, saying this case was urgent but not at the expense of his health.

Sach grabbed my shoulder. "Head in the game now," she murmured in my ear. "Body in vat of acid later."

"Yeah." I walked over to the sink and splashed some cool water on my neck and forehead like I could wash off my hurt and anger and watch them swirl down the drain. My hand tightened on the tap. It would be so easy to stay wrapped in these dark emotions, but there was too much at stake. Not just for me personally with my promotion, but getting justice for these victims and stopping the killers before anyone else died.

I took a deep breath. I was going to the Crypt, and I would do so in top form.

Silas dropped some zip ties in the trash. "Aviva?" he said softly, one eye on Ezra, who'd moved to the other side of the room and was speaking on the phone. "When you're with him in Babel…" He jammed his hands in his pockets. "Keep an eye on him, okay?"

"Obviously. He's my partner."

"Not that. Everyone wants a piece of him and that doesn't leave a lot of people seeing the whole of who he is."

"Oh…" I shook my head. "I'm not… I don't…"

"Yeah," he said simply. "You do." He patted me on the shoulder and walked away.

I gripped the counter, staring at a water spot on the wall to keep from running after Silas and yelling at him for dumping that on me. It was one thing to have Ezra's back, but to be responsible for his mental well-being was, quite frankly, cruel.

Except Silas didn't strike me that way, so why put this on me? There was no point speculating. I'd observe Ezra on this side mission and form my own conclusions. I loosened my grip on the Formica.

"Darsh." Ezra slid his phone into his pocket. "I've

arranged a private jet to drop you off before taking Sachie to Manchester. Okay?"

"Private jet?" I spun around. "Hang on."

"Too late," Darsh sang. He nodded graciously at Ezra. "That is acceptable."

To add insult to injury, my so-called best friend stuck her tongue out at me. "Have fun in the Brink." Sachie snapped her fingers. "Give me your keys so I can grab my passport."

"I was going to drive to the laundromat," I said.

Darsh groaned. "I meant to ask Sach for a lift to the airport, but I'm not riding in your student starter car. Last time, it took me ages to scrub away the stench of beach and despair."

"Don't insult my car freshener. You're the freak for not liking coconut."

"Yet you don't defend the vehicle." Darsh stroked his chin. "How telling."

"It's settled. You'll take a cab." Sachie held out her hand.

"Apparently, so will I," Darsh muttered.

Sighing, I deposited my car keys in Sach's palm. I tucked my wallet in my back pocket, debating whether to take my phone, since it wouldn't work in the Brink. I couldn't say one way or the other if I'd get reception in Babel, but I decided to chance it.

Humans were forbidden to carry weapons in the megacity, and if a vamp needed one against a fellow undead foe, their thinking was they deserved to die. However, I tucked a silver lighter that we'd brought over in the weapons box into my suit jacket pocket. It looked and acted like a regular lighter until a groove in the bottom was depressed, at which point it activated the red magic stored inside and became a flame thrower.

Ezra raked a slow look over me. Not a sexy one. More

like he was weighing my organs for some trafficking of his own.

"Something you want to say?" I asked.

"Go home and change. You look like a gift-wrapped package in all that pink. The vamps will come after you like you're candy."

"Let them unwrap me." I cracked my knuckles. "They'll be in for quite the surprise."

"No one is unwrapping you," he snarled, his eyes flashing.

That was quite the possessive tone from the man who couldn't answer a simple question about whether or not he'd kill me on Daddy's orders. I unclenched my fists, chanting *Stay professional* in my head. "Listen, Count von Cardoso—"

"Suuuuupeeeervillain," Darsh said with a wave of his hand.

I snapped my mouth shut.

Sach snickered, and even Silas tried to unsuccessfully hide a grin.

"The fuck?" Ezra said.

I grimaced, not wanting to apologize, but Ezra started laughing. It was loud, rich, totally unguarded, and zinged directly into my bones, blowing away the heat of my anger to fill me with a syrupy warmth. I gritted my teeth.

"Do I have a costume to go with your supervillain casting, Aviva?" He slapped a hand on the table, his face aglow.

"You still got that Clark Kent outfit from Zara's hundred and fiftieth birthday?" Silas said. "Or should I say what's left of the Superman number you had on underneath it?"

"Was that the party in Barcelona?" Ezra snapped his fingers. "No, that was Violetta's. Zara's was Rio. Carajo, that night was a blur." He shook his head, still chuckling.

"If she hadn't shown me photographic proof that I—" He caught Sachie, Darsh, and me staring at him. "Well, the less said the better."

Trust me, you've already said too much. I took another deep breath. At least I was getting a lot of oxygen today. Okay, we likely had our fourth murder victim, I was going to the Crypt, and Darsh and Sachie would return with solid leads from their trips to Greenland and Manchester respectively.

See? I had all of that in the plus column against the con side that my ex was a globe-trotting player with questionable photos possessed by female vamps with sexy names, and given his mafioso connections, it likely wouldn't go well for me if I stabbed him in Babel.

Was Zara a friend or a lover? Was she on the list of recipients for knitted goods? If he was currently seeing someone that would have come up, right? I mean, he wouldn't allude to our relationship if he was with someone else, would he?

Ezra and I had never declared our love even though I'd fallen hard for him. We were together only six months, and I hadn't expected reciprocal feelings, but I'd hoped he'd say it eventually.

Has Queen AF been stung by Count von Cardoso? Shut up, stupid announcer voice.

Ezra gathered up his belongings. "Aviva, go home and change into something inconspicuous. Hide your hair, make yourself unmemorable. Please? I'll meet you at the laundromat in an hour."

"Don't even think of going without me," I said.

"I won't." He grabbed his coat and headed outside, Silas accompanying him to get the details in case he had to take care of anything while Ezra was in Babel.

Sach wandered over. "Remember your whole 'lust hath forsaken me' lament?" She slung an arm over my shoulder. "That better still be the case when you get back from Babel, because if I find out that any mission bonding naked shenanigans happened?" She smiled—sans dimples—a dangerous gleam in her eyes.

"He couldn't answer whether he'd disobey an order to kill me," I said. That inability had snagged into me like a barbed hook, releasing an overwhelming emptiness inside. My bones felt hollow, like they—*I'd*—been stripped of all substance. Regardless of our past, Ezra's denial should have come swift and strong.

Sach nodded thoughtfully. "Okay, that's a deterrent." She clapped me on the shoulder. "Now let's go home and get you dressed to kill."

I brushed off my sorrow. That emotion wouldn't help me on this mission. "Literally?"

She held up crossed fingers. "A girl can dream."

Chapter 15

Darsh accompanied us home. I changed into a black sweater and T-shirt, dark jeans, and flat shoes, and tucked my hair under a black baseball cap. After transferring the silver lighter to my back pocket, I bade my friends goodbye and good luck in England.

My taxi pulled away from the condo tower and onto a busy downtown thoroughfare.

Out of curiosity, I pulled out my cell and punched Ezra's name into the Maccabee employee database, but nothing came up. I tapped my finger against the screen. Was he in there under a code name or did I not have the security clearance to even get a search result?

It made sense that the Maccabees had buried his profile since he was a public figure who was intel gathering. Prime Playboy and Crimson Prince went together. Throwing Maccabee spy into the mix did not. I imagined those hands, which had so tenderly caressed me, choking the life out of someone or snapping their neck, and shivered.

The driver turned up the new song playing, and I scowled. I would have preferred a different anthem for my first visit to the black market than this Nickelback tune. Suzi Quatro's "The Wild One" or The Runaways' "Cherry Bomb" would have set the vibe. (Yeah, I appropriated the name for the Baroness. Yeah, I thought it would bring mom and me closer together. I was wrong. Maybe I should have paid attention to the lyrics when I named Cherry as a kid. Moving on.)

At least this post-grunge rock chorus I was subjected to right now didn't include the lyrics "You're gonna die, you're gonna die, bwahahaha, you're gonna die," so while the song sucked, it wasn't prophetic.

Putting my phone away, I stared out the window at people going into bars, shoppers on bustling retail streets, and patrons in restaurants enjoying dinner and conversation. Normal everyday life was so far removed from mine at the moment that it was like watching a documentary on aliens.

Fully absorbing where I was going and who I might run into was kind of insane. I warned Cherry that she was not to fight me for control. If worst came to worst, I'd give her the lead, but I called the shots.

I'd never made it far enough across the Brink to reach Babel. Would I see much of the sprawling vamp megacity before reaching the Crypt?

Would I face the infamous Kosher Nostra?

Would Ezra behave like a Maccabee or his father's son?

Did the Maccabees have some unofficial policy to stay out of Natán's way? They didn't have jurisdiction in Babel, but if Ezra killed any humans, he'd done so here on earth.

By all accounts, Natán had been an excellent operative back in the day. What did he think about Ezra's moonlighting gig? Was there a sliver of allegiance left to the organization he'd given so many years to?

After Natán killed a vamp in self-defense on a job, her undead lover came after him, bent on vengeance. She could have murdered Natán as an eye-for-an-eye payback, but upon learning that he and his wife, Eva, were religious Jews, she struck a much worse blow.

The vampire turned the couple.

Between Judaism forbidding the consumption of blood and the importance of light to Jews, my people historically had protected ourselves from becoming vampires. It was a large part of why the Maccabees as an organization had been formed.

The taxi sped through evening traffic along the viaduct leading out of downtown, headed for the laundromat in the Strathcona neighborhood.

No amount of vamps' sex appeal in popular culture could overcome even secular Jews' deep resistance to being changed. It didn't help that over the centuries, many vampire stereotypes were based upon the Jewish people: the outsider as a threat, the beaky nose, the fact that their day began at sundown, they showed an aversion to the cross, and they dressed in black. Hell, in the movie *Nosferatu*, the vampire was depicted coming from Transylvania surrounded by rats—an animal that Jews were compared to. But the worst of all the antisemitic propaganda tying us to vampires was blood libel, the crime of drinking Christian children's blood, which sparked the Spanish Inquisition.

So yes, turning Natán and Eva into vampires was a fate worse than death. What their maker didn't know was Eva, an Eishei Kodesh, was five months pregnant with a son.

Initially both parents attempted to carry on as operatives by switching to the Spook Squad in Natán's hometown of Caracas, Venezuela, but when Ezra was about five or six, Eva couldn't live with the shame of what she'd become any longer and walked into the noon sun on a record hot day.

According to Michael—though she didn't tell me this until after the rumors about Ezra being an enforcer first surfaced—everyone tried to help Natán once Eva was gone, but he was so lost to grief and rage that he moved himself and Ezra to Babel. He used his Maccabee knowledge of vampire Mafias to take over a smaller, weaker outfit, systematically growing it over the years into one of the most powerful criminal organizations.

Vamp Mafias didn't exist only in Babel; their tentacles spread to earth, where they'd either wiped out most human Mafias or folded them into their own organizations.

Natán renamed his group the Kosher Nostra after the nickname given to the Jewish-American Mafia in the early twentieth century and raised Ezra to be his Crimson Prince.

I frowned. Raised or honed?

Regardless, Ezra was a grown-up now. He didn't have to follow his father anymore if he didn't want to.

Speaking of parents, I'd promised to keep Michael in the loop. I fired off a text saying that we were making progress and following some promising leads and that I'd update her further when I had more concrete information.

A rap on my window made me jump. The taxi now idled at the curb by the abandoned laundromat, and Ezra stared at me through my window. He opened the door while I was paying the cabbie.

He'd dressed up for the journey. Under his trench coat he wore a moss-colored suit, the gold cufflinks on his light green shirt winking from a streetlight. He oozed power and masculinity, the lines of the suit emphasizing his broad shoulders and muscular thighs.

"What?" Ezra said grumpily.

"Huh?"

"You're staring at me with a weird look."

"I'm calculating how much I could get for a well-timed photo of you." I waved a finger around his face. "Are you student loan payoff material or just a fancy dinner?"

His silvery-blue eyes twinkled in amusement. "Paparazzi do crazy things to get the money shots."

"Phrasing," I chided.

He grinned unrepentantly. "How far are you willing to go?"

"Much more fun to keep you in suspense."

He harrumphed, waiting for me to get my receipt. (I'd have a better shot at winning a popularity contest as an infernal than being reimbursed by Maccabee accountants without one.)

Slip in hand, I thanked the driver and got out.

We crossed the broken parking lot, Ezra strolling beside me with his hands in his pockets, while I checked for power-happy vampires or thrill-seeking youth.

It was a rite of passage for local teens to see if they could make it inside the laundromat, through the rift, and into the Brink. None ever did. Younger children didn't even reach the door before they'd be scared off by a vamp baring their fangs. Older ones might get close enough to see the brightness of the portal from inside the building, then they'd be unceremoniously tossed outside onto their asses.

That was strike one.

Strike two involved more than baring their fangs, and vampires never forgot a face.

If there was a strike three, the families were too scared to report it, because neither the Trad police nor the Maccabees had ever heard of one.

Adults weren't prohibited from crossing. They were of legal age. That was consent enough for whatever might happen to them at any point in their journey. Operatives were supposed to be exempt from harassment, but as my previous visit to the rift had proven, that wasn't always the case.

"Why are you really so desperate to accompany me?" Ezra said. "Skip the part where you want to make my head explode. That's a given."

"Batten down your ego. I wanted to go with Darsh. I'm tolerating accompanying you on account of my ability to see the double knot, which I was about to bring up in the meeting when you executed your nonexistent veto powers to prevent me from going."

"We'll see."

"Do you plan to second-guess everything I'm doing?" I let the door to the laundromat swing closed without holding it behind me for him, hoping it would hit him in the face.

"Like you aren't doing the same with me."

I patted his cheek. "It's cute that you think you're worth the time expenditure." I paused.

"You think the vamps who control this neighborhood recognized you?"

"If they haven't, they need to get better subordinates."

Someone had half-heartedly cleaned the cream and mint tiles inside, though the broken metal table still lay on its side and the florescent light fixtures hung down from ancient cables. The sole washing machine had been repainted beige with a tag reading "OTTO FUCKS!" on it.

"Good for Otto," Ezra said. "The world needs more joyous sex."

I squelched all images of Ezra contributing to that and squinted at the light pouring out from the back office, shielding my eyes from the portal. "True."

He glanced over, an unasked question flitting across his face, then shook his head, and crouched down. "Hop on."

I'd rather have slathered honey on my body and rolled in fire ants than have Ezra piggyback me, our bodies pressed together, my arms around his neck, and my cheek resting against his soft curls at the nape of his neck.

"Absolutely not," I said.

I used to play with those curls while I drifted off to sleep. Ezra would give these little half shivers when my fingers brushed the back of his neck because he was ticklish there, but whenever I asked him if I should stop, he'd push his head against my hand in encouragement to keep going.

"Well, I'd rather not cross the Brink at a snail's pace," he said.

Technically, vehicles worked in the Brink, but practically, the chances of getting across on a motorcycle or in a car without the chaos magic taking control of the vehicle and killing you was slim.

Vamps were willing to take that chance since they bounced back a lot better than humans did. I'd always refused to risk it, though it seemed like the better option now. Sadly, bicycles always ended up with flat tires. Not that a vamp would be caught dead on one.

"I'll run," I said.

"Not as fast or for as long as I can." He tapped his back. "Can we please save our energy for the Crypt and not this argument?"

Since I had no reasonable rebuttal, I climbed on, piggyback style, and squeezed my eyes shut.

The rift's hug was tighter than normal, and when Ezra broke free into the Brink, he stumbled. I lost my balance, and we both almost toppled over.

"None of that," Ezra said lightly. He readjusted his hold on me and sprinted off.

Fifteen minutes later, we'd gone deeper into the Brink than I'd ever been and encountered six types of weather, including a hailstorm of pine cones that we had to wait out under an overhang at the bottom of a sheer cliff that had sprung out of nowhere and almost killed us.

"Have I mentioned how much I hate this place?" I said, wrapping my arms around myself for warmth despite my heavy sweater and T-shirt underneath it.

"Take my coat," he said.

"I'm fine, thanks." Going to Babel with Darsh had sounded like a heavenly respite from Ezra's presence, but instead of that, I was pressed close to the one person I needed a break from, smelling cardamom, cloves, bergamot, and the windswept scent of a summer breeze. I was suffocating. Forget wearing his jacket, being piggybacked was my limit on up close and personal Ezra experiences.

"Stubborn." Ezra poked his head out, looked up, and was bonked in the face with a pine cone. He swore in Spanish, throwing me a mock chiding look when I laughed, and leaned back against the cliff, his knee bent and his foot pressed flat to the rock. "The Brink on the other side of the Moscow rift once sprung up a lake, so the vamps hauled in boats to get across. For seven years, vampires bitched about that lake, but what could they do?" He shrugged. "The Brink is what it is. Then one day, the lake disappeared." He snapped his fingers. "It was all land again with no evidence the lake had ever been there at all. And when the water vanished, so did all the vamps crossing it at the time."

"Your point?"

"Even vamps are subject to their environment."

Silas's comment sprung to mind. Was Ezra offering me a piece of his history to keep me from seeing the whole of him? "Is that a warning that you're your father's son? I got it the first time."

"*No.*" He crushed a pine cone under his shoe. "I'm saying that vampires are so convinced of their infallibility and of always being the most powerful that they discount simple things that could destroy them."

"Your word choice of 'simple' aside," I said, "point taken."

Ezra stuck his hand out; the pine cone shower had ended. "We're good to keep going."

No, the only good thing was the lack of supe-vultures.

"Are they asleep or what?" I had to yell over the wind that Ezra battled, slowing him from blur to vertigo-inducing breakneck speed.

"Don't bother trying to figure them out. I haven't."

We jumped a pile of logs that were riddled with diseased mushrooms and into an invisible barrier that blanketed us in absolute darkness. I closed my eyes, convinced that the entire universe was beneath my feet, and if I glanced down, even blind as I temporarily was, I'd plummet like Wile E. Coyote acknowledging gravity. Except my fall would last for eternity.

Ezra grunted and pressed forward. The barrier excreted us with a soft pop and the scent of burned baby powder into an airport with a soft jazz version of "Bridge over Troubled Water" playing.

I slid off his back.

The terminal was lined with tasteful signs in cursive letters hanging from the ceiling. "Vancouver" was sandwiched between "Stockholm" and "Quito."

Cherry Bomb, the Brimstone Baroness, roared to life, viewing the world with a hunger. The colors here were so saturated that they hurt, voices and music rubbed against my skin like a cheese grater, and the collective smell of soaps, shampoos, sweat, and blood made me gag.

Cherry hissed at me to let her protect us.

I swayed on rubbery legs. How was this protection?

Blinking in confusion, I stared at the blue dots blinking throughout a nearby vamp's body. Every injury she'd ever sustained was laid out for me. It didn't matter that she'd have instantly healed them with her vamp magic, the sites all bore traces of weakness.

As with humans, these spots were more susceptible to reinjury, but seeing them was impossible.

Not impossible. Demon realm. Oddly that thought was in my voice, not Cherry's.

While the Brink was an in-between habitat where the demon realm and earth engaged in a constant battle, Babel was a long-abandoned shedim space that had been claimed and tamed by vamps.

Not in my wildest dreams had it occurred to me that I'd have different abilities here.

I tapped Ezra on the shoulder to tell him about my newfound power.

He blanched, a bright blue dot from some previous injury spiking across his chest, and shoved me back toward the rift.

Scientists don't believe that the universe has a true edge. They're the experts, but wrapping my head around the concept of something that doesn't physically end made my brain break, so I tried not to do it often.

However, the wall we'd come through was made of such a flat black mesh it almost curved in on itself. It was the length and height of the waiting room, and yet I had a bone-deep certainty that, like our universe, it had no end.

I wasn't going through it unless absolutely necessary.

"What the fuck, dude?" I smacked him away, accidentally snagging the sleeve of his cashmere coat with one of the claws on my left hand. *Oh, shiiiit.* Those had not been there a second ago. I squeaked, my pulse hammering in my throat. What was happening to me?

"Your eyes," he hissed. "They're glowing green. And

your skin. It's…" His mouth fell open, his upper lip curling back.

I touched my face with a trembling hand, flinching at a sharp edge, then peeked down the front of my sweater. My hands, arms, and whole body were covered in scales frosted the same toxic green as my eyes. They weren't merely strips like on those rare other occasions the scales had surfaced. No, all my skin had become scaley armor. Pushing through the vague claustrophobia, I poked one of the two spots throbbing on the top of my head, encountering bone.

Needle-sharp horns? What. The. Fuck. My stomach lurched queasily at this new development.

I, Aviva Jacqueline Fleischer, the woman who'd spent her life hiding her shedim side, stood here, exposed in the vampire megacity. I should have been the most horrified about this, but looking at Ezra's face, I wasn't.

Chapter 16

"Cherry isn't in control. If you're wondering," I said, staring at myself with my phone's camera to see the full extent of the change. "She's smart but like in the id sense of instinct. Primal drives. Mobile phones frustrate her, so opening my lock screen is all me."

Most of the vamps nearby had barely given me a second glance. Evidently, demon visits to Babel weren't uncommon. Filing that knowledge away, I pulled the baseball cap off my head and shook out my hair. My thick, dark brown waves were now crimson.

I tilted my head, my eyes narrowed in examination. My poison-green eyes really popped against this new hair color. Honestly, even my frosted scales were pretty.

I'd packed on more muscle mass, too, going into She-Hulk territory. When I lifted my sweater, those last five pounds of belly fat I could never lose were gone, replaced by a wicked six-pack. My biceps were jacked and cut like a female weightlifter's and my hard thighs strained against my denim jeans.

I glanced back. You could bounce a coin off my tight ass. Whoa.

I was used to my green eyes and claws, even very occasionally, a strip of scales on my skin, but crimson hair, full body armor scales, a more toned form, and horns were next level. I made a flirty face for the camera, though I knew better than to take a picture of my badass self.

"This could fuck everything up," Ezra snapped in a low whisper.

I didn't use my synesthete vision on team members without their consent unless they were in dire straits and couldn't grant it. So while I didn't use it on him now, I also didn't require it to sense his fury. It rolled off him in waves.

"Why didn't you say something?" He grabbed my arm, directing me back to the rift.

"About the thing I had no clue would happen, in the place I'd never been to before?" I tore free and put my phone away. "If anyone should have known, it should have been you. It's your home turf. And I'm not leaving. Keep bugging me and we'll find out what other abilities I've gained."

"Coño. Keep a low profile and let's move on."

"Fine by me." I tried not to rubberneck my way through the building, but every single vampire was lit up in my synesthete vision, with the best places to weaken them before staking or decapitating them marked as clearly as exit signs. Vampires were a lot stronger than me, so my strategy was to strike first and strike hard. Seeing their weaknesses now helped immensely should I need to battle one.

Not that I planned to.

None bore my shifting shadows at the backs of their heads in their hindbrains.

Some people maintained that demons had created the first vamps, but I'd always believed the rumor I'd heard growing up that vampires were descended from the human workers who built the Tower of Babel and had been cursed by God. It seemed plausible, given vamps named their megacity after the tower like a fuck-you reclamation.

Whether or not a higher power was involved in their creation, judging by what I saw, the undead had no trace of demon in them.

I smiled grimly. *All the better for us.* I blinked at the thought, which hadn't come specifically from Cherry. Come to think of it, there wasn't our usual divide, and despite my new physical attributes, my eyes didn't have that pins and needles tingling, I didn't emit any scent of brine, nor had a hum like locusts in my veins presaged my scales and new form bursting out.

Cherry and I simply existed here. Together.

Still, there was no reason to get violent. I'd defend myself but I wasn't starting anything.

Some hairy bloodsucker gave me the once-over, his gaze lewdly roaming my body.

My heart thumped like a drummer on a breakout rock solo—had I been made?

"You scared, demon?" the strange vamp sneered. He and his two buddies moved in on me. "Too far from home?"

Demon? They didn't realize I was half-human? A weight lifted off my shoulders, and I clamped my lips together to keep a grin from springing free.

"I'm exactly where I mean to be," I growled.

I kicked one in an old thigh wound, snapped a twice-broken wrist of another one, and slammed my elbow under the chin of the third. He didn't have a previous injury on his face, but he bit his tongue hard enough to bleed and the other two vamps fell on him.

Chaos broke out.

Ezra grabbed my shoulder. "That's your low profile?"

"They started it." I bounced on my toes, craving more of an adrenaline rush and looking for my next opponent.

Ezra blocked a punch from another vamp and tossed him halfway across the building like he was a pillow, then barreled toward an exit like a linebacker ploughing through the opposing team.

I ran behind him, elbowing and punching any vampire who got too close, whooping with the unhinged glee of a sugared-up toddler.

When Ezra finally slowed to a stop several blocks later, pronouncing us safe, I craned my neck up in awe with a soft gasp.

The sky was smudged dark blue and indigo with a single faint smear of peachy gold, caught in those last precious seconds of dusk that, on earth, would flip to night in the next blink. Babel existed in a state of permanent twilight.

I snickered, wondering about the origins of a certain popular fiction series; however, despite the sky's beauty, it wasn't soothing. Rather, I felt like the vamps had captured part of our galaxy by force and pinned it here. The velvet air didn't caress my skin so much as nip at it while the breeze carried a metallic bite like a rainstorm threatened.

It would never come.

The temperate weather didn't change, and any plants or animals here were imported. It was like I was trapped in those hazy moments between a nightmare and waking, unsure whether this was real.

Perhaps that, too, was part of Babel's careful construction.

Skyscrapers extended in every direction, but they sprang from the ground like alien wildlife, instead of being built upon concrete foundations. One was a slab of obsidian, another, a twisting steel and glass creation that swayed gently, dislodging muted showers of delicate flower petals.

Neon signs not only floated in mid-air above the towers, they streamed down the sides like code, reflecting over sleek hovercraft pods with tinted windows, which prowled streets paved in the same crimson as my hair.

Ezra crossed his arms. "I didn't scent any injuries on those vampires, yet you were very precise in your strikes. How?"

"I saw their weaknesses."

His eyes flickered down over his body, almost involuntarily. "You once told me you couldn't read vampires."

"I can't on earth. It's different here. But don't worry. I won't read yours."

"I'm supposed to trust you on that?" His fangs descended.

Were infernals perceived as a threat by vamps?

The few like me that I'd heard of, thanks to their infamous criminal exploits, were Eishei Kodesh. I'd assumed that shedim genetics either killed Trad fetuses in the womb, or never took hold in the first place. But that left me with some demon capabilities plus my magic, an ability denied to vampires who'd once had flame powers in life.

I notched up my chin. "Yeah, you are. I don't read my team members without their consent, unless it's a life-or-death situation, but I give you my word." I flashed him a tight smile. "I won't even read you then."

"You're just full of surprises today, princess," he said in a low, dangerous rumble.

Had Ezra assassinated infernals? He'd insisted he didn't kill operatives, but if my ring was the only thing that had ever kept me safe from him, how much of a guarantee was that?

In going for my dream of becoming the youngest level three operative in Maccabee history, would I one day find myself face-to-face with Ezra, where the "ex" stood for executioner?

Was that day today?

I squashed the urge to run. The worst thing I could do was make myself prey. Besides, I wouldn't escape quicker than Ezra could grab me. Matter settled. I refused to show weakness or doubt myself. Not here in Babel. Not in front of Ezra ever.

"Believe me or don't," I said impatiently. "I, for one, would like to get on with the investigation."

He studied me for a moment longer, then he nodded and his fangs disappeared.

My sphincter unclenched, and I glanced around to verify we were still alone. "This place reminds me of Los Angeles—tons of vehicles but no pedestrians. How many vamps live here in Babel anyway? Hundreds of thousands? Mill—?" I shuddered like someone had dumped a bucket of cold water over me and stomped around in a circle. "Fuck! Fuck! Fuck!"

"What?" Ezra looked around, but there weren't any threats in our immediate vicinity.

"There's no alarm in my head that I'm one puny human in a land of predators. My fear should have overloaded me and reduced me to a terrified puddle, but I'm fine."

"You didn't think of this before?"

"You didn't either." I jabbed at him with my index finger, and he jumped back so my claw didn't take out his eye. Whoops. "We were so busy arguing back at the office that we failed to consider it. It was a major fuck-up on all our parts."

"You're right." He stroked his hand over his cropped black beard. "If your human fear responses are gone, how are you going to stay safe? You saw how those vamps reacted to you."

"I don't know that they're gone entirely," I said. "Just that I'm not melting down at the thought of all the vamps outnumbering me. But in terms of the ones back in the terminal, the first guy presumed I was scared, that I was demon prey, and he reacted. Not that he suspected…you know, since some demons have heartbeats. The others just jumped on the violence bandwagon."

"That doesn't make you safe."

No, but it didn't make me stand out either. Not to other vampires at least.

"Perhaps I don't have to worry about that like a human would. Vamps are taking what they see when they look at me at face value. Their perceptions aren't true, but it's the belief that matters. That means I can employ different thinking and different reactions. Since, you know." I ran a hand along my shedim tricked-out body, with no desire to hide from Ezra, or cringe in shame. It was liberating.

"Wonderful." His face puckered. I resisted the urge to check out his ass and see how deep the clench went.

Perhaps it was petty to feel such a deep and smug satisfaction forcing Ezra up against this side of me, but mostly I hoped he choked on his discomfort.

Meanwhile, I drank in this strange, marvelous place. I was in a vampire realm, a place where the police didn't exist, the fire department never came, and the morgue was never used. To forget its danger or be lulled into complacency here was a death sentence.

I licked my lips, up for the challenge.

Ezra sighed and flagged down a sleek hover pod that, to my eye, looked indistinguishable from all the others. A center panel slid away, allowing us access to the inside, which smelled like bourbon and money. There was no driver, only two cushioned benches facing each other. Ezra announced our destination, and the pod shot into traffic.

I avoided looking down since the floor was also glass, and even though it seemed thick, one little crack would freak me out. The road whipping past about a foot underneath us was making me nauseous.

"What do vamps offer the talented people like engineers, architects, even aerospace mechanics who they lure here to create tech like these pods?" I said. "Is it money? The challenge? Are they forced?"

Not all Maccabee chases through the Brink were to apprehend criminal suspects on the run. Sometimes, we were stopping a particular person from bringing knowledge developed on earth into Babel. The vamps were the foreign spies smuggling them out against our homeland security trying to stop a widening tech gap.

Maccabees had never cracked the secret of how vampires helped law-abiding humans who lived here not short-circuit from the fear of living among these supernatural beings, though there were hotly contested debates over whether it was drug-based or some form of exposure therapy.

Ezra either didn't know or wasn't saying.

Criminals who came here willingly tended to be psychopaths and/or extreme narcissists, neither of which allowed for regular fear functionality in the brain.

"Experts who come here get to take their human know-how and Eishei Kodesh abilities and integrate that with the inherent demon magic here in Babel to create buildings that defy what's possible on earth or tech that can only exist here," Ezra said.

"Unless it was smuggled back, which the vamps won't allow."

"Of course not." He shrugged. "The carrot works better than the stick."

"The Mafias don't have a hand in it?"

"You'd have to speak to the vamps specifically engaged

in making this realm function and enhancing its beauty." His mastery of the evasive answer was almost impressive.

The deeper we drove into the city, the more signs of life there were and the more the architecture changed, losing its Blade Runner vibe. In one neighborhood, characterized by crescent windows and minarets, vamps sat around outdoor tables smoking hookahs and wearing abayas, the loose-fitting Arabic robes. Bright tiles adorned arched doorways, and round fountains shot up plumes of water in large plazas.

In another area, Eastern European–looking vamps with gloomy expressions patrolled in front of ornately painted buildings with onion-shaped domes. A foot soldier was being read the riot act by a female vamp outside a busy hair salon.

Eventually we reached a boisterous beachfront area along a lake. A predominantly youthful-looking population strolled the streets, some waiting in a long line outside Blood Gelateria, others at outdoor pubs where servers slung pitchers of blood.

Nowhere did I see children. How lonely had Ezra's childhood been?

We'd been driving for over an hour by now, and I'd long since shut down my synesthete vision because all the blue was overwhelming me, though my sensory fatigue didn't stop me from practically pressing my face against the tinted glass to take in the sights.

We hit the fringes of the beach, the pod propelling us over narrow streets past large windows spotlit from above, some with their curtains open, others tugged tightly closed.

I did a double take.

Not because Babel had a red-light district, but because the vamps on display looked bored. More than one was scrolling on their phone, and even the workers engaged in negotiations with clients looked put out, like this was a mundane task they'd just as soon be done with. Which, I guess, was fair.

I squinted against the flashing lights now strobing over the glass thanks to casinos lining both sides of the street. They went on for blocks, with adult vamps of all ethnicities streaming through the doors.

The casinos were followed by an area populated with bars bearing names like Xtacy, Dragon, and A-Bomb, all drug slang. They were mixed in among nightclubs called Silver, Mystic, and Spotlight, which I assumed were regular dance clubs.

The lineups outside each of them varied in terms of age and flashiness, but no one had a "broke college student" vibe.

Newer vamps weren't necessarily rich, but everyone acted the role. Power plays on power plays. How exhausting.

Ezra slapped a hand on my thigh, and I practically jumped out of my seat. "Try not to get us killed in the Crypt," he said. "But if you must?" He winked at me. "Let's have fun."

Chapter 17

My first sighting of the Crypt was astoundingly anticlimactic. It didn't resemble a carved stone mausoleum, it wasn't an open-air market where vamps hawked lethal wares, and it wasn't a hole in the ground with a ladder leading to untold dangers. My imagination was zero for three.

The Crypt was a squat windowless building ringed with blue floodlights pointing up from the ground, which rippled over the concrete, lending it an underwater mood.

Ezra pressed his thumb against a flat pad in the hover pod. It glowed green and gave a soft bing to indicate payment was successful.

I tried not to bounce like Tigger when I got out of the car.

Ezra waited for it to drive away before leaning in and brushing a lock of hair off my face, his eyes boring into mine with an intensity that made me shiver. His odd behavior became clear when he tapped my Maccabee ring. "Lose it," he murmured. "There are no demon operatives, ergo you'll be outed." He traced a finger across his throat.

I scrubbed a hand over my face, the roughness of my scales rubbing together producing an odd, itchy sensation. No one would ever learn that I'd removed the ring and I'm sure that other operatives had, but none of that mattered. *I* hadn't. I'd wanted to be a Maccabee since I understood what my mom did. My entire life had revolved around that, my identity bound to it.

"Choose," Ezra said in a low but hard voice.

I could justify that this was for our investigation and vital to catching a killer, but I wouldn't. Tikkun olam. In this vampire realm and in this shedim physical form, my vow felt more important than ever.

"I'm not breaking my oath." I twisted the ring around so only the gold band was visible. "Vamps will look at me and see a demon wearing a gold band. If not, I'll deal with the consequences."

With that I marched up to the door of the Crypt, which was twice my height, grasped the handle, and leaned my weight into it.

It didn't budge.

"Even if it's not in triplicate, I'm not filling out paper-work if you get maimed," Ezra said, and pushed the door open with one hand.

The air inside smelled sweet and electric, like ozone, and was warm and moist, which made sense since the dominant—and only—feature of the space was an Olympic-sized swimming pool.

"Uh…" I walked across the smooth concrete to the lip of the pool and crouched down, trying to see past the surface tinted a dark green from colored sconce lights on the walls. "Are you pulling my leg?"

"Nope. And don't touch."

Careful of the claws on my left hand, I pulled off my sweater, leaving me in a T-shirt, and tied it around my waist. "You may not have a problem breathing underwater, but if I'm supposed to free dive, that's not happening."

Ezra laughed. "I wouldn't advise that." He crouched down next to me and dangled his hand in the pool. "Look."

A thick, dark shadow shot up toward us, the gentle swells turning to a furious roiling.

I screeched and stumbled back, Ezra catching me before I fell on my ass.

"Don't worry," he said. "It can't break the surface."

"What is it?" I inched closer, fascinated.

"A demon of some sort that got left behind long before the vampires ever took over."

I peered into the water, but it was too dark to see where the creature had gone. "There is a bottom, right? It's not some portal to the actual demon realm?"

"There's a bottom, and no, it isn't." Ezra tapped my shoulder. "This way."

We walked around to a metal ladder attached to one side.

Ezra grasped the railing and squeezed twice. He tugged me back a few feet. "Watch."

A glass pod silently rose up like Aphrodite from the waves. Awesome, another pod, though the glass on this one was clear, not tinted. That didn't make it better. It bumped gently against the edge of the pool, bobbing there with the center panel open in invitation.

Oh no. Not this again. I gave a panicked laugh. "I am not getting in that death trap."

"It has oxygen," Ezra said. "You're not the first human to visit."

"That demon down there could crush us."

"Well, yes." He stepped over the lip of the pod. "But you could be hit by a bus tomorrow."

I reluctantly joined him. "People always say that, but

honestly, how many deaths are attributed to bus smushing per year?"

The elevator pod felt even more slight and unstable once the panel slid closed and the capsule bobbed in the water.

"Organ market, please," Ezra said.

I held my breath while we sank beneath the surface and might have continued to do so for the entire trip, despite Ezra snickering, if I hadn't gasped once the water closed over our heads. "Holy. Shit."

The swimming pool was the watery inner courtyard of a round stone building, which reminded me of the Colosseum, complete with a huge section on the far side that had crumbled away. I looked through the glass between my feet, finding broken pillars and enormous stones littering the bottom far, far below.

There was also a pod that had been partially smashed on a wide set of shallow stairs that should have been topped with a throne, but which led to nowhere. I squeaked, then jumped back because a giant eye had opened in the water underneath us.

"Steady," Ezra said. "It won't hurt us unless it's provoked." He paused. "Or they sound the alarm."

"What would cause that?"

"It's not so much a predetermined set of rules as a fuck around and find out scenario," he said.

"Huh." I thought I'd said it noncommittally, but he narrowed his eyes at me.

The water creature kept swishing around the pod emitting a vibrating hum. Oh brother, had she identified me as kin or something?

I peered into the arch-shaped windows of the building. Some were lit, others were dark. Inside one bright room, a vamp stood on a platform, making her a head taller than the gathered crowd. I couldn't see what she was demonstrating, but given her customers' appreciative nods it could have been anything from a set of "slice through a tin can and still stay sharp" knives to a rocket launcher.

Suddenly, the heavy wooden pillar next to the female vamp was engulfed in flames, which disappeared a half second later. The pillar imploded in a cloud of ash.

The customers clapped.

Through a gap, I spied a dejected-looking man with a collar around his neck and fire dancing over the fingertips of one hand.

A strangled moan escaped my lips. They were selling Eishei Kodesh?

Ezra slapped his hand over my mouth, his lips to my ear. "So much for not thinking like a human," he whispered harshly. "You insisted on coming here, so suck it up, buttercup, and do not react. To anything. Even if you don't think anyone can hear you. Do you understand?"

Seething, I nodded, but Ezra was right. Looking skeptical, he left his hand where it was, so I bit the fleshy part of his palm.

He removed his hand, tracing over the bite with one finger, a crooked grin on his face. "I've killed people for less."

A squirmy sensation shot through my core. Huh. It seemed lust had not forsaken me after all. To ensure that Sachie didn't murder me for that, and also because I wasn't a masochist, I stomped any lust and lust-adjacent emotions to dust and speared Ezra in my acid-green gaze. "Try it," I said coolly.

A male vamp stood alone at another window, staring out into the water with the dead-eyed resignation of a cubicle worker counting the minutes of their sentence until they were free.

The floor below that appeared to be an extension of the red-light district with one notable difference: it was no longer sex on offer or vamps on display. They were human blood slaves.

The people in the small, narrow rooms were collared and chained, terrified, drugged, or all of the above, and grouped under large signs according to blood type. Undead customers scrutinized them with a flat-eyed detachment. In one room, a female vampire sank her fangs into a young woman's wrist in front of two customers. When the woman fought back, the vampire roughly grabbed the prisoner to hold her still.

The fiend gesticulated while blood spurted out of the woman's wrist, and one of the customers bent and drank like the human was a water fountain.

I swallowed my growl, my entire body going rigid with the force of not reacting.

"What did you think happened here?" Ezra said softly.

I shrugged helplessly. "Weapons? Drugs?"

"The only weapon vampires crave is access to more magic and most drugs can be bought openly here in Babel, same as sex. Those things are controlled by the various Mafias but easily accessed. Vamps don't suffer from the same moral hang-ups as the living. Dying changes them."

"What about Primes?"

"Didn't you hear, princess?" His silky voice hid an undercurrent of venom. "We never had a soul to guide us in the first place."

I had many ways to describe Ezra, but "soulless monster" wasn't one of them. He cared about our murder victims, and his affection and loyalty to Silas was evident. Did he go around the world charming people because he was trying to convince them of his worth?

Convince himself? Did he think he only had pieces to give?

"Ezra..."

He stepped back, his expression shuttered.

The water demon slithered around our pod, still humming.

"This is so messed up," I muttered.

There were powerful humans who used Babel as a meeting ground to escape detection. They generally had the money and connections to return, if not unharmed, then at least alive. They were also in the minority.

Had I saved Heloise and Clément Toussaint from being the latest couple on tap? I consoled myself that I had, but who was I kidding? Even if I was right, it was a drop in the ocean.

"I've always prided myself on being smart," I said, "yet here I am, so naïve. If vampire morality is more flexible than ours, why hide these humans away like— Fuck!" I flinched as the pod sank past a window right as blood splattered against it. Someone's back hit the glass with a dull thud, the body sliding to the floor and smearing the blood in a glistening trail.

"Because of *your* morality," Ezra said. "Some criminals who come through here are human traffickers. They make other people endure unspeakable horrors, but they'd be up in arms if they saw us monsters doing the same because that's suddenly less a window into our actions and more a mirror on theirs." He stared off through the glass into the dark water. "There's a reason humans claimed that vamps don't have reflections. Propaganda to distance yourselves." He shrugged but there was a weariness in it. "We do what we must to survive. There are far, far more humans than vampires, you know that, and we can't have you storming our gates."

"At least humans try and stop this kind of shit. Babel is lawless." My voice shook.

"Babel rules on power, not law." He paused. "So does earth. You're not *that* naïve."

"No," I said with a quiet sigh. "I'm not."

The water demon nudged the pod with something that wasn't a tentacle and wasn't a flipper. I squeaked and grabbed Ezra's shoulder. Our transport tipped sideways before righting itself.

He nudged me. "It likes you."

I let go of my ex, my heart in my throat. "How can you stay so calm?"

Ezra rapped on the glass and waved at the sea monster. "If it's my time, it's my time."

I smacked his hand down. "You are quite the ray of sunshine. Besides, you're immortal. It's easy for you to be so nonchalant."

"Immortal doesn't mean unkillable. I'm sure you plotted out my demise a time or two."

I tutted him with my finger. "You persist in your misguided belief that I've wasted any time thinking about you."

"Since we only recently met, and I've been a dream to work with, right?"

"Positively Kafkaesque," I said sweetly.

About three-quarters of the way down, the pod glided to a stop against one of the building's arched windows. A shimmery seal appeared, encasing the gap between it and us, and both our panel and the window slid open.

We stepped into the organ market and I shivered. It was colder than our chapter morgue. At the sound of a soft thwap, I turned back to the pod, but the window had closed, the pod was already descending to a lower floor.

When I was a kid, my mom took me with her to Tokyo for some meeting at the Maccabee HQ there. We had a bunch of time to sightsee, and one of the attractions we visited was the now-closed Tsukiji Inner Market, waking up early to catch the tuna auction. The complex was so huge that I got tired before we saw all of it, but I'll always remember the chaotic energy and stall after stall selling fish in every shape and size conceivable, their lifeless stares following me.

The organ market here in the Crypt had that same energy. Too many dead eyes as well.

And that was just the vamps.

Ezra raised an eyebrow. “Ready?”

I steeled my shoulders and followed him into the belly of the beast.

Chapter 18

This floor wasn't broken up into individual rooms. Instead, the narrow market hall followed the circumference of the building until it reached the broken part, which was closed off from the water by a sheet of glass.

Thankfully, the ventilation system here was next level because all I smelled was the faint tang of bleach and not the human parts set out on tables with beds of ice like samples in front of freezers. It wasn't just organs for sale here—the whole human was used. How nice of them to cut down on waste.

Some of the vendors had added garnishes like fern leaves or radishes carved into delicate flowers. How many people had died to stock this place? What were the buyers doing with this stuff?

A vampire picked up a marble-pale leg off a bed of ice and sniffed it. Licked it. Knocked the limb twice against a pallet like it was a croquet mallet.

My head pounded, and I forced down a scream. An organ market was going to be categorically awful, but I hadn't expected the vampires to act so normal. On the plus side, my scales prevented me from getting goose bumps or looking pale and scared. I pasted on a fierce expression and strode forward.

The vamp holding the leg saw Ezra and dropped the limb, causing the vendor to glance up and see us. He then whispered something to another patron.

Murmurs of "The Crimson Prince returns" rippled out in our wake, everyone turning to stare. One or two vamps even bowed nervously.

A darkness had fallen over Ezra. He moved with deadly intent, his eyes flat and assessing, and his trench coat swirling around his legs. The menace that rolled off him kept the other vampires from approaching, but it made me want to hurl myself through the window and take my chances with the water demon.

What the fuck, man? Dozens of vamps and they don't faze me, but Ezra goes super alpha and that's when I felt cowed?

Screw you, Cardoso. My fierce expression grew fiercer.

Two vampires placed themselves in our path. One, a Black man with a shaved head, was the picture of elegance in a double-breasted black suit with a dark red vest and black tie that popped against his white shirt. My first impression of him was a wolf in well-tailored wolf's clothing.

I glanced sideways at Ezra and snorted softly.

Mr. Elegant shot me a brief, dismissive glance.

His friend, a weaselly-looking white dude with a blotchy complexion, scraggly facial hair, and an oversize neon orange bomber jacket, leered at me.

Yeeees, was it fight time?

"You've got a hell of a nerve showing up here, E," the stylish vamp said in a broad British accent.

I peered closer because his suit jacket exaggerated the line of his shoulders, and I didn't see this man wearing padding. However, it wasn't cloth at all. It was armor, made of a dark liquid that flowed and shifted under the surface of the hard shell. More vamp tech. I wanted to poke it and see if it was stronger than my scales but, ever the picture of restraint, I didn't.

Ferret Vamp cracked his knuckles. Upon closer inspection, his bomber jacket was also armor, not fabric.

Ezra flashed a smile like a whetted blade unsheathed from its holster, cold and hungry for battle. "Has my father taken over the Crypt?" He scratched his chin. "I didn't get the group text."

Oh, we were so going to fight. I flexed my clawed hand.

"Don't be daft," the Brit said. "We all have to present ourselves to Natán when we return to Babel. Even his enforcer."

Ezra pressed a hand to his heart. "While I'm ever the dutiful son—"

The Brit raised his eyebrows.

"I'll speak with him later and make my apologies, but right now, I have pressing business."

A number of the vampires looked visibly nervous, like perhaps Ezra meant them. One rangy bloodsucker bolted so fast, I could practically taste the dust he stirred up in his wake.

"It'll have to wait." The Brit motioned with his index finger for Ezra to come with him. "You can bring your friend." His lips twisted in distaste on that last word.

"I'll handle my father, Alastair." Ezra made a shooing motion at the Brit.

"That's not how this works, mate. You know that. We've all gotta dance the dance." Alastair motioned at his partner. "Remy?"

I bit the inside of my cheek to keep from laughing because this guy sharing a name with the *Ratatouille* rat was too perfect.

Remy grinned, his three gold front teeth glinting in the light. He puffed out his chest, all the better to smack it with both hands. "You'll show Natán respect. The only question is if you're gonna do it the easy way or—"

Ezra stepped in close, calmly tilted his face down toward the slightly shorter male and placed his finger to his lips. "Shhhhh."

Remy's mouth opened. Closed. He furrowed his brows together so deeply that the "V" threatened to slide down his face, and smacked his fist into his palm. "I'm gonna—"

Ezra edged his face so close to Remy's that under other circumstances I'd have assumed they were going to kiss. "Uh-uh-uh," he murmured and tapped his finger twice against his lips in reminder.

I swallowed to get moisture into my dry mouth, something heavy and carnal snaking through me, catching fire.

A female vampire next to me fanned herself. "Ooh, Crimson Prince, shush me like that," she said in a breathy voice.

I took two steps toward her, my claws flashing and the blood roaring in my ears before I forced myself to stop.

Ezra and Remy stayed in their poses, the rest of the room spellbound, until the shorter vamp deflated and bowed his head in submission.

Finally, after another interminable pause, Ezra inclined his head and tugged sharply on his cuffs, breaking the spell he'd cast over the room. He may have released his hold, but the tension still lingered.

No one moved.

As Ezra turned away, he snagged me in his silvery-blue gaze.

I dropped my hand because I'd been raking my claws gently against my collarbone.

His lips quirked, then he clapped Alastair on the upper arm. "I'll speak to my father at the first opportunity."

"Bloody hell, E, Natán's going to be in a right state now. You've just turned the rest of my day to shit. Fuck you very much."

Ezra grinned, clasped his hand around the back of Alastair's neck, and brought their foreheads together. He said something for only his friend to hear, which made the Brit roar with laughter.

Alastair playfully shoved him. "That doesn't make it better, you arsehole." He shook his head. "Remy, let's go."

Remy shot Ezra a wounded look like a puppy being separated from his most favorite person, then lumbered after his superior.

Ezra spun in a slow circle, one brow arched. "Does anyone else have something to add or can I get on with my visit?"

The vamps all averted their eyes, resuming trade and conversation with a forced joviality.

I licked my finger then touched it to my ass with a sizzle, winking at Ezra.

He sighed and walked on.

Natán sounded like a real piece of work, making everyone in his crew pay their respects to him whenever they arrived in Babel. He had everyone on a leash, even his own son. The question was: how long was Ezra's?

I picked up my pace against the unwanted rush of sorrow and empathy that surged through me. Though that was better than the lingering desire to find the nearest storage closet and fuck my ex's brains out.

What even was that thought? I shook my head. Talk about intrusive. This place was getting to me.

Ezra stopped in front of a stall with a small pile of fleshy gray matter piled pyramid-style on the display table.

I almost laughed because seeing that many brains laid out like a buffet for zombies was absurd.

Then the vendor opened one of the freezers, which

was packed with vacuum-sealed children's brains, and my laughter died in an instant, a growl escaping my lips before I could smother it.

"Yum," I said, licking my lips vigorously to cover it.

The owner shook his head. "Demons."

Like your vamp customers were buying from you with the purest of intents. I swiped my claws through the air. "You dissing me?"

Ezra swung his arm in front of me like I was a purse about to fall off the front seat at a sudden vehicle stop. "Demon women. Feisty, right?"

The other vampire chuckled. "You're a braver vamp than I am."

"She knows who's boss." He ruffled my hair.

My breath caught at his touch, but I snapped my teeth at him to cover it.

Time to bash my head into a concrete wall one or two hundred times. I'd been in a good place where I'd forgotten Ezra existed, mostly, but now I was stuck with him. To be fair, working together had been better than expected, but seeing these different sides of him along with the rest of it was making it hard for me to keep slotting him as my asshole ex.

Damn you, Silas.

While Ezra engaged in predetermined small talk with the vendor, I slid into my synesthete vision and walked around the market, paying close attention to any places selling torsos.

None of them had a fat blue double knot in their center.

I tore my gaze away from a pulpy chest being squished at the bottom of a pile.

"You looking for a hard body?" a female vamp said. She had the upright posture of a ballet dancer.

"Who isn't?" I examined one torso. "Actually, I'm

looking for a special ingredient for a client of mine fixing to whip up some stamina elixirs." Any potion promising a magic cure was a con, but some people believed in them enough to claim that they worked. It kept an underground industry afloat and allowed me to create rapport with this vampire.

"For that you only want the bones. Like the old fairy tales? 'I'll grind your bones to make my bread'? The giant wasn't doing that for taste reasons, if you get my drift." She pointed at a vendor farther down the market. "Phaedra could help you."

"What about magic marks like large double knots in the chest? Ever get anything like that?"

She shrugged. "Can't see them so I wouldn't know, but no one's ever asked for that before. What do they do?"

"I heard if you distill the magic in it, you get an anti-love potion." I lied.

Her eyes gleamed greedily. "A lot of people would pay big bucks for a new formula for that. Thanks for the tip."

"No problem."

"Over here." Ezra beckoned me from a doorway. "I've ruled out organ trafficking," he said once I'd joined him. Even though he stood next to a loud generator that muffled our conversation, he spoke quietly.

"I haven't made any progress, either," I said. "Where else can we get answers and hopefully find a different motive?"

"This may well be the only one, so the sooner we stop them, the better our chances of preventing an all-out war." His expression brightened. "You know the good thing about serial killers?"

"They have the most memorable dinner party stories?"

He laughed. "That too. No, they practice."

I frowned. "We're *not* looking for someone with

surgical training, then? Because they'd have plenty of practice."

"You forget that the bodies were also exsanguinated. Drinking all the blood from a human is not something most vamps do more than once." He grimaced. "It's very frat boy. Absolutely nauseating. Far too much blood goes to waste and the hangover?" He shuddered. "Now, I could pull it off without losing a drop, but I'm extremely talented."

"You're extremely disturbing right now."

Ezra chuckled and opened the door. Gee, I couldn't think of anything better than following the good-to-the-last-drop bloodsucker into an empty stairwell while he was in this giddy mood.

I shrugged. On second thought, it could be fun. I increased my pace to catch up.

"Even if I bit an artery," he said, "which has far faster blood flow than a vein, it's impossible to keep the blood circulating long enough to completely exsanguinate a human *without* the constant contact of my fangs." He jumped the entire flight of stairs to the next landing down. "It's the enzymatic release in my bite that keeps the blood flowing past the heart giving out. If I'm not still biting, that stops pretty quickly."

"Then the vamp kept biting our murder victims," I said, hurrying down the next flight after him. "So what?"

"The amount of time that the killers left themselves vulnerable to discovery bothered me." Ezra shook his head. "There's only one way that they kept the blood flowing after the initial bite to painstakingly collect it, and do it fast."

I peered over the railing. "How far down are we going?"

He jumped down another flight. "All the way."

Chapter 19

Sighing, I kept moving, ignoring the burn in my thighs. I swear, my scales had increased my body weight by twenty percent and I was stronger, so where was my comparable increase in stamina? Stupid stairs. "How did the killers drain the victims?"

"Claret."

"The wine?"

"The very expensive, very rare, and, for purposes of our discussions about practicing, very difficult to administer drug. But it speeds up the exsanguination process immensely."

"We're going to find a dealer?"

"Manufacturers don't openly deal Claret, not even here. But the one thing we can get? Information. With the right incentive, of course." He got to the bottom of the stairwell three flights earlier than me and disappeared through a door.

Information? Why didn't he lead with that? I hurried after him, bursting into a dimly lit tavern that looked like it had been there since the 1700s. It had vaulted stone ceilings, a window with a view into the dark depths of the water, and a vampire reaching for his severed spine with spasming fingers.

In the whole minute before I'd arrived, Ezra had cracked this dude open like a lobster tail.

Incentive. Riiiight.

It took every ounce of willpower I had to keep my expression neutral and body language relaxed, Ezra's earlier warning to not react to anything ringing in my ears, because all I could smell was blood, and I had the worst urge to lick gristle off Ezra's cheek. Eww. Kind of.

Being in this tightly wound Cherry-Aviva state was messing with my head because I was finding things hot that should not have been a turn-on.

Blood pooled under the deconstructed male, draining into a hole set into the concrete.

Kudos to my co-leader; he'd done a remarkable job of directing the spray away from himself. His shirt had gotten dirty, but he'd tossed his trench coat and suit jacket over a chair before engaging.

The wounded male made a gargling sound, then fell apart in clumps of ash.

Ezra tucked a wild curl behind his ears with an oddly elegant movement for someone with blood dripping off his hands. Grimacing, he plucked a red bandana off the head of a massive vamp in biker leather. The vamp pushed his chair back, but at the look Ezra shot him, hastily assured him to go ahead.

Perhaps the most disturbing thing about this scene was the other vamps' lack of reactions. They kept talking or drinking or conducting whatever business they were engaged in.

"Now, Maeve." Ezra cleaned his hands off and deposited the wadded-up fabric in its owner's lap. "Care to answer my question?"

The female vamp he addressed was about four feet

high, with sagging boobs the size of large gourds, and two beady black eyes in a jowly face. "Och, but you don't have to be getting showy," she said in an Irish accent. "I was putting up with you when you were in short pants, laddie, so don't be pulling the Crimson Prince with me."

Ezra raised his eyebrows.

Maeve peeled away with a huff from a group standing around one of the crude wooden tables. "The Claret manufacturers were in Thailand, but they closed that shop down about a month ago. I have no clue where they've relocated."

"You're sure I can't jog your memory?" Ezra said.

"Try it."

He grinned at her. "And get my nose broken again? No, thank you."

"I'd hope you have more sense than when you were seven."

A server carrying an enormous tray with pint glasses of blood walked past me. She didn't seem to be having difficulty with it, but the thick glassware was sliding back and forth, making the tray sway precariously.

I stepped back out of splash range right as a tiny hand with the strength of a mighty god clamped on to my forearm.

"This one yours?" Maeve said, hauling me across the floor.

"I mean, he doesn't feed me or walk me," I said, "so define 'yours'?"

Maeve roared with laughter and slapped one thigh. "Good one. What's your name?"

"Cherry," I said perkily.

Ezra glared at me.

"Nice to see you consorting with better company than those humans you cat around with in the papers," she said to Ezra. "What did I teach you about playing with your food?"

Heh. I liked her.

Still, the frosted edges of my scales darkened as I imagined all the people he was catting around with in exquisite detail. Damn my excellent imagination. "We're not consorting. He's my temporary associate." I smirked at Ezra. "He knows who's boss."

A handsome Asian vampire stood up. He had thick, lustrous hair and killer dimples. "Lucius Lee, at your service." He gave a courtly bow, which was absolutely charming. "I'd be happy to consort with you. Perhaps guide you around our fine city?"

I shot him a crooked grin, twirling a clawed finger around a crimson curl. I wouldn't really take him up on it for reasons ranging from this being a murder investigation, not a vacation, to being identified and my safe cover of being a full shedim blown, but my body vibrated like I'd been caressed by a featherlight touch. Under Lucius's admiring gaze, I felt desired, but it was cut with disquiet because I was still hiding, still keeping a part of me invisible.

I didn't want to live by halves.

"I'm sure Cherry would love your company, Lucius," Ezra said before I could answer. He smoothed a hand over his short beard. Really? He was fine with this? In the middle of an investigation? No, this had to be some ploy to throw my unprofessionalism back in my face and get me off this case.

"Another time perhaps," I said. "Business comes first."

"My offer stands. Anytime." Lucius sat back down.

I gave him one last admiring glance. "Maeve, any idea who's bought multiple doses of Claret in the past year?"

She rubbed her thumb and forefinger together, looking at me expectantly.

I pulled out a wad of cash. Information was never free, and I'd come prepared.

"Aren't you cute, lassie?" Maeve said. "I only deal in gold. That ring of yours looks like good quality."

I folded my hand over my Maccabee band. "No can do. It has sentimental value."

"Then we're done here." She shrugged and turned away.

Nice try, but she wasn't getting off that easily. Maeve knew something useful. I was sure of it.

Had I appeared human, I'd have let her go regardless, but for all intents and purposes, I was a full shedim. I was face-to-face with a predator who registered me as a demon and now, more than ever, I had to commit to the role.

A good leader couldn't show fear to her adversary. And honestly? I didn't really feel any.

I grabbed Maeve's stringy dirty blond hair, yanking her head back. "I'll say when we're done, Squash Tits."

Oh sure, now the entire room gasped.

Maeve tore free, leaving a greasy clump of hair in my fist, which I immediately dropped. "What did you call me?"

I leaned in, getting eye to eye. "Squash. Tits."

Ezra's shoulders shook, and though his lips were pressed tightly together, a snort escaped.

"Claret." I snapped my fingers under Maeve's chin. "Who's bought multiple doses in the past year?"

"The woman with one leg," she stammered.

Given her slack jaw, it may not have been my epic badassery that got the answer but her shock at my impudence. Either way, she made no move to retaliate, so I won.

Also, we were looking for a woman, huh? The vampire that had been caught on the security camera at Roy's was male, so she was our Eishei Kodesh. Female serial killers were unusual, but a higher purpose, a fervent belief, could easily transcend gender.

"There've been some murders of humans with a magic double knot in the upper area of their chest," I said. "What does the mark signify?"

Maeve scrunched up her face. "How would I fecking know? Why do you care—" She grabbed my ring and twisted it painfully around on my finger. She recognized the engraved flame and five tiny gems because her eyes widened. "A shedim Maccabee? That's a sorry state of things." She'd spoken in a low growl, but as everyone in the room had vamp hearing, it's not like she had to project.

Dozens of pairs of eyes flicked my way.

A shiver ran down my spine, but the key word to remember in Maeve's pronouncement was "shedim." Infernals were so rare that it hadn't even occurred to any of these vamps that I might be one, instead of the stranger occurrence of a demon operative.

"That's reductionist. I'm many things, none of which require apologizing for." I extracted my hand with the fierce smile of a warrior counting the bloodied corpses of their enemies on a muddy battlefield. "I also didn't give you permission to touch me," I said coldly.

"You're as low as those vamp traitors who work there," Maeve said. She spat on the ground, then spun to face Ezra, her eyes flashing. "Tell me you're not one of them."

Chairs scraping against the stone floor, the sound bouncing off the walls, and the patrons ready to jump in to this conversation.

Ezra crossed his arms. "Claret comes in handy in my line of work, and someone is muscling in on that," he said impatiently. "I'll use whomever I must in order to hunt them down. Even a—"

I tensed, feeling small and vulnerable and hating him

for, yet again, inducing a negative emotional reaction in me.

"Maccabee," he said.

"You'll do as you will," Maeve grumbled. "That much hasn't changed, but I have my pride, and I won't be helping the likes of them."

Think again, vamp. I was proud of being an operative and had worked hard to get where I was. "Maccabee or not, you'd do well to remember that Babel is built on a *demon* realm. We tolerate your existence here but make no mistake that if provoked, we could extinguish your presence like that." I snapped my fingers.

"Is that a threat?" She swung her gaze to Ezra. "Curb her, lad."

His lips were pursed, his head tilted, and his eyes narrowed. "I think not."

I smirked at Maeve. "Told you I was his boss. Now, what does the magic double knot signify?"

She flapped her hand at us and turned away.

Activating my magic vision so Maeve's old injuries lit up like traffic lights, I swung her around and threw a left uppercut to the side of her head.

She blocked the punch, but I followed up with a swift heel kick that crunched her nose. Blood streamed down.

The other patrons sat up hungrily.

Before Maeve recovered, I executed a roundhouse kick and blew out her previously broken left knee.

One of the vamps stepped forward, cracking her knuckles.

Ezra, examining his nails with a put-upon expression, deigned to spare her a glance. "I wouldn't."

She nodded sharply and dropped into a chair like a stone.

"Almost done?" Ezra asked me.

"Bored, are you?" I kicked Maeve in her previously shattered ribs, making sure she was both down and out.

"Feeling a little unnecessary," he replied. "How will my ego cope?"

I rolled my eyes then nodded at a vampire whose body vibrated with the strain of keeping herself in check under Ezra's watchful eye. "You did kidney dialysis in life, didn't you? Wonder how those puppies would feel with a few strategic punches? And you." I directed this at a guy with mutton chop sideburns. "Those were some pretty badly broken vertebrae. Bet they snap easier the second time around."

"Enough." The bartender came around from behind the bar, his apron slung over his broad shoulder. "Out of respect for Natán, we'll allow you to leave unharmed, provided you do it now."

"Thank you." Ezra placed a hand on his heart, dripping sarcasm. "Your permission means the world to us." He grabbed his coat and suit jacket and strode out.

I pointed from my eyes to the barkeep and backed out of the room with an extra swagger in my step.

Lucius blew me a cheeky kiss and I winked back.

Ezra and I were quiet while we took the glass pod up from the depths to the surface of the pool and stepped onto the pool deck.

A group speaking in some Slavic language was waiting to descend. Most of them weren't human, unless the others had some hard-core breath-holding skills, but all possessed an unfortunate love of leather vests and chains. A few checked us out, but they were more interested in their conversation.

All except one man, whose every inch of exposed skin was tattooed. He kept darting horrified looks my way.

I bared my teeth at him.

He instantly looked down at his feet. Heh.

"Was that your half-human side prevailing?" Ezra said when we got outside. "You sure could have fooled me."

I inhaled deeply to clear the itchy smell of ozone from my nostrils. "What?"

"You enjoyed scaring that man."

"So? He was a piece of scum."

"He was still human." Ezra caressed the scales on my cheek. "Did you forget all those rules and filters you so desperately cleave to and for once relish being a monster?" he purred.

I stepped out of touching range. "I'm in a place brimming with shedim magic. This is how I survive here. I can't change my form so there's no point living according to my human side."

He gave me an oddly dark smile. "I never said otherwise. I merely pointed out that your humanity didn't win out and you enjoyed it."

I turned away from his knowing gaze. I'd spent my life attempting to do good, and less than one day in this place, I was inciting violence, playing top of the food chain, and loving it. Were other humans right to force infernals to stay hidden?

Another pod with dark glass pulled up to the curb and the panel slid open. I'd once called a taxi, waited forty-five minutes on a downtown corner in a snowstorm, and then walked home for another forty minutes before getting a call announcing my taxi was close. The service here was superb. Creepy, but superb.

Ezra climbed in after me and announced our destination to the Vancouver Departure Lounge. He pulled out his phone and texted the info about Claret and the lady with one leg to Silas, explaining that Babel had telephone capabilities, including being able to phone or text anywhere on earth, but no net access.

Ordinarily, I'd have been interested, but now my head

pounded. I was no longer certain of where the truth of who I was ended and my personal beliefs began. Was I fundamentally evil but my self-perception was so strong that I'd deluded myself? I searched deep inside but didn't find an answer.

Suddenly, all the exhilaration of publicly showing my shedim side blew away, leaving a flatness inside me and tight, itchy scales. I didn't want to pretend I was a demon, and I didn't want to pretend I was fully human.

I wanted to be me.

"How do you switch between those different aspects of you?" I asked, scratching at my scales. "Without losing yourself to one?"

Ezra caught my hand and pulled it across my lap so it rested palm up in his. "I don't switch." He pulled a crumpled linen handkerchief from his coat pocket and carefully cleaned off the claw that I'd blooded in my attempts to pick my scales off. "I also don't hide any part of myself, except the undercover work. I told you that."

My hand remained in his even though he'd wiped the blood away. I craved contact with someone who'd seen all of me, not just pieces, even if his acceptance had lasted only one short night.

Maybe Ezra craved it too because he didn't pull away. He absently stroked his thumb over my palm.

Silas had been right. And so had my mother.

God help me. I did see all of Ezra; I did know him better than anyone.

What I mistook for different masks were actually Ezra's way of protecting his core self. I'd observed him interacting with other people, his charm and charisma were undeniable, but they felt like distractions so no one would see the entirety of him.

I turned my head and looked into his eyes. Really looked. There was a darkness behind the silvery blue that made me uneasy. It was like he was always hiding something, a core part of himself that he didn't want the world to see.

"Aviva, stop," he muttered, breaking the stare.

"You're not part of the Kosher Nostra anymore, are you?" I said softly.

"Of course I am." He glowered at me.

I'd seen too many suspects lie to me not to spot the tells. Maybe not always or even on all vamps, but now, on this one, I could. His menace was merely bluster. Another mask. "Everyone thinks you're still your dad's enforcer, but Silas knows the truth, doesn't he? Does Alastair?"

After a long moment, Ezra reluctantly shook his head.

"Why did you really join the Maccabees? Was it a way out? Protection from your dad?"

He pulled his hand free. "There's no protection from him."

"Then what's going on? You keep up this myth of being his enforcer and he allows you to live?"

"Having a son nicknamed the Crimson Prince comes in handy for him."

"I imagine for you as well. You schooled Remy by shushing him."

Ezra chuckled.

"But having a son actually *be* the Crimson Prince would be handier," I said.

"Yeah, well. There's that."

I gnawed on a fingernail. A regular right-handed one, not my leftie claw. "Did you agree to become an assassin because of me? Did Natán find out I was an infernal?"

Ezra leaned his head against the padded headrest. "No."

"To which?"

"Both. I didn't have a problem taking out shithead vamps."

"You said you killed humans."

"I didn't say it was for Natán though, did I?"

I pressed against our shared leather seat like I might release some sudden insight into whatever he was still hiding. "You implied it."

"You inferred it because you wanted to believe it," he corrected wearily.

We were silent for a while. What was true about Ezra versus what I believed, or even what he believed?

"What humans have you killed?" I said. "Who do you still want to kill?"

"At the moment?" he said mildly. "Only you."

I flapped a hand at him. "Pshaw. I'm only half-human."

"And I only half want to kill you. Can we drop this, please?"

"No." I poked his side.

"You're a real piece of work."

"I'll take that as a compliment," I said.

"You do you." There was no heat in his words. No teasing either. Just a bone-deep weariness. It was all kinds of wrong on a man who ordinarily took up so much space and whose presence was usually larger than life.

I worried that I'd somehow shrunk him with this conversation. I didn't want to be the person who made him small.

"Luscious, I mean, Lucius would have done me too," I joked. "Scales, horns, and all."

"Aww, princess." Ezra mustered up some much-appreciated snark. "Want to go back and take him up on his offer?"

My teasing mood vanished. "You seemed eager enough to push me his way."

"I trusted you to be professional enough to turn him down, but once we'd gotten answers?" He turned his face away. "I lost all claims to your personal time," he said quietly.

I had no response to that, simply sorrow at what we could have had all these years. It killed any last trace of adrenaline from my visit to the Crypt. I meant to stay awake for the rest of the ride because I'd probably be run out of town if I ever came back to Babel, but I was wrung out and crashed in no time flat. When I woke up, we'd arrived in the skyscraper area with the neon streaming down the sides of the towers.

Ezra was looking at his phone and frowning. "Change of plans," he announced. "London terminal, please."

The pod pulled a smooth U-turn.

"What's up?" Yawning, I rubbed my eyes.

Silas had sent the details of a flight landing in Manchester in a few hours, presumably Sachie's. Guess we were meeting her plane. There was also a link Ezra didn't want to open while we were in Babel, saying he didn't trust the security or privacy here.

The London departure lounge looked identical to the Vancouver one, to the point that I'd swear the pod went around a few blocks to throw me off while they switched the sign inside.

Traveling through the wall of black mesh on our way out was no less unnerving the second time around.

We landed in a different part of the Brink than I'd ever traveled—the one closest to the rift in England—but I couldn't tell what it looked like, because the entire thing was shrouded in a thick fog that smelled like seaweed and felt like nails lightly scraping against my skin. I shivered, partially from cold, and partially because I wanted to nope the fuck out and go back to the place where the nice vampires lived.

At least my scales were gone, and when I felt for my horns with my blessedly claw-free left hand, I didn't have those either. While I couldn't see them, I guessed that my eyes and hair were also back to normal. I'd been fairly confident my shedim features would disappear in the Brink, but that sliver of doubt had been a malicious bitch.

I patted my belly. Hello, pouchy. My relief at being fully human once more was mixed with wistful loss.

Cherry sighed, our seamless unity from Babel already relegated to a memory.

I was Cherry and Cherry was me, but I wouldn't feel whole until I could live authentically. I was doing everything to craft a world where I could live as my true self. With one hundred percent fewer scales, but still. Who was to say I wouldn't want to rock some horns or my kickass crimson hair on a night out?

"This isn't ideal." Ezra was a disembodied voice next to me.

At first, I thought he meant me and Cherry, but no, he meant the fog. Beyond supe-vultures or other vampires concealed by the gloom, the Brink could decide to open a chasm in front of us, and we wouldn't see it until it was too late. I couldn't even see my hand held out a few inches in front of my face.

A puff of wind lifted the hair off my neck, the fog caressing me with a dank touch. I reached out, fumbling for Ezra's sleeve, but for one heart-stopping moment, I couldn't find him. "Ezra?" I said, sounding pitchy.

"I'm determining our best plan of action."

Orienting myself with his voice, I caught his elbow. "Go slow and be trapped here longer with more potential for something to go wrong, or go fast and not see an attack coming." I made a hmm sound. "I vote fast. If I'm going to die, I don't want to spend a lot of time anticipating it."

"Agreed. Hop on."

I groaned. "Again?"

"Yes, again. Your antics in Babel could have blown up

spectacularly. I was very patient, but I've hit my limit. Don't push me."

"Says the guy who ripped out a dude's spine."

There was silence. I couldn't see his face, and he couldn't see my death glare.

Ezra laughed. "That felt so good."

"It looked pretty badass." I chuckled. Then immediately checked that Cherry hadn't seized control of my vocal cords *and* my sense of humor (though we both enjoyed a good British comedy), but no, that amused approval was all mine. *Nonononononono.* Why couldn't I have a sick attraction to a different dude who could rip a spine out with his bare hands?

"You looked badass too," he said.

Fantasy number four (a second tier wish in that it didn't involve bodily harm to Ezra) of the post-breakup years had partially come to pass. The man who'd left me was admitting how cool I currently was. It wasn't accompanied with a sorrowful sigh and him rending his shirt at how he'd been a fool to let me get away, but it still sent a shaft of warmth through my chest.

I groped up his arm for his shoulder. "Crouch down, little pony."

"Stallion," he corrected, squatting so I could get on his back.

"What is it with every single male and that deluded belief?" I tightened my arms around his neck and he stood up, gripping the backs of my thighs.

Our inbound journey through the Brink had been so plagued by pine cone storms and shitty geographical transformations that it didn't leave time to lust over Ezra. Being enveloped in the heavy fog now, however, heightened my other senses.

I was acutely aware of the press of his fingers against my legs, and the slight double twitch he gave with his right thumb when his jog became a vampiric blur. Of course, I only sensed our speed because the initial warm damp from the fog turned to a cold, stiff breeze.

"You all think women get hot and bothered by that suggestion," I said. "Have you ever seen a stallion's dick? Would you want that telescope stuffed inside you?"

"Aviva Jacqueline Fleischer, you have a sick, sick mind," he said. "We simply wish to help you run free with the wind in your hair."

"So chivalrous." I turned my face into his neck to better inhale the smell of his light sweat mixed with his cologne, sinking deeper into the firm warmth of his back against my body.

"We made a good team," Ezra said.

At his words, a hollow ache throbbed in my chest. They said a picture was worth a thousand words. If you took one of me right now, would you see my thousand emotions flitting across my face?

"Yeah," I said softly. "We did."

Chapter 20

We made it to the rift in North Yorkshire without incident and stepped onto the moors. Hay-brown grass and blooms of heather gave way to emerald fields laid out in gentle hills under a bleached-out late morning sun. The air was cold and clean, and the only sound was the wind, which reminded me of ocean waves.

A female Maccabee bundled in a wool coat asked us for our passports. I explained that I didn't have mine because I'd had business in Babel and had expected to return to Vancouver. Ezra had no passport either, no Maccabee ring, and she couldn't find him in the system.

We were told to go into the lone structure, a thatch-roofed pub, and wait for clearance to enter the country.

The pub, built and controlled by our organization, was paneled in dark wood with beer company signs running along the tops of the walls and down the pillars. Maccabees and non-operatives sat at a long narrow bar, enjoying their beverage of choice, while there was a heated darts tournament happening in the corner.

"This place is adorable," I said.

The portal here in Northern England was unusual in

that it was located on the moors in the middle of nowhere. Maccabees had seized ownership before vamps could. This pub had been built and was controlled by our organization. The closest town was a ten-minute walk away, but apparently, the locals didn't mind the short trek.

Ezra ordered a couple pints, which we both half-heartedly sipped at while seated by a cheery fire. Neither of us were fans of dark beer. I appreciated the salt and vinegar crisps a lot more.

There was no cell signal so we couldn't check the link that Silas had sent yet.

The existence of rifts was a political nightmare for governments. Vampire Mafias owned all the real estate in a several-block radius around urban rift entrances, making it impossible for political bodies to set up any kind of border control. The Maccabees did their best to keep tabs on who was coming and going, but it was a constant struggle.

Governments had tried to seize control, bless them. Various countries had called in their armies—which just ended in insane amounts of bloodshed. They'd also attempted to appropriate the vamp-owned properties through legal challenges and bring all that land under federal control. See above result.

Appealing to residents and business owners in these neighborhoods or even surrounding ones didn't work either, because the vamps were savvy enough to put a lot of money back into community improvement. The streets were clean and well lit and crime was nonexistent. A mom could take a crying baby out for a soothing walk in the dead of night and come home safe and sound. People longed to live and work in these areas. I'd even heard of cities where civil wars raged, but no bomb or bullets touched the vamp-owned areas.

The female Maccabee returned, saying we were

cleared, but that we were to present ourselves at London HQ, the main British chapter.

I stopped in the restroom for a desperately needed pee. I also sponged down my pits and face and fixed my ponytail.

Ezra and I agreed that since a time frame hadn't been specified for our London visit, we'd continue as planned to Manchester and deal with London at some later point. Ezra had decided to set up base there, since Sach had to investigate the tattoo, and it was easy enough for Darsh to reach us after Greenland.

We made a quick stop in the nearby medieval village for Ezra to buy a shirt to replace his bloodstained one, which he dumped in the trash. He'd kept his coat buttoned up inside the pub so he wouldn't spook the locals.

After a short cab ride to a larger town, we caught the train to Manchester.

The travelers in our car took one look at Ezra and moved, giving us all the privacy we desired. Brilliant.

Ezra went on a nourishment run, returning from the dining car with a tray, which he set down between us on the table.

I unwrapped my roast beef sandwich excitedly. "How did you score me an entire extra pickle?"

"I have my ways," he said in an exaggerated German accent, waggling his eyebrows.

I bit into my appy pickle with a small smile. He'd remembered my fondness for the double pickle? *Phrasing*. I clamped my mouth against a snort.

"What I never understood, though," he said, cradling a steaming mug of blood between his hands, "was that if this is your appetizer pickle and the other one is dessert, to be consumed after your sandwich main course, what happens when you have an actual dessert?"

"The pickle becomes the inter-course palate cleanser." When he smirked, I hurriedly cut him off. "I mean, inter dash course. Being between meals."

His smirk grew wider. "Keep going. Please."

I kicked his shin. "Open the link Silas sent."

It led to a drop box.

While we ate, we leaned over Ezra's phone, reading the profile that Silas put together on Dr. Athena Metaxas, age thirty-seven, from Greece. This Yellow Flame Eishei Kodesh was a critical care surgeon who'd lost a leg in a boating accident when she was a teen. She had a seaside apartment in Thessaloniki but was currently on leave from her hospital, whereabouts unknown with no credit card usage. The doctor was divorced, with no children or close family, and, like Kyle Epstein, was Jewish.

"Hello, lady with one leg." I munched on what was left of my dessert pickle. "Silas found her really fast with very little data. He is good."

"Told you."

I wiped my mouth with a paper napkin. "Why do our killers believe they can cure vampirism? Read one book on the topic and you'll see it's never happened. Not only that, no expert believes it's possible. You can't take some essence of a good person to negate the evil of vamps. Even if all vampires were bad, it doesn't work that way."

"I don't know. What about you? Have you given up on the double knot in Kyle's chest being relevant?"

"Since I still can't find any explanation for it?" I shrugged. "I've tabled it for the moment. I think we'll learn more if we dig deeper into the doctor's and vamp's backgrounds."

"I'm sure Silas is working on it," Ezra said.

From movies and television shows and not any personal experience, I knew that private jets had internet connection, so Sachie would have seen the profile. Same for Darsh in Greenland, though neither had texted.

"Regardless of whether our victims have this weird knot," I said, "the bigger issue is that they lived all over the world. How did the murderers find them?"

Ezra peered at me over the rim of the mug, his eyes hardened to steel. "If I had the answer, I'd be there to greet the psychos on their next attempt."

By the time we arrived in Manchester and taxied out to the airfield, the flight had landed. I told the employee in the small terminal who we were meeting and was escorted onto the airstrip where two limos awaited. Was another flight due to land?

I hugged myself for warmth, wishing I'd brought a coat to wear over my sweater and watching flies buzz around one of the motion sensor lights on the airplane hangar.

Ezra was still inside the terminal, dealing with something.

Sachie bounded down the mobile staircase looking as relaxed and glowing as if she'd just exited a spa. She waved vigorously, then caught herself mid-wave, and hurried over, grabbing my arm while speaking a million miles an hour. "How was the Crypt? Wild? Private planes are the bomb. Tattoo shop time, am I right?"

My best friend could cold-bloodedly stare down a vampire and bluff her way into victory, so whatever had her acting like she'd mainlined a case of Coke must have really upset her. Especially since my bitchy behavior had already been forgiven. I expected to have to grovel and feed her before that happened.

The knot of unease in my stomach tightened. Had something happened with the mission? Had she received bad news about one of her parents? Before I could ask, Sachie glanced over at the plane, so I did too.

My mouth went dry.

Darsh escorted one of the most beautiful women I'd ever seen down the staircase rolled up to the plane. Laughing and chatting, they descended like gods bestowing their divinity on earth.

Her blond ringlets tumbled artfully past her shoulders, framing a heart-shaped face with expressive features and a wide smile. She wore jeans and a white T-shirt under a short maroon leather jacket, and the outfit was sexier on her than a designer dress with a plunging neckline.

"Who is she and why was she on the private flight?" I said, confused.

"Orly!" Ezra's shout made me jump. His arm was raised in a wave.

This goddess was the woman who Ezra knit gifts for?

She squealed and ran down the stairs to him, her arms outstretched and her tresses streaming behind her.

I ran a hand over my lank ponytail, licking my chapped lips and wishing I had some lip balm. My self-confidence regarding my attractiveness was fine, so it wasn't the difference between Orly and me that made a small "oh" fall from my lips.

It was the way Ezra looked at her, like she was full sunshine and he'd happily burn up so long as he could be near her. Did he slide one hand along the nape of her neck when he kissed her? Take his time to divest her of her clothes, making her bathe in moonlight, her body wound tight in a lust-filled anticipation while he prowled toward her, naked and magnificent? Had she been bent over and taken from behind, his sweat-slicked chest pressed against her spine as he whispered filthy words in a mix of Spanish and English?

My heart twinged like it was a muscle I'd sprained, and I rubbed my hands quickly over my goose-bumped arms.

Darsh arrived in time to catch this and gallantly draped his beat-up brown leather jacket over my shoulders.

Smiling gratefully, I burrowed into the warmth and the scent of sandalwood from his favorite soap, which he'd gifted to Sach and me after we'd pestered him for the name of the local company that made it.

"She's really nice," Sach said miserably, and then the happy couple was upon us.

"Aviva," Ezra said, draping his arm over the blonde woman's shoulder. "Meet Orly Attias."

I looked at my ex—and his whatever she was—and took my conversational skills to a new level, with a flat-out "No."

"No?" Ezra wrinkled his brow.

Cherry had taken over all my brain function, busy calculating the easiest way to rip that woman's shoulder off without Ezra noticing.

I repossessed a couple of brain cells. "I mean, no, we haven't met before. Hi." I stuck out my hand. "I'm Aviva."

"I'm so happy to meet Ezzie's team," she pronounced in a throaty accent, shaking my hand with a respectably firm grip.

"Not as happy as we are to meet you," Darsh said. Hearts practically floated around his head.

Readjusting his jacket around my shoulders, I forced my smile wider.

"Orly scored us the plane," Sachie said.

"When Ezzie called asking for my help, how could I say no?" Even the blonde's hand gestures were charming.

Let's see how charming they are when we rip them off and she's left with stumps, Cherry murmured.

"Right?" I said.

Sach threw me a confused look. Whoops.

"I mean," I amended, "we're all grateful for the help."

“It was nothing. I simply arranged for my flight to start in Vancouver,” Orly said, “and pick me up in Toronto. Why waste an opportunity to hop over to London and go shopping?”

I’d initially placed her accent as French from the way she pronounced her “R”s but listening further, I concluded she was Israeli.

“More stuff,” Ezra teased. “That’s exactly what you need.”

“I’ve seen your closet, you hypocrite.” She leaned against him.

Was her side welded to him or something?

I could help with that, Cherry purred.

“You didn’t go to Greenland?” Ezra said to Darsh.

He shrugged. “Wasn’t much point once I had the profile that Cowpoke rustled up, but I phoned the hospital director from the plane. There was nothing she could add.”

“We were having too good a time to let Darsh leave,” Orly said firmly. “Now be nice so I can enjoy my five minutes with you.” She elbowed Ezra. “He’s so hard to pin down.”

“I wouldn’t know,” I said blandly. “We’re just work acquaintances.”

“Actually,” Ezra said in an amused voice, “I’m Aviva’s personal nemesis. Her own supervillain.”

Orly laughed. “You probably deserve it. And now I will have more friends the next time I visit Vancouver.” She beamed at Sachie and Darsh.

“This winter,” Sach agreed. “All the holiday light displays.” All three of them high-fived, though my former best friend darted an anxious glance my way.

I was frozen in place, Cherry raging inside me. My head throbbed and my fingers twitched with the need to stamp my claim with friendship bracelets and a secret language. This interloper could have Ezzie, and may they live happily ever after, but my two closest friends were off-limits.

"Such fun. In the meantime," I said, "we have work to do. Sach, you and Darsh find a registered vamp with that soccer league tattoo."

"While you and Ezra do what?" Sachie said suspiciously.

"Pay a visit to Maccabee HQ in London," I said. "Since it's one of the largest chapters, I'm hoping someone can point us to an expert on certain cures. We have to present ourselves to the director anyway. Might as well try this line of inquiry one last time."

"Okay," Ezra said. "We'll split up."

Orly clapped her hands together. "This is perfect. Sachie, Darsh, the limo over there is for you to take into town. Use it however long you need to. The three of us will drive to London together in the other one."

So perfect. What could be more fun than spending the next few hours as the third wheel to their happy reunion? Also, I barely had one functional car, but Orly had *two* limos? Ezra would have grown up with money. Ill-gotten riches, but still. Was this level of wealth still normal for him? Had he been slumming with me?

The drivers of each vehicle got out as if magically summoned and opened their respective back doors.

"Are you sure?" Sach said.

"But of course," Orly replied. She said goodbye to Sachie and Darsh and got in her own limo.

I hugged Sach, aware that her question had been for me. "I'll be fine. You be careful and find that vamp. And I'm sorry."

She hugged me tighter. "I want to hear every last detail of your visit later. Don't skimp on the bloodshed."

"How do you know there was bloodshed?" I joked.

Darsh looked between me and Ezra. "We can but hope," he said cheerfully.

Suddenly Sach jabbed a finger at me. "Stay forsaken," she said pointedly.

Any lust had vanished the second I saw Orly. "No worries."

"Hang on." Ezra tugged on my sleeve. "You should return Darsh's jacket."

I held the garment closed with one hand. "I'm cold."

He shrugged out of his cashmere trench and held it out.

I hesitated, still against the idea of wrapping myself in him. His *coat.* Plus, if it bothered him that I wore Darsh's jacket, then I perversely wished to wear it forever.

Ezra waved his trench coat like a bullfighter with a flag. He looked like he was trying to hold back a laugh. Asshole.

Darsh gave an annoyed sigh. "Take it, AF, so we can be off already."

I handed the leather jacket over and put Ezra's coat on. It smelled like him, that spicy fragrance mixed with a summer's breeze, and somehow, even though it was as soft as a cloud, I felt like I was wrapped in barbed wire. "Stay in touch."

"We will." Darsh blew me a kiss and ducked into the back seat after Sachie. A moment later their limo glided away.

I took off Ezra's coat. "I can't wear this. It's way too nice and I'm murder on clothing."

"Aviva." He raked a hand through his hair, his Orly-inspired happiness wiped away in favor of an annoyed expression. "Wear the damn thing. I don't want you catching pneumonia."

"I had a perfectly warm jacket. You didn't have to piss on me like a dog marking his territory." I clamped my mouth shut before I lost my moral high ground by saying something petty and jealous like *Especially when you've got Orly*.

"We're going to an HQ that I'm not familiar with," he said, his voice hard, "to ask questions about curing vampirism, which will undoubtedly upset people, especially given that I'm one of the ones asking. I don't know who I'll be meeting or where else we may end up in the course of stopping these murders, and I'm not going to do it with you smelling like another vampire. It will severely undermine any position of power that I have."

"That's why you insisted I switch?"

"Yes," he said with forced patience.

My co-leader had accepted me accompanying him to Babel. It was only fair that I play along with vampire rules, like the scent thing. It was even good that he'd clarified this was a vampire politics thing and not him being weirdly possessive of me around Orly.

I quit grinding my teeth and shrugged back into the coat. "Understood."

In the next two and a half hours back to London, I learned several things: Orly liked to talk. A lot. And it was a full-body experience. Were she forced to sit on her hands, I'm not sure she could speak. When she really got going, she would lapse into animated Hebrew, using the word "ke'ilu" a ton, which I figured was equivalent to how we used "like."

Ezra would remind her, sometimes in English and sometimes in Hebrew, to speak English at which point she'd laugh at herself. Orly had been in Ezra's life a lot longer than I had, though in what guise, I had no clue and didn't ask. She had a master's degree from the Barcelona School of Economics, spoke six languages, worked for a global think tank, and had a party-sized bag of M&Ms in her giant red purse that she shared with me.

By the time she dropped us off at Maccabee HQ, I'd bonded with her over our love of psychological thrillers, found myself agreeing to let her fly me to Toronto for a noir film festival, and was almost depressed that I couldn't date her myself, because damn.

She kissed both of us on each cheek while holding our hands, then drove off, hanging out the window, waving, while I stood on the sidewalk, shell-shocked. Like I'd been hit by a sparkly meteorite.

"She's really something," I said, meaning it in the best way possible.

"Yeah." Ezra smiled. "She really is."

I couldn't even hate him for agreeing. Instead, I squared my shoulders and looked up at the modern glass and steel building, surprised there weren't gothic towers and a doorman in full livery standing at attention. "Want to catch our killers?"

Ezra pulled the front door open, a hint of predator lighting his eyes. "You have no idea."

Chapter 21

We checked in at reception and asked to meet with the director. Twenty minutes later, we were taken up to the top floor. Booker Harrison was a dapper Black man in his sixties with an upper-class British accent, a trim goatee, and an unhinged love of tweed.

He greeted us in a room that was library porn with its floor-to-ceiling bookshelves, rolling ladders, gorgeously bound rows of first editions, and a large crackling fireplace. Despite the many cozy seating areas, he led us to a smaller, utilitarian room in the back that held a conference table and chairs that were so hard that my butt and back were in agony in under a minute.

We were not offered refreshments.

"I've spoken with Michael," Director Harrison said briskly. "This entire carte blanche situation is highly unorthodox. Maccabees serve everyone equally. I don't hold with people pulling strings, whether they're on the Authority or not."

"With all due respect, Director," Ezra said, "a child was murdered. So were four others."

"I'm not unsympathetic to that," the other man said,

"but what makes them more important than anyone else who's met with foul play? On top of that, I have a vampire who has spent the majority of his time in the field as an intel gatherer and a level two operative co-leading this investigation?" He steepled his hands together under his chin. "That is not how we do things here."

"I'm sure Michael vouched for us." I flipped through my new Canadian passport. Ezra and I had been provided with them when we arrived. Mine had the same horrible photo as the one in my passport back home. It was equally terrifying and terrifyingly efficient.

The director regarded me evenly. "I'm sure your mother had no choice in the matter." He paused. "Since I'd hate to believe that Michael was playing favorites too."

I tensed and sat up straight. *Oh no you didn't.*

Under the table, Ezra placed a hand on my thigh. "It doesn't matter what you think of our presence here," my partner said. "At the end of the day, we *do* have carte blanche and you *will* assist us."

Director Harrison gave a quiet unamused laugh. "Like father, like son."

A muscle ticked in Ezra's jaw.

I placed my hand on the small of his back, which was as hard as a sheet of plywood, and spoke up before this got ugly. "Let's cut to the chase. What do you have in the archives on the subject of curing vampirism?"

"Very little, since it's a myth. There are some journals containing detailed failed attempts. Nothing has ever been proven to reverse that magic, though many have tried. You think that's the motive for these murders?"

"Yes," Ezra said.

A vein throbbed in the director's forehead. "Heaven help us."

Disappointing as it was that they didn't have any useful resources, it wasn't particularly surprising. Operatives got a history lesson in all those pointless attempts back when we were Maccababies.

"There's an old and established Jewish community here in London," I said. "Since Maccabees were originally only Jews, perhaps this group has relevant oral tales that our organization didn't record. Could anyone there help us?"

Only Jews were recruited as operatives for several hundred years, though from the start, the positions were offered to both men and women. However, even once we welcomed non-Jews, the organization remained a secret until after the Salem witch trials in the late 1700s.

The one big caveat to our reveal was that we kept demon and vamp hunting a secret—until our hand was forced, and supernatural beings became public knowledge in the 1960s when vampires stepped forward for the first wave of their public relations offensive.

Director Harrison sat back in his chair, drumming his fingers on the table. "Rosemary could help you." He texted his assistant, who showed up a couple minutes later with the woman's information.

"Will that be all?" he said.

"That's it." I closed my contacts app. "Thank you."

"James will show you out." The director headed for the door but paused on the threshold. "Do remember that you're guests in my city and keep a low profile. I don't want messes that I'll have to clean up."

James did not encourage us to linger, and we were back on the street in no time.

"His faith in us was touching," I said, already calling Rosemary Durwood at Palace Imports & Exports to set up an appointment.

"I especially enjoyed how he got digs in at both of us through our parents." Ezra positioned himself between me and the curb like he always used to when we walked together. "That was a highlight."

Ms. Durwood was surprised by my request to discuss cures, but once I said that Director Harrison had given us her name, she was amenable to meeting right away.

I flagged down one of London's famous black cabs. "You're not making friends with this whole carte blanche deal."

"Like I give a shit," Ezra said, holding the door open for me.

I gave the driver the address, then stared out the window watching famous landmark after famous landmark pass by. It was almost as surreal as being in Babel, but it didn't hold all my attention because my head was swarming with questions.

When had Ezra become so hard? Cherry perked up, and I scowled at my reflection in the glass. *Down, girl.* Hard in spirit. What was he really after by solving this case? Because I still didn't buy his whole human hitman spiel. There were other questions, but I pressed the palms of my hands into my eyes until I saw white dots and could force those questions away.

"You okay?" Ezra said.

I dropped my hands in my lap, blinking to clear my vision. "Yup."

By the time we were dropped off in an industrial park close to Heathrow Airport, it was almost 8PM. The corridor of dark blue warehouses with tan loading bay doors was homogenous enough to be located in any city.

"There's a distinct lack of British pip pip tally ho," I muttered, peering at signs, half expecting Director Harrison to have pulled a fast one to get rid of us.

"That's where you're wrong." Ezra pointed at a row of compost bins, one of which had been turned over.

Two furry white heads with black stripes and narrow

snouts were digging through the offerings.

I blinked dumbly at him. Did he expect an animal rampage?

"That's Pip Pip," he said loftily in a British accent, "and the badger on the right is clearly Tally Ho. Sod Off and Bollocks stayed back to have a bit of a lie-in and a cuppa."

There was a twinkle in his eye, and a slight curve to his lips. Ezra had shed his residual anger and was actually trying to lighten the mood.

The tension in my body melted away, the corners of my mouth twitched upward, and before I knew it, I was laughing. "Goof."

The smile he bestowed on me wasn't the adoring one he'd given Orly. It was full of mischief yet boyishly charming.

It caught me off guard, my heart swelling with adoration for him.

I cleared my throat a couple of times. "Ms. Durwood's company is just over there."

Palace Imports & Exports was closing up, the loading bay door lowering and employees streaming out through the front.

When I asked one of them for Ms. Durwood, saying we had an appointment, she told me to wait in the showroom and went to get her.

The unifying theme of all the items on display was their bright colors: painted dishware from Sicily, glass lampshades from Spain, throw pillows from Portugal, and tiles from Morocco. For the first time, I envied people like Orly who could surround herself with beautiful pieces instead of much cheaper knockoffs with none of the same vitality.

I glanced at Ezra idly browsing a jewelry case, wondering not for the first time what his place looked like and where his home base was. It was better than questioning whether he was looking for something specific right now.

"Hullo. I'm Rosemary." Somewhere in her mid-sixties, the business owner wore a rainbow-colored skirt, a light blue flowy blouse, and large chunky pieces of jewelry, while her hair was a riot of red curls. Despite her WASPy-sounding name, I'd bet my meagre savings that she was Ashkenazi like me. Jews identifying Jews: a long and honored schtick.

Ezra and I introduced ourselves and took seats across from her at the small reception desk, declining her offer of tea.

I shrugged out of Ezra's coat. "That's very kind, but you're already staying late to meet with us. We don't want to put you out further."

"Not at all," she said, stacking phone messages into a neat pile. "Booker and I go way back. He consults me from time to time but never with any notice." She shook her head, her expression fond.

Though Ezra dwarfed the slender chair he sat in, he didn't appear to make her anxious. Rosemary must have interacted with the London Spook Squad.

"If you're Maccabees," she said, "you already know that curing vampirism isn't possible. I spent years studying that from both a scientific and a medical standpoint before taking over my dad's business. I was also interested in folkloric mentions but never found anything that amounted to much."

"Did you ever come across anything about a fat double knot in a person's chest seen via blue flame magic in relation to curing vampirism?" I said.

Rosemary had been putting a package of sticky notes in the desk drawer but at my question she stilled, the color draining from her face. "Someone had that?"

"Why does my question upset you?" I countered gently.

She braced a hand on the desk like she was steadying herself. "The Spanish Inquisition, which brutally persecuted the Jews, lasted a few hundred years. It was finally suppressed in 1808 but reinstated in 1814, following an on-again, off-again pattern until it was abolished for good in 1834." She slid the drawer shut. "But the reason it was reinstated was largely because some alchemists claimed the missing ingredient to curing vampirism was the blood of a Jewish woman. Jews had been dispersed around the globe by this point, and many were now Conversos, people who'd been forced to convert." Rosemary looked off into the distance, her lips a flat line.

"What happened?" I prompted when she didn't continue.

"These alchemists teamed up with a Blue Flame who claimed that he could spot anyone with even a drop of Jewish blood because of a specific identifying mark. The exact nature of that mark has been lost to history, but they could have claimed it was anything. The mark itself doesn't matter."

"Just what people believed." I twisted my fingers in my lap tight enough to make them go white. "Accuse any woman of having a mark and she'd be killed for her blood."

Rosemary nodded. "The number of innocent women, especially Jewish ones, murdered for that evil agenda was horrific. If this is happening again..." She buried her face in her hands.

"People are being murdered," Ezra said, "but they haven't all been Jews or women."

"True," I said, "but one of the victims was Jewish, another was female, and all the murders involved a ritual purification using aspects of making meat kosher. Our suspected Yellow Flame is also Jewish. What if she knew about this event and wanted to resurrect that potion?"

"It feels like a stretch to me," Ezra said. "Like you said, she's a Yellow Flame, and there's no evidence that a Blue Flame is involved."

My phone rang. I glanced at the screen, about to hit dismiss when I saw it was from Darsh. Icy tentacles slid through my blood because he always texted, and I hit the answer button so hard that I bruised my thumb. "Darsh?"

A burst of static deafened me, and I flinched.

Ezra rose up from his chair, watching me intently.

"Darsh!"

He answered, but I couldn't make out what he was saying through the noise.

"I can't understand you," I said helplessly.

Another burst of static. "...operative...."

"Operative? What operative? Did something happen to Sach? What's going on?"

"Trap!"

With a final crackle, the line went dead, and the front window of Rosemary's business exploded. She screamed and ducked behind the desk.

A half dozen vampires raged through the gap, their heels crunching over broken glass.

Cherry roused herself to coldly assess the situation, but I'd already flagged a lanky male and wiry female duo on the left as the vamps who'd get to Rosemary first.

Ezra was already in the center of the action, fists swinging and fangs out.

Yelling at Rosemary to stay down, I grabbed a thick decorative glass item that looked like a tall genie's bottle and hefted it in my hand. Its bottom was weighted, which was perfect.

Holding the bottle by its neck, I smashed it into the side of the wiry female vamp's skull. She stumbled sideways and fell against a display of dishware, bringing the plates crashing to the ground.

My eyes didn't tingle, my skin remained normal, and I didn't feel any horns, but the craving to violently take these attackers down wasn't human. Sadly, I wasn't in Babel, and I couldn't blame an infusion of shedim magic. This urge was all me. Before the Crypt, I'd have agonized over it.

Now, I owned it—and used it.

The lanky male twisted away, my blow only grazing his shoulder. He shook off the hit, cracked his neck from side to side, and rushed me.

We grappled for the bottle, my legs intertwined with his in a back-and-forth dance, but he easily wrested it from my grip, brought it up high, and—

I slammed an uppercut into the underside of his jaw. He staggered, off-balance, and missed, the heavy glass narrowly whistling past my ear.

I jerseyed him by grabbing his shirt and pulling it over his head, a dirty fight move learned from watching 1980s Canadian NHL brawlers. My opponents were vamps, and I was a proud half-demon Canuck; gentlemanly warfare did not apply. I kept him pinned and blinded, driving my knee repeatedly into his face until he crumpled and the bottle fell from his hand.

Cherry was singing LL Cool J's "Mama Said Knock You Out" in my head. I appreciated the catchy soundtrack.

My original attacker grabbed me from behind, her fangs grazing my neck, but I seized a fistful of her blond hair and yanked her head away, straining to keep from being bitten.

The male recovered and drove a punch into my kidneys that made me flinch and escape the female's bite. Lucky me.

Exhaling with a hard grunt, I shoved my weight backward into my female attacker, giving myself the leverage to push off her and kick the lanky dude in the solar plexus, then I snatched up the discarded bottle and brought it down with such force on the crown of his head that the glass cracked in half. While he swayed dizzily, I slashed him across the neck.

He disintegrated into ash, dead.

Suddenly, my breath was knocked from my lungs, and pain blazed up my side. Doubling over, I pressed my hand to my waist. It came away sticky, a jagged piece of ceramic stabbed through my sweater into the same place where the male vamp had punched me. Luckily, when I examined my wound with my synesthete vision, I saw that the puncture had missed any vital organs. Lacerating muscle and fat still hurt like a bitch though.

Sneering, the female vamp pitched me across the room. The piece of the bottle that I held went flying and smashed against a wall, while I hit the corner of the desk with my shoulder, jostling the embedded shard in my side. I screamed.

Ezra glanced over, his eyes narrowing for a fraction of a second at me bleeding out, but he still had three vampires to take down.

One swiveled, his nostrils flaring at the scent of fresh blood.

I snapped my fingers at the eager beaver. "Eyes on your own work."

The hungry vamp's fangs elongated.

Ezra fisted the vamp's shirt and punched him. His blow went clean through the other vampire's skull, Ezra now elbow deep in the hole, blood and gore dripping off his arm.

Fuuuuck. I fanned the neck of my sweater out.

He winked and kicked the vampire's ashes aside.

Cherry nodded in approval, while I questioned my sanity in finding that hot.

The female vamp reached under the desk and pulled Rosemary out by one leg. The woman was screaming and crying, clawing uselessly at the ground with her fingernails.

My legs buckled and I slid down the wall onto my ass. The last thing I wanted to do was move, but I had to save Rosemary. I quickly scanned the room for the best weapon to end this once and for all.

Ezra grabbed one of his two remaining attackers and punched him in a series of fast taps until his nose cartilage caved in. Amazingly, that didn't deter his foe much. He leapt on Ezra, tackling him to the ground, the two of them rolling and wrestling for dominance, while the other bloodsucker that Ezra had been fighting dogpiled on top of them.

Thanks to my blood loss, I didn't have the energy to fashion a stake out of something. Besides, I was operating at about forty percent: any attack I launched would be easily brushed off.

Blood smeared along the ground, and the room stank of hot copper.

The eyes of our three remaining undead attackers took on a feverish sheen.

Ezra's had as well.

Cherry stopped singing.

There was no way I was getting up off the ground. I removed my sweater to stanch the blood, shifting my weight, and something dug into my butt cheek. Oh, hello. I'd forgotten about the wonderful gift from my past self in my back pocket.

The female vamp dropped to Rosemary's side, grabbed her arm, and sank her fangs into the woman's wrist.

I pulled the lighter out with a trembling hand, crawled to Rosemary, and flung myself over top of her with a hiss of pain. Placing my back against her chest, I dislodged the vampire from further feeding, putting myself squarely between the two.

I flicked the silver lighter open, its small flame jauntily popping up.

The vamp laughed, but it turned into an eerie cry when I found the groove and a column of fire shot out, engulfing her and knocking her backward into the legs of one of the two vamps that Ezra was fighting.

Whoosh. The second attacker burned like dry timber.

Moving off Rosemary, I snapped the lighter shut, watching the blaze consume the two of them with satisfaction. "Tikkun olam, motherfuckers."

Ezra dispatched the last vampire by snapping his neck.

Rosemary curled into a ball, still crying. She had a nasty wound on her wrist, but she wasn't bleeding or physically injured anywhere else. However, when I locked eyes with my ex, I decided that comforting her had to wait.

Ezra's shirt was slashed in several places, although the gashes raked across his arms and torso were already healing. The issue was that his pupils were enormous, he was covered in gore, and I was still bleeding like a stuck pig, despite the pressure I was applying with one hand. I couldn't tell how rational he was.

I flicked the lighter open again and readied my thumb on the groove.

"You're a little..." I circled my own eyes. "Gleamy," I said carefully.

"Planning to test how fire resistant I am?"

I shrugged, my breathing turning shallow at a fresh wave of pain. "Craving toasted marshmallows."

Ezra scrubbed a hand over his face, his eyes once more

clear and bright, and dropped onto his knees beside me. "Should I get you a stick?"

I raked a slow gaze over him, ascertaining that he wasn't a danger to us, then dropped the lighter. "Another time."

"Can't wait." He grabbed my sweater and wrapped it around the embedded shard, his hands pressing down on top of mine. His touch was gentle yet firm, but he looked like someone holding in a roar.

A shiver ran through me, Ezra's eyes snapping to mine. "Help Rosemary," I said. "I'll be okay."

He seemed doubtful, but he touched the woman's shoulder, speaking in a low, calm voice and asking for her help in stabilizing me.

Rosemary agreed in a shaky voice, which was good because it would keep her focused until we got her to a healer to help with the psychological trauma.

Ezra positioned me with my head in her lap and placed her hands on the fabric. "Press down on either side of the shard."

She obeyed him, her shallow breathing growing slowly steadier, though her gaze remained vacant. I rested a hand over hers, hoping the connection would pierce the fog of shock she was lost in.

"You couldn't have led with the fire when the vamps first arrived?" Ezra said, wiping blood off his hands so he could open his phone.

"I figured I'd try not to destroy the shop. I have this reputation for being reckless and impulsive that I'm really trying to fix." I gave a shuddery laugh but even that tiny effort made me shiver violently.

"That's it." Ezra's fangs elongated, and he bit down on his wrist, pressing it to my mouth. He wasn't attempting to turn me—he couldn't even if he tried. He only meant to provide a hit of healing blood.

Years ago, I'd been combing through the Maccabee archives and came across a record of an experiment in the 1970s involving a half shedim with reality-warping powers. They didn't come from being Eishei Kodesh, since the man was a Red Flame.

Seeing an opportunity to further their limited knowledge on infernals, the "researchers" (torturers) made a vampire bite their subject multiple times, but they never succeeded in changing him. The poor human died of multiple puncture wounds, but it *was* death and not undeath.

Regardless, I didn't dare ingest Ezra's blood. I'd never found evidence that vamp blood on an a half demon, even in a healing capacity, had an inverse effect, but I couldn't risk its magic properties pushing Cherry to some kind of extreme behavior. Especially not when I was wounded, exhausted, and in close proximity to a human. I clamped my lips shut and shook my head, flicking a pointed glance at Rosemary.

Ezra figured it out. "Right." He dialed a number. "I'll get you both to a healer."

"Not me." I was down to a whisper. The world swam around me dizzily, and my heart hammered so hard, I was positive I would break a rib. "Can't trust London HQ."

He brushed a hand over my forehead. "I know, Avi. Trust me, okay?"

"Aviva," I said.

"We'll discuss your name preferences later. For now, shut up, and save your energy for getting better."

I hated letting him have the last word, but I was too tired to do anything other than nod. *This round to Count von Cardoso*, the announcer voice in my head proclaimed. Yeah, well Queen AF was down, but she sure as hell wasn't out.

Chapter 22

Healers could play all the meditative instrumental music in the world, no amount of flute was soothing enough to overcome the certainty that my insides were being twisted, rearranged, and slotted back into place with hot pokers.

I pounded a fist on the massage table, my naked torso covered in sweat, and gritted my teeth. "Motherfucker."

"Almost done, duckie," the matronly Yellow Flame said.

She'd better be. The strain of keeping Cherry from punching her in the throat was only slightly less exhausting than undergoing this treatment.

There was a sharp jolt on my left side—like I was a pinball machine on tilt and the healer had knocked her hip into me to dislodge the ball.

"You're all sorted now." Rubbing her neck, she got up off her stool. "I'll go see how your friend is doing." She meant Rosemary. Ezra had bundled us into the healer's car and stayed behind to deal with the mess at the showroom.

"Thank you." I sat up gingerly.

Michael once mentioned that the strange thing about

childbirth was that the second a baby was out, that was it painwise. It didn't gradually die away like a stomachache or a headache. It was the same with being treated by a healer. Once they were done, that was it. I was pain free, but it always took my brain a few moments to be convinced of that.

I took a fast shower in the bathroom connected to the clinic's treatment room and put on the sweatsuit that the healer had provided me with since my poor clothes were ruined. Rubbing condensation off the mirror, I checked to see how awful I looked. My popcorn white skin and strained expression were not improved by an outfit where the shoulders were too baggy for my frame yet too tight across the boobs and butt. Somewhere out there was a body made for these sweats, but sadly, the clothes were stuck with me in this darkest timeline.

I turned my phone on to check if Ezra had contacted me. He hadn't. Nor had Sachie or Darsh.

My mother had, though. Or rather, Director Fleischer had. Eight increasingly angry texts, the final reading *Check in now, Operative!*

I winced. Being reduced to my job title was worse than being called on the carpet when I was a kid with my mother using my full name. I phoned her back on an encrypted line since it was easier to inject contrition into my voice that way than via text. "Hi, Mi—"

She ripped into me about upsetting Director Harrison and involving a civilian in a vamp attack.

I held the phone away from my ear until she'd finished yelling. "May I speak now?"

"I put you on that team to keep Cardoso in check, not go stampeding with him like two bulls in a china shop."

"Okay, well, that saying's been disproved—" At her sharp inhale, I skipped ahead. "If we're being technical, you put me on the team to spy on him and test my leadership. Ezra has carte blanche. Take it up with Council Member Pederson, not me. We presented ourselves as per protocol, and if anyone has reason to be pissed off, it's me, because Maccabee procedure is not supposed to involve operatives setting traps for other operatives." My voice had risen. I checked myself and tossed my hair—like my mother could see it.

"Are you fucking kidding me?"

I fumbled the phone. I could count the number of times my mother had dropped an f-bomb on one hand and have four fingers left over. She certainly hadn't said it in her official capacity. "I wish I was."

"Booker is a fourth-generation Maccabee," she said musingly, already pushing away her anger to sift through all the angles of this problem. It was part of her effectiveness as a director. "He's legacy. He mustn't have known."

I was legacy too, yet Michael had never crowed about my stature that way. She'd usually brought it up as incentive not to make her look bad. "Well, only he and his assistant could say where we were going. Six vamps showed up at that civilian's shop, and something's happened to Sach and Darsh on their assignment. We can't get hold of them or track them, so forgive me if I don't give a shit about legacy."

"Three of my operatives in two different attacks?" I could feel her mind whirring. "Come home, Aviva. I'm pulling you out."

"Don't order me home like I'm a child," I said coldly. "We survived the attack and protected the civilian. I'm not leaving until my friends show up."

"I'm not worried about you," she said. At her matter-of-fact admission, my shoulders dropped down from my ears. "This is a politically delicate situation. Booker wants you gone. As a legacy and a director, he has the clout to retract Ezra's carte blanche."

There went my shoulders again. "If we weren't getting close to finding the killers, we wouldn't have been attacked."

Michael was silent for a moment. "I'll placate Booker. If the London office is aiding or abetting these killers in any way, root out who's involved. I want constant updates."

I'd successfully expressed my argument to Michael and gotten the director—gotten my mother—to throw all her power behind my cause. I did my happy dance around the room, the one that was all sultry hips and sharp shoulder struts accompanied by Nina Simone's version of "Feeling Good" playing in my head. "You'll get all the updates. Thank you."

"You're welcome. And Aviva?"

"Yes?"

"Watch your back." On that warm and fuzzy note, my mother hung up.

I tried my friends again, but like the first two attempts in the taxi and here at the clinic, neither of them answered. Powering my cell down so it couldn't be tracked, I bowed my head.

My friends were trained operatives, and they were with each other. They'd be fine.

They had to be.

Beyond those fears, the idea that London HQ might be compromised, since only Director Harrison and his assistant were aware of our visit to Rosemary, turned my stomach into a hard lump. Not that they were necessarily traitors; neither had any reason to believe our visit had to be kept secret. However, their involvement wasn't off the table either.

Now it was Michael's problem too. Heh.

Yawning, I transferred my belongings to the pockets of my sweatpants and went to find Rosemary. Seeing to her safety was something actionable that let me feel in control. I wandered down the corridor, pressing my ear to a couple of closed doors but unable to hear if she was behind them. I peeked in the waiting area, but no one was there, so I headed the other way, finding her in a small lounge with a pot of untouched tea in front of her and a woman who had to be her sister sitting holding her hand.

The night sky was brightening with pre-dawn gold.

"How are you doing?" I said.

"I'm a Trad," she said in bewilderment. "A Trad."

Okay, she was still, understandably, somewhat stunned, but she was as fine as she could be if a healer had set her up here. I poured her a cup of steaming tea, stirred in an enormous spoonful of sugar, and gently pressed it into her hands.

"Drink this." I took a chocolate digestive cookie from the plate, put it on a napkin, and set it in front of her. "And have a biscuit."

"Thank you for saving Rosie," the other woman said. "I'm her sister, Lily."

"It was the least I could do given we brought this trouble to her door." I folded the sleeves of the sweatshirt over my hands, my cheeks growing hot.

"That wasn't you," Rosemary said in a low, fierce voice.

Lily poured another cup of tea and set it in front of me. "You look like you could use this too, luv."

I took a sip, then nibbled on a cookie. "Until we have the name of the person who sent the vamps after us, do you have somewhere safe you could go for a few days? I don't think you're in danger," I said when Rosemary paled, "but let's not take any chances."

"We'll go to the place in Brighton," Lily said. "I can get a few days off."

I swallowed my bite of cookie. "Is that somewhere

associated with you two?"

She shook her head. "No one will look for us there."

"Pay in cash and don't give your real names, if possible," I said.

"What about my store?" Rosemary seemed to be speaking past my shoulder.

For a second I thought she didn't want to make eye contact.

"The glass and lock have been replaced." Ezra strode forward, now wearing his trench coat, which was once more buttoned up so that the bloody vamp didn't terrify the humans. That man was going through shirts like crazy. He dropped a set of keys in Rosemary's hand, along with a card. "I swept up best I could, but a lot of merchandise was broken in the fight. Once you've estimated the damage, call the man on that card. He's my banker, and I've already authorized him to cover the full amount."

Rosemary blinked at him. "I have insurance."

"Which could take months to pay out if they even do. Vamp attacks are hard to get compensation for," he said. "For now, don't think about it. And call your employees. Tell them to take a week off. I'll cover their wages. You should be fine to return after that."

Rosemary stood up and gave Ezra a hug, though Lily's gratitude, while heartfelt, was said from several feet away.

My saint of a co-leader protested that it was nothing, and I bit into my second cookie hard enough to snap it. Honestly, I admired Ezra for the compassion he showed people, but why hadn't he shown any to me?

"Promise me you won't contact Director Harrison," Ezra said.

"Booker would never hurt me," Rosemary said. "We've been friends for years."

"Of course not," he lied smoothly, "but someone was able to find us."

"Oooh." Lily clapped her hands together. "His office was likely bugged."

"Right." The tension in Rosemary's shoulders eased.

I hoped that these Trad sisters never faced anything to upset their innocent worldview again.

After another round of thank-yous to both of us, the women left.

Ezra dropped into the chair and snagged a cookie.

"Don't ascribe any nobility to you, huh?" I said. "That rule is just personal to me then, is it, Mr. I'll-Pay-For-Everything?"

"There was always a different set of rules for you, Aviva," he said in a tone I couldn't decipher.

"Don't I feel special?" I muttered, though it didn't have any heat to it, because he'd sighed deeply, throwing his head back and massaging his neck.

I reached for him but dropped my hand in my lap. I wasn't his person that way anymore. "Have you stopped for even a second yet?"

"Messes to clean, rats to flush out," he said. "There's simply never enough time."

I snorted. "Have you gotten hold of Sachie or Darsh?"

He shook his head. "Silas can't find them either. He got their last pinged location in downtown Manchester, but after that it's a mystery."

My fears about their safety flared up like a sore tooth that I'd poked with my tongue. In situations like this, I was trained to compartmentalize and focus on the mission, but I was barely succeeding. "Is it safe to contact Silas? Are we all being tracked somehow?"

"We have an encrypted communication channel. It's fine." He stood up. "Right now, you and I need to go to ground and figure out what the fuck happened."

I took one more swallow of hot, strong tea and pushed to my feet. "Sounds like a plan."

Chapter 23

When Ezra said we were going to ground, I expected a shabby hotel with staff who were either uninterested in us or open to bribery to forget we were there, not a townhouse on a quiet traffic-free cobblestoned street in one of the most prestigious areas of London.

We'd taken the tube, Ezra wearing a baseball cap whose brim he'd pulled low and me with the hood of my sweatshirt pulled up. We kept our distance from each other on the journey over, doing our best to avoid CCTV cameras.

Some of the passengers threw nervous glances Ezra's way on the Tube, but he kept his body relaxed and scrolled on his phone and no one panicked.

"These homes are amazing," I said, openly rubbernecking while I followed Ezra.

"They're mews houses." He punched in the code on a red front door. "They were originally built as stables and the servants lived above." That explained why the garage door looked like it had been lifted from a barn.

"And you happen to have one handy as a safehouse, why, m'lord?" I shifted the bag of groceries I'd bought at the Tesco Express on our way over onto my other hip. It also held a bottle of wine with my name on it. The second the clock struck noon, I was cracking that puppy.

Ezra glanced around one last time, opened the door, and escorted me inside. He disarmed the alarm. "It belongs to Orly's family."

He had the entry and security codes to this place, did he?

"Oh," I said tightly and toed out of my runners and socks. Noon was really only a suggestion for wine anyway. Why wait? The cool tile under my throbbing feet was heavenly; the certainty that he and Orly were more than friends was less enjoyable. "Is she coming back? I don't want her to get in any trouble or inconvenience her." Whatever my complex emotions toward Orly, I genuinely didn't want her hurt.

"She has a hotel she prefers when she's in town." Ezra moved through the open concept kitchen and living room, closing curtains and turning on lamps. "Her family only uses this place in the summer. We'll be fine."

"Did you want to shower before we debrief?" I placed the bag on the counter and put the groceries, including synthetic blood, in the fridge. I'd gotten enough supplies for both of us for a few days, though I'd bought sandwiches and prepackaged food because I wasn't up to cooking.

"Yes. I'm going to nap, as should you. Neither of us is in any condition to keep going right now."

"I'll take the sofa. Is there a blanket and pillow I could use?"

"There's a guest room." He strode off, discarding his coat on a chair with an ease born of familiarity.

The bed was comfy, and my eyes were already fluttering shut by the time my head hit the pillow, which spared me listening for the sound of the shower or imagining Ezra's naked body streaming with rivulets of water, clouds of steam billowing around him.

Too bad my stupid imagination went into overdrive while I slept because I woke up flushed, tangled in the sheets, and super horny.

I considered getting myself off for a split second, but no matter how quiet I was, he'd hear me.

Which made me consider it for slightly longer.

Bad, bad idea.

Now profoundly irritated, I beelined for the fridge, unscrewed the wine bottle (only the classiest of vintages for moi), and poured myself a healthy slug. I wouldn't say it was fruity or plummy, but it was alcohol, which was good enough for me.

My stomach rumbled, and I checked the time on the stove. I'd been asleep for seven hours. I brought my wine over to the mid-century modern cream sofa along with a container of tabbouleh and some crisps. Dinner of champions.

Ezra padded out wearing jeans and a sweater, his feet bare, and his black curls messy. He cracked the cap on a pint of synthetic blood and downed it in one go before bringing another serving to the living room in a beer glass.

I held up my glass of wine. "L'chaim."

He clinked his second pint against my glass, choosing a comfortable chair across from me. "Do you think Darsh and Sachie were caught in a trap, or did he get a heads-up that the vamps were coming for us and the call was a warning?"

"Both." Tucking my leg under me, I wolfed down a couple of forkfuls of tabbouleh, even though thinking about my friends made my stomach hurt. However, with the curtains drawn tight and the lamps throwing honeyed pools of light on the white walls and cream furniture, it was almost cozy enough in here to forget the shitstorm we were caught in.

"They're okay," Ezra said.

"Are any of us?" I dug my fork into the container for more tabbouleh. "It's infuriating that every new piece of information seems to reinforce that the killers are creating a cure for vampirism. What else would they use the blood, eyes, and heart for if not this bullshit potion?"

He swirled the blood in his pint glass around. "Rosemary's comment about a Blue Flame being able to identify Jewish women for their blood makes me lean toward this all being a con to sell snake oil to the highest bidder. The ritual is the smoke and mirrors."

"Con or not, it won't stop a war if vamps learn of it."

"I know." He frowned. "How strongly do you believe that our killers are connected to Maccabees, given the attacks and Darsh's phone call?"

"Silas would have mentioned in Dr. Metaxas's profile if she had ties to the group," I said, licked salt from the crisps off my finger. "But the vamp—"

"Could be an operative. I agree. He'd have the resources to track anyone asking questions." Ezra placed his glass on a coaster. "How many British Maccabees can there be? A dozen tops?"

"Narrowed down by Manchester?" I took another bite of tabbouleh, barely chewing before I swallowed. "I'd be amazed if we end up with more than one name. Do you think that's what Sach and Darsh learned? That they were attacked because they sussed out this vamp is an operative? But why go after us?"

"He didn't want us confirming motive? Let's loop in Silas. We'll be trackable for a few minutes but I'm willing to risk it." Ezra turned on his phone and typed a message.

Once I'd finished eating and disposed of the empty containers, I wandered around the living room getting a sense of the owners. There were photos of various family members, some candid, others more formal. The books on the shelves were a mix of literary fiction in Spanish and English, though there were also some dog-eared economic texts and anatomy books. Guess the whole family were underachievers.

Ezra shut his phone down once more and crossed to the stove to set the timer. "Silas will have an answer for us in half an hour," he clarified at my puzzled look.

I stopped in front of a painting of a nude woman reclining on a chaise longue with her head resting on her hands, gazing directly at the viewer. I couldn't look away from the stark eroticism of the image: her pale plumpness, the blush on her cheeks, her expression of languid satisfaction.

"It's beautiful, isn't it?" Ezra murmured from beside me.

"Who painted it?"

"Goya."

I wasn't a huge art connoisseur, but I recognized the name of a master when I heard it. I gogged. "This is an original Goya? Just hanging here?"

Ezra chuckled, the sound sliding through me like syrup. "That's what paintings generally do."

"You know what I mean." I glared at him and returned to the sofa, refilling my wineglass. I twisted around to check the timer, but there were still twenty-six minutes left until our check-in with Silas. The silence was stifling, and I wasn't up to making conversation. "Put on some music, would you? There's a stereo on the counter under the microwave."

It was such a perfectly vintage-looking player that it had to be modern and extremely expensive, but I'd have taken a crackly transistor radio so long as the two of us didn't have to talk.

The room filled with a sultry version of "It's a Man's Man's Man's World" with a Middle Eastern vibe to both the melody and the way the female singer performed it.

"This okay?" Ezra said. "I left it on the programmed playlist."

"It's wild. I really like it."

He sat back down, both of us checking the timer more often than necessary. I guess he was as uncomfortable with me being in his girlfriend's family's place as I was being here.

My second glass of wine and three songs later, I was feeling no pain. So what if we were stuck here for another nine minutes until Silas got back to us? I swayed, my eyes closed, grooving to the woman's magnetic voice as she sang in a mix of Arabic and English.

The next song hit the ground running with a funky Arabic drum beat with hip hop stylings and horns recalling carefree summer nights. I was totally down for it.

Until she sang the first line. The title of the song. "I Put a Spell on You."

I stiffened, digging grooves into the cushions with my fingernails.

Ezra was bobbing his head to it. "This is a great cover."

As the melody of the song drifted through the air, memories flooded back to me like a tidal wave crashing onto the shore. Did he even remember this was the song playing when he first kissed me? Or was I the only one stuck in the past, unable to wipe away that first brush of his lips against mine and how our bodies molded together in perfect harmony?

I'd spent so long trying to forget him, trying to forget the way he made me feel. Now he was sitting there, so close to me, yet a million miles away, forcing me to confront those emotions once again. My disappointment and dread were almost suffocating.

"Yeah. It's great." I stomped over to the stereo and snapped it off, then dumped my glass in the sink. When I turned, he was a foot away facing me, his back to the quartz island. "Could you wear a bell or something?" I shoved at him to move.

Walls were more accommodating.

"Why are you so pissed off?" he said. "You were the one who set the no history rule."

"Which you broke about ten minutes into our charming reunion, but it's fine. I agree this isn't the place for those types of memories."

"What the hell are you talking about?" He wrinkled his brow.

I shoved him again, just as uselessly. Was he really going to make me spell it out? "Orly? Your girlfriend?"

He unfurled a slow, dangerous smile. "You think she's my girlfriend?"

"Lover. Whatever." I gave up trying to move him and extricated myself instead, but he wasn't having any of that either, smoothly stepping sideways to block me. I planted my hands on my hips. "I saw how you looked at her."

He tilted his head. "How?"

I dropped my gaze to my feet. "Don't do this."

He tipped up my chin with one finger. "Would it help if I said that I wanted Darsh's jacket off you because so long as you smelled like him, I was a breath away from ripping his head off and branding you?"

I viciously uprooted the tender stalk of hope out of my chest and smacked his hand away. The sting of my flesh on his was a poor substitute for staking him. How dare he act possessive? Especially when the exact nature of him moving on was documented in thousands of articles and social media photos? "That doesn't make it better, asshole."

"You think I don't know that?"

I swallowed. My heart was in my throat and my breath was stalled out somewhere before my lungs. I gripped the sink edge behind my back.

The apex predator was polite enough not to mention my imminent cardiac arrest.

My stomach had grown rubber bands that were being pulled taut under his caveman admission. "You left me, remember?"

"Leaving" was an action verb. Being left was also an action, despite what grammatists said, because spending months picking up the pieces of your shattered heart and finding the energy to fake functioning like a normal human required a fuckton of active effort.

"I haven't forgotten." That wasn't an apology, but it did sound a little tormented, and his gaze flicked to my mouth, his eyes heated with desire.

I felt a surge of satisfaction. Poisonous satisfaction, but life wasn't perfect. The smart thing to do would be to ask him why he'd done it. Pour his rejection like cold water over my flushed skin so it didn't spark and catch fire from the charge flowing between us. If I could switch the trajectory of the two of us moving achingly slowly closer so I'd brush past him instead of back into his arms, that would be good too.

"Orly," I prompted.

"She's my cousin. I said so when I introduced her."

"Nuh-uh. You introduced her as Orly Attias. Full stop."

"Did I?" His look of confusion looked so fake. "After my parents were turned, my mother's relationship with her sister became strained, but once she...died, and my father moved us to Babel, my aunt pestered him until he let me spend time with her family in Israel. Orly is like a sister who I love more than anyone, but that's it."

Whoops. I sent up a silent apology for visualizing porny situations involving the two of them.

"No girlfriend," he said. "No lover." He reached out his hand, tentatively brushing it against my side. It was a ghost of a touch, and I briefly closed my eyes with a shiver. The sensation was as acute as if he'd branded the swirls of his fingertips on my skin. "You?"

The louder my brain screamed "Danger!" the hotter a spiral of desire wound tight inside me. Logic was a losing battle against Cherry Bomb's interest and my betraying body's reaction.

Why hadn't I listened to Sachie and found a nice guy that I could trot out now? I opened my mouth to lie about the lovely man from accounting I was seeing, or to tell Ezra I had stage six leprosy with a side dose of the clap. Anything that would stop this madness.

Ezra edged his face close to mine. There was no mask. His expression was unfettered, vulnerable.

Honest in its longing.

It swept every barrier away, leaving me with nothing but honesty as well.

I shook my head. "There's no one."

"One chance to walk away," he murmured.

One chance to consume and be consumed.

I rose onto tiptoe and nipped his bottom lip.

The floodgates tore open, his mouth punishing mine, hard, fast, and hungry. I pushed up against him, raking my nails along the nape of his neck, hoping to slash him open.

I also longed to relearn his new, more muscular physique and map every inch of him, preferably with my tongue, and leave him desperate.

His fingers dug into my hair, but his touch went deeper

than that. It went to parts of me that no one else had ever reached. That I'd forgotten were there.

Ezra snaked his arm around my waist and hauled me against his rock-hard chest, changing the angle of the kiss, deepening it, demanding more. He groaned, tangling his tongue with mine.

When he kissed me six years ago, he'd been a nice guy with sweet kisses and smooth skin.

He wasn't a nice guy now.

And there was nothing sweet about this kiss. It was electric, dirty, messy—a declaration of war. I scraped my fingers up the ridges of his abs, along dark ink. His beard rasped the skin under my jaw when he sucked and nipped there.

Ezra slammed me up against the cabinets, my hands pinned above my head. The edge of a rounded handle dug into my shoulder and I shifted.

He pulled back, his eyes seeking mine. "Are you okay?"

In my mind Cherry howled and I joined in, a lament of pain and lust and fury. "No," I hissed, and launched myself at him. The deeper I drowned in his kiss, the more I marked him with my nails and lips and teeth. I wanted to leave claw marks in his soul like a painter signing their masterpiece.

My sweatshirt rode up, and when he splayed his hand on my bare skin, I gasped, all my nerve endings suddenly concentrated in that one spot.

I wedged my leg between his, and he ground against me with a moan that left no doubt he was mine for the taking.

All I had to do was ask.

I was the human, and he was the vampire, so why did I feel like I'd found myself standing in the hot blaze of the midday sun about to burst into flame leaving nothing behind but ash?

I shoved him away from me.

His hair was messy, his shirt untucked and half-unbuttoned, and his pupils were wide and drugged out. He absently ran his thumb over one of the scratch marks I'd given him.

But his wounds were already healing.

The oven timer went off in the loaded silence and I jumped. "You should…" I cleared the huskiness out of my throat. "Call Silas."

"Yeah." Ezra ran a hand over his hair and smoothed down his shirt.

I curled my hands into fists, so I didn't reach for him, but Ezra tracked the movement.

He stepped back, once, then again, like he was fighting against a magnetic pull, and opened his mouth.

I held up a hand. "Apologize and die," I growled.

His lips quirked up in the faintest smirk, then he found his phone and turned it on to an insistent ringing. "Silas? Yeah. I'm here." Ezra listened for a moment while I got a drink of water, watching his expression turn grimmer and grimmer. "Got it." He disconnected. "There's been another murder."

Chapter 24

Today was Saturday; it hadn't even been a week since Kyle was killed. Had we accelerated the murderers' timeline by investigating?

Sachie and Darsh were still unaccounted for. I'd have hied off to Manchester to look for them, but I had to examine the new corpse with my synesthete vision, so I booked a ticket on the last express train to Amsterdam. I'd be harder to track by rail.

Ezra had Silas send our missing teammates an encrypted text with the address of Orly's mews house before he joined us via Babel. The two of them would monitor the situation in addition to figuring out where my friends' tattoo-finding mission had gone tits up.

Ezra was reluctant to let me go off on my own, but I insisted that he stay here. Did I want my friends to see a familiar face when they showed up? Yes.

Did I need a body of water between us after that kiss? Also yes.

Our goodbye was perfunctory, even if my lips were still puffy. Since anyone who'd profiled me would be familiar with my love of stylish business wear, I left on the sweats

I'd gotten from the healer, borrowed an old fleece jacket that belonged to Ezra's aunt, and wore no makeup, determined to be as nondescript as possible.

Silas had only learned of the murder because he'd coded software monitoring police channels around the world for specific keywords and gotten this hit. He didn't have any details, but it was better to experience this going in cold and making my own determinations.

Five hours later I was at the morgue at Netherlands HQ.

Instead of presenting myself to the director in Amsterdam and possibly getting another lecture about carte blanche and proper procedure, I called a former colleague of mine who'd moved to the city when he got married, apologizing for the late hour.

Jacob was a rule-happy operative, which worked in my favor because no one would suspect him of doing something sneaky like giving me access to the morgue without any record. Our acquaintanceship wasn't strong enough to buy me any favors, but he and Sach had dated for a while and remained friends. When I explained in confidence that she was missing, that I suspected the Maccabees to have a mole, and that solving this murder was key to it all, he stepped up to the plate without hesitation and got me in undetected.

It was a lot harder seeing this woman's corpse than it had been seeing Kyle's because the woman was close to my age. Her dark hair framed a narrow face with empty eye sockets the same pale color of natural candle wax.

Had she stared death in the face or had it snuck up on her? While I despised her killers for robbing her of life, I hated Dr. Metaxas almost as much for purifying this woman with her yellow flame magic. This woman's loved ones should have been allowed to learn if she'd fought back, but any traces of that, along with any possible skin or hair from her attackers, were cleansed away.

The fat blue double knot in her upper chest, however, was clear as day. I ghosted a gloved finger over the top, as perplexed and frustrated as the first time I'd seen one. It wasn't a coincidence that I'd seen the magic mark on two victims, but what did it indicate?

And did we also have to look for a Blue Flame, since neither Metaxas nor the vampire operative could see the mark?

Did we have *three* serial killers working together? That seemed outlandish.

I rubbed the goose bumps on my arm; the cool temperature in the morgue had nothing on the grind of this case. "Who was she?"

Jacob flipped through her chart, frowning. "A real piece of work. Rie Bleeker. She's got a rap sheet a mile long."

I did a double take. "You must be mistaken."

He handed me the chart, and I whistled. Rie had packed a lot of activity into her twenty-eight years. Two arrests for aggravated assault, one for being drunk and disorderly, and her most recent charge: a string of home invasions.

So much for our theory that the killers were harvesting goodness for their bogus cure. Even if this was all a con to start a war between vamps and humans, they wouldn't select someone with a rap sheet.

I dropped the chart hard enough to send some of the papers flying. Murder number six and we were back to zero?

Jacob picked up the fallen pages. "She didn't deserve to die this way. Poor woman. She was born with a disadvantage."

"What do you mean?"

"Look at this photo." The picture in the file had been taken on a CCTV camera when Rie was still alive. She had numerous tattoos, none of which appeared on her body now because of the ritual cleansing. He tapped the ink in question, a small bomb on Rie's wrist. "That's a gang tat," he said. "The leader likes to brag he's an infernal and that he only recruits people with shedim blood."

The victims were half-shedim?

"Wh-what?" I caught myself from feeling the back of my skull. It's not as if Jacob labeling Rie half-shedim had caused my shifting shadows to pop up above my head like a giant arrow pointing down at me.

Part of me wanted to lash out, overturn tables, and fling surgical instruments, and another part wanted to curl up in a corner and forget I'd ever heard this. Sadly, I couldn't do either, because I was chilled down to the marrow of my bones, the air knocked from my lungs.

I pressed my hands to the sides of my chest and dragged in a breath, looking down like I had to watch my torso inflate to prove I was getting oxygen.

My inhale turned into a choked cough. I'd still been using my synesthete vision, which is the only reason I saw the blue double knot in the center of my chest, linked to shifting shadows swimming down from my head.

I gasped and raced for the closest bathroom, slamming and locking the door with shaking hands. Holy fuck! I had a double knot?

I heard my mother's logical voice. *Break it down, Aviva. Deal with one part at a time.*

I'd checked the back of Rie's head in my cursory examination of her corpse, but, like Kyle, there were no shifting shadows in her hindbrain. I'd have clocked that immediately.

Jacob knocked on the door. "Aviva, are you all right?"

"One moment," I squeaked. I bunched up my shirt in my fist and pulled it away, like that would help get air through my tight rib cage and into my lungs.

Why were my shadows moving down to form the double knot in my chest? I'd obviously examined myself with my magic sight, both calmly and when injured, but apparently never when I'd experienced such a sudden and profound mix of shock and fear. That was the only explanation I could come up with.

Shock and fear, however, were precisely what all the victims would have felt in their final moments. They were also emotions that people experienced in the center of their chests.

I'd seen other murder victims though. Emotions didn't transcend death to be seen with my blue flame vision, nor did fear in life manifest as a double knot. It was a dot or maybe a swathe of blue. I narrowed my eyes. However, that was with Eishei Kodesh magic. I had no evidence for how shedim magic processed lethal attacks.

Until now.

I exhaled hard. I'd gotten this all so wrong. I didn't see my shadows because my blue flame magic perceived being an infernal as a weakness. I saw them because my *shedim* magic allowed me to see evidence of my demon side.

The same magic that allowed me to see the knot, triggered by a deadly attack on my shedim half. It didn't have to be physical. Look at me. The shock and terror of this revelation had been enough.

When our demon part came under attack, in the most terrifying, shocking situation, it all coalesced in the shifting shadows migrating and twisting up into the double blue knot.

I finally had the piece of the puzzle I'd been seeking, and all I wanted to do was throw it away and pretend it didn't fit.

I, also, now had a large problem because I'd been telling everyone about the double knots. I shook my head and splashed some cold water on my face before returning to the morgue. I'd deal with that later, along with whether or not the killers knew about me.

Speaking of those two monsters, I ruled out the vampire Maccabee as being the one who'd identified these infernals. He wasn't a half shedim because infernals couldn't be turned. Nor was any Blue Flame involved. Dr. Metaxas was our culprit. She'd seen their shifting shadows with her shedim magic and killed her own kind.

Our kind.

"Here." Jacob walked into the morgue with a glass of water. I hadn't even noticed his absence. "You look pale."

"I was looking at how pieces of Rie were carved away. It's..." I glanced at her magic double knot again and grabbed the glass, drinking quickly to prevent a moan from escaping. "Where does this infernal gang hang out?"

Jacob gave me the name of a motorcycle shop but warned me against going there on my own, especially now in the middle of the night.

"I won't," I promised. I'd have Cherry. And yes, I was still aware she was me, but I'd have said anything to get out of there. Besides, I didn't plan to ask questions or cause trouble.

The neighborhood where the bike shop was located wasn't seedy, but with its tightly locked-up businesses, no pedestrians, and guys on big fuck-off hogs roaring through the streets, it wasn't on the tourist circuit either.

I hid in the shadows down the street from the shop, watching the comings and goings of the crew. The leader was a pompous, loud-mouthed man with a shock of red hair. He wasn't a half shedim and neither were any others of his crew, save one: a jittery older teen with hunched shoulders who was at the others' beck and call. He was the only one with the blue shifting shadows at the back of his head like I had.

At one point, the leader sent him off on some errand, and the teen headed down the block. When he reached the corner where I'd hidden, I stepped out and knocked into him, giving a startled cry and grabbing his arm to steady myself.

Pressing through any embarrassment that I'd expected some kind of instant connection with this stranger, I visualized my shedim magic flowing into him. I'd never done that before, and Cherry perked up in interest. There was a quick, gentle buzz between my palm and his arm, then it turned sharp like a sweater snagged on a nail.

I laughed weakly and dropped my hand. "Electric shock. Sorry."

He looked at me oddly but muttered that he was sorry to have frightened me. He had only a regular blue dot in his chest that was already fading, but no double knot. Maybe his shedim magic recognized mine and understood that it wasn't a threat?

I was disappointed that I hadn't been able to re-create the double knot in him, though I was sure my hypothesis on the matter was correct.

Regardless, when he walked away, I saw that the blue shifting shadows at the back of his head had been joined by a white pulsing dot. It reminded me of the kill spot I saw on full shedim.

Did I have one? I'd never seen it, but it made sense, right? What would happen to me if I was stabbed in the back of my head?

The kill spot in full shedim was located all over their bodies, making it tougher to determine where to aim. Apparently, we were different.

Were we the "easier to kill" progeny?

I involuntarily stepped backward, but there was no

amount of space that could protect me from these revelations.

There was no point going to the crime scene. Ezra could use his carte blanche to get the photos, but as every site looked the same, I didn't expect this one to be different. I checked into a cheap hotel for a few hours' sleep, hoping to be struck with inspiration on how to tell the others without outing myself.

Ezra knew about my blue shifting shadows, and he was too smart not to immediately catch on. He was so invested in this case that I didn't trust that he'd keep my secret about Cherry Bomb if I brought up the topic of infernals without a plausible reason for how I'd made the leap from a blue double knot to shedim genetics. The others would question my findings, and in the interests of expediting the investigation, Ezra would answer them if I wouldn't.

I dragged in a breath through my tight rib cage, turned off the light, and tried to nap. When the alarm went off, I was groggy and no closer to how to share this news. I proceeded directly to the train station and ate a shitty overpriced breakfast on board that left me queasy. Though that might have been because someone was killing my kind, Sachie's and Darsh's voice mails were full, and Ezra hadn't contacted me to say they'd shown up.

My phone died before I could call Ezra. A blessing in disguise.

Obsessing over my friends wouldn't help. I borrowed a pen and wrote down on a napkin everything about these murders. The vics were killed via vamp bite and Claret was administered to speed up the exsanguination. But the murderers took an enormous risk with the length of the ritual and leaving the corpses in the woods.

Did they honestly believe that half shedim required purification before their blood, eyes, and heart were ground into a ghastly potion? They were using them to rid the world of vampires, for fuck's sake, not cure cancer.

It was bad enough that these poor people were killed for a quirk of birth that they had no control over. I mean, it was a miracle any of my kind were born in the first place, but to still be seen as dirty or abominable?

My eyes tingled, and I hurriedly turned my face to the window until I'd calmed myself down enough to remain human in appearance.

It was only in appearance, however, because I wanted an eye for an eye, and to rip those puppies from the murderers' skulls with my bare hands.

The train slowed down, now approaching the station, and people gathered up their belongings. I drummed my fingers on the plastic armrest, impatient to get back and praying that Sachie and Darsh had shown up.

At least traffic was light on this Sunday morning, and I got back to Orly's townhouse reasonably quickly.

The front door was opened before I could knock, Ezra blocking my way. His eyes were wild, and he held himself rigidly, his teeth audibly grinding together.

"What's happened?" I said frantically.

He reached out and touched my cheek tentatively, his brow wrinkling, before he crushed me to him in a hug that knocked the air from my lungs.

"Can't. Breathe." I bashed him on the shoulder a few times until he let go, then I grabbed his arm. "They're dead, aren't they?"

It took him a moment, but he shook his head. "They're here. Sleeping."

I closed my eyes against a surge of relief that left me weak-kneed. "Then what was with that weird behavior?"

"I thought *you* were dead," he growled.

"Why?"

"You didn't check in and we couldn't trace you—" He

threw up his hands with a stream of Spanish cursing, a lot of jabby fingers my way, and what I guessed were some musings about my intelligence or lack of self-preservation.

I grinned at him, the first moment of lightness I'd experienced since my grim realization about the victims. "You were worried about me."

He crossed his arms. "You were reckless. This isn't how you co-lead a team."

My grin faded. First, he was so jealous he could have ripped Darsh's head off over a jacket, now he couldn't admit to worrying about me, even as a team member? I was done with him blowing hot and cold. I darted my tongue over my lips, trying to wash away exactly how hot he'd gotten, and stomped past him, kicking off my shoes.

"My phone died. Now, if you're done your performance review, then I'm going to see my friends and update my team with my findings." I'm sure I'd come up with some plausible explanation.

I strode into the living room.

Sachie and Darsh were crashed out on opposite ends of a sofa, sharing a blanket. She had an ugly bruise along her jaw, and her left arm was in a cast. Resisting the urge to fling myself on top of them and smother them with hugs, since they'd likely kill me when they woke before I could identify myself, I crouched by my bestie—out of throat-grabbing range.

"I have approximately 337 new gray hairs because of you," I said, sloughing my rage at Ezra to focus on this reunion. "Wait and see how I sign your cast."

She chuckled, turning it into a weird yawn partway through, and opened her eyes. "I want you to bedazzle the damn thing. Dumb Trad doctor almost amputated my arm instead of setting it. I am not cut out for a life on the run."

"Oy, the drama." Darsh sat up, flinging one hand

against his forehead. "We lay low for a day and a half, and he was a perfectly competent medical professional. And where's *my* love? I saved your life with my timely warning."

I jumped on him, nuzzling his neck. He grabbed me and pretended to hump me from under the covers, tickling me when I tried to get away.

"Y'all are the strangest team I've ever worked with."

"Silas!" I hugged the other vampire. My arms didn't close around his chest, and his pecs against my cheek had about as much give as an anvil, but I was deliriously happy that we were all together.

Grumpypants von Cardoso watched our reunion with a poker face before sitting down in a club chair and tapping his foot impatiently.

Fun as it would be to piss him off further, that would delay our team meeting. And possibly getting first crack at Sachie's cast. When it came to broken bones, healers were hit and miss. It was best to go to a Trad doctor in the first place, set the bones, then when the cast came off, follow up with a healer.

I found some colored markers in the junk drawer in the kitchen—*rich people! They're just like us!*—then I got comfy in between Darsh and Sach, the blanket across our laps.

"Pushy," Darsh said.

Silas pulled up a dining room chair and straddled it backward.

There was always this moment in an investigation before all the threads came together where I balanced on a knife's edge of tension, like a hunter with a finger on the trigger, waiting to sight our quarry.

We'd taken some shots to flesh them out; some had hit, others missed, but they were still out there in the woods hiding from us. Eagerness or moving too quickly would scare them away for good, but being hesitant or second-guessing our aim would leave us empty-handed. It was a split second of exquisite anticipation that was almost mouth-watering and entirely dependent on lining up all the various pieces into one perfect sightline.

I uncapped a red marker and propped Sach's cast on my lap. A good leader listened to her team and went last. "Tell me everything."

Chapter 25

Sach and Darsh told their tale with a lot of mutual interrupting, but the gist of it was that they found a tattoo artist who recognized his work from the photo and gave them the name of his client, Gabriel Mendoza.

Silas frowned. "That's not the name of the vamp operative I came up with."

"Hold your horses and let me tell the story in order," Darsh said. "We showed up at Mendoza's house to a welcoming committee."

I was partway through a masterful drawing of their epic battle, showing Sach in all her fighting glory, when she nudged me.

"Why am I fighting a cow with a bumblebee riding it?"

I gasped in outrage. "That's a vampire on a Hell stallion. I'm exercising artistic license."

"Have you ever seen a horse?"

Darsh, recounting how badly outnumbered they were, waved his hand in front of my face. "Hello. Speaking here. And respect cows, please."

"Yeah, yeah," I muttered, adding a spraying arc of

blood to my drawing. Darsh, like most vamps, was atheist, but once upon a time he'd been Hindu, like many of the Roma of old. He hadn't eaten beef when he was alive and didn't drink cow blood now.

"I fought zero deformed cows yesterday," Sach said, "but after I was injured, we decided to get out of there." She tensed, a distant expression on her face. "We barely got away."

I added a rainbow to the drawing and nudged her shoulder, eliciting a smile. One dimple. Good enough.

My stubborn friend insisted on paying a follow-up visit to the tattoo artist before she got her arm fixed, while Darsh snuck back to spy on their attackers.

The tattooist was terrified and baffled when she burst in on him. He didn't know anything about a trap and couldn't believe that Gabriel would do such a thing, especially since he was deeply Catholic.

"A religious vamp?" Ezra said, clanking together chunky needles. He'd unearthed an unfinished sweater in hot pink yarn that he swore was a project his aunt had abandoned. Yeah, right. "Don't see that often."

"I twigged on it too," Sachie said.

My masterpiece completed, I signed my name to it, along with the inscription: H.A.G.S. aka "have a great summer." What everyone wrote in the high school yearbooks of people they weren't really friends with.

Sach snorted a laugh and got up to rummage through the fridge. "I asked him for a description of the vampire and guess what?"

"Gabriel Mendoza wasn't a vampire at all," Silas said.

Darsh mock-pouted at him. "It's not fun when you already have the answer."

Sachie returned with an orange in one hand and a transparent package of synthetic blood for Darsh tucked under her good arm. "Gabriel is a level one human operative with the London office. He's a White Flame." She handed Darsh the drink and peeled her orange.

"There's nothing to indicate that anyone other than Dr. Metaxas and a single vamp are involved." Ezra flattened out the bunched-up stitches and started on his next row. "But after Aviva and I visited London HQ, someone leaked our location for a second attack. We got hit right when Darsh phoned."

I switched to a chair so I could massage my tired feet without constantly elbowing my friends.

"Mendoza might still be the person who sent the vampires to Rosemary's store and who helped capture the victims," Ezra said.

"I doubt it," Darsh said. "Because when I caught up with our merry band of assholes, one of them was having a heated phone call with someone he referred to as 'that Maccabee vamp fuck' when he hung up. Such eloquence."

"Confirmation he's an operative," Ezra said. "Excellent, but also damn."

"Can I jump in now?" Silas said to Darsh goodhumoredly.

"Knock yourself out."

"We're looking for Roman Whittaker. He was a level two Maccabee in London before he was turned four years ago and chose to stay with the organization." Silas pulled up a photo of an unremarkable white guy with sandy-colored hair in a buzz cut.

The knitting needles clicked in a steady rhythm, the pink fibers sliding through Ezra's strong fingers. This lethal predator was creating this warm, comforting garment. The memory of him being my place of strength and comfort rushed over me. I wriggled my fingers, chasing away phantom sensations.

Unfortunately, I then pressed my thumb into my instep

slightly too hard and winced. "So Roman set Gabriel up to be the fall guy. What a team player."

Did Director Harrison know that Roman was murdering half shedim? Did he give tacit approval by looking the other way?

"What a clusterfuck." Darsh tipped his drink back to get the last drops.

Silas half put up his hand like an excited kid in class.

It was adorable, and I shot Darsh a pre-emptive glare in case he made fun of it.

"Get this." Silas rocked onto the back chair legs. "When Dr. Metaxas was born, her family was part of an extremist Jewish sect with fundamentalist practices, but they left soon after the boating accident where she lost her leg. It raised some flags about why they didn't want their community around them after this tragedy, so I dug a bit deeper. No accident, no boat. It was a vampire attack, and the family was expelled from their community for her contamination. This confirms the cure motive."

"No," I sighed. "It doesn't." I rubbed each of the toes on my left foot, totally stalling. Telling everyone about Rie wouldn't out me, but I'd spent my life steering clear of any infernal-adjacent topic, and I had to gather my courage to keep talking. "The latest victim, Rie Bleeker, had a rap sheet and belonged to a gang."

"That blows our theory that the victims were chosen for their innate goodness to counteract the evil within us big bad vamps," Darsh said. He recapped the empty drink and placed it on the coffee table. "Their targets were from all over the globe, but they weren't randomly chosen. They'd have known Rie was a criminal."

"Oh shit!" I slapped the table, the final piece falling into place. "We've been assuming that Dr. Metaxas was looking for a way to rid the world of vampires by creating something for vamps to ingest to combat their magic. But this potion is for *humans*. Those fuckers aren't using innate goodness to overpower vamp magic, they're using demon magic to protect people in the event they're bitten because vampires can't turn infernals. They're creating a vaccine."

Ezra shot me a hooded stare and laid the knitting on the table. "Our victims are infernals?" he said silkily.

"I—uh…yes." I felt like my blood was reversing in my veins, each synapse flaring up in a dark, deep dread. The room zoomed away, as if viewed through a long, narrow tunnel. I'd been so determined to solve this, never realizing that it would thrust my darkest fear from the shadows into the light. "Uh, well, the leader of the gang that Rie was part of claimed to be an infernal and to only recruit people with shedim blood."

Silas frowned. "Just because Rie is a criminal doesn't mean she's an infernal."

"Not all criminals are infernals but are all infernals criminals?" Darsh mused.

"No," I snapped. "They're not."

They didn't realize that the sheer effort of being decent to other people when you had a force constantly begging you to go off the rails meant it was all or nothing. Either you fully embraced the evil or you were more likely to be an actively good person than the average individual who didn't live with a demon voice in their head.

Since I couldn't share that, I shrugged lightly. "I'm extrapolating from the fact that not all vampires are bad."

"It's not the same though, is it?" Darsh said. "Demon blood negates any human impulses."

My eyebrows shot up. "Are you fucking kidding me right now?"

"I'm simply pursuing our murderers' thinking, dear heart," Darsh said, "not playing arbiter of good and evil."

"Most of the victims weren't just regular people," Sachie said, "they were actively doing good. Infernals might lead normal lives and not hurt anyone, but do you honestly believe they'd be such outstanding citizens?"

My heart plummeted—as did my secret hope that my best friend recognized that I was a half shedim and didn't care. My biggest nightmare hadn't played out as a monster coming for me in the dark of night; it blinked curiously at me with brown eyes that I knew better than my own.

"I've met an infernal," Ezra said, "and I guarantee they were a deeply compassionate person."

His pity was a slap in the face.

"Infernals are individuals," I said to Sachie. "They don't work off some evil hive mind like the Borg."

She frowned. "You don't need to take this so personally."

"Regardless, vamps can't find infernals, and Metaxas isn't a Blue Flame, so unless they're working with someone who has Aviva's specific abilities," Silas said, "we still aren't sure how they found the victims."

"Or that the blue knot on Kyle means he's an infernal." Sach gathered her orange peels into a neat pile.

"If Rie had it," Darsh said, "I'd say it was conclusive."

The three of them looked expectantly at me.

My mind was blank. I couldn't figure out how to answer to save myself. What if I said yes, and then one of them learned that there was no precedence of Blue Flames identifying half shedim? Not even those Eishei Kodesh with my particular abilities.

I only could because I wasn't just human.

Casually mentioning that I was a half shedim was unthinkable. When I did finally come out, there was an order to which people would be told, and Sachie was head of the line. She was my chosen family. My sister from another mister. (A much better mister; Ben wasn't a demon.) I carried enough guilt over having told Ezra about Cherry in a love-induced haze; blurting it out now to everyone would be unforgiveable.

Liar, the Baroness hissed. *You're ashamed.*

No, I was a coward. I trusted my best friend with my life, but the thought of trusting her with this, especially after her comments, made my throat go tight and sticky and my veins fill with ice. She wouldn't betray me.

But she might walk away.

"I…um…"

"Aviva," Ezra said sternly.

I swung a panicked gaze at him.

He crossed his arms. "Did you forget to check her?"

He was throwing me a lifeline? Why? Who cared. I grabbed hold.

"Sorry. I was so thrown by her rap sheet and the gang connection that it flew clear out of my head." I mimed it flying away. Laughed weakly. Added the motion and sound of a bomb going off.

Someone stop me. Please.

"We get it," Silas said. "It doesn't matter though. This makes sense. I agree that the victims are infernals and Roman and Metaxas are using shedim magic to protect humans from vamps by creating a vaccine."

He, Sach, and Darsh talked through whether that affected the likelihood of war breaking out if this became public knowledge, while I listened with half an ear.

Ezra hadn't outed me. Except it wasn't only relief coursing through me—or victory for that matter. It was heartbreak and a profound bafflement. How could he have hurt me so badly over Cherry Bomb but behave this way now? The initial rush that my secret remained safe now drained away.

"You don't look so hot." Sachie pointed at the kitchen. "Maybe you should eat something. Want an orange?"

"I hear gingko biloba helps aged brains," Darsh said.

"In that case, I wouldn't want to deprive you of your stash," I said sweetly. He'd expect me to tease him back, and I didn't want to make things worse by behaving out of character.

More out of character.

"Ooh. Meow." Darsh made cat claws.

Ezra's shoulders were rigid, and he massaged a temple with his index finger, glaring daggers at me. Flaming, poisonous ones with serrated blades, all the better to tear into my flesh. Oh. That's why he'd thrown me the lifeline. He planned to kill me himself.

"I need coffee," I said, rising. "Let's take ten."

Chapter 26

I bolted for the coffeemaker and popped in one of the coffee pods, watching each drop fall with a totality of attention generally saved for holy miracles. Once my drink was ready, I took it outside into the backyard that was walled off from public view and tipped my head up to the sky.

Ezra joined me, closing the sliding door behind him. "Want to share what's really going on in your head?" He held a ginger cookie.

The sun was shining brightly, and even though it wasn't hot, being October, he kept to the shadows.

I moved closer to the townhouse and stood beside him. "Is that for me?"

He shrugged. "Depends on what you tell me."

All mention of white dots and kill spots were information overload at this particular juncture.

I cupped my hands around my mug. "Rie had the blue double knot."

"I figured."

"Blue Flames can't identify half shedim, but even though Metaxas must be an infernal, she'd have trouble locating others. It would be like finding needles in a haystack."

"Depends how long she'd been looking," Ezra said. "She might have spent years setting this up." He sighed. For dramatic effect, not breathing purposes. "You'll have to come up with a plausible lie to explain seeing the double knot. You've told too many people about it."

"Maybe the less I say the better." I rubbed my eyes. "I don't know anymore."

Ezra handed me the cookie.

"Thanks." I bit into it, a rich ginger molasses flavor hitting my taste buds. "Mmmm, so yummy."

Ezra snagged a piece and popped it in his mouth.

I pulled the rest out of reach. "Get your own, bloodsucker."

"Wow." He pressed a hand against his heart. "I rescued you from having your deepest secret exposed and that's the gratitude I get?"

I broke my cookie in half and shared it. "Yeah, thanks for the pity. Good times."

"It wasn't pity. You're not ready to tell people yet. Despite what I think."

"Really," I said tightly, taking a sip of coffee.

"What's that supposed to mean?"

I shook my head. "Nothing."

"That's it." He grasped my shoulders and spun me to face him. "I'm aware of what you believe, and we're dealing with this once and for all. I didn't break up with you because of Cherry."

"All evidence to the contrary, but great. Thanks for clearing that up."

He swore in Spanish.

"Actually, no." I flung my cookie into the grass. "If that wasn't the reason, then what was? Use precise words."

"It wasn't you or anything about you."

"You used the 'it's not you, it's me' excuse last time. In Los Angeles. The first time, I wasn't given much of an explanation at all."

He sighed audibly, rubbing his forehand with one hand. "Cherry's existence was never an issue. The timing simply wasn't right for a relationship."

"Because of your father pulling a Don Corleone to bring his son into the family business?"

"That didn't officially happen until later, but yes," he admitted. "It was the expectation."

"Did you ever murder infernals?"

He flinched, his shock genuine. "No, Aviva," he said coldly.

I matched his icy stare. "It was a fair question."

"Have you ever once considered that the breakup was hard on me too?"

"No, because you wouldn't have given up what we had together if it was. And for what? Playing hitman? Playing spy? Catting around?"

"It must be so nice to get to live your life in black and white. Not all of us have that luxury," he fired back.

"Then explain the shades of gray," I fumed, white-knuckling the mug's handle.

"You wanted us to be a fairy tale; the Maccabee princess looking for a prince who didn't exist."

"Fuck you, Ezra. I'm not a princess and I sure as hell never wanted a prince. Plus, you're seriously deluded if you think I ever saw *you* as one." My head throbbed like it was going to explode. "As for me being a Maccabee…" I gestured sharply at him. "Pot, meet kettle."

"I wasn't one back then." He opened his mouth, then shut it with a pained expression, scrubbing a hand over his face. "Do you have any idea how hard it was to put that in place?"

"You said they came to you."

"I made sure they did." He slumped against the wall. "Look, I was caught up in the two of us as much as you were, but ultimately, one of us had to get real." He sighed. "I'm sorry. I never meant to hurt—"

I raised my hand to shut him up, turning away to blink the tears out of my eyes.

Ezra had fucking broken me. There was a point, months later, when Sachie had peeled me off the sofa and told me about the Japanese art of kintsugi, repairing broken pottery by mending it with gold seams. It showed that when something broke that didn't mean it was no longer useful. Rather, that even its breakage was valuable. It was called the art of embracing damage.

I loved that concept.

It had taken the shattering of my heart to realize how valuable it was, but now that it was imperfectly but beautifully mended, I'd be extra careful with who I gave it to.

I might lust after Ezra and crave his touch, but he'd never again be given the precious gift of my heart. However, since he was the person who'd broken it in the first place, sorry didn't cut it. Cherry bared her teeth, and I think I did too, because he took a step back.

"You had no business coming back to Vancouver. No business…" I sucked my bottom lip into my mouth, besieged with the memory of our kiss, then ruthlessly shoved the image away. "You owed me that much."

"I had a murder to solve."

"It didn't need to be *you*," I said, tightening my grip on my mug so I didn't brain him with it. Or so I'd have more power in the swing if I did. "Don't feed me more bullshit about this being your way to keep killing people. For once, be totally honest with me."

"I've been more honest with you than anyone."

"Then I pity everyone else in your life."

Pulling away from him was a slow process akin to

freeing myself from a web of sticky taffy. The air between us grew thinner and thinner until it snapped.

Our mission wasn't over yet, so why did this feel like our final moment together?

I hurried inside, catching one last glimpse of Ezra standing motionless on the other side of the glass.

Sach scooped her hand under my elbow and led me away. "What was that?" she said suspiciously, holding up her phone to show me she had "Gaston" queued up.

"No Disney," I said hollowly. "I swear I'm not going back there."

Darsh placed his hand on the small of my back and steered me to the kitchen. "Listen, the three of us had a little confab, and we've come up with a plan." He leaned on the island.

"What?" With the self-control of a saint, I passed over the bottle of wine and settled for a breakfast sandwich on an English muffin, which I toasted in the oven.

"We're going to buy out the world's supply of Claret." Darsh bopped the end of my nose. "If you can't beat 'em, join 'em. Brilliant, right?"

"Sure, except when it's completely ridiculous." I drank some coffee, made a face, and dumped the lukewarm brew down the drain.

"Hear us out," Sach said, standing next to Darsh. "Can I get one of whatever you're toasting?"

"I'll tell Ezra what we discussed, so we don't need to repeat it," Silas said, walking out the sliding door.

I gave Sachie my food and popped another sandwich in the oven. "All right," I said, once it was toasted, and I'd taken my first bite. "How do you see this working?"

"Claret can only be produced in small amounts," Darsh said, "and has to be administered within days of it being concocted."

"Why? What's it made of?" I polished off the first half of my meal and dove into the second.

"Many things," he said with an evasive hand flap, "but it also requires an insanely skilled Orange Flame to handle the delicate magical mechanics of the procedure. The upside is that there's not usually a ton of demand for the drug. We go in as Maccabees and use our official authority to buy an exclusive contract to regulate the use."

"Preventing people from being drained of blood falls under our purview," I agreed, "but the manufacturers will assume the organization will get a few doses to analyze, then shut them down. We've done it before. Why would they agree?"

"The alternative is we raid them and they get nothing." Sachie wiped her mouth with a napkin. "This gives them a chance to set up shop in the future, and the Maccabees can make a big deal about this win. It's bullshit but it's the game."

"That's depressing," I said. "Okay, we get hold of a dose, take it to the closest chapter for analysis, and see if Roman goes after it?"

Darsh nodded. "He's the muscle, so that's the plan."

"Claret's short shelf life also explains killers' timeline," Sachie said. "The interval between getting doses."

I gathered our plates and my mug and took them to the sink. "Why did a new dose show up days after Kyle was killed when it was weeks between murders before? What changed?"

"During the phone call I overheard," Darsh said, "the vamp on my end asked how the new Orange Flame was doing."

"Still not following," I said, washing up.

"The amount of magic expended to make Claret takes an enormous toll on the Eishei Kodesh," Sachie said. "They can only create one dose before they need to rest, and if they've been doing it for a long time, the cumulative toll means it can take weeks, sometimes months, for them to rejuvenate enough to make another single-use dose."

"But if they're new to the game, their re-up time is a matter of days," Darsh said.

I put everything in the drying rack and wiped my hands off on a tea towel. "When did you both get so knowledgeable about Claret?"

"We didn't." Sach poured herself a glass of water. "Darsh mentioned hearing there was a new Orange Flame to Silas, and it was like lights going off in his head as he put it all together."

Darsh narrowed his eyes. "He's a mystery, that one."

"How do we make sure we end up with the Claret instead of our killers?"

"Money," Darsh said.

I laughed. "Michael won't authorize enough to outbid murderers buying a rare drug for some holy crusade."

Sachie washed her glass and set it in the drying rack. "Silas didn't think it was a problem."

"That's probably where Count von Cardoso comes in," Darsh said. "He's obscenely loaded."

"His dad is, but I'm not sure about Ezra," I said. "I mean, he's well-off, but obscenely loaded?" Then again, he had offered to personally reimburse Rosemary for all the damage. "Okay. Maybe."

"No maybe about it. I've seen the building in Babel where Ezra's penthouse is." Darsh rubbed his thumb over the tips of his index and middle fingers.

Ezra entered the room. "Great idea to buy them out."

"You going to ask Michael for the funds?" I said, embracing my original "Ezra and I have no history" intention with everything I had. I'd deal with any residual emotions once the killers were caught.

He and Silas joined the rest of us around the kitchen island.

Ezra laughed then blinked. "Oh, you were serious. No, we don't have time to get caught in red tape. I'll get the cash."

Darsh shot me a "told you so" look.

"We still don't have the location of the manufacturers," I said. "They were in Thailand, but they've relocated."

"I've got a wide network of contacts. I'll work them and shake something loose," Ezra said.

"What about Burning Eddie?" Sach said. "He lives in England."

"Nooooo." Silas dropped his head in his hands with a groan. "Not him."

"Not anyone's first choice," Darsh said, "but he'd know."

I looked at my teammates, my brow wrinkled. "Who or what is Burning Eddie?"

"A shedim with a side business selling human blood," Sach said.

Despite the fact that I habitually fought shedim, Sachie's desire to work on the Spook Squad meant she'd done a deep dive into the Maccabee files on all known demons currently operating on earth.

I shuddered. "Ewww. Why isn't he dead?"

"No one can pierce his permanent magic shield," Ezra said. "To the point he holds competitions to let others try. He's perfected how to keep vamps alive over a low fire for hours."

Sach snickered. "Really he's more like Slow Roasting Eddie."

"That's…" I shook my head. "Nope. No further details necessary. Why would he help us?"

"Eddie lives on a farm about an hour outside

London," Ezra said. "His hatred for humans and vamps is only surpassed by his love of horses. And he tolerates cowboys." He clapped Silas on the shoulder. "Especially this one."

His friend glared. "I hate you."

"Great," Sachie said. "Silas and I will go visit him."

"No disrespect," Silas said, "but I don't think that's smart."

Sach crossed her arms. "When's the last time you were in the saddle?"

Darsh cough-laughed.

Silas blushed. "Not for decades."

Darsh opened his mouth, and I shot him a warning glance. He sniffed, as if to say, "Can't blame a guy for trying."

Sach ignored us. "Whereas I was on the Canadian national eventing team when I was eighteen. Dressage, cross-country jumping, and stadium jumping." She unleashed her dimples. "Eddie will adore me."

"No one is more proficient at cowgirl," I said.

"Or reverse cowgirl," she added.

"I didn't need to know that," Ezra said with a grimace.

Silas pursed his lips thoughtfully, then nodded. "Okay, we'll go together."

Look at that. Nary a word of protest or caveman command from Ezra at Sachie accompanying Silas. I glared at him and he blinked, his brow furrowed.

"I call dibs on doing the buy," Darsh said.

I nodded. "Once we've got the info and the meeting's been set up, you and Ezra go together."

Darsh sighed theatrically. "If we must."

"Where will you be?" Ezra said.

"Waiting for my minions to do their share." I grinned at the others, but my amusement leached away, leaving only a cold smile. "Once that Maccabee vamp fuck is caught, I want first crack at him. I'll get Metaxas's location." Her crusade to cure vampirism had led to the deaths of six infernals. I intended to look her in the eyes as I wrung answers out of her. The more painfully, the better. "The good doctor is mine."

Chapter 27

The universe cut us a break and the first part of our plan went off without a hitch. Sachie and Silas returned from Burning Eddie unharmed, bearing the location of the Claret manufacturer, though the vamp was walking bowlegged and stiffly.

"Not one word," he growled to a smirking Darsh.

Sach had charmed the psychotic shedim so thoroughly that he'd not only signed her cast "Slow Roasting Eddie," along with a bloody thumbprint, but given her a cowboy hat to remember him by. The amount of pride with which she wore it was "a sleep with one eye open" level of disconcerting. Then again, she was too lazy to break in a new roommate, so I was probably safe.

Darsh announced he and Ezra were ready to meet the drug producers and show them the new sheriffs in town.

Silas winced. "Don't actually say that."

"I won't just say it." Darsh snatched the cowboy hat away from Sach, but before he could put it on his head, she'd lunged at him with a small, lethally sharp blade to his throat.

"I didn't hear you say please."

Darsh rolled his eyes, easily pushing her off him. But he did return the hat.

Ezra and he headed off to the Greek island of Kos.

I couldn't decide if it was more or less weird staying at the mews house without Ezra, but he insisted that Orly, who'd gone back to Toronto, was all "mi casa es su casa" and it was for the best if we stayed together. He'd commandeered one of the bedrooms for himself, Sach and I were bunking together, and Silas had the third bedroom, which left Darsh on the sofa.

With Darsh and Ezra gone, the emotional temperature ratcheted down several thousand degrees to a lovely mellow vibe. Silas radiated laid-back. It rubbed off on Sach and me, not that we were particularly high strung, but the three of us were much more relaxed without the other two.

The only tension-inducing hitch was that Michael was owed an update. I shut the bedroom door, went into the en suite bathroom, and turned on the tap and shower. The things I had to do to get past vampire hearing.

I sat on the closed toilet lid and got on an encrypted video chat with her.

It was close to noon on Wednesday here in London, but not even 4AM Tuesday morning in Vancouver. Not that I was under any delusion that a sleepy director would be an easy-going one.

Other than her silk pajama top and a slight flatness on one side of her silver hair, there was nothing to indicate she'd been asleep. No trace of puffy sleep face or a single piece of crusty eye granola. She wasn't on the call in bed on her laptop, she was sitting at the small desk in her bedroom. Michael took one look at my face and sighed. "Is there any good news?"

"We have motive. We believe they're murdering their victims to create a vaccine for humans."

"Serial killing their way to a better humanity," she said contemptuously. "Dangerous, misguided fools. Why choose these people specifically?" She adjusted the desk lamp, casting herself more in shadow while throwing the glare on the screen like an interrogation light.

I squinted and blinked rapidly. Her reaction so far had been what I'd expected. Maybe this final bombshell wouldn't include me in its blast zone. "We believe they're killing infernals."

I was more familiar with Michael's full range of expressions than anyone. I could decipher anger or amusement in the tiniest twitch, but I'd never seen her go slightly cross-eyed while her jaw pumped in a way that reminded me of the monster in *Alien* about to push out a second mouth filled with razor-sharp teeth and dripping mucus.

I may have leaned closer to the screen of my phone, my eyebrows raised, instead of checking that she was all right, but this was a once-in-a-lifetime spectacle. Besides, if her first reaction wasn't to be horrified, immediately followed by her deep concern for her only child, then I was going to schadenfreude the fuck out of this moment.

She scrubbed a hand over her face, wiping away all emotion. "How did you deter—" She sucked in a breath. "The knot that you told Malika about? It represents infernals?"

I dug my fingers into the toilet paper roll. "Yes," I said. "And yes. After death."

"If it's just Malika?" My mother looked off, her expression distant. "I can contain it." She faced the screen directly again. "Who else knows you've seen it?"

I flinched, but her anger made my blood pump and my jaw harden. "The general public. I had a T-shirt made saying 'Infernal detector. Ask me how.'"

"Watch your tone, Operative."

"Show some compassion, Director. Someone is out there killing my kind."

"They aren't your kind."

I shook my head like I could dislodge her words. "Yes. They are. What are you going to say next?" I leapt up, pacing the narrow track along the bathtub and holding my phone up by my face. "That the thirteen-year-old or the man who'd devoted his life to promoting education in rural Pakistan must have done something to deserve it? Even our one criminal victim didn't deserve to be killed for that."

"Stop twisting my words."

"What if I'm on the list? What will you say then?"

"Enough!" She slammed her hand on her desk. "Sit down."

I stopped pacing but stood where I was.

"Did you learn anything further about the London office and the source of the attacks?" she said.

"A vamp operative there is one of our killers. Roman Whittaker."

"Then they aren't the infernal."

"No, that's a Yellow Flame. Dr. Athena Metaxas. She's a Jewish surgeon."

"This just gets better and better," she muttered. "When you apprehend them, they'll need to be transported back to London HQ for Booker to deal with." When I didn't immediately reply with my affirmation, Michael crossed her arms. "This is non-negotiable. The operative, in particular, is not to be killed. Take him alive and hand him into Booker's custody. Is that understood?"

"Yes." My tone echoed Cherry's growl in my head, and I modified it. "I understand."

"Good. What do your team members know?"

"Don't worry, Michael. My secret is still safe. They only know that I saw that knot on Kyle's body and not on the criminal who belonged to a self-proclaimed infernal gang." I propped the window open, the cool air failing to kill the flush on my cheeks. "That association allowed them to put the pieces together without me saying anything further. Happy?"

"Delighted," she said dryly. "Anything else I should know?"

"We're in the process of taking over a drug called Claret that—"

"I'm familiar with it. Where's it being made now?"

"The island of Kos."

She drummed a pencil against her desktop. "That makes Bodrum the closest HQ to take it in for analysis. A small outfit, no Spook Squad, not a lot of prying eyes there, though I'm not sure how efficient it is. I've heard… Well, you'll have your team."

Awesome, a bum chapter. That was unusual, but not unheard of. Poor leadership or a lack of individuals willing to live in a specific place could really impact the quality of operative found at a chapter. They were still trained; they just weren't necessarily the cream of the crop.

We didn't have much choice though. The Claret had to be taken to the closest office to be analyzed before the magic went dormant, and while the flight to Athens wasn't that much longer than to Turkey, traffic in the Greek city would hinder getting the sample to the lab quickly enough.

The Turkish chapter was unique. Not only was it the smallest Maccabee chapter, it also had the distinction of having the only underwater rift on earth into the Brink, roughly thirty feet offshore.

Once it was discovered, Maccabees moved into position with lightning speed, buying up the closest stretch of land and keeping it out of vampire hands—just like they'd done on the moors.

Controlling the two rifts in isolated areas was a drop in the bucket compared to vampires owning the ones in packed urban centers, but we did what we could.

Unfortunately, the Maccabees there didn't have the budget for dedicated water surveillance. They relied heavily on the fact that it was a hassle for anyone to use that rift. Vamps could travel underwater, no problem, but they didn't enjoy being soaking wet while crossing the Brink to Babel. Same with humans, but add scuba gear, and it resulted in a little-used portal.

Hopefully Roman and Metaxas believed it was the best undetectable approach to us and worth the effort.

"Once this is wrapped up," Michael said, "I expect you to immediately come into the office to debrief."

My heart plummeted like a freefalling elevator. This promotion hinged on her approval, and there was a distinct lack of that in her tone.

"You said I had to keep you in the loop," I said tersely, "and I have. You never claimed you had to like what I told you. Don't penalize me for this."

She regarded me with an even stare and then tilted her head. "Good night, Aviva."

Her screen went dark.

I stormed into the bedroom, threw my phone on the bed, put a pillow over my face, and screamed.

"Aviva?" Silas called out from downstairs. "You good?"

I opened the door. "I'm fine."

Sach trundled up the stairs. "The report went over that well, huh?"

"I'm going on a food run, then I plan on eating my body weight in British junk food until we hear back from the guys. Coming?"

"You bet. There's a bar of Flakes with my name on it."

IT DIDN'T TAKE ALL that long for Ezra and Darsh to fly to Kos, meet with the distributors, and get them "on board." Waiting for them to get the dose of Claret was the time-consuming part, so we didn't meet up with them at the small HQ in the Turkish beach town for another few days.

Before I left London for Bodrum on Saturday morning, I left a message for Director Harrison with his assistant that in the course of our investigation, we'd taken over Claret distribution and were bringing a sample to the Bodrum office. Ezra and I would be out of his hair.

Ezra and Darsh had told the manufacturers to spread the news to their clientele, so one way or another, Dr. Metaxas and Roman Whittaker would learn about it and come for the drug. It's not like they could harvest the blood without it, and none of my team believed these murders were a thing of the past.

Sach and I had gone shopping for clothes and makeup before she'd visited Burning Eddie. She'd declared that the demon cow on her cast demanded a certain level of panache, so we'd hit up some fashionable boutiques in Kensington.

I was glad to have a decent wardrobe to bring with me on this trip. It made me feel more like myself, and given the nature of this investigation, I'd take any advantage.

We flew out of Heathrow in the middle of a rainstorm.

After some high-profile lawsuits ruled that airlines couldn't ban vampires, the airlines deemed that vamps could only travel on certain flights. This was supposedly so they could cater to that clienteles' specific needs, stocking blood and coating windows with special sunlight-blocking sealant, along with installing lie-flat beds throughout the cabin. For Trad vamps, flying during the day was like taking a red-eye for the rest of us. On shorter flights, they slept in the cabin on the tarmac until dusk.

Humans willing to take these flights were given steep discounts. There were also human stewards who'd made a killing working these shifts and retiring early. There were also ones who never lived to cash in on their pensions.

I wasn't willing to risk it, and neither was Sach. All it took was one drop of spilled blood and a single vamp with low self-control and we'd be trapped on that plane and hunted like motherfucking snakes.

We took a separate flight from Silas and met up in the Bodrum airport.

Our Uber was blessedly air-conditioned, though the driver took one look at Silas and charged us danger pay and an extra fee in case his suspension system broke.

Bodrum was a charming town on a peninsula dotted with gleaming white homes, ancient cobblestoned streets, and an enormous stone fortress overlooking boats bobbing in turquoise water. It was also as hot in October here as Vancouver was in the summer. I was grateful I had some lightweight blouses to go with my A-line skirt, because within minutes outside, I was sweating.

Sach had dressed up for her first contact with this new Maccabee group in gray pinstriped trousers and matching wrap shirt. Silas had brought a duffel bag with changes of clothes when he came from Vancouver, and he'd forgone jeans for black trousers and a tight, dark green button-down shirt that earned him a lot of second glances at Heathrow.

HQ was located in a repurposed luxury hotel right on the beach. They'd kept the balconies, pillared covered patios, and swimming pool, which was a hell of a perk. Cushioned sitting areas were grouped in the shade under lemon trees and broad-leafed palms, while one wall was covered in a riot of scarlet bougainvillea.

Operatives should have been lining up to live in this slice of paradise, but perhaps it was too sleepy a town. We Maccabees did love our thrills.

We checked in with Director Yildiz, a good-humored woman in her fifties, who struck me as taking everything in stride. The director, who insisted we call her Defne, had met with Ezra and Darsh only an hour ago, learning of the analysis and expected arrival of a couple murderers for the first time, and yet she'd already sent the dose of Claret into her in-house lab and was familiar with our professional résumés. If she hadn't crossed paths with Ezra socially before and if our descriptions had not been provided, we would have found ourselves with a very different welcome.

It's true there weren't as many operatives here, and the shoreline appeared unwatched, but that wasn't the case at all. Defne had deliberately cultivated her chapter's reputation for being barely staffed and barely skilled, preferring to be underestimated, but this all-human crew was more trained than Navy SEALs.

Her people were always on high alert, and it was to her credit that none of us, not even Silas, had detected that our approach was tracked the moment our plane had touched down. No one got past them—not on land or in the rift.

For once, Roman being a Maccabee worked in our favor, because if Michael believed the story that the Bodrum chapter was second-rate, then Roman would as well.

Defne took us down to forensics in the basement, her sandals slapping quietly against the large tiles. "Here you go." She left us in a comfortable conference room with one-way windows looking onto a small yet meticulous forensics lab.

A level three operative in a lab coat and gloves checked a chart in front of a bank of machines, none of which I could identify, but which I catalogued as science-y.

The sight of Ezra and Darsh sprawled in chairs, however, tossing a foam football back and forth, made no sense, despite the dozens of explanations I rapidly sifted through.

Ezra kept clothes at the mews house and Darsh had done some shopping because they were both in Testosterone Black, a color popular with action heroes and of a similar hue to Slimming Black. That's why those people never had fat asses. Fat heads were another matter.

Sach nudged my shoulder. "Make them stop," she whined. "Darsh is being sporty. It's unnatural."

"Oh!" I brightened. "You're practicing your undercover act."

"Women," Darsh said and tossed the football to Silas, who caught it one-handed.

"Excuse me?" Sach slid her small sharp blade out of her sleeve.

Darsh ran a hand along his body. "I'm genderfluid and comfortable with my feminine side. It was an objective statement, not an insult."

I stepped away from Sach's blade. "How did you get that through security?"

Sachie grinned. "You really want to know?"

"Probably not," I admitted.

"I do." Ezra caught the football that Silas threw.

"My man." Darsh air high-fived him.

"My God." I shook my head. "Darsh is rubbing off on you." Ezra pitched the football at me, and I caught it with a grunt.

"Well, he clearly needed a positive role model," Darsh said.

The guys had bonded over their dislike of the arrogant human drug producers: two Dudebro Trads and a smarmy Eishei Kodesh. They were almost giddy recounting how they'd made the trio their bitches.

Darsh and Ezra were friends. Oh, goody.

I studied the photo of the vial of Claret they'd brought. The operative running the tests had left after informing us that it would take time to break down the components, but we'd been given permission to stick close to the lab. One thing the man told us was that the burgundy fluid was the magic version of a vasodilator, which was medication to increase blood flow.

"What's so complicated about administering this?" I asked after he left.

"Inject too much and the victim goes into extreme vasodilatory shock involving loss of consciousness, weak pulse, and rapid breathing among other symptoms," Ezra said. "That sets off a domino effect of multiple organ damage and death. More importantly for this scenario, there's no more blood flow to exsanguinate their victim."

"Claret also has to be administered in the femoral vein," Silas said. "That's a deep vein with a lot of risks, requiring precision. The magic works in tandem with leg muscles that help push blood upward to the heart and out through the puncture wound in the neck at an insanely fast rate."

Twelve hours later the Claret was still being analyzed, there'd been no attack, and we were all getting punchy from boredom and waiting.

Sach went to ask the resident healer if she could lose the cast yet. She swanned back into the room with a "Behold the wonders of magic," receiving applause for her fixed arm, though she'd kept my demon cow drawing, claiming she'd hang it in a place of pride back home.

It was totally going over the toilet. I just knew it.

After a delicious dinner of freshly grilled seafood with baklava, tiny cups of strong espresso for Sach and me, and synthetic blood that Silas pronounced the equivalent of a bottle "1947 Château Cheval Blanc," making Darsh openly gape at him, we were all stuffed.

Defne bade us good night, explaining that her second-in-command, Mo, was here to help us with all our needs.

We changed into more comfortable clothing while we waited, which for me was a baggy T-shirt and a pair of shorts.

For all of Ezra's smart fashion choices, he'd put on sweats that slid so far down his hips they were hanging on only through sheer tenacity. His faded T-shirt had a giant hole in it, spotlighting his pelvic bone, which curved inward like the flourishes on a Stradivarius.

Silas and Darsh, playing yet another round of black-jack, didn't note it, but Sachie, standing slightly behind Ezra and out of sight of anyone except me, pointed from her eyes to mine with a glower.

I raised my eyebrows like I had no clue what she meant and continued watching Ezra play solitaire.

Wrong response. She shot me one last death stare then mimed licking up Ezra's body, humping him from behind, and giving him a blow job, her tongue bulging out her cheek in time to her hand job.

"Spit or swallow?" Ezra said dryly without turning around.

Sach bit her tongue. "Kusoyarou!"

Silas glanced up and flipped over a ten to go with his three threes. "That was random, Ez."

Darsh, who'd gone over twenty-one, narrowed his eyes at Sach, who'd recovered remarkably quickly.

"Here's a fun fact," she said. "The first known blow job happened after the Egyptian god-king Osiris was murdered and chopped up. His wife, Isis, put his body back together, but when she couldn't find his dick, she made one out of clay—"

"Shit," I said. "I could have been making more interesting things than dreidels as a teen?" I threw up my hands. "Now you tell me."

Ezra snickered.

"Then what happened?" Silas said.

"Looking for tips, Cowpoke?"

The large vampire braced his hands on either side of the ottoman they were using as a table and leaned forward. His biceps flexed, his sleeves shifting and pulling tight around the muscles. "Enough," he said slowly and firmly.

Darsh generally didn't keep prodding people if they drew a hard line. He'd ragged on Silas longer than others, so I wasn't surprised to see him shrug as a faint blush hit his cheeks. "Sorry."

"You're trying too hard," Silas continued. "It's embarrassing to watch."

Darsh's head snapped up, and his eyes locked on to Silas's. A slow smile bloomed over his face.

Fuck me. He'd love him and leave him as roadkill, like he did with all his conquests. I didn't want to see how a 300 lb. solid-muscle vampire got over hurting after he'd been tossed away like a used tissue. It sure wasn't with a chilled Lambrusco and Amy Winehouse's "Back to Black" on repeat. I whipped the football at Darsh's head.

He caught it one-handed before it connected, his eyes back on his cards.

"Back to my story," Sach said loudly. "Isis stuck it on his crotch and blew life into him by playing his love flute." She mimed the actions.

"I think you mean love recorder," I said.

"So, to answer your question of spit or swallow?" She tapped her chin with her index finger. "In the interests of historical accuracy, I'd have to go with chop off."

"Ha!"

Ezra raised an eyebrow at me, unamused.

"I stand by my statement." I shook off my restless energy. "I'm going for a walk around the grounds."

Darkness had settled over the compound. A warm breeze kissed my skin, and the stars and the sound of the waves kept me company.

Two sleepy-looking operatives lounged in the back. We briefly chatted, the pair showing that their fatigue was a total charade. I was impressed at how thoroughly hoodwinked this chapter had everyone.

A shrill alarm sliced through our conversation, and the operatives bolted up.

Vamps poured over the walls to either side of us like a plague of locusts. The air was thick with their bloodlust, their howls a chorus of rage and hunger.

I had no weapons and no magic ability to defend myself against this onslaught. There were only two ways for me to survive: run and hide—

Cherry scratched against my skull—

Or burn my life down.

Chapter 28

The first wave of vampires closed in, dressed in all black like a sea of undead mercenaries.

The operative who I'd been joking with seconds ago sent magic flames dancing over his arms and hands. With a cry, he plunged into the undead horde while his colleague yanked out a scimitar from under the lounger she'd been reclining on, taking off a vampire's head with one clean swipe.

I ran toward the building, hoping to find a weapon, but I'd barely made it a half-dozen steps across the lawn when a rank-smelling vampire grabbed me from behind, choking me. My lungs burned. I tugged ineffectively at his hand, but he squeezed tighter.

In my head, Cherry growled but my fear of exposing her to the world was greater than my fear of dying.

Seconds later, I amended that stance, but even thrashing in panic to get air, with dark spots flickering at the edges of my vision, I couldn't bring myself to drop the bindings I'd so carefully honed over a lifetime.

Everyone would see me. The real me.

Sachie and Darsh would see me. Maybe they'd appreciate my presence during the fight, but it was one thing to be tolerated in the darkest night. Daylight would come, and they wouldn't see their friend Aviva anymore.

Just a monster who should have stayed hidden.

I flickered in and out of consciousness, death's chilly touch dancing over my skin.

My will to live kicked in, and summoning all my courage, I tore free of that sticky web of fear.

Time to stop living by halves.

I let go.

Scales exploded over my body, snapping my armor into place with such a sharp suddenness that they tore my T-shirt and shorts.

The vampire hissed and snatched his bloody hand away. He stared at me, the gash already healed. "Your eyes. You're an—"

I ripped his throat out, shook ash clumps off my claws, and kicked free of my garments. It wasn't the same as being naked since my scales covered my beefed-up physique, rather I appeared to be wearing a form-fitting armor. Plus, no one could recognize me by my clothes if I wasn't wearing them.

Human Maccabees desperately fended off vampires, battles waging atop the thick compound walls, on balconies, and even on the roof.

Three vamps approached me. One raised his hands. "We have no quarrel with you, demon."

"Awesome. Stand there and die." I twisted his head off and slammed it into the chest of another vamp. "Tag!"

Surprised, she caught it, then flinched and dropped it. It imploded into ash, which funneled along the ground in a tiny whirlwind, disappearing into the night.

Cherry and I took on the other two vamps, my crimson hair flying around my face. It was the first time I'd allowed myself to enjoy the pleasure of my full-demon form. Unlike in Babel, I didn't need to keep myself in check.

I leapfrogged over one vamp to land a barrage of punches on her surprised partner, my muscles surging with a newfound strength and power.

While I reveled in the freedom of my shedim physique, something nagged me deep inside.

I was whistling jauntily. Not Cherry, *me*.

Was it right to enjoy this violence? My attention lapsed, and it cost me. One of the vampires landed a blow to my head that sent me staggering sideways dizzily.

My armor did not make me infallible. Got it.

We dispatched the vamps, but part of the compound was on fire, smoke making my eyes and throat scratchy.

Carefully tucking all worries about everyone inside in a deep, dark box, I zigzagged toward the building, swimming through a sea of vamps who lashed out with claws and fangs, their beady eyes beacons of death.

A hot torment blazed up my side and frosted-tipped scales rained to the ground. I was gashed open, the sight of glistening muscle making me queasy. Gritting my teeth, I barreled into my opponent, and tore her chest apart with my needle-sharp horns.

She crashed onto her knees, her eyes wide and scared, then she dropped her pair of small axes and fell face-first in the dirt.

I gasped. She was an operative.

A human.

I swallowed hard, tasting bile. I'd given in to my infernal side and taken a woman's life. I flipped her over, but no amount of CPR could compensate for a mangled heart, half sliding out of her body.

You were defending yourself, Cherry hissed. *This won't be the last time. Now get your shit together. You need to live.*

I stared at painted fingernails belonging to the dead

woman's hand that I held. Tears blurring my vision, I closed her eyes, and pushed to my feet, rejoining the fight.

Or rather, Cherry rejoined it.

I retreated to a safe corner of my brain where reality stuttered past like an old movie that belonged in someone else's life story. The fatigue in my limbs, the mix of dried blood and ash tightening my scales—it all felt distant. My brain cocooned in layer after layer of fuzzy blankets, dulling the roars of fury and pain that surrounded me like Dolby sound, until I was barely there at all.

I came to awareness, sprawled on my back, fully human, naked, and covered in gore and dirt. I stretched my sore limbs and wriggled all ten fingers and toes.

I was human. On the outside at least.

Cherry was barely a whisper of a presence inside me. *Thank you*, I thought, watching the sun slowly creep across the horizon. I'd lived to see the dawning of another day thanks to her, and I was grateful, but the rest of my emotions were too complex to unpack right now.

My fingers brushed powder. The ground was white with ash. The world swung vertiginously, and, off-kilter, I scrabbled to find grass, some sign that this wasn't a permanent apocalypse. I gave a deep sigh at the blades of green and flecks of dirt that came free. Then, snickering in a somewhat deranged manner, I waved my arms and legs and made an ash angel. Maybe that could be my code name should I need one.

"Aviva! Avi!" Sach's terrified bellows drilled into my head.

I weakly sat up with a hiss, my body throbbing like I'd been used as a battering ram on a steel door. "Over here."

She sprinted over, clutching something to her chest, and when she got close, chucked two filthy garments at me.

My clothes had been trampled on so many times that

the tatters were mud brown, save for the parts streaked with dark crimson and gray. How Jackson Pollock. I tossed them aside with a grimace.

"You idiot!" she said. "I was positive you were dead and eaten or something." She wrinkled her nose. "Why are you naked?"

I didn't share that it was the result of my more muscular half-shedim form busting free along with not wanting to be recognized. "I didn't want to do laundry?"

Sachie laughed, the sound pitchy with hysteria. She brushed an ash-covered lock of matted hair off her forehead with a filthy hand. Her clothes and a solid eighty percent of her skin was covered in blood.

"May I?" I pointed at my eyes.

She wrinkled her brow in confusion, then nodded. "Okay, but I'm fine."

"Better to be safe than sorry." I jumped into my magic synesthete vision. Her ribs on her left side had a dark blue dot, as did the nasty cut at her temple, and there were some lighter blue dots in her left thigh, but nothing that couldn't be healed.

"No internal bleeding and nothing serious." I let out a relieved sigh and pulled my knees into my chest, wrapping my arms around them to cover myself. "How's everyone else?"

"Our team is alive. Eight operatives are dead though. Everything was pure chaos inside, and I kept looking for you, but I couldn't find you, and rumors were flying that the devil had appeared, so Ezra went to go find out, and then I lost track of everything except fighting." She'd blurted it all out without taking a breath, so she dragged one in now.

Devil? That felt like an unfair escalation. I double-checked my left hand for claws. All clear. "I didn't see any devil."

"Really?" Ezra said, striding toward us. He hadn't cleaned himself up after the battle yet either. "It was hard to miss." He held a bundle: a blanket and a set of sweats. He draped the blanket over Sachie's shoulders and handed me the clothes. "Hoping to start a new trend of naked fighting?" His tone was light, but his eyes were flat.

"Pfft. Someone doesn't know his battle history. Nudity in combat goes way back." I put clean clothes over my disgustingly dirty body with a grimace. I didn't care about these two seeing me naked; it wouldn't be a first for either. "Besides, tell me that wouldn't go viral."

"You can never have too many likes and shares," Sachie agreed, still looking a little wild about the eyes, like she remained lost in the fog of war.

"Sach, can you give me and Aviva a moment?" Ezra asked tightly.

I reached for my friend's hand, because hard pass on alone time with the pissy Prime, but she stood up. "Sure. I need to get some food in me. Later, gators."

Ezra sat down beside me, his legs splayed out in the ash.

"Spare me a lecture," I said. "I would have been dead if I hadn't let Cherry out."

"You almost died six times over as it was," he growled. "You know how many operatives I had to distract until they realized you were fighting for us not against us? Which I'm sure no one will have questions about," he added snarkily.

"You kept people from killing me?"

He uprooted blades of grass. "Why do you sound so surprised?"

"Because…Cherry…"

"Oh, you mean the half shedim that I already told you I didn't have a problem with?"

I tugged at a loose thread on the hem of the sweatshirt, the gesture pulling a plug out of my soul. I shook uncontrollably, my teeth chattering. "You wouldn't have helped me if you knew what I did."

He rubbed my back slowly. "You didn't mean to kill Pinar."

I expelled a hard breath. Knowing the woman's name made her death more real and much worse because with her name came a thousand questions about her life. I hadn't simply killed a nameless operative or written the final moments in the story of an anonymous protagonist, I'd slammed the book on the rich fiction of a specific person's life. Pinar's. "You—you know?"

"I figured it out when I saw her wounds combined with someone who'd cared enough to close her eyes."

"How am I supposed to live with this? And don't say it was her or me, or that it will get better. She's never going to laugh or eat or yell at people in traffic ever again and it's all my fault."

"It only gets better if you're a complete psychopath."

I stared at him, shivering. How could he say that and then maintain he wanted to kill people?

"You'll live with it because you have to. It's done." Ezra moved his hand away and began shredding blades of grass. "We caught Roman," he finally said, "and since things have calmed down, we can question him. This investigation is almost over, and then it won't matter what I think. I'll be gone from your life, just like you wished."

I wrapped my arms around myself, totally spent on a physical, spiritual, and psychological level. "Great," I said hollowly.

Our progress through the charred building was slow going, partially because of all the debris and partially because we checked in with every single operative, all us survivors hugging in the aftermath.

When I told Director Yildiz how sorry I was for the

loss of her Maccabees, I could barely get the words out, feeling like the worst hypocrite. Defne had treated us with kindness and respect and put her chapter at our disposal, her generosity worlds away from the crap we'd had to endure in London. In return, we'd brought a bloodbath to her door.

As for me? I'd killed her friend, and she'd never know the truth. Her hug was almost painful to accept, and I did the only thing I could: hardened my emotions into a sharp spear and headed for our prisoner.

Roman Whittaker was being held in a bare room with a concrete floor and three sturdy iron bars over the single glassless window. He was gaunter than in his photo.

Michael was going to freak the fuck out about the battle, but all was not lost for the successful outcome of this mission. Technically she hadn't mentioned vamps couldn't be collateral damage—especially when they'd attacked first—just that Roman was to be handed over to Director Harrison.

I'd make sure of that.

I spared a moment to drink in the rest of my team, weary but alive. "Hey, gang, thanks for not starting without me."

Roman lay on his back at Darsh's feet, his forearms and shins broken in a way that made them look like a swastika.

"That's offensive," I said.

Silas nodded. "That's what I said."

No sooner did Roman heal one leg, the bones snapping back into position, than Darsh broke it again.

"There aren't a lot of pattern options once I break his bones," Darsh said and tossed me a pair of nulling handcuffs. Okay. My friend wasn't being antisemitic, just practical.

I squatted down next to Roman. "I've got some questions. We can do this the easy way or the hard way."

He spat a phlegmy glob at my face.

I wiped it off with a shudder. "Sach?"

She circled Roman, drumming the fingers of one hand against her thigh. "I could slow roast him. Burning Eddie shared some good tips."

"Praise be to Burning Eddie," I said.

"But I feel this calls for a blunt approach. Silas?" She pointed at one of the bars on the window.

He lumbered over, snapped it free with little more than a grunt, and tossed it to her.

Sachie jammed the bar through Roman's shoulder, leaning into it to pin him to the floor.

The vampire gave a furious howl.

"Nice." Darsh nodded approvingly. "Your upper body regime is really paying off."

"Thanks." She flicked her fingers, and the metal bar glowed.

Roman let out a stream of inventive curses.

I waved my hand next to the bar. Heat poured off it. "Now. From the top. Why kill those people and stage a ritual murder that pointed to finding a cure for vampirism when there's no way to protect humans from being turned?"

Our prisoner grabbed the bar to pull it free, but it burned his hand. "I wasn't killing infernals to help weak, pathetic mortals."

My mouth filled with a bitter taste. I'd nurtured a tiny hope that the victims weren't all half shedim and that there was another reason why they'd been chosen. It was depressing having that confirmed, but I accepted the fact that nothing about this conversation was going to make me happy.

"Might want to keep the comments on who's the most

pathetic to yourself at the moment," Silas remarked blandly, "but that's just my opinion."

Did our Yellow Flame share Roman's view of humans being some lesser species since she was half demon? I couldn't ask that without explaining how I knew that fact to my team, so I went for a safer question. "Okay, you weren't killing infernals to help humans. How about Dr. Metaxas? Where would I find her to get her take on this?"

Roman was panting, his face contorted in pain, but he tried to sneer. "Oh, Athena believed she was saving the world. You should have seen her face when she discovered that instead of protecting people from vampires, she was —" He cut himself off sharply.

"What?" I kicked him in the ribs. "Instigating a vampire-human war using a bogus vaccine?"

"It was worth killing her to shut her up." He mimed crying.

She was dead? My vision narrowed down to a dark tunnel, and a roaring filled my ears. I forced it away, focusing on what I was missing, but it was getting harder to think, much less speak, because Cherry's baying for Roman's blood had joined the other noise in my head that I couldn't block out.

Seven infernals had been murdered, and with this last one, my chance to understand how the doctor could have killed our own kind was gone. Plus, Roman hadn't confirmed he was trying to start a war or disclosed his agenda at all.

I had to ask him, but I was too angry to speak.

Ezra walked slowly around our prisoner. "Why kill Metaxas now? Did she learn that you'd used her and refuse to help with whatever you were up to?" He squatted down with an expression of mock sorrow. "Did you lose your temper?"

It was a common technique to pepper a hostile suspect

with questions from all different angles to keep them off-guard and get them to eventually answer something that we could use to pry the full truth out, but Roman remained obstinately quiet.

Silas placed his boot on the top of the heated bar and drove it deeper into Roman's flesh.

"Fuck. You." His face was flushed and his sweaty hair was matted to his temple. "I'm not telling you shit."

I twirled the cuffs around my finger. "You've already confirmed the ritual was a sham. Why stop now? What was the point of all these murders?" I waited a moment. "Nothing?" I nodded at Darsh.

My friend stomped on Roman's hand. The bones broke with a series of loud snaps. "Killing your Eishei Kodesh co-conspirator didn't matter," Darsh said, "but you still came for the Claret. Why?"

Roman was breathing heavily, his eyes closed.

"In order to use the doctor," Sachie said, "you sold her this story complete with a showy ritual that fit into her own tragic history of the vamp attack that took her leg. Truth is irrelevant," she said in a voice thick with disgust. "Only belief matters."

"That's it!" I jabbed my finger in the air. "The lady with one leg bought the Claret. She had the connections to get the drug, not Roman." I toed his side. "As a Maccabee, it was too risky for you to try. The eyes, the heart, the purification, those were red herrings, but in pursuit of what?"

"You can't become an infernal or gain shedim abilities by drinking their blood," Ezra said. "But if you were convinced otherwise, then why kill them? Just drink from one. You didn't need to drain them with the Claret."

Roman gritted his teeth, his skin sizzling, but he still refused to answer.

"It's not about drinking the blood," Darsh said slowly.

"Is it? That was another reason for the sham. Make it so people didn't look beyond the mystic combination of eyes, heart, and blood to the properties of blood alone."

"Blood magic?" Ezra said. "Only rare demons have that ability."

"Not true," Darsh said. "Long ago blood was used to amplify magic. It wasn't an inherent ability but a taught technique. Use blood to call to blood. Six bodies' worth of infernal blood and the correct power words would go a long way."

Seven, I thought dully. I whirled on Roman. "You took their blood to make vamps untouchable? Why not just kill full shedim?"

"Blood magic requires human blood," Darsh said. "Or, well, partially human at least."

Silas eyed him like he had follow-up questions for my friend, but simply shook his head.

Whittaker gripped the heated bar, his flesh sizzling, trying to outlast the pain long enough to pry it out. His hands slipped off, and he bowed his head in defeat. "Go ahead and kill me. Another will take my place, and more infernals will die."

How? Metaxas wasn't around to suss out half shedim. I gasped. Unless…

Roman was a cog in a larger machine, and someone else was calling the shots.

"Drop the magic," I told Sach.

"What?"

"No," Ezra said.

I clanged the two manacles of the nulling cuffs together like a pair of maracas. "Drop. It."

Roman laughed. "Tell you what, sweetheart, I'll give you one free punch before I tear your throat out."

I smiled coldly. "You heard the fuckbag. Drop the magic. That's an order."

Muttering under her breath about how she was keeping my damage deposit when I died, she did it.

Silas, Darsh, and Ezra had gone tense. They'd step in, but I didn't need them.

I'd sunk into the eye of the hurricane. A place of perfect calm and clarity.

Roman pushed shakily to his feet, his hands loosely at his sides, and his burned skin already returning to normal. "Like I said. One free pu—"

Gripping the metal cuffs securely, I clapped them against his ears. He recoiled, and I followed up with a kick from behind that blew out his knee. I didn't have the vamp-weakness sight that I'd had in Babel, but I'd seen his injuries. "Who's in charge?"

"Fuck you." He got up, favoring one leg.

"Now you're just being repetitive." I struck down onto the crook of his elbow with a chopping motion while whipping his arm up.

His elbow snapped, but his leg had healed.

"Should we stop her?" Silas said.

"You're welcome to try," Sach replied.

"Give me the name." Every blow I landed tasted like cotton candy and acted like a pure sugar rush.

Roman charged me, head down, knocking into my belly and sending me crashing back against the wall so hard, I saw stars.

The cuffs went flying.

Ezra moved, but I yelled at him to stop, and he froze. His jaw was so tight he looked like he was about to start spitting teeth.

Roman bobbed on his toes. "You've got spirit, I'll give you that."

"The name," I snarled. I snatched up the iron bar, which Sach had cooled enough to touch, but I barely had it in my hand before Roman slammed me against the wall and tossed it away.

He leaned in close, his fangs brushing the side of my neck. "They'll find you." His words were a muted whisper against my ear. He licked up the side of my neck.

Roman knew what I was?

My shocked gaze locked with his knowing one.

He nodded. "Blood calls—"

I gouged his eyes out with my fingers.

Screaming, he spun around blindly, blood pouring down his face.

Once more I grabbed the metal bar and staked him—right through the windpipe. I was under orders not to kill Roman, but there hadn't been any clear directive on maiming.

While he gurgled, I nodded at Sach. "Burn his hands."

The vampire would be alive, but he couldn't speak, couldn't write—and he couldn't share my secret.

"Girl, you are in one bloodthirsty mood." Sachie made a circular motion. "I like it."

Roman's hands shriveled into stumpy twisted lumps.

"She's been hanging out with us for too long." Darsh beamed at me like a proud parent.

I still wasn't ready to reveal Cherry to the world in her full glory, but perhaps I'd underestimated my friends. Perhaps I'd stuck to a comfortable, easily palatable lie of what would happen, not because they'd walk away, but because by putting the onus on them, I didn't have to face a final truth.

I didn't simply like and tolerate my shedim side: I relished it.

Cherry hummed happily in my head, content for once to stay on the sidelines. After everything we'd been through lately, enough of the Brimstone Baroness had bled into my baseline that she'd reshaped my moral line.

Maybe that made me a bit less human. So what? I *was* less human.

I smiled. "Yup. You've broken me."

"Finally," Darsh said.

"Y'all are an interesting bunch," Silas said.

Sachie grinned. "You have no idea."

Ezra strode over to me, his face a grim mask. He picked up the nulling cuffs and waved them in my face. "How the hell am I supposed to put these on him when you burned off his hands? Really, Aviva."

I started laughing, deep belly laughs that I couldn't stop, even though they hurt. Alison, Zayn, Aleksander, Lynd, Kyle, and Rie had died for something they had no control over. No one asked to be born a half shedim, and even though some of them had left our world a better place for their existence, I could trumpet that fact from the rooftops, and it wouldn't be enough to overcome humanity's prejudice against us.

Whoever was pulling the strings was proof of that.

But I was keeping the record book now, and one day I'd use it to change people's hearts and minds.

In the meantime… I whipped out my phone and dialed a number. "Director Harrison?" I smirked at Roman, writhing in pain on the floor. "You've got a mess to clean up."

Chapter 29

"You gave me your word." I sat in Michael's office, staring at the living bamboo wall, which once again utterly failed to calm me down. I unclenched my fists and folded my hands in my lap. "We successfully wrapped up this investigation five days ago, and although you grilled me thoroughly the moment I got back, you didn't say a word that my promotion would not be happening. Then, you made me undergo a psych eval before I was cleared to return to work, which I sailed through with flying colors." I took a deep breath to loosen the sensation that a vise tightened my chest, but it didn't help. "Imagine my surprise when I came in today to find it was business as usual. Aviva Fleischer, level two operative. You could have told me when I came home that you had no intention of keeping your word."

"That's enough," Michael warned. "I had every intention. However, you burned an operative's hands off and rendered him mute. I had to promise Booker something to calm him down."

"Roman was a traitor. He attacked fellow Maccabees and he was killing half shedim!"

"No one cares about infernals!" She slammed her hand on her desk, the crack sounding like a gunshot.

I flinched. "Thanks, Mom," I said bitterly.

"You know what I mean." She pinched the bridge of her nose. "The vampire attack on the Bodrum compound was horrific. Your team fought well, and you stopped a corrupt operative from killing again. That counts for a lot, which is why no one else on your team was penalized."

It was a minor miracle that she hadn't heard the rumors about "the devil" who fought alongside the operatives. Or if she had, that she was ignoring them.

I bit my tongue, seething. Of course I was glad that no one else had gotten in trouble, especially not Sachie or Darsh. Sachie had even achieved her dream and been transferred to the Vancouver Spook Squad. I was thrilled for her.

"Someone else is hunting half shedim," I said. "We have to stop them."

"You can't prove that all the victims had demon blood. You said yourself that when you visited Mr. Epstein's body in the morgue again upon your return that you didn't see any mark."

"Roman confirmed it."

"He's not a reliable source," she said in a steely voice.

I wasn't going to let Michael bury this.

"Then let me find a way to prove what these victims were." I stood up to pace and shake off the spiky energy under my skin. "My whole life I've been told I was unique. Alone. Hell, the rare documents involving half shedim only proved that they were just as bad as full demons, which was why I had to hide that part of myself. But these victims were good people. Not just nice to their neighbors but actively changing the world for the better. Someone couldn't stand the deviation from the narrative and killed them, hoping to use their blood for dark magic to make vampires untouchable."

"Do you hear how insane this all sounds? In the same way you can't cure vampirism, you can't use infernal blood to turn them into super soldiers."

"According to who? The Maccabees? We both know how little our organization knows about half shedim. That's the problem. We are exactly the ones who should start asking questions about this narrative we've all been fed, because if we don't have the correct information, our world could be headed down a dark path. Tikkun olam."

"We've been fighting darkness for thousands of years. Surely this would have surfaced before now. You're upset that a couple of infernals were brutally murdered and that's understandable. But there is no way that all those victims were half shedim and there isn't any big-picture sinister agenda going on. End of story." Michael opened a file folder marked with signature tabs and rummaged among the clutter on her desk for a pen. "I shared with Malika and Booker that you were under stress from the investigation when you examined Mr. Epstein's body, and that made your magic glitchy."

"How convenient," I murmured.

She shot me a sharp look, but I didn't recant with an apology like I normally would have. Maybe she took off her director mask to simply be my mother in this moment, because she didn't get angry.

"Booker has his people combing through every aspect of Roman's life. If there is someone else involved?" She sounded doubtful. "They'll find that person. Meantime, you should be thanking me for preventing any blowback and ensuring no one is any wiser about you."

What had my mother convinced herself of in order to love me and keep me safe? To keep *herself* safe?

I longed to snap a snarky retort about my deep and

abiding gratitude at having my identity swept under the rug like dirt. But although I'd reached a new equilibrium with Cherry, I wasn't ready to come out of hiding.

Perhaps that's what burned most of all.

Someone was still out there tracking my kind. Unfortunately, I couldn't hunt that being if the rest of the world was hunting me. I wasn't strong enough—yet—to take that person down with a target on my back, and after the battle in Bodrum, I didn't want to expose my friends or family to that level of danger again because of me.

So, no, I wouldn't be revealing my truth to the world today. Still, it wouldn't happen as far in the future as I'd originally presumed.

"You won't be able to hide what I am forever," I said.

Michael signed a page and flipped to the next without glancing up. "We'll deal with that day when it comes."

I stood up, my head throbbing. "Can I go?"

She motioned at the door. "Be my guest."

I shut the door quietly behind me, taking a moment in the corridor beyond her assistant's desk to lean back against the wall and breathe, wishing none of this had happened. How was I supposed to go back to regular Eishei Kodesh policing when this heinous agenda was out there? How could I keep investigating it when I was stuck being told which jobs to work on?

I rubbed my shoulder blades against the drywall like that would release the hot, itchy energy that had gathered during that conversation. Maybe I should go for a long run, just like I'd done every day while in limbo waiting to hear about my promotion? I sighed. Now that I'd been delivered the bad news, I couldn't dredge up the energy.

"Is Michael going to tear a strip off me too?" Ezra said.

I jerked my head up.

He was in another bespoke three-piece suit, this one gunmetal gray.

Michael's office was soundproofed against vampire hearing. He was simply reading my body language.

I didn't bother moving, happy to let the wall brace me. "Why aren't you in England?"

Ezra and Silas had delivered Roman to London the day after our Bodrum interrogation of the vamp. I'd expected Director Harrison would have kept them longer, since I'd gotten a text that they'd found Dr. Metaxas's body.

My ex raked a gaze over the top two open buttons on my fitted black shirt and down along the curve of my short houndstooth skirt with an unreadable expression.

I clasped my hands behind my back so I didn't give in to the temptation to fix the wayward curl at his temple.

"Michael ordered me in." His lips curved into a wry smile. "I think she wants to tell me in person that future visits here will not be welcome."

I tore my eyes away from his mouth and the memory of that kiss that even now made my cheeks flush. "Explain you have your dream hitman life to resume."

"Right." His face shuttered.

Suddenly the air around us tightened. It was like I'd put on a dress that almost fit, but now, trying to get it off, it had gotten stuck.

My shoulders slumped. None of this mattered. Our working partnership was done. The team office had already been disbanded. I'd run past it the other night and seen movers bringing in furniture for the new occupants.

"Good luck with your next assignment," I said, straightening up and pushing off the wall.

He caught my wrist lightly and leaned in. "Roman is dead," he murmured.

"What?" I practically shouted it.

He placed his hand over my mouth. "Quiet."

I bit his finger, and his eyes flared to burning silvery-blue spears. He dropped his hand to his side.

"How?" I whispered, glancing down the hall to make sure we were alone.

"His jail cell in London HQ. Cameras were disabled." He stroked his neatly cropped beard. "Someone or something got past the guards. Booker is keeping it quiet."

On a first-name basis with the director now, huh? "I'm sure he'll find whoever it was. It's not my problem anymore."

"Pull your head out of your ass," Ezra said harshly.

I crossed my arms. "Excuse me?"

"You're missing my point." First he was a jerk then he insulted my intelligence? "We couldn't figure out how the victims were found."

"At first," I replied frostily. "Until we realized Metaxas was a half shedim."

"How did they find Metaxas to begin with?"

"Roman admitted there's someone else."

"Right. And where would one operative find another person with those resources?" Ezra challenged.

A sick, sinking feeling ballooned inside me. The Maccabees. But who? Someone like my mother? My mother specifically? I didn't believe she was killing infernals, but did she know there were more of us out there than I'd been led to believe? Had she been lying to me all these years about what she knew? Telling me a convenient story because it was easier—for her—to frame infernals in terms of black and white?

On those rare occasions we even got to be part of a story at all?

I twisted my fingers together. "You think that someone higher up in the Maccabees knows how to find infernals?"

"I don't know that it's even just one person," Ezra said grimly.

I shook my head. The Maccabees were the good guys. We *had* to be the good guys.

Silly girl, Cherry said. *You're not evil, so why would they all be good?*

"Aviva?"

Ezra Cardoso was about to leave my life, but this time, I was still standing. The smart thing to do would be to wish him the best and let him go.

But he'd kept my secret, and he had my back.

"You interested in continuing this partnership?" I tilted my head. "Professionally and off the books?"

He held out his arm, and with an intrigued gleam that was nothing like the shy expression he'd worn the first night I met him, but had my heart racing in the same way, said, "Can I buy you a drink?"

THANK you for reading BIG DEMON ENERGY.

While you're waiting for Aviva's next adventure, I'd like you to meet Miriam Feldman in THROWING SHADE (MAGIC AFTER MIDLIFE #1).

Middle-aged. Divorced. Hormonally imbalanced. Then she got magic.

Underestimate her. That'll be fun.

It's official. Miriam Feldman is killing it in the midlife crisis department. She's mastered boredom, aced invisibility, and graduated Summa Cum Laude in smiling and playing nice in her post-divorce life.

Then her best friend gets tangled up with some vamps and goes missing. If that's not scary enough, Miri snaps, and in a cold dark rage, unleashes a rare and powerful shadow magic.

Now, with only a mouthy golem and a grumpy-yet-sexy French wolf shifter to help her navigate this world of hidden magic, she's in a race against time to rescue her friend and keep her loved ones safe from the skeletons in her past.

Sure, she's caught in a spiderweb of supernatural power plays, but she's a librarian, she's over forty, and she's definitely done with being sidelined in her own life.

She's turning her invisibility into strength; they'll never see her coming.

Featuring intelligent snark, a slow burn shifter romance, and a midlife heroine who takes no crap and makes zero excuses, this first in series mystery adventure will take you on a hilarious wild ride.

Binge it now!

Turn the page for an excerpt from Throwing Shade…

Excerpt from Throwing Shade

A man kneeled next to Alex's body. He seemed a few years younger than me, probably in his late thirties, and was about six inches taller, putting the shifter at about six-foot-two. His hair was a riot of dark curls.

The man's jaw was firm, his lips full, but right now, they were set in a severe line. Moonlight kissed the olive skin of his broad shoulders and leanly muscled torso, a trail of hair leading down to—

Jeans. I gusted out a breath.

The man huffed softly. "You came back," he said dryly, with a slight accent I couldn't place. "You've got balls, I'll give you that."

I gave a weak laugh and he locked his brilliant emerald gaze onto mine. Thickly lashed, his eyes were what I would have called beautiful in his human form, but there was a hardness to them—like he'd seen too much and all innocence was long gone.

Eli had looked that way after his first year in homicide. Fuuuuck! This guy had to be a Lonestar. Okay, looking on the bright side, he could help me find Jude—if he didn't destroy me. I'd been so bent on getting answers from Alex that I'd thrown away every single safety procedure that I'd lived by and shown a stranger my magic. I could have left when the shifter took off with Alex but no, I had to play detective.

I reached behind me, clutching the railing because my legs felt rubbery.

The Ohrist reached into a duffel bag, revealing a nasty silver jagged scar that ran halfway up the left side of his back, and pulled on a faded blue T-shirt that said "Bite Me." This wasn't a gym rat with a six-pack for show; he was a warrior and his body was his well-honed weapon, in or out of wolf form.

Ohrist magic was based in light and life, while Banim Shovavim powers were rooted in death and darkness. Historically, they'd taken that as clear-cut signs of good and evil. They pitied Sapiens but had hunted my kind into near extinction.

There was even a skipping game sung by Ohrist kids: "Clap for the light, 'cause light is right. All other magic is a blight. How many shadow freaks will we smite?" At which point they'd jump as fast as they could while counting.

I eyed the wolf shifter with a sinking feeling that he'd probably counted pretty damn high.

Maybe he didn't remember the exact details of his time in his wolf form? Could I bluff my way out of here?

"Did you want something?" he said, impatiently.

My brain short-circuited. "I'm guessing that light magic allowed you to cut through his breastbone and rib cage only using your claws," I said, "but why isn't there blood all over the place?"

I could have smacked myself. This was not the time for curiosity or further questions like "How do you have more than one magic ability?" It was the time for well-crafted lies.

"The magic cauterized the blood vessels." The man rolled his "r's." He grabbed a box of table salt from the duffel bag.

"Regular sodium," I said thickly. "How bland. I prefer Pink Himalayan to balance the delicate flavor of human flesh."

"I'm not eating him." He dumped the salt over the corpse. "It interferes with the scent so animals don't show up before Ohrists get here to retrieve the body."

"That's good, because cannibalism can make you sick. You get this brain disease called kuru and—"

"Like mad cow?" He tapped the last of the salt onto the body with a contemplative expression.

I blinked. People didn't generally come back with follow-up questions to my random facts. "Not quite. People can't get mad cow disease, but in rare cases they get a form called..." I shook my head because cows, mad or otherwise, were not the issue. "Was Alex human?"

Or was he some other species entirely and did that make a difference to the answer? He had looked human, even if what was inside of him wasn't.

My moral compass was having trouble finding true north.

"Not anymore," the wolfman said.

I knelt down beside Alex to close his lids because his lifeless stare felt accusatory, but the man batted my arm away.

He lay a hand on the deceased's forehead and stared into his eyes as if committing him to memory. There was both a gravitas and a resignation in the shifter's expression, and I couldn't tell if he did this to honor the dead or torment himself with a parade of his kills. Maybe it was one and the same.

When he was done, I checked Alex's back pockets for his wallet.

"The man's body isn't even cold and you're robbing him?" Wolf Dude said.

"I'm looking for identification," I said through ground teeth. There was a cracked phone but no wallet. It must have fallen out at some point during the fight. A vise tightened around my chest and I shoved the Ohrist, banking on the fact that if he'd intended to hurt me, he'd have done it already. "You ruined my chance to get information about—"

"I saved you." The man stuffed his bare feet into motorcycle boots, which also came out of the duffel bag. "I don't know what interrogation skills you think you have, but I can assure you that dybbuk wouldn't have given up shit."

"Dybbuk?"

"Merde," he said in perfect French. Ah. "You went after him without knowing what you were dealing with?" His full lips twisted. "Fucking BS."

He remembered.

I took two wobbly steps back, Delilah by my side, but he didn't come after me.

He laced up his boots. Okay, he was a derisive son of a bitch, but he lacked the horror others of his ilk displayed upon meeting my kind, nor did he seem inclined to kill me.

I'd take the win.

"Alex had attacked me once already," I said, "and if he did something to my friend—"

The shifter pulled out a beaten-up brown leather jacket and shrugged into it, his shoulders bunching. "Then she's gone. Sorry for your loss."

My eyebrows shot up. Yes, this guy was an ass, but surely he was connected to an infrastructure that could help me find Jude. "Sorry for your loss? How about you help me find her? Aren't you a Lonestar?"

He laughed without an ounce of humor. "Hardly."

Then what was he? He'd already killed one person, and yes, that dybbuk thing seemed to justify Alex's death, but I was alone out here. If he was working on his own vigilante moral code, how safe was I?

I eyed the stairs. How many were there? Thirty? Then perhaps another fifty feet to lose myself in the crowds in Terence Poole Plaza? He'd be faster than me, even as a human. I bit my lip. If I screamed for help, would anyone come?

Screw that. I had magic and could cloak and get away at any point, but his rudeness was grating. I threw my hands up. "That's all you have to say?"

"No." The man raked a shrewd glance over me. "Should we ever have the misfortune to meet again, get out of my way."

"Or what? You'll huff and you'll puff and you'll blow my house down?"

He bared his lips, briefly shifting his canines to wolf form. *My, what big teeth you have.* A strangled laugh burbled out of me. My epistemological crisis involved a hell of a Freudian undertone.

"I'll do whatever the fuck is necessary," he said.

"Is that your action hero catchphrase or something? Because it's a little on the nose."

He zipped up the duffel bag. "My reputation doesn't precede me? Shocking." His voice was laced with bitterness.

"Wow. Someone is full of themselves. I've got no idea who you are."

He peered at me suspiciously. "Are you new in town?"

"No."

He shrugged. "Then you know who I am."

"Hate to disappoint you, but you're just some rando who crashed my party and ruined my plan—"

"To get answers from someone who wouldn't tell you anything you actually wanted to know. Brilliant strategy. You've the mind of a tactician. Even if you did get something out of him, did you think he'd let you walk away after?" His accent thickened when he got annoyed.

"I had my shadow."

"I wouldn't brag about that if I were you."

"For your information, I'm doing an admirable job. Before yesterday, the only monsters I had to worry about were of the human variety." I shot him a pointed look.

"There's no way you didn't know about dybbuks. You're too—" He snapped his mouth shut.

Delilah puffed up behind me. "Oh, no," I said. "Finish that sentence."

The man crossed his arms, rustling the leather. "Old," he said levelly.

My shadow bopped Wolfman in the nose with a swift jab. Ha!

The man pinched his nostrils together to staunch the bleeding, his emerald eyes glinting dangerously.

My amusement drained away, my magic swirling around my feet, ready to cloak me, but I'd hit the wall and I was out of fucks to give.

"Should we ever have the misfortune to meet again, get out of my way," I said.

"Vraiment? Why?"

"I'm a woman in my forties who's remembered how powerful she can be. Don't fuck with me, Huff 'n' Puff." Head held high, Delilah and I sailed past him into the night.

Become a Wilde One

If you enjoyed this book and want to be first in the know about bonus content, reveals, and exclusive giveaways, become a Wilde One by joining my newsletter: http://www.deborahwilde.com/subscribe

You'll immediately receive short stories set in my different worlds and available only to my newsletter subscribers. There are mild spoilers so they're best enjoyed in the recommended reading order.

If you just want to know about my new releases, please join my list at: https://deborahwildebooks.com

Acknowledgments

My deepest thanks to Rabbi Eliana Jacobowitz for letting me pester her with the weirdest questions as I built my world and my magic system for this book. Her suggestion for the Eishei Kodesh made everything fall into place, and I am very grateful for her patience and good humour.

To my awesome friend, Elissa Vann Struth, I don't know what I'd do without our talks—both personal and professional. You understand the joy of planning, make me laugh, keep me sane, and are always always a beacon of truth about my writing. Thank you for all of that and the last minute "special read" you did for me.

Dr. Alex Yuschik, my most fabulous editor, can you believe we're starting another roller coaster of a series? There is no one else I'd rather go on this crazy ride with and I thank you for pushing me to be my best writer self with each new book.

My husband and daughter continue to humour me for spacing out in the middle of conversations when I get an idea, and making them talk plot ad infinitum. I love you both impossible, ridiculous amounts.

Finally, much love to all my Wilde Ones. You people are my happy place and it is an honour and a delight to share my stories with you.

About the Author

A global wanderer, former screenwriter, and total cynic with a broken edit button, Deborah (pronounced deb-O-rah) writes funny urban fantasy and paranormal women's fiction.

Her stories feature sassy women who kick butt, strong female friendships, and swoony, sexy romance. She's all about the happily-ever-after, with a huge dose of hilarity along the way.

Deborah lives in Vancouver, along with her husband, daughter, and asshole cat, Abra.

"Magic, sparks, and snark!"

www.deborahwilde.com

LIGHTNING SOURCE
JULY 19th.

CPSIA information can be obtained
at www.ICGtesting.com
Printed in the USA
JSHW021133090723
44409JS00006B/31